THE THINGS
THAT CANNOT
BE FORGOTTEN

THE THINGS THAT CANNOT BE FORGOTTEN

A VIC LENOSKI MYSTERY

PETER W.J. HAYES

LEVEL
BEST BOOKS

First edition

ISBN: 978-1-68512-828-9

Cover art by Level Best Designs

This book was professionally typeset on Reedsy.
Find out more at reedsy.com

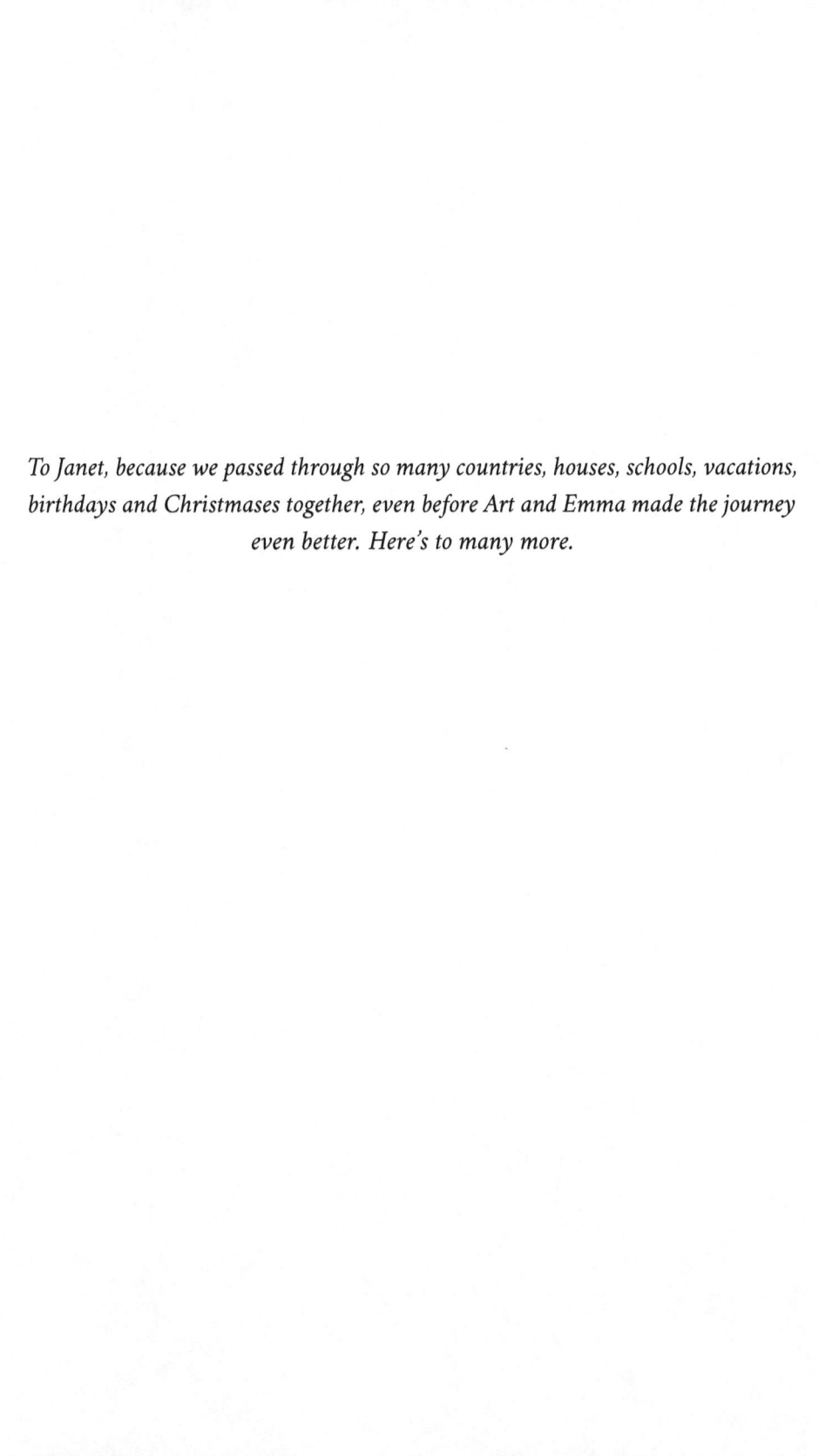

To Janet, because we passed through so many countries, houses, schools, vacations, birthdays and Christmases together, even before Art and Emma made the journey even better. Here's to many more.

Life doesn't run away from nobody. Life runs at people.

— Joe "Smokin' Joe" Frazier
World Heavyweight Champion, 1968 - 1973

It is not the size of a man but the size of his heart that matters.

—Evander "The Real Deal" Holyfield
World Heavyweight Champion, 1990 - 2001

Chapter One

The stench of paint thinner drove Jake Kittery back from his garage door. He stared at the ghostly remains of the letter he'd tried to rub away, smeared but still readable against the white paint of the door. He squeezed the rag of paint thinner in his hand.

"Power-wash and repaint?"

Jake turned to his wife. Ellie stood ten feet away, carefully upwind of him. Her blue nurse's scrubs were tight on her plump figure, but he thought she still looked good, even after thirty-six years of marriage and everything he'd put her through.

Ellie shifted on worn white sneakers, arms folded against the autumn cool, staring at the message. "He hasn't gotten any more creative, has he?"

Jake glanced at the spray-painted words. *Dam Commie Pinko*, they read, finished with a crossed hammer and sickle, or perhaps a jittery 'x.' Rivulets of paint streaked from the bottoms of the letters and sickle handle.

"Or figured out how to spell and write with spray paint," Jake added.

"You're asking a lot."

"People should take pride in their work."

Ellie glanced at a burned-out patch of their front lawn. "Sometimes it's more about doing it over and over again." She turned her amber eyes on him in the way he'd seen hundreds of times before. Ellie laying down the law.

Jake knew he needed to listen. He also knew what was coming.

"He was due, you know that, right? He's like the damn seasons." She nodded toward the burned-out grass without breaking eye contact. "Tire

1

fire was July. Summer." The 'i' in each of the first two words of the sentence was lengthened by her broad Pittsburgh accent.

"I can't stay up every night waiting for him."

Ellie balled her fists and planted them on her hips. "Almost fifteen years he's been doing this crap. We even moved here to get away from him." She swept her arm at the end of the cul-de-sac, where the ground fell away into a steep valley. They'd chosen the house to minimize the number of neighbors who might require apologies. "It needs to stop. You need to stop it. Or call the cops."

"He *is* a cop. Or was. Cops aren't going to help us. He's one of theirs."

"Then *you* need to stop it." She stared at him hard before breaking her gaze. "My shift starts soon." She walked toward the house but turned when she reached the front door.

"Aren't you supposed to be at work by now?"

Jake tossed his rag into a nearby bucket. "Yeah. Stevie said he'd pick me up. He hasn't shown. I was just doing this until he got here."

Ellie frowned. "He's usually on time. Why don't you drive me to work and take my car?"

"Sure."

Ellie disappeared into the house, the screen door banging behind her. Jake lifted the garage door and put the bucket and rag away. The clean-up could wait until he got home.

Outside again, he closed the door and ran a garden hose to wash off the thinner, shook his hands dry and called Stevie on his flip phone. The call went straight to voice mail. He crossed to the curb and waited beside Ellie's blue Ford. She'd wanted a Japanese car, but he'd insisted on American-made. Which also explained his flip phone. No way he would buy anything manufactured outside the United States.

Ellie locked the front door and skipped down the walk, her purse strap over her shoulder, the purse itself clamped under her arm. His heart gave a lurch. Even after all these years, he thought.

But she was right. Stevie, their son, was always on time. This wasn't like him at all.

2

Chapter Two

Detective Vic Lenoski closed the driver's side door to his Toyota and surveyed the area. The bluff on Mt. Washington overlooked the city of Pittsburgh, and the blue sky felt huge and cold. Wind gusted, and he zipped his Carhartt jacket. Hands in his pockets, he glanced both ways and followed his partner, Liz Timmons, across the narrow two-lane road toward the crime scene tape and the large blue van of the crime scene investigators. To the right, life-sized statues of George Washington and Guyasuta, the Seneca war chief, sat leaning toward one another, gazes intent, noses inches apart.

As he stepped onto the sidewalk, Vic wondered if Guyasuta, all those years ago, ever sensed Washington's future—or his own—as he guided the twenty-one-year-old Washington through the western Pennsylvania woods. If Guyasuta had any inkling of how many battles he and Washington would fight in the years to come.

Vic shifted his shoulders, glad for the jacket's roominess. He liked this coat. It wasn't just that Anne, his wife, gave it to him. The heavy canvas felt substantial and the tailoring let him move his shoulders easily. Perhaps it was time for a change. For years, he'd suffered sport coats that always clenched at his back and armpits. After all, Liz always wore a black leather bomber jacket, which wasn't exactly department dress code. But Liz was Black, and he knew the jacket was her way of leaning into the color of her skin. Combined with her black jeans and gray shirt, the way she carried herself intimidated more than a few suspects. None of their commanders had ever wanted to take that away from her.

Ahead, Liz spoke to a uniformed officer, who lifted the crime scene tape. They scooted underneath. Vic led Liz down a narrow gravel path that ran parallel to the road to a small, grassy area. There, three people in white Tyvek suits and blue masks— one on their knees running gloved fingertips through the grass—worked around a prone body.

Vic stopped halfway down the trail, next to the railing that separated them from the sidewalk. To their right, a sheer cliff fell perhaps eight hundred feet to railway tracks, a four-lane road, and the Ohio River. The wind rushed up the hillside and battered them.

"Forrest," Vic called, knowing Forrest led the team of crime scene investigators.

One of the androgynous, white-clad people raised a head and started toward them. He peeled off his mask as he walked, revealing Forrest's five-day stubble and wattled neck. "You guys got this one, huh?" He stopped a few feet away.

"We're born lucky," Liz said drily.

"Not sure you'll want it." Forrest matched Liz's tone.

"Is there anything worth wanting?"

"How about the crime scene?" Vic cut in as Liz finished talking, thinking that if Liz and Forrest kept trying to outdo each other, they might clasp hands and hop off the cliff.

Forrest turned to him. "Young male, late twenties, I'd guess. No ID. Or phone." He smirked at Vic. "Which is why I said you might not want it."

"Okay, a John Doe." Vic stared at Forrest, willing him to keep talking.

Forrest got the message. "Stabbed. Some kind of long blade. There's blood on the nearest stone." He pointed at two large, flat rocks visitors used as benches to admire the view of Pittsburgh and its three rivers. "If I had to guess, victim was standing talking to someone. Assailant was sitting on the rock and stabbed upwards. Person standing collapses, catches the edge of the rock on the way down, ends up on the grass and expires."

"Well now." Vic smiled at him. "You'll have to fingerprint the stone, won't you?"

The corners of Forrest's mouth turned down. "Yeah, thanks. Already figured that out. Can't be more than a couple hundred prints."

"I bet they were sitting on that other stone as well." Liz's high, falsely happy-to-help tone hung in the air.

"No." Forrest's retort was immediate. "I already made that call. Just the stone with the blood." He shot a baleful glance at the sky. "Might do that next, in case the weather turns on us."

"Anything else?" Vic asked.

Forrest shook his head. "No murder weapon, no wallet, no cell phone. Tourist called it in about eight this morning. We got here a little after nine. I'm guessing our victim was stabbed sometime after midnight, but no way I can really tell."

They were all silent for a second as the wind shifted. "Okay," Vic said finally. "Victim's belongings might have been thrown over the edge. Better have the fire and rescue guys check the railroad tracks for his wallet and phone before some train shreds them. Then rope their way up the cliff in case they got hung up somewhere."

"Yeah. I thought about that." Forrest didn't sound happy.

"And the railing along the sidewalk," Liz added. "If the perp walked back up the trail and took a right onto the sidewalk, I bet they looked over the railing to check the body. Human nature. Did I really do that? Is the guy really dead? Chances are good they put a hand on the railing right then."

Forrest sighed. "I didn't think of that."

"That's why we all get paid the big bucks." Vic grinned at Forrest. "We'll tell the uniform at the top of the trail to tape off that area for you. Call us if you find anything, okay?"

Forrest nodded. "We'll do the autopsy tomorrow. I'll let you know. We'll be done in about half an hour if you want to walk the scene."

They said their goodbyes, and Liz led Vic back up the path. Vic instructed the guard to tape off the sidewalk to protect the railing where it overlooked the crime scene. They moved off several feet to the statues of Washington and Guyasuta.

"What do you think?" Liz asked.

"Doesn't sound easy." Vic held up his phone. "I'll tell Craig to watch

Missing Person reports, see if a young male goes missing. Let's hope we get a fingerprint match."

Liz shifted to get a better look at the arrowhead of Pittsburgh, shoehorned between the converging Allegheny and Monongahela rivers.

"Or maybe we find his wallet *was* thrown over the hill."

"Is it ever that easy?"

Liz glanced at him. "Not since I started working with you."

"And yet we do close cases."

"Not all of them."

"Well, yeah. Who does?"

Liz didn't reply. Her words were so pithy he knew she was thinking about one particular open case. It predated her move from New Orleans to Pittsburgh and happened in the days immediately after Hurricane Katrina. Her husband and his partner, patrolmen for the New Orleans Police Department, were lost in the flooding, looting, and confusion in the days after the hurricane. Their bodies were never found, just two of the roughly seven hundred people still missing. That open case still chafed Liz raw.

Vic didn't know what to say. Any kind of encouragement was a lie, and he knew Liz would consider it an insult. He waited, the wind pushing at them.

Finally, he gestured at the statues. "Guyasuta there, he had an interesting life."

Liz gave the seated statues a baleful look.

"He scouted for George Washington, when Washington was in the English army. Then, he sided with the French and helped them defeat General Braddock and Washington just south of here. Braddock died in that battle, and they named a town after him. Guyasuta might have been one of the guys put a bullet hole through Washington's uniform. After that, Guyasuta fought for the French in the French and Indian War, and was a war chief for Cadillac, fighting the settlers around the Great Lakes. After the American Revolution he gave up and started looking for a peaceful way to live with the settlers. Never figured it out. Died a drunk. Do you know the problem with that?"

"You mean dying?

"No, drinking yourself to death because you can't solve a problem."

Liz shrugged, her attention back on Pittsburgh and the formation of the Ohio River.

"Think about it. There actually wasn't a way for him to live with the settlers. There just wasn't. Settlers were going to take Indian land no matter what. Kill him if they had to. So fighting didn't work, and neither did cooperation, because there wasn't a solution. Was never going to be. He couldn't figure out how to make peace, and it killed him."

Vic saw a flicker in Liz's eyes as she grasped the parallel to her own lack of closure in her husband's death. She turned to him. "God save me. You're my partner?"

"Flesh and blood."

"And that's how you try to make me feel better? What the hell did I do in a past life to deserve you?"

"I ask myself that same question, sometimes."

Liz laughed, actually laughed out loud. Vic felt lighter for it. He braced himself in case the wind found him easier to lift.

Liz let her laughter run out and shook her head. "Okay," she said, sobering. "Let's figure out who this kid is. I don't want anyone else lost."

Chapter Three

C arty Swain felt good. Sharp. The New Orleans mid-morning heat might be hotter than dragon's breath, but his tan poplin slacks were light and comfortable on his legs, and his white shirt was loose enough to catch every dainty trickle of moving air. Even better, a loose shirt meant he was unbuttoned far enough to show off his Spanish doubloon on its gold chain, neatly nestled among his thick, auburn chest hair.

It was a real doubloon, according to his coin-collecting friend in Costa Rica. Perhaps rescued from a 1600s Spanish shipwreck, and worth about forty-five thousand dollars. And he was here because he knew there was more for the taking.

Around him, the city was just waking up. What time, nine-thirty? The city of hangovers, he'd always called New Orleans when he lived here.

He took his time, continuing from the Canal Street Ferry toward the Garden District. He looped blocks and checked cross-streets, memorizing as he went. What had changed since Katrina, what was the same. This part of town hadn't been damaged or altered much, but, as always, he liked to be careful. He wanted to imprint the local map in his mind again, after all the years.

Tomorrow, he would enter the Garden District and start his search.

My reconnaissance and renaissance, he thought, grinning at the wordplay.

The house he sought was a fixture in his mind. A Victorian structure with six ground-to-roof pillars and narrow first and second-floor porches overlooking the street. He remembered the sloshing sound of shin-high water as he and his partner walked by, not long after the second levee broke. How the pink wooden siding had contrasted with the electric gray of the sky. "That's the place. Keep moving," his partner had hissed.

He didn't know why he felt it was important to revisit the house. He'd never been inside, never seen the coin collection his partner, Demond, told him about. Despite wearing one of the coins today.

He just wanted to feel grounded. To know his starting point.

Circling another block, he noted a new row of townhouses, ugly in their sameness, on a block where one-story houses once stood. He wiped his forehead with a white handkerchief and gave himself until noon, when it would be too hot to walk, even as appropriately dressed and accustomed to the heat as he was.

He turned the corner, and his mind drifted back to the late afternoon when Katrina started to abate. The roads still mostly impassable, the water still rising. Radio systems down and cell service a joke. The ramshackle shack off Route 90.

He remembered Demond turning their patrol car onto the dirt road—the muck fuck, Carty had christened it—that led to the shack. Following Demond over downed branches and sticky mud to the front door. They'd stepped inside, not worrying about their muddy footprints on the sagging floor. Used Maglite beams to see.

Demond had pried up a floorboard in one corner and extracted a metal box. Placed it on a listing chair and opened the top so the lid blocked Carty from seeing the contents. From inside, Demond retrieved a coin and flipped it to him. Carty remembered catching it, the flicker of gold in his palm, and how his heart skipped a beat. The warmth he felt at the weight of it. And distantly, Demond saying he'd changed his mind. That he planned to return the collection. That in the moment of checking the house before the storm, he'd simply lost his head. Been misled by greed.

Carty remembered his heart thudding with rage at those words, at Demond's betrayal. He'd known instantly what to do. Looking up, the center cross on the doubloon imprinted in his mind, he'd shrugged and agreed they should return the collection. Then, with a lazy movement, he'd tossed the doubloon back to Demond in a high arc. The moment Demond reached for it, Carty drew his .38 and fired twice into Demond's chest.

Demond crumpled to the ground. Carty flipped the metal box around to find it empty. Curses escaped his mouth like sulfur. "Where's the rest?" He screamed the words so loud his throat hurt. He looked down at his partner on the dirty floor.

"Never. Trusted you." Demond blinked and took several short, whooping breaths. Pink bubbles formed at the corners of his mouth.

"You're lung-shot," Carty said, scrabbling for a way to make Demond talk. His gun was loaded with hollow points, and he knew the wounds were fatal. But what he said was, "You want help, tell me where the collection is. All of it. We can give it back. Get you fixed up."

His words sounded ridiculous, even to his own ears.

Demond coughed, strained, and went limp.

Only the wind remained, keening, swallowing the shack in an excruciating exhale.

Carty walked to the corner and picked up the doubloon. Pocketed it. Stood over his partner's still body.

"Yeah, well, I never trusted you either. Asshole."

He noticed that Demond had his Glock in his right hand. Demond had suspected that Carty would refuse to return the collection.

He sighed. Maybe Demond really had stolen coins worth a fortune, maybe he'd only taken one. He had no way to know, now. But he wasn't going to risk a murder charge. He would dump the body in the Mississippi, leave the cruiser somewhere in a flood area. Become one more of the lost.

The body and cruiser disposed of, he spent the rest of the night in the Garden District searching houses. He scrounged cash, jewelry and clothes from abandoned homes and hitchhiked west at dawn, the rides frequent and accommodating, everyone surfing a wave of goodwill in the storm's wake. He spent three months in Dallas rebuilding his identity. Purchased a new birth certificate and social security number. And finally, wrangled a new passport under the name Devon Blair. Then, he took a bus to Mexico and continued south into Costa Rica.

He parlayed being a nightclub bouncer into a job as a bodyguard. Eighteen months later, that became close security for a wealthy banker named Luis Manuel Arias Vargas. Mostly, Carty managed the logistics of Vargas' meetings with his two mistresses, who needed to be kept secret from the long-legged German model Vargas had married. But Carty's life, and luck, changed one night when he spotted Vargas' wife returning home unexpectedly. In an inspired moment, he spirited one of the mistresses out of the house unseen. A few weeks later, Vargas gave Carty a management position in the bank's security group. Two years after that, Vargas promoted him to commander of the security team.

By then, Carty and Vargas were friends, and Carty knew that Vargas collected coins.

Katrina faded from memory. Carty did the math, and after several more years, knew the missing person cases from Katrina were likely shelved.

One night, as he and Vargas smoked rich Tres Humanos cigars on a country club patio overlooking a golf course, Carty showed Demond's doubloon to Vargas. He said it was passed down to him from his father. Was it real? Worth anything?

Vargas, who liked whiskey and cigars as much as his mistresses, turned the doubloon in his hand, considered its glint in the fading light.

"Very much so," he'd said. "A fine specimen. Perhaps from a shipwreck."

As the light faded, the banker recounted the blood-soaked history of the coin. How the Spanish stole Aztec and Inca gold figurines and artwork at sword-point and melted them down to cast doubloons. How the legacy of those civilizations was destroyed to finance Spain's trade and colonialism, and accidentally launched the pirate era. That doubloons were traded as far west as China, the Philippines, and Thailand.

Carty barely listened. He sipped his whiskey, reliving the buck of his .38 in his hand, Demond collapsing to the shack floor. Saw once again the pink bubbles at the corners of Demond's mouth. Heard that keening wind.

And then Vargas asked," Where did your father get this?"

Carty shrugged himself into the present, his senses tingling, warning him to be careful. "He never said."

"Really?" The banker returned the doubloon to him. "That is unusual. People who own things like this, they always say. They can't help themselves. Even my wife knows the history of the few coins I own."

Carty puffed on his cigar, trying to appear unconcerned.

"Coins like that are remembered," Vargas added, looking into the distance. "Collectors discuss them. I will give you an example. There was a collection of doubloons in New Orleans that disappeared in the Katrina hurricane. Never found. That collection is still talked about. Magazine articles speculate about it. Extremely valuable. Worth millions."

As his friends' words glowed like coals inside him, Carty forced himself to stay silent. He sipped his whiskey. Because now he knew. His old partner, Demond, actually did steal the collection. It was out there somewhere, waiting for him.

Even better, Vargas had given him a roadmap to find it. He'd said anyone in possession of a collection would tell people about it.

Their friends. A wife.

And Demond did have a wife. Chances were good he said something to her. Not about the theft, but where the doubloons were hidden. Perhaps something she didn't know was a clue.

He couldn't personally approach her. His reappearance would be impossible to explain. But there were ways around that. He just needed to be careful. As he always was.

Driving home that night he dredged up the names of everyone he knew from his days as a NOPD patrolman. Scoured his memory for one particular name.

The name of Demond's wife.

Her name finally came to him, settling through the wafting heat from the palm fronds above the road, or perhaps drifting east from the endless Pacific.

Liz.

Liz Timmons.

Chapter Four

J ake Kittery guided his wife's Ford into the parking space reserved for him beside the renovated three-story brick building that held their offices. He'd made the builders take down the sign that read 'Reserved for President of TU Health," but everyone left the spot open for him anyway. He liked that quiet respect, despite feeling vaguely guilty about it.

The office building stood in the land rising gradually from the Monongahela River and railroad tracks toward Braddock's main street. The area was once block after block of row houses and small family homes, but most were gone now, leaving a crisscross of streets, overgrown yards, and the occasional standalone house. Their office building was once part of a row of narrow two-story buildings that held ground-floor shops below family apartments. It stood alone like a sentinel now, the bricks on the four corners scarred from their separation from the adjoining buildings.

Jake opened the back door and stepped into the office kitchen, thinking about the building's history.

He'd first seen it as a kid in the nineteen seventies. Then, only three of the houses in the row still contained residents, usually living in second-floor apartments. The shops were long closed. When the elderly resident of this particular building died, the structure was bought by a hulking ex-steelworker nicknamed Boots. Named for his size thirteen steel-toed shoes, Boots knocked out the ground floor walls and installed a bar that ran almost the entire depth of the first floor. He placed a red neon sign spelling out Whiskey Rebellion in the front window, and by the time Jake turned eighteen, he knew that Whiskey Rebellion's draft beers and Jim Beam shots never cost more than a dollar. The bar's two pool tables—marred with cigarette burns and chalk-marked felt—were always playable. The standing joke was they were still more level than any contract offered by factory management.

When Boots died in 2010, almost two hundred people crammed St. Pete's for the memorial service.

Only then were the surrounding buildings torn down. Jake didn't know if keeping the shuttered Whiskey Rebellion was a miracle of city planning, or unvarnished nostalgia. But when the idea for TU Health took shape five years ago, Jake remembered the shuttered bar.

He bought the structure for a song with the first of their grant money. He and Stevie removed the long bar and gutted the walls to the studs before rebuilding. Stevie, despite his college and graduate school degrees, took to the manual labor and held his own. Jake didn't say anything to him, but he'd been proud.

He knew that Stevie would carry the work around with him. Would appreciate the offices more for having done the work himself.

Jake stepped through the kitchen into the bullpen of desks at the front of the building.

Edna turned to him from the low-walled cubicle where she worked. "Nine-thirty?" Her throat sounded like she needed a cigarette. "Life of Riley, I guess."

Jake knew Edna was in her early sixties, but she looked older, the skin around her eyes and mouth a patchwork of creases. She'd buried her husband twenty years earlier after a mill accident and lost her son in Afghanistan. The largest objects on her desk were two eight-by-ten frames holding photos of her two granddaughters. The words "love and faith" were engraved on each frame. She polished the glass every day the same way most people said their prayers.

"Stevie was supposed to bring me in." Jake glanced at Stevie's dark office. "He never showed."

"Young men," Edna rasped, a smile curling her lips. "Probably met some sweet young thing. Doesn't want to leave her. He's sleeping in." She emphasized the last two words.

That was something Jake always liked about her. Sixty-some years old, and her mind still worked like a prowling tomcat.

"He's got a job to do," Jake shot back roughly, although he liked her suggestion. It crossed his mind, not for the first time, that Stevie needed to find someone and settle down. He wouldn't mind some grandchildren of his own, and Ellie had hinted about them enough.

Jake turned to a large whiteboard opposite the offices. "Anything going today?" He skimmed the list of doctors and their planned visits for the rest of the week.

"We lost Charlie Klug last night," Edna said quietly. "Charlie's wife Mary called me. I guess he passed away in his sleep. Doc Loost was scheduled to visit him Friday, so I marked her free."

"I remember Charlie." Jake pictured a night when Charlie ran the pool table at the Whiskey Rebellion, taking fifty dollars from some young suburban kid trying to be tough. But clearest was the memory of Charlie beside him in 1986, during the union march along Grant Street, Pittsburgh's main boulevard. That was a day. Forty-thousand union members, rallied together, protesting the employment of non-union labor for the renovation of the Pennsylvania Railway Station.

They'd won the jobs back.

And later that same year, the six-month strike against U.S. Steel. Charlie on the picket line that helped bring the continuous caster mill to Braddock, another big win. Charlie finished his working years there, lasting long enough to see his son through college.

Where was Charlie's son now? Washington D.C.? At the funeral, Jake decided to say something to the young man. Tell him about Charlie's loyalty to the union. A real brother. And maybe about the night Charlie ran the table on that greenhorn kid. Bought beers for the bar with the winnings.

He fought down a surge of loss and glanced at his son's dark office.

He turned to Edna. "Is Mary doing okay? Anything we can do?"

"She seemed alright." Edna touched the frame holding the picture of one of her granddaughters. "It's a mercy, sometimes." She looked at Jake. "What

Charlie had, he was wasting away. I don't know how much more Mary could take."

Jake had no response, but he didn't need one. Edna's words were the truest he knew. Charlie's cancer, it went unsaid, came from the lousy air at any of the several mills Charlie worked. Now, he was just another data point proving the higher cancer and pulmonary disease rates among retired mill workers. Which was exactly why Jake agreed to put his name behind TU Health.

"Send Mary some flowers, if you think it's the right thing to do." Jake stepped into his office. The motion detector flicked on the overhead light as he slid behind his desk.

The brightness made him think of the graffiti on his garage door and that Ellie was right. Conor Byrne was to blame, and it had gone on too long. Today's graffiti, the burned tires on his lawn, the roadkill deer dumped in the center of his driveway. The anonymous whispered calls to the local police, accusing Jake of being a wife beater.

Coincidentally, the incident that started Conor after him was that same 1986 union march down Grant Street.

Perhaps he deserved Conor's rage, perhaps not. No matter how frequently Jake replayed that day in 1986, it was always a blur. The marchers taunting the cops, the charge of the police line. Him shouting not to give ground, the crush of bodies and punches. The grunts and screams, his own breath, hot in this throat. One of his union brothers folding to the ground beside him, how it uncorked him, freed him to swing his fists at the blue uniforms. Then a separation, almost by agreement, the sides reforming, members tending to and lifting the fallen, the police officers helping two of their own away.

Jake rose and stared at the office wall, tingling with the memory of it. He'd led the way, he knew that. As head of his local, he had to. He'd also felt his punches connect, but against what? Who? But none of that mattered. Conor Byrne's rage didn't distinguish between Jake's leadership of his local and his thrown fists. In Byrne's mind, they were the same.

Jake sat, the tingling subsiding to a slight nausea. There were no answers, he knew. He'd covered this ground hundreds of times. In depositions, in court, with Ellie, and most of all, alone in bed at three in the morning, Ellie asleep beside him. If it was his punch, he would willingly take responsibility, but he just didn't know.

He swallowed and slowly, with an effort, made himself stare at the one true fact of it all.

Conor Byrne Jr., named after his father, a rookie cop just starting in the same profession as his dad, was the only death that day. A brain hemorrhage from a blow to the head that somehow went undiagnosed. Or, more likely, Jake believed, a blow that went unreported. Conor's son wouldn't want to let down his unit. Or his father.

And Conor Byrne Sr., with his spray paint and rotting roadkill, was never going to let Jake forget.

Chapter Five

Vic and Liz finished their coffee sitting in Vic's car, buffeted by the wind staggering over the bluff. They talked about Jayvon, Liz's son, now in his second year of college. Liz grudgingly admitted he seemed to be doing well. Vic updated Liz on his granddaughter, Lettie. Almost seven years old, set to start first grade in the coming year.

Family updates exhausted, Liz turned to him. "When does the new girl start?"

"Our new commander?" Vic stuck his empty cup in the cup-holder. "Sandy Vrail. You might not want to call her *girl*. And you saw the memo. Next Monday."

"You're going to miss your one-on-ones with our DA. I think you kinda like her country-club hair."

Vic thought about his last meeting with Hana Richards, the county's first female DA. She'd been matter-of-fact and decisive, as usual. He'd come to know Hana well over the last six months, but couldn't read anything into the way she told him about his new commander. He didn't hear excitement, and she didn't hint at what Sandy Vrail's priorities might be. It surprised him. While Hana was always direct, her asides and jokes always gave him a sense of direction and tone. He received none in that meeting.

"Hana didn't give me any kind of read on Sandy."

"Lotta military," Liz said quietly. "I read Sandy's bio from Hana's e-mail. Twenty years in the Army, most of it in military police CID. Criminal Investigative Division is no bullshit. And that wasn't a small job she had for the last four years. Commander of CID at Fort Hood?"

"Texas. Great. Any idea where she's from originally?"

"I called someone I know from the military. Army brat, they said."

Vic thought about that. Liz could have talked to Levon, her live-in boyfriend. He was ex-military, but he was also out of the country and out of touch. Vic had also heard Liz speak less and less about Levon over the last few months, and he made a note to ask Levon about that next time they met.

Vic also knew Army brats were different. Most people had their thinking framed by their family and where they grew up. Their new commander's world-view was the military, plain and simple. "Hope she doesn't want us all to salute her."

"We're cops, of course we salute her. Do you understand what the word *commander* means?"

"You're the one who called her *girl*. And I meant salute her all the time."

Liz looked at him out of the corner of her eye. "Oh yeah. You're going to get along just great with her."

"Let's hope." His phone buzzed, and Vic checked the text. "Forrest. He says we can walk the site."

Without speaking, Liz swung herself out of the car. Vic followed, noting that the coroner's van had appeared along with a Fire and Rescue team. Two young men were strapping on rappelling harnesses, preparing to scour the bluff-face for the victim's phone and wallet.

He and Liz passed a small group of onlookers and ducked under the crime scene tape. They walked the path to the grassy area and the large rocks, Forrest waiting for them, his mask and hood pulled down. The wind tousled his salt-and-pepper hair.

"Anything new?" Vic called.

"Nah. And we fingertipped the whole area." He nodded toward some tall weeds on the far side of the clearing. "Even went through there as far as we could. If the killer dumped the wallet and phone here, they went over the cliff."

Liz's eyes narrowed. "That means the killer searched the victim's pockets?"

"Possibly. We'll check the pockets for DNA. As soon as we get the body

19

to the morgue, we'll fingerprint him as well."

Vic considered the figure prone on the ground, now covered by a weighted plastic sheet. "Can I take a look?"

Forrest led them over to the body, and after a quick glance back up the path, stepped around the body and lifted the sheet so it blocked the onlookers from seeing the victim.

Forrest had rolled the body over so it lay on its back and placed the hands inside paper bags. Vic considered the young man, vaguely aware of Liz snapping photos on her phone. Vic guessed the victim was in his late twenties or early thirties. Lean and muscular, he wore designer jeans and a trim grey shirt. His shoes were brown with some kind of white sole, a style Vic hadn't come to appreciate yet.

"Money," Liz said quietly. "See the haircut?"

Vic glanced at the neatly groomed hair. "Yeah. And take a picture of the belt. Have you seen one like it before?"

Vic studied the supple, rich-looking black belt. The silver buckle was one thing, but the leather was pockmarked all over. He wasn't sure he'd seen anything like it.

"Nope." Liz adjusted the zoom on her phone and photographed the belt.

Vic studied the wound in the solar plexus area of the man's body. "Was there much blood?" he asked Forrest.

"Yeah. Ground absorbed it. We took samples. Stabbed and expired here. He wasn't moved."

Liz lowered her phone. "You mean right here?"

"Oh yeah. He didn't walk down from the statues or anything. We'll know when he's opened up, but I'm guessing the blade stabbed his heart."

"That's a very long blade." Vic glanced at Forrest.

Forrest shrugged. "Well, I'm hoping that's what happened. That way, it would be quick. He'd pass out before he really knew what happened."

Vic didn't believe him. His sense was anyone would feel the pain of the blade entering, know from the sluicing hot blood it was fatal. Be overwhelmed by the terror of knowing there was no coming back, that this was the end. He glanced from the body to the city of Pittsburgh below. At night, lit up, with the cars streaming over the bridges, the wind on your face, perhaps it wouldn't be such a bad place to die.

That was ridiculous, and he knew it. More likely, the man's last thought was about what he got wrong. The mistake he made that led to this. What he would never get to do. He looked at Liz, his throat tight. "Good?" Even to his own ears, the word sounded strangled.

Liz stepped to the victim's feet and took one last photograph. She nodded to Forrest. Squinting in concentration, she then looked around. "Anything from the rock?"

"About two thousand prints. So yeah."

Vic recognized two of the people who worked in the coroner's department manhandling a stretcher down the path. He looked back as Forrest tucked the cover over the body again.

Liz slid her phone into her pocket. "That's everything I need."

Together, he and Liz walked up the path, stopping long enough to let the coroner's office personnel pass them.

They ducked under the crime scene tape. Vic glanced at the uniformed officer and saw strain and boredom. Vic guessed his feet were starting to hurt. He thanked him.

A short woman stepped toward them from the statues of George Washington and Guyasuta. Her hair was pulled back over her head so severely Vic thought her scalp must hurt.

"Are you the lead detectives on the scene?" She looked from Vic to Liz, her voice direct and expecting an answer.

Normally, Vic would ignore the woman, but a small voice in his mind noted her hairstyle looked military. "And you are?"

She squared up in front of him, her feet spread. Vic noted hiking boots. He also had the sense of an implacable force.

"You're Detective Vic Lenoski, correct?" She shifted her gaze to Liz. "And you're Detective Liz Timmons?"

Liz gestured toward Vic. "What he said."

The woman cut a look back at Vic. The corners of her mouth were tight. "I'm your new Commander. Sandy Vrail." She waited for the statement to sink in. She didn't extend a hand.

Vic settled himself. "Well, good to meet you, I guess. I didn't think you were going to start work until Monday?"

Sandy blinked, and her face strained for a split second as if she was about to deliver a reprimand. She caught herself. "I thought I should get an early start, meet some of the detectives. DA Richards told me to start with you two. I called the detective pool and talked to a Craig Luntz. He reported you were here. What do we have?"

Sandy's words were almost a force of nature and Vic straightened to attention. "John Doe. Early-thirties, maybe. Stabbing victim. Happened last night, discovered this morning. Victim looks middle class."

Sandy looked from Vic to Liz, skeptical. "That's it?"

Liz cocked her head. "Yes. Until we get an ID."

Sandy considered Liz for perhaps fifteen seconds. "Next steps?"

Vic saw Liz tense, and he jumped in before she said something she would regret. "Hoping for a fingerprint ID, and we'll have DNA. No wallet or phone on the body." He gestured to the Fire and Rescue team, who were lugging coiled ropes along the path, their equipment jangling. "Fire and rescue will search the hill-side and the bottom of the cliff, in case those items were tossed over."

"Good. Keep me updated." Sandy hesitated, as if unsure what to say next. She looked at Vic. "We should have lunch." A blotch of red appeared on her neck. "I mean with both of you." She gestured at Liz. "I'd like your take on how things are done and what we can do to improve the team." She searched their faces.

"Sure," Vic answered. "Um, when?"

"Next week. We'll finalize on Monday."

Sandy glanced from Liz to Vic, her eyes settling on Vic's jacket. A sour look crossed her features. She looked up. "Carry on." Her right arm shifted just slightly, and she pivoted sharply on her heel and hiked toward the road.

Neither Liz nor Vic said anything for thirty seconds. They just watched Sandy, her back ramrod straight, march toward the parked cars.

"Did you see that?" Liz asked.

"What?"

"Her face got all tight after she introduced herself, and you didn't react."

"I saw it. So?"

"She was expecting you to salute. Was about to jump down your throat when you didn't. Then she remembered she's out of the military. And she almost saluted right before she walked away. Moved her arm, but caught herself."

"Well, shit." Vic finally relaxed.

The wind buffeted them.

"Shit is right," Liz breathed.

Chapter Six

Vic and Liz waited in Vic's car until they were sure the body was on its way to the morgue. Only then did Vic head for Allegheny County Police headquarters, with a detour for coffee and takeout sandwiches that took longer than either expected.

When they reached their desks, Craig rose from his chair. "Hey. I talked to our new commander, Sandy Vrail. Did she find you guys?"

"She did." Vic removed his jacket, remembering the sour look Sandy gave it. He sighed.

"Well?" Craig couldn't keep the excitement out of his voice.

Vic looked at Liz, encouraging her to speak. She rolled her eyes and turned to her computer screen, leaving Vic to answer the question.

"Hard to say. She seems very…military."

Craig turned from Vic to Liz and back again, disappointed at the limited description. Still annoyed at the look Sandy gave his jacket, Vic studied Craig's shirt and slacks. There was no question that since Craig started dating Eileen Liang, his dress had improved. Clearly, Eileen helped him pick out his clothes, or at least required a higher standard. His shirt sleeves even showed traces of a crease from an iron.

"Let's give her some time to settle in," Vic said, loud enough for Liz to hear. He bored a look into Craig. "You ready for next week?"

Craig gave him a lopsided grin. "Good to go."

Craig's detective test was the following Tuesday, and while Vic wasn't too worried about Craig passing on the first try, he still felt the need to push him about it. He owed it to Craig's father, a retired police sergeant who looked out for Vic as a rookie.

"Mess it up and I'll kick you back to CSI." Vic thought his threat sounded about as dangerous as a kitten.

Liz glanced at him from her computer screen and raised her eyes to the heavens.

Craig beamed an unintimidated smile, but his phone rang before he could respond.

Vic turned to his computer screen and tried to look busy as Craig took the call and hung up. "We have an ID," Craig called out.

Vic looked up, surprised, catching a similar look on Liz's face.

Craig was hunched over his computer, studying an online form.

"That was fast." Skepticism riddled Liz's words.

"Yeah." Craig turned away from his screen. "I called the coroner's office while you guys were getting lunch, told them to fast-track the fingerprints. Turns out the guy has a local police record. Much faster ID than the national databases."

"Okay," Vic called, urging him on.

Craig turned back to the screen. "Name is Steven Kittery. Pittsburgh guy."

"What's he in the system for?"

Craig hunched closer to his screen, reading. He sat up a few seconds later. "Two years ago. Assault." He kept reading. "Oh wow. The guy he assaulted, get this, he's a retired Bureau police officer. Officer Conor Byrne."

Vic and Liz exchanged glances, but Liz was quicker to the next question. "Did it go to trial?"

Craig scrolled the document on his screen. "No. Byrne dropped the charges after a couple of weeks."

Vic knew Liz was thinking the same thing as him. If a retired police officer dropped an assault charge, there needed to be a very good reason.

"Do you remember Conor Byrne?" Liz frowned at Vic.

Vic shook his head. "No. But the name sounds familiar. I'll ask around." He turned to Craig. "Do a workup on Steven Kittery. We need his address. If he posted bail related to the assault charge, find out who paid. That might give us next of kin. Then, do the normal run-up. Address, phone records, financials, you got it?"

"On it." Craig bent to his computer screen.

Vic thought about the Fire and Rescue team working their way down the hillside. It was Steven Kittery's phone that mattered now. Maybe this was one of those cases where the pieces fell into place. The kind that almost solved themselves.

Vic turned back to his computer screen with a wry smile.

Right. Was that likely, when the first person they discovered with a possible grudge against Steven Kittery was also a retired police officer?

Chapter Seven

Steven Kittery's place of residence was the city's East End, a surprise given that Steven's workplace was in hard-bitten Braddock, a ghost-ridden mill town clutching the last functioning steel mill within an hour's drive of Pittsburgh. The East End address was a newly gentrified neighborhood favored by the city's swarm of college-fresh high-tech workers.

No one answered the lobby bell to the four-story, sleek building housing Steven's condominium. Vic found a sales office at the corner of the complex, and after a brief explanation showed his ID to a brightly interested young woman named Ashley. It wasn't until Ashley led them along the third-floor hallway to Steven's condominium that reality seemed to strike her. She turned to Vic and Liz without breaking stride. "I guess Steve was involved in some kind crime? Was he robbed or something?"

They reached the door to Steven's condo and stopped. Ashley's dark, pretty eyes settled on Vic. "Is he okay?"

"Do you know Steve well?" Vic asked.

"Well, he was one of my first sales. I see him in the gym sometimes. He works out pretty hard. He always stops and talks to me when we see each other. Which is nice."

Her dark hair was long and parted in the middle, and she brushed some strands away from her face. "I mean, he seems like a good guy."

From the way Ashley said the last sentence, Vic thought she'd hoped for more attention from him.

"I'm sorry," Vic said slowly. "We aren't in a position to discuss the case.

All we can say is that Steven was the victim of a crime, and we're trying to find out what happened. Does he live with anyone? Roommate, partner perhaps?"

Ashley glanced from Vic to Liz and back. "No. He's by himself." She turned to the front door, and Vic was sure her eyes were damp. Vic realized Ashley was smart enough to understand the implication behind his words.

She turned her key in the lock and pushed open the door, stepping back to let them pass. "I'll wait out here. I want to make sure it's locked after you leave."

Vic thanked her, and he and Liz stepped inside. The door thumped shut behind them. They both looked around.

The living room, dining area, and kitchen adjoined one another. The appliances were stainless steel and new. A large screen TV occupied one wall of the living room, the furniture arranged to face it. The furniture's black leather upholstery, white kitchen cabinets, and black granite of the countertops made Vic think of a bachelor's apartment.

"Not thinking he had a woman in his life," Liz said quietly.

"Maybe Ashley should have talked to him a bit more instead of waiting."

"Well, that chance is gone." Liz stepped toward a hallway. "You take out here, and I'll look down the hall?"

"Works for me." After a sweep of the living room, Vic headed for the kitchen. Within a few minutes, he'd established that Steven liked to cook. Instead of frozen dinners, he found a stocked larder, and neatly divided and hand-labelled frozen meat in the freezer. The refrigerator drawers contained a variety of vegetables. Stuffed into a small box on the countertop were print-outs of recipes from a variety of sources, several with hand-written notes.

Liz appeared in the hallway. "One thing you need to see."

Vic followed her down the hall to a bedroom converted into an office. She pointed at the desk. "Actually, it's what you don't see."

The center of the desktop was empty except for a straggly charging wire.

"No laptop," Vic said quietly.

"Can't find it anywhere. He's got a backpack, and I didn't see it inside."

"Maybe it's in his car?"

"Wherever that is. We didn't look for it on Mt. Washington."

Vic thought about that. "Have Craig check the car registry databases and send some uniforms to look for it. Make sure they check the parking lot at the bottom of the Duquesne Incline. He might have parked there and ridden to the top."

Liz called Craig and passed along the instructions. "We should check the parking lot here," she added, putting away her phone.

"Agree. Maybe we'll get lucky. Reminds me there's security cameras in the incline car and the top and bottom stations. We might get a time when he went up the hill."

"Good point. Didn't think of that. Maybe we'll see him with someone."

"That would be something." Vic didn't believe it. He already had the sense the murder was premeditated and well thought out. Late at night, a lonely location, a murder weapon that was transported to the scene, a murderer with the presence of mind to dump Steven's wallet and phone, and possibly his laptop. If it wasn't for the lucky hit on the fingerprints, they would still be floundering around for an ID.

Vic turned to Liz. "Okay. Anything else from this end of the condo?"

"Not really. No evidence of a steady girlfriend, but he does have women over. Condoms in the bedside table and good sheets and pillows on the bed. Couple of toothbrushes still in the packaging in the bathroom. Woman's comb and brush and a box of tampons in a drawer. The bed's even made. He's prepared."

"A modern bachelor."

"Or one who doesn't want women to have an excuse to leave."

Vic glanced at her. "Well, when you put it that way."

"There was no hair in the woman's brush. He'd cleaned it. That's working way too hard. Do you smell anything? I don't. What guy in his twenties doesn't have a smelly apartment?"

Vic headed back down the hall so Liz didn't see his smile. "He cooks, too," he called behind him.

Liz followed him. "If I was twenty-three and walked in here, I'd go find the handcuffs you know he's got hidden someplace and leave him chained to his fancy refrigerator. This place ain't natural."

Vic stopped in the living room and looked around. "Did you see any photographs anywhere?"

"Just one. On the bedroom dresser. Photo of a dog. Big fluffy white people kind of dog. Guaranteed to make the girls ooh and aah. Like I said, this place ain't natural."

Vic stopped at the front door and turned to her. "No address book? Planner?"

Liz stared at him in disbelief. "Really? They're on his phone and laptop. What century are you in?"

Grinning again, Vic twisted the door handle. "Whichever one helps me catch the bad guy."

Chapter Eight

The drive to Braddock took Vic and Liz almost an hour. No highways led there, only twisty and roller-coaster two-lane roads, regularly interspersed with faded stop signs and dingy yellow-painted traffic lights sagging from overhead wires. Narrow wood-frame houses in need of paint crowded the road. As they entered Braddock, Vic felt he was travelling back into his childhood. He'd grown up in Homestead, another Monongahela River mill town with the same rows of narrow, high-peaked homes clinging to the long hillside overlooking the mills, river, and railroad lines. He remembered sitting at his bedroom window high on that hill, staring through the sooty glass, hearing the shift-change whistles and echoes of the jarring, irregular slamming sounds that his father explained away as the working of the foundry. From his perch, he'd only glimpsed the river beyond the flat, low ground that held the factories and mills. Depending on the time of year, the river water was grey, brown, or a turgid dark green, the opposite bank a steep, tree-covered bluff that made him think the mill was held in the palm of a hand.

"You okay?"

Vic shook away his reverie. "Yeah. Reminds me of Homestead, where I grew up."

"This?" Liz pointed at the buildings lining North Braddock Avenue. Stretching ahead of them were shuttered storefronts, the names above the doors faded or missing letters. Here and there, an empty space between buildings sat like an empty tooth socket. Incongruously, they passed at least three bright wall murals.

"Mayor put some effort into this town." Vic eased the car past a job retraining center and a forlorn park. In the distance, mill stacks etched the skyline.

Liz checked the map on her phone. "Mayor is a senator in Washington now, right?"

"Yep."

"We'll see if he ever comes back." She pointed ahead. "Next right."

Vic slowed and turned onto a street that ran several blocks in the direction of the railroad tracks and river. Most of the buildings on the left side of the road were gone, but one three-story building remained, surrounded by overgrown grass, the rough brickwork of its side wall showing that it was once connected to another building.

As they passed, Vic spotted a small sign that said, TU Health." He stopped quickly, just before the entrance to a parking lot tucked against the far side of the building. Only three vehicles sat among the six empty spaces: a Ford sedan at the very back of the building, a battered mini-van near the street, and between them, a gleaming Mercedes SUV.

Vic wheeled in and parked between the minivan and the Mercedes.

They let themselves out, Liz giving the Mercedes a long appraisal.

Vic was surprised at her interest. "Your next ride?"

She considered the car for another few seconds before turning to follow him to the building's front door. "Trying to figure out how that fits here."

"Did you ask it?"

Liz didn't answer. The front door led into a small entry and a second door that opened into the offices. Clusters of desks separated by low walls covered most of the floor space, with glass-fronted offices and a conference room along the back wall. A large whiteboard hung from the bare brick right-hand wall. Two people were sitting at desks, and both raised their heads so quickly, Vic knew that walk-ins were unusual.

"Can I help you?" The gravelly voice was from a woman in the center of the room. Vic guessed she was in her mid-sixties, and from her pale face and permed hair, he knew she was Pittsburgh-born and bred. The woman sitting nearby wasn't. Her black hair and liquid brown eyes suggested

Indian descent, and she looked as sleek as the SUV parked outside. Vic dubbed her Ms. Mercedes.

Vic crossed to the woman who welcomed them, introduced himself and Liz, and showed his ID. Ms. Mercedes didn't take her eyes off them.

"We have information that a Steven Kittery works here," Vic told the elderly woman, lowering his voice. Vic noted two oversized framed photographs of young girls on the woman's desk. Grandchildren, he guessed.

"Stevie Kittery is our CFO," she replied, frowning.

Beside him, Liz shifted position, and he knew she also caught the nickname Stevie.

"Great. Is he here?" Vic hated this dance, but he had to be sure they had the right Steven—or Stevie—Kittery.

"He hasn't come in yet today."

"Has anyone heard from him?" Vic used his patient voice, although Edna, as he saw from the nameplate by her desk, was sticking to terse replies that were starting to annoy him.

Edna cut her eyes from him to Liz and back. "We've been expecting him," she conceded.

Vic didn't like having this conversation in the open, especially with the fashionably dressed and overly interested Ms. Mercedes watching as if they were all part of a TV sitcom.

Edna solved it for him. "Wait here." She gave Ms. Mercedes a look that said, "Keep quiet," crossed to a glass-walled office, and leaned inside. Vic saw a rangy man place a hand over the mouth of his telephone and listen to her. He looked through the glass wall of the office at Vic and nodded to the woman. He returned to his telephone conversation, but stood.

The woman moved to the door of the glass-walled conference room next to the office. "You can wait here," she called and waved at them to enter the conference room. "Mr. Kittery will talk to you."

When Vic reached the doorway, he asked her, "Another Kittery?"

"Right. Jake Kittery. Our CEO. Stevie's dad."

Vic's stomach twisted. They'd walked in unprepared. Vic thanked her and stepped into the conference room, annoyed at himself. He hadn't done a death notification in months. He rarely needed to anymore. But if Jake Kittery was Stevie Kittery's father, that was exactly what was going to happen next.

They sat at the table, and Liz pushed her phone over to him. "We should have checked." She pointed at a photograph on her phone. "That's Steven Kittery." She flicked her finger on the screen. "And that's Jake Kittery, CEO. They even look alike."

"Great. I'll do it, okay?"

As Liz nodded, the rangy man entered from the office next door, his face set, eyes alert.

He already suspects something, Vic thought.

"What can I do for you?" The man's question was pointed.

Vic rose, introduced himself and Liz, and presented his ID.

"Sure, right. Now, what is it?"

"Perhaps we could sit down?" Vic gestured to the chair nearest the man.

"Look. My son didn't come in to work this morning, and now you two show up. I can do the math."

Vic hesitated. "You are Jake Kittery, is that correct?" Vic made a point of sitting down, hoping that Jake would follow suit. He didn't.

"Yes."

"And your son is Steven Kittery?"

"Yes. Now what's happened? Is he in jail?"

Vic took a slow breath, hoping to slow his heartbeat. "Sir, we discovered the victim of a crime this morning. A suspicious death. We believe that victim is your son, Steven Kittery."

Jake's eyes widened in confusion. "What are you saying?" He leaned over the table toward Vic. "I don't understand."

Careful not to look away, Vic spoke slowly. "We're investigating a suspicious death. We took the fingerprints of the victim who died, and they matched fingerprints we have on file for your son, Steven Kittery."

The color drained from Jake's face. "No. It's a mistake." Jake's right knee quivered. "You're saying Stevie's dead? You made a mistake." The desperation in his voice was unmistakable. Jake grabbed the nearest chair for support.

"We don't believe so. We made the identification through fingerprints. But if you or someone you trust could view and confirm his identity, we would appreciate that. If you aren't feeling up to it, there are other methods we can use."

Jake wrenched a chair from underneath the table and collapsed into it. "It has to be a mistake." His voice was barely more than a whisper.

"Can I get you some water?" Liz asked.

Jake gulped a breath, as if he'd found himself plunged into the ocean. "You're saying he was murdered? Somebody killed him?"

"We have to conduct an autopsy before we can confirm the crime as a murder, but at this time, we believe the death to be suspicious."

Jake dropped shaking hands into his lap. He closed his eyes and swayed for a few moments before going rigid. His eyes flashed open. "It'll be Conor Byrne." His neck flared red. "He did it. I guarantee it. Have you arrested him?" He grasped the edge of the table, knuckles white. "Have you arrested him?"

Vic was confused, and Liz gently cut in. "You're talking about the man who brought charges against Steven for assault?"

"Yes! He's been out to get me for years." Jake slammed a fist on the conference table. "He painted crap on my garage door this morning. Do you understand? He thinks I killed his son, and now he's taken mine."

Vic struggled to breathe in the tight air of the room. "One step at a time." He glanced through the glass to the outer room, wondering if the others could hear their exchange. The elderly woman's head was tilted toward her computer screen, but Ms. Mercedes was watching them, eyes wide. Perhaps she couldn't hear, but Vic knew the tone and intensity of the exchange was obvious.

Vic leaned forward and repeated himself. "One step at a time, Mr. Kittery. First we need to confirm the identity of Steven Kittery. We need to be sure."

Jake stared at him, disgust suffusing his face. "Yeah. Of course you don't want to go near Conor Byrne. He's a cop." His voice rose. "Protect your own. So how does my son get justice?" He took a ragged breath. "Doesn't sound like it'll come from you two. Or any of your goddamned type."

"Okay." Vic fought down a surge of anger. "We're going to follow the facts. Right now, we hardly have any. You want us to find who killed your son? Then work with us. For starters, we need to find his laptop. Is it in his office? But even before we get to that, we need to be sure we have a correct identification. How about we start there?"

"Jake?"

Everyone in the conference room turned to the door. The elderly woman stood there, clutching the doorframe, hanging onto it as if she was teetering at the edge of a pit. As if she knew the horror at the bottom. Vic thought she'd aged fifteen years since they arrived.

"Jake." Her voice was gravelly and low. "Not yet. Let them do their job. Tell Ellie. Right now. Tell Ellie. Then bury your son. Bury Stevie." Her eyes searched Jake's face. "Then worry about Conor."

Vic saw the flush on Jake's neck fade. "Mr. Kittery." Vic watched Jake blink and turn to him. "We have to do this a certain way. The right way. Edna understands. Tell your family. Focus on Steven. That's what you need to do now. And understand something. I don't play favorites. My partner and I," he gestured to Liz, "We don't play favorites. Let us do what we do best, and we'll catch who did this. Whoever it is."

"You're going to find it's Conor Byrne." Jake's words were obstinate, but the vehemence was gone. Vic had seen Jake flinch at the mention of Ellie, and guessed that was Jake's wife, Steven's mother. He had the awful, wrenching memory of telling Anne, his own wife, that their daughter Dannie was missing. And again, almost eighteen months later, of telling her Dannie was dead. Nausea rose in him, and his eyes burned. To hide it he reached inside his jacket.

Carefully, he separated a business card from the pile he kept in his pocket, his hands below the table to hide his shaking fingers. He pushed one over the table to Jake. Took a breath. "If you feel up to doing an identification, call me, and I'll set up a time for you. Okay?"

"Or me." Liz slid her own business card over the table. "In case you have trouble reaching Vic. Although he always answers his phone."

Liz's last sentence surprised Vic. He'd never heard Liz make a positive comment about him. He didn't have time to dissect it. He rose and handed Edna a card as well. She took it with a disjointed movement.

"Thanks, Edna." Vic sat and turned to Jake, who looked dazed, his hands again clutching the edge of the table. "Mr. Kittery, we'd like to take a look in Steven's office. With your permission. Maybe you could get started with any notifications you need to do?"

Jake blinked. "Right." He turned to Edna. "Show them Stevie's office." Almost as if he was in pain, Jake rose from the table, left the room, and returned to his office. But Vic saw something else in his movement. It was as if Jake was unbalanced, a part of him missing.

"This way." Edna's voice was barely above a whisper.

Vic and Liz followed Edna's heavy steps to a smaller office next to Jake's. As they passed Jake's office, Vic noted the door was closed. Jake was sitting at his desk, staring at nothing at all. Vic looked the other way and saw that Ms. Mercedes, or whatever her name might be, was gone.

Edna stepped aside at the door to Steven's office and waved Vic and Liz inside. "Let me know if you need anything else." Her voice was thick.

"Thanks, Edna." Liz was already behind the desk, looking at the files stacked on the surface. The overhead light flickered on.

Vic nodded to Edna and followed Liz inside. The desk faced a bookcase, and he checked the three framed documents hanging above it. He read each one, identifying a diploma from the University of Pittsburgh, a diploma from Pitt's MBA program, and a Pennsylvania CPA License. He photographed each one.

"No laptop," Liz said from behind the desk.

Vic turned to her. Liz gestured at the desk surface. "But there's a charging wire here. Looks like he moves his laptop between his home and here."

"Did Craig find Steven's car?"

"Haven't heard yet."

Vic turned back to the bookcase and examined the items arrayed on top. Two were acrylic awards. He scanned them, the words not really registering.

They were from the dominant health insurer in the Pittsburgh area. Out of habit, Vic photographed each one. The third item was a photograph. Vic picked it up. Inside the frame were two people wearing black graduation gowns, arms around each other, their free hands showing diplomas. One of the two was Steven Kittery. Vic didn't recognize the other man, but from his age he had to be a classmate.

"Finally have a photograph." Vic held up the frame for Liz to see.

"About time."

Vic stared at the photograph and compared the diplomas held by the two men to the ones framed on the wall. The photograph's diploma clearly matched the MBA diploma. Vic took a photograph and returned the frame to the bookcase. He gave the two acrylic awards another glance and focused on the books, skimming the titles. They were all business or accounting-related.

Behind him, Liz shifted something on the desk, and a moment later, he heard a drawer rumble open. Vic weighed his phone in his hand, swiped to the Favorites screen, and called Craig. Tapped the phone onto speaker.

"Vic," Craig answered, almost immediately.

"Craig, three things." He pivoted to face Liz. "Anything on Steven's car?"

Liz stopped her search of the desk drawer and listened.

"Not yet. There's a black and white checking the incline lot now."

"Okay, second, can you call the Medical Examiner and let her know we've done the family notification? Turns out the father works at the same place as Steven."

"TU Health?"

"Right. We need to be ready for Steven's parents to come in for an identification. And third, we visited Steven Kittery's apartment, but we forgot to ask if they have security footage in the apartment hallways or stairwells." He glanced at Liz in time to see disgust as she realized their mistake. "We can't find Steven's laptop, and if it isn't in the car, that means someone may have entered Steven's apartment and taken it. We need to see if we have footage of that. We talked to an Ashley in the condo building sales office. Track her down. She seemed pretty competent."

"On it, and I'll let you know when they're finished with the parking lot."

"Good. And pull the security footage from the incline. Pretty sure they shut down at 12:30. Keep that in mind."

Vic ended the call.

"Are we off our game?" Liz asked.

"Kind of. Maybe just slow pulling ourselves together. We talked about the incline footage, but I didn't think it through. Forrest thought Steven was killed close to midnight. The spot where he was killed was maybe a hundred yards from the Duquesne Incline station. Maybe our killer took the incline down. It's one thing to see if Steven rode up on it; maybe just as interesting to see who was on board for the last couple of runs down."

"Works for me."

That was more like Liz, Vic thought. No compliment in that response. He stepped into the office doorway. Edna was at her desk, head bowed and face in her hands. He looked through the glass into Jake's office. Jake was hunched over his desk, office phone pressed hard to his ear, his wide shoulders rounded, a large knobby hand over his eyes. As Vic watched, Jake's chest heaved in what had to be a sob, or a suppressed wail.

Feeling slightly sick, Vic let out a slow breath.

Chapter Nine

Carty Swain eased his rental car off Route 90 and onto the dirt road that led to the shack. He'd found the Garden District house faster than he'd expected. As he sauntered past its stately front yard and studied the stacked verandas from the corner of his eye, he'd thought it looked about the same, like the neighborhood itself. Despite the flooding he'd sloshed through after the second levee broke, the Garden District had maintained its character.

With time to spare, he'd found a downtown car rental location, visited a hobby store, and driven Route 90 looking for the shack's turnoff. The rusted, dark green gate told him he'd arrived. The gate shut behind him; he eased the rental along the hard and rutted track—no longer the muck fuck he remembered from his visit with Demond—and circled behind a screen of trees.

The shack's roof leaned at a rakish angle, the left edge planted into the ground among a scattering of broken boards. The right wall leaned at a forty-five-degree angle toward the right edge of the roof, which somehow was still upright. The front door was gone, the dark interior leering at him like the tunnel of a hollow eye socket.

At some point over the years, someone had spray-painted the word *toots* in fat red letters next to the front door.

Carty cut the ignition and got out, assaulted by the heat and the screech of insects. He studied the dark, weathered boards and tilted roof.

He'd decided to visit on a whim, but he knew his reasoning was sound. After tossing that doubloon back to Demond and firing, Carty had completed a quick search of the shack's interior. But that was it. He'd been too nervous and jazzed about hiding the body to search properly. He needed to be sure the rest of the doubloons weren't hidden right here.

He opened the car trunk and the large box he'd bought at the hobby store. From inside, he slid out a metal detector. If the doubloons were buried outside the shack, this was his best chance of finding them.

Putting the detector together took ten minutes, and several rereads of the instruction sheet. It took only five minutes to acclimate himself to the squeal when the detector skimmed over a buried nail. Satisfied he knew what to expect, he started from the right side of the shack, working in even rows twenty feet out from the walls and back again.

It took him two painstaking hours to circle the sides and back of the shack. Each squeal of the detector meant a minute or so of digging to unearth a variety of rusted nails, bottle caps, and, on one occasion, a dirt-encrusted pair of pliers.

He discovered little more at the front of the building.

He stopped finally, sweat dripping from his chin, and swatted left-handed at the insects dive-bombing his face. Behind the screen of trees, cars whooshed by on Route 90. Flat grey clouds spackled the sky, dimming the sun and concentrating the humidity. He turned to the shack's ghastly doorway.

It was unsafe to go inside, of course, but it was more than that. He'd kept the trapdoor into that moment of his life shut and locked for years. Vapors escaped, sometimes, as they had that night with Vargas sipping whiskey and discussing the doubloon, but he had no doubt that ducking into that darkness beyond the doorway would bring everything back.

The kick of the gun in his hand. Demond Timmons on the floor. That last sigh of wind.

He stepped toward the door, stopped, and weighed the metal detector in his right hand. He knew that inside, the detector would squeal like the vitals monitors of a dying man.

He stepped to the door, inserted the detector inside, and flipped the switch. The squeal was immediate. He swept the detector in an arc, searching for a pattern. It took two more sweeps for him to spot the repetition. The ancient floorboards were nailed to joists, and the detector squealed as it passed over each nail head. He slowed the sweep until the squeals became a timed repetition. He nodded to himself.

He wiped his face with the inside elbow of his free arm to remove the sweat, squatted, and duckwalked into the darkness and stench of mold and rot. He reached the rear wall, and, sweeping the detector back and forth, thighs burning, backed out of the shack, the detector squealing at regular intervals.

Outside, he straightened, dropped the metal detector, and breathed deeply. He hadn't taken a breath the entire time he was inside.

Arms on his hips, he walked around the shack one last time. The humid air was thick in his lungs. But now he knew. The doubloons weren't hidden in or around the shack.

He stopped at his car, staring into the shrubs and stunted trees. He spoke aloud to anything that would hear him, "Nothing's ever simple."

He scooped up the metal detector, dropped it in the trunk, and wedged himself behind the steering wheel. Turned on the engine and blasted the air conditioner.

Where were the doubloons? After Vargas told him about the collection's disappearance during Katrina, he'd searched the internet. Several articles discussed it, even providing a name. The St. Augustine Collection, after the shipwreck that produced the doubloons. And Demond had taken it. The collection was out there somewhere. He knew it.

Once he'd convinced himself of that fact, he'd researched Liz Timmons, on the chance she'd found them. He discovered she'd moved to Pittsburgh and was now a detective for the county police. He knew it was unlikely she kept the collection. When Demond first introduced him to Liz, he'd known immediately she was the right or wrong type. If Liz had discovered the collection while moving out of the apartment, she would have turned it over to authorities. He was certain of it.

Looking back, he guessed a large part of Demond's decision to return the doubloons was driven by the strength of Liz's principles.

"Your damned marriage got you killed, Demond," Carty breathed, staring at what was left of the shack. "In a dump of mouse shit and bugs."

Engine running and windows closed, he picked at his shirt where sweat pasted it to his body. He still had one good card to play. He needed to check the apartment where Demond lived with Liz. He'd visited once and been able to reconstruct the location before he left Costa Rica. And he needed to be sure Liz and Demond hadn't owned any other property in the area. If Demond didn't use his apartment as a hiding place, which was likely, he might have hidden the doubloons on some other property he owned.

The car engine rumbled. High above, the layer of gray clouds was cracking, revealing slivers of blue. He tapped the steering wheel. "Okay. In for a penny, in for a doubloon."

He put the car in reverse and started the turn that would take him to his hotel and what came next.

Chapter Ten

Outside TU Health, Vic and Liz leaned against their car's closed front doors, Liz with her elbows on the car roof reading her phone. Vic watched her, his gut tight, as if he'd sparred a few rounds with someone who'd targeted his abs. He twisted his shoulders side to side experimentally.

Perhaps it wasn't too bad. He faced Liz. "Anything new?"

She pursed her lips without looking up from her phone. "This place. TU Health. Getting a feel for them." She kept reading.

Vic pushed himself off the car. The Mercedes was gone, but that wasn't a surprise. He looked beyond the parking lot, past several more deserted city blocks, the occasional small home standing like a gravestone. The far horizon was marred by the long metal roof of the steel mill's rolling shed and the stubby upright fingers of the blast furnace chimneys. Above that loomed electrical transmission towers, the wires so thick Vic could follow them for at least two miles across the river toward the sunset. He breathed deeply. The air had a texture he remembered from growing up. Not really an electricity, but something freighted, with a vague metal tang.

"Yeah, it's interesting."

Vic looked at Liz. "What's interesting?"

"TU Health."

"Such as?"

"It's a non-profit. It helps retired steelworkers and other union retired. The TU stands for Trade Unions. They organize doctor and nurse home visits to union members with debilitating diseases. I guess the illness rates

44

for retired mill workers are way higher than the rest of the population. More cancers, lung diseases, mobility problems, you name it. Takes pressure off the families to transport the sick to doctor appointments and makes sure patients get more regular care. Doctors are all volunteer."

Vic opened his driver's door, and Liz took the passenger seat, still reading. Vic started the car and steered onto the main road that led to Pittsburgh. Imprinted in his mind was Jake Kittery, hand over his eyes, round-shouldered, as if he'd lost the instinct to see anything coming toward him.

"Anything on Jake Kittery?"

"Short bio. Steelworker early in his life, then full-time head of his local and labor activist. Union through and through."

"And his son? Steven?"

"Nothing we didn't already know. CFO, worked at one of the health insurers after his MBA. Doesn't say which one. Finance department. When TU Health started he became their CFO. That's about it."

They drove in silence for a mile. "Makes sense, though." Vic glanced at Liz. "Jake Kittery has the union contacts. If he was head of his local, union membership will trust him as head of TU Health. They'd go along with the doctor visits. His son knows finance. Good match."

"Feels a bit too homey to me. Non-profit run by a father and son?"

Vic didn't agree, but skipped over it. "How about Ms. Mercedes? Does she show up? She got out of there in a hurry. I bet she overheard us or knew it was bad news. The place wasn't exactly private."

"I'm thinking she's one of the doctors. Explains the Mercedes. And she looked about the right age."

"Whatever that means. But we should look at the doctors. Edna can give us a list. They might know something about Steven."

Liz looked thoughtful. "And what was all that Jake was saying? Graffiti? He thought we were there for another reason. Something related to Conor Byrne."

"We need to get into that as well." Vic accelerated his car along an on-ramp. Evening traffic whizzed around them.

Liz's phone rang, and she answered it. Vic drove in silence, listening to Liz's grunts of agreement. She finished the call with a thank-you.

"That was Craig. He's got all the requests out for video. Port Authority said they'll have the incline footage tomorrow; he's going to pick it up. That girl at the condo said they have stairwell footage. She'll pull that."

"Anything about Steven's car? His laptop and phone?"

"They found the car in the incline parking lot. It's being taken to impound. Uniform who found it gave it a visual, he didn't see a laptop. Might be in the trunk. We'll know tomorrow. Nothing from Fire and Rescue yet."

"If we can't find the laptop," Vic said quietly, "The question is why."

Liz looked at him. "I had the same thought."

"I get the phone disappearing. That's instinctive, even if most people know we can pull the phone records. They just want to get rid of the thing. But why the laptop?"

"You can get your texts on your laptop, you know. Maybe the killer was just being thorough."

Vic frowned. "What I meant was, what if Steven had the laptop with him on Mt. Washington?"

"Killer would have seen it. He took it with the phone."

Vic smiled at the windshield. "He?"

Liz hissed a breath. "You know what I mean."

He did, but his suggestion that Steven carried the laptop to his Mt. Washington meeting bothered him. Nobody would do that normally, especially not at midnight. It didn't make sense. Not unless Steven needed the laptop to show something to the person he was meeting. And if that was the case, whatever he wanted to show was important. It might even have got Steven killed.

Vic slowed as the traffic into the tunnel thickened. His impatience thickened with it. The missing laptop was the first thing they'd discovered that didn't make sense, and he knew from long experience that what mattered were the things that didn't make sense. They needed to track it down. The video footage from the incline might help.

He knew instinctively that would be a better place to start than the doctors

CHAPTER TEN

volunteering at TU Health.

Chapter Eleven

Jake barely remembered driving to the hospital to pick up Ellie. She was standing outside the ER entrance, arms wrapped around herself, her face pale and stricken. When he pulled up she didn't recognize the car for a few seconds, and her hesitation somehow sharpened him, made him more aware of his surroundings.

When she settled into the passenger seat, she didn't say anything.

"I'm taking us home." His words came out hoarsely, barely above a whisper.

"I want to see him," was all she said.

"Let's go home. We can arrange it."

"No. Now. Call whoever you have to call." Her voice was high and brittle, on the edge of a scream. She rocked in her seat.

Jake sank back into some kind of remote operating state. He found the business card given to him by the detective. He called one of the numbers and talked to a young man named Craig, and several minutes later, was on hold with some county department. Five minutes later, he was driving again, now toward a building in Pittsburgh's Strip District, just east of downtown.

As he drove, one face gradually emerged in his mind, gazing at him hungry-eyed. Not Stevie's, but Conor Byrne. Jake saw Conor's pale face and loose jowls, as if a good shake of his head would slough off the skin. Conor's long black hair gleamed, swept back from his forehead, and held in place with a lathering of product. And always, those hungry, blue, hollow eyes.

That image of Conor lingered in his brain even as he and Ellie were shown into some kind of tiled room that smelled of disinfectant. Even as the sheet was pulled back from the prone figure to reveal Stevie—gray-skinned, lips discolored, and so still, so very still. When Ellie's knees gave out, and Jake caught her, it felt as if Conor caught her as well.

The drive home barely registered with him. Again and again, he touched a set of xeroxed sheets folded into his shirt pocket, given to him by the man who showed them what used to be Stevie. They were instructions on what would happen next, when Stevie's body would be released. For Jake, those pages were a lifeline. The architecture of his next few days. The distance that he had to travel.

At home, Ellie collapsed on the bed. Jake sat in the living room, staring at the television. He couldn't bring himself to turn it on. And no matter how much he tried to avoid him, he knew Conor Byrne was beside him, taking each breath with him, his sunken, hungry eyes ablaze with satisfaction.

Chapter Twelve

Vic couldn't sleep. Not really. Anne lay beside him, her breathing regular. Their bedroom door was ajar and Vic found himself listening for noises from Lettie's room, even though he knew she was too far away. At some point between three-thirty and four, he rose, padded down the hall, and stood in the doorway to Lettie's room, staring at her under the comforter. Anne had let Lettie grow out her hair, and in the nightlight, he saw several lanky strands across her pale cheek. He slipped into the room and gently hooked them behind her ear. He wanted to kiss her, but didn't want to wake her.

Back in bed, he stared at the ceiling. He knew the real reason he couldn't sleep. He'd seen Jake Kittery's face at the moment when the truth about his son struck home. That split-second when Jake's life changed forever.

Jake's expression was a direct line to the moment when he'd learned, finally, that his own daughter was dead. He remembered the North Dakota state trooper standing before him on the asphalt of that parking lot overlooking Lake Sakakawea. How he explained that Vic's DNA sample was a parental match to an unidentified burn victim.

That split second when he knew Dannie truly was dead, after eighteen months of searching. After eighteen months of chasing a sliver of hope that she might be found.

He knew any chance of sleep was gone. All he had was the memory of Dannie. And Lettie, Dannie's daughter, sleeping down the hall.

His throat tight and stomach heavy, he wondered at his arrogance. Those days and nights as Dannie grew up and he acted, and thought, that nothing would ever happen to her. To him or Anne. The sheer, audacious arrogance of it.

The stupidity.

He waited for sleep. It came, finally, more like revenge than anything else, and trapped him inside a dreamworld. There, the light was the gray of low-scudding rain clouds. Wherever he looked he glimpsed his mother and father fading into sooty air that carried a metallic tang. Shift whistles shrieked without any sort of time logic. He jerked awake and saw it was five-thirty. He got up and took a shower. By six-thirty, he was at his desk, working in the morning gloom, several of the overhead lights still extinguished as an overnight cost-cutting measure. He searched his emails for the security footage from the incline or the report on the contents of Steven's car. All he found was an update from Craig, telling him that Jake and his wife had visited the morgue and confirmed Steven's identity.

He read the message and tried not to think about what the morning looked like for Jake and his wife. How their night had been.

"Do you have time for an update?"

Vic started. Sandy Vrail stood in front of his desk, looking down at him. Her hair was again pulled back into a tight bun, not a single hair out of place, and he wondered what led someone to prefer that hard, committed look.

Vic struggled out of his thoughts. It dawned on him that Sandy wore a short leather jacket similar to Liz's.

"Sure." Vic gathered his thoughts, glad for the distraction.

Sandy reached into Liz's cube and dragged out the chair. She sat in the hallway, not crowding him exactly, but certainly blocking his escape.

"So," Sandy said. "The murder on Mt. Washington."

Vic was glad she didn't try to assign a clever name to the case. Not the Incline Murder or the Statues Death.

Vic walked her through the identification of the body, the notification of next-of-kin, and their progress to date. Sandy watched him as he talked, very still, barely blinking.

When Vic finished she nodded once, sharply. "Good progress. Fast work."

"Well, now the tough part starts."

Sandy didn't have an answer for that. She rose and pushed Liz's chair back into place. Turned back to him.

"I, uh, came in to find my office. My ID was ready yesterday. Thought I would get familiar with where I'll be sitting and have the IT people come in so I can be up and running when I start."

"Sure." He was surprised she felt the need to explain herself. "Don't think I've ever heard of IT showing up before ten."

"I'm used to being at work this early."

Vic couldn't tell if the sentence was supposed to be rueful or wry. Or both. Or just a statement of fact. Her face gave nothing away.

Her eyes narrowed. "Are you okay? It looks like you had a rough night."

"Oh." Vic glanced at his computer screen to avoid her gaze. "Liz and I did the death notification. The father was pretty broken up. It was a bit rough."

"It reminded you of your daughter."

Vic stayed silent. Hana hadn't told him much about Sandy, but it was plain that Hana and Sandy had talked about him. He was vaguely annoyed, and wasn't sure if it was with Sandy or Hana. He raised his head and stared at her.

"I, uh, read your file." Something like an apologetic smile flickered on her face, just for an instant. "It's in there. I thought it must have been rough to be sidelined on the investigation. And I guess Hana said something about it."

Vic guessed that Sandy thought she'd overstepped and wanted to explain herself. But he liked the way she focused the blame on herself, didn't try to pass it off on Hana.

"Well, I'll be starting full-time in a couple of days." Again, Sandy's delivery was flat, without a trace of facial expression to help Vic understand her feelings about what she said.

"Right. Monday."

"I'll see you then." Sandy turned sharply on her heel, a perfectly executed right face, and headed along the aisle toward her office. Vic watched her go, and a moment later the overhead light to her office illuminated, followed, coincidentally, by the remainder of the overhead lights. Vic thought about that. She'd said she wanted to find her office, but she certainly seemed to know where it was. And her arrival clearly meant it was time to get to work.

He turned back to his computer screen. He was overthinking the situation, and he knew it. But he had the distinct feeling that finding common ground with Sandy, and a good working relationship, might be prickly. She also apologized a lot for a commander. He wondered if there was something behind that.

Several new emails had appeared, and he was glad to see one from the Crime Scene Investigation unit with the topic line: Impounded Vehicle, followed by the case number. He clicked on it.

It only took a few minutes to skim the report and inventory of items found in the car. Steven's laptop was not among them. Instead, the list included a charging wire for an iPhone plugged into the storage compartment between the front seats. A collection of take-out plasticware sets, paper napkins, several music CDs, and against all odds, an actual pair of gloves in the glove box. A travel umbrella was found jammed into the rear pocket of the passenger seat, and a tube of cherry Chapstick in the passenger-side door cubby. The trunk included a ragged towel and spray bottle of Armor-All.

Vic sighed. The car could have belonged to anyone, and they were no closer to the laptop. He idly wondered how long the CDs had sat unused in the glove compartment. The car was new enough to run the entertainment system from a smart phone, and the wire suggested Steven did exactly that.

Karen, the floor administrator, appeared and plopped into her desk chair. An undertow of tiredness tugged at him, his restless night already affecting him. He went to the building's break room and poured himself a cup of coffee. When he returned to his desk Liz was sliding out of her jacket. Craig, he noticed, still hadn't arrived.

"Car inventory is in," Vic called to her as he took his seat.

"Anything?"

"Could have been my car. And no laptop."

Liz nodded thoughtfully. "I was thinking. We need to speak to that Conor Byrne, the retired cop?"

"We do."

"Let me research him before we do."

"Sounds good. Craig said we won't get the Incline video until later today. And I got a preliminary report from the Fire and Rescue guys. So far, they haven't found anything on the cliff or below it. No wallet or phone." Vic pointed in the direction of Sandy's office. "And we have company."

Liz nodded. "I saw the light." Her voice notched lower. "Lucky us. A hard charger."

Chapter Thirteen

C arty Swain started his day on the ground floor of his hotel, navigating the breakfast bar crowd. He scooped up rubbery scrambled eggs and bacon that smelled like shoe leather and looked about as tough. With a large paper cup of coffee and a handful of creamers, he retreated to his room. Sitting at the desk, he checked news reports and tried not to think about what he was eating. He missed Costa Rica's piled helpings of Gallo Pinto and the way their bitter coffee somehow reminded him of blue sky. Even the corn texture and taste of chorreadas with sour cream would have been enough. Or fresh fruit. He'd grabbed a few cubes of melon from the breakfast bar, but the Honeydew was harder than chunks of tire tread, the cantaloupe dispirited.

He pushed the food to one side and sighed. If he found the doubloon collection, he could eat any breakfast he wanted, so it made sense to get to work. He searched out the landing page for the Office of the Clerk of Civil District Court for the Parish of Orleans. If Demond or Liz owned any land or property in the parish, this was the place to find it. The system listed all the land and building ownership, sales, and mortgages. He sipped more coffee, the acrid taste overpowering however many creamers he added.

The property would need to be somewhere in or close to Orleans parish, close enough for Demond to hide the coins quickly as Katrina made landfall.

After a two-hour search, he'd found nothing. No property bought or sold in Demond or Liz's name within the correct time frame. No record of a mortgage.

They must have rented. He'd never paid attention at the time; who did?

Carty rose and dumped the remains of his breakfast into a garbage can and set it outside his hotel room door. Back at his computer, he wrote down the seven parishes that made up New Orleans. He placed Orleans at the top and crossed it off. With a sigh, he began his search of the real estate database in each of the remaining parishes.

It was early afternoon when he finished.

Nothing. No real estate transactions or mortgages in either of their names. He rose and checked himself in the mirror. His pants and shirt were creased from sitting. He changed his shirt, smoothed his pants, and went to find his car. He couldn't stand the thought of eating the hotel food again.

He bought a Po' boy for lunch, and after eating, cruised the neighborhood where Demond and Liz once lived. He soon spotted the blue Victorian house. It was still divided into apartments, the detail along the high gables still yellow. It was on his second pass that he noticed it. A stand-alone garage, partially hidden behind the house. It looked unused, the paint faded, the garage doors sagging and held shut by hefty padlocks.

One car sat in the gravel driveway.

Carty drove to the nearest convenience store, bought a bottle of water, and drank it slowly while sitting in his car. He felt a tickle of excitement. Demond would never have risked hiding the coin collection inside his apartment, in case Liz found it. But the garage was a different possibility.

He decided to take one more pass, but not immediately. He didn't want it obvious he was checking the house.

Fifteen minutes later, he cruised past the house and checked the garage. He spotted a side door. That was his access point, he decided. Now, he just needed darkness. And a decent dinner.

"I'm famished for Spanish," he said out loud, ignoring the tortured rhyme. "Oh yeah. In tune for doubloons."

He tapped his hand against the steering wheel, trying to find a rhythm that matched his wordplay.

Chapter Fourteen

Vic didn't say anything when Craig hurried into work twenty minutes late. Liz, however, couldn't pass up the opportunity.

She leaned back in her chair and called across to Craig, just as his email inbox appeared on his screen. "Glad you could join us."

Craig's shoulders tightened. "I was studying for the detective's test." He turned to her. "I didn't get to bed until late."

"Test day isn't until tomorrow, right?" Vic called to him.

Craig glanced Vic's way, and Vic thought he spotted an appeal for help in Craig's eyes. "Right. But I want to get a good night's sleep tonight, so I did my cramming now."

"With Eileen." Liz said the two words with disbelief.

Craig reddened, but his voice stayed level and he held Vic's gaze. As Vic watched, Craig centered himself and turned to Liz.

"Yes. She was helping me. She didn't get much sleep either. And she's got a full symphony practice today."

Liz watched Craig for a moment, then lifted her palms toward him. "Okay, okay. You get a detective's exam pass." She looked slightly annoyed that Craig had handled himself so well.

Craig glanced at Vic and turned back to his computer.

Vic typed out a short note and emailed it to Craig. "Next time," he wrote, "Text me and let me know what's up. It's easier if we know your schedule."

Vic watched Craig open the email and absorb the message. He turned to Vic and gave him a nod. He looked relieved.

Vic rose from his chair and called to Liz. "Conor Byrne?"

Liz finished typing and clicked on the send button. She gave him an odd look but rose as well. "I could have spent more time researching him."

Vic told Craig they planned to visit the retired police officer assaulted by Steven Kittery, and together, he and Liz took the elevator to the first floor and found their unmarked Malibu in the parking lot.

Liz rearranged herself in the front seat. "That Craig is still a bit too thin-skinned."

"He's getting there." Vic merged into the bumper-to-bumper traffic, headed downhill to the tunnels and downtown Pittsburgh. "He isn't sure of his girlfriend yet, and his job depends on passing the test. When he gets those settled, he'll start giving it back to you."

Liz was silent for a few moments. "I like that Eileen, though. When he says she was helping him study, I believe it. She didn't get where she is by laying off. She's been good for him. You see how he's been dressing lately?"

"Agree with that."

"Now, you going to explain this to me?"

Vic eased the car along in traffic. He knew what Liz meant. It would be more useful to interview the Kitterys first, finish the background on Conor Byrne, and then see how the interview with Conor aligned with their research and the Kittery's account.

Vic took a slow breath. "I thought I would give the Kitterys the morning to pull themselves together. We can always circle back on Byrne if we need to."

Vic didn't say he needed the morning just as much as the Kitterys, that interviewing parents who had just lost a child was raw for him as well. He needed to prepare himself.

"Uh-huh." Liz made the sounds vaguely, and Vic knew she understood him. "Then Conor Byrne it is."

Forty minutes later, Vic pulled up to the curb in front of a small house on the eastern side of Pittsburgh, close to the Allegheny River, near the town of Oakmont.

Vic studied the front yard as they exited the car. The shrubs edging the front porch needed pruning, and autumn leaves littered the patchy lawn.

The plastic covers on the porch furniture looked as if no one had removed them for years.

As they approached, Vic saw Liz studying the flimsy screen door. He followed her gaze and saw spots of green lichen blossoming on the white metal.

Liz leaned to one side to look down the driveway that ran beside the house. "I guess he uses the back door?"

"Or doesn't get out much."

They climbed the steps to the porch, and Vic pressed the bell. It chimed inside the house, a four-tone sequence that reminded Vic of a children's song. He couldn't place it.

As they waited, the wind rose and fell like a restless animal. Vic pressed the bell a second time.

It was easily another fifteen seconds before the doorknob on the opposite side of the screen door turned. The door opened, and a tall, thin man with black hair swept straight back from his forehead stared at them with unusually large, blue eyes. His pale skin, jowls, and the dark smudges under each eye gave his face a rumpled look. Vic raised his ID wallet to the man's face.

"Detectives Lenoski and Timmons, Allegheny County Police. We need a few minutes, Mr. Byrne."

As Vic lowered his ID, he saw Conor's lips draw tight in something between a resigned smile and a grimace. He held Vic's gaze.

"And if I say no?"

"Well, we can do it here or in an interview room downtown. Which is easier for you?"

"Neither." Conor held Vic's gaze a beat longer and nodded at the screen door. "It's unlocked." He turned, and, leaving the door open, retreated into the house.

Vic tried the screen door, swung it open, and led Liz inside. Vic caught a whiff of burned toast and something stronger.

"In here," Conor called from the left and farther inside the house. Vic saw Liz pull her jacket away from her hip and place her hand on the butt of her

Glock.

Vic couldn't place the smell, but he recognized it. He turned toward Conor's voice and stepped into a room that ran the entire depth of the house, starting as a living room and ending with a dining table and breakfront. Conor was standing with his hands on the wooden back of a chair set at the center of the table.

"You can sit here." Conor gestured to the seats opposite him. He pulled his chair out from underneath the table and sat, waiting.

Vic led Liz past a matching couch and armchairs clustered around a coffee table that held a large piece of colored glass. It was a woman's touch, Vic thought, yet he didn't have the sense a woman lived in the house. He couldn't explain why.

And then Vic knew what he smelled wasn't an odor. It was entropy. The house was permeated with a sense of decline and disorder so strong it emanated into the air.

"Are you alone in the house?" Liz asked, as they approached the dining table.

Conor nodded. "Yep."

Vic and Liz sat across from Conor. Conor watched them, his thin lips now a straight line. On the wall behind Conor, high enough that Vic could see it over Conor's swept-back black hair, was a color photograph of a young man's face and shoulders. The man looked like Conor, but his skin was smoother and suffused with energy. He wore a Pittsburgh Bureau of Police cap, dress blues, a black tie, and white shirt. Vic recognized a Police Academy graduation photograph. Segmenting off the right upper corner of the frame was a one-inch band of black ribbon.

Vic lowered his gaze and met Conor's blue eyes. Vic knew Conor sat him in this chair on purpose, to make Vic and Liz look at the photograph and remember that Conor's son was a police officer who died in the line of duty. The photograph wasn't a memorial, it was a cudgel.

"If that's how you want to play it," Vic thought. Vic stared at Conor. "Like I said, we have questions."

"Okay." Conor interlaced his fingers on the tabletop.

"What can you tell us about Steven Kittery?" Liz asked. Her tone was forceful, and Vic knew that she also was annoyed at being manipulated by the portrait of Conor's son.

The question seemed to surprise Conor, but he hid it quickly. "You're talking about Jake Kittery's son?"

"Yes." Vic copied Conor's posture, even interlacing his fingers. He knew the copycat action sometimes irritated people, and he decided to see how Conor reacted to it.

Conor shrugged. "Bit of a hothead. Rash. But he's a kid, really. Why?"

Vic noted Conor's use of present tense. "We're interested in the assault charges against him. The ones related to your claim he attacked you." Vic stressed the word "claim," needling a bit more.

"He did attack me. Threw a punch at me. Through my car window."

Liz leaned forward. "Yeah. We read the report. And that upset you, a big tough guy like you? When a *kid* did that? As you said."

Vic knew Liz had picked up on his approach to Conor, and was adding her own needling pricks.

Conor didn't respond. He glanced from Liz to Vic and sat back, this time crossing his arms on his chest. "What's this all about? I dropped those charges. You aren't here to talk about that."

Vic remembered what Liz had told him about the arrest report as they drove to Conor's. How Conor had stopped his car outside the Kittery house one evening, window down, and according to Steven Kittery's statement, shouted an insult at Jake Kittery as he and Steven were standing in the front yard. When Jake didn't respond, Steven had chased the car and thrown a punch through the open driver's side window as Conor pulled away. Steven's punch had glanced off Conor's shoulder.

Vic sat back and crossed his arms over his chest, continuing to imitate him. "So where were you two nights ago between eleven-thirty p.m. and one-thirty a.m.?"

"What the hell is this about?" Conor sounded annoyed, and Vic was surprised. He'd expected Conor to better handle the interview.

"It's a simple question." Liz shifted in her chair enough to remove a small notebook and pen from her jacket pocket. She placed them on the table. "Actually, let's expand that time frame. Eight in the evening two nights ago until eight yesterday morning."

Conor glanced from Liz to Vic and back. "Look. You want me to say anything, you have to explain why you're here, and why you need that information."

Liz stayed quiet, giving Vic the opening. Vic kept his arms crossed. "You have history with the Kittery family. It goes back a long way. More than that, you brought charges against Steven Kittery, for what looks like a pretty minor incident that you instigated. But it suggests you have a grudge against the Kittery family, and Steven Kittery in particular."

Conor frowned, as if he couldn't quite understand where Vic's comments were taking them. He released his arms, and from the way he positioned them, looked as if he'd moved his hands to his thighs. "You've got that wrong. I thought about it and dropped the charges against Steven. Steven's got nothing to do with what's between me and his father. I decided to keep Steven out of it."

"You would say that," Liz said quickly. "Now that Steven Kittery is dead."

Conor shuddered and his right arm dipped as if the hand had slipped off his thigh. "What?" The word came out hoarsely.

"You heard me." Liz leaned over the table. "He was found dead on Mount Washington yesterday. Suspicious death. A stabbing."

"So you can see why we need to know where you were two nights ago." Vic said the words mildly, counterbalancing Liz's sharpness.

"Jake Kittery's son?"

Vic thought Conor sounded genuinely surprised.

"As identified by his parents," Liz shot back.

Conor sat back, folded his arms over his chest again, then let them drop, as if he couldn't find a comfortable posture. His face was drawn, and his gaze inward, reliving something.

"Again," Vic said gently. "We need to know your movements. I think you can understand why."

Vic saw something flicker in Conor's eyes, but he wasn't sure if the reaction came from the gentler appeal, or the reminder that as a cop he should understand why Vic and Liz were there. Vic was again aware of the house around them, of the sense that something within these walls had eroded and collapsed.

"Right." Conor refolded his arms over his chest. "Eight o'clock?" He looked at Liz.

"Good place to start."

Conor nodded to himself, as if telling himself to gather strength. "I was here. Watched TV and did some other stuff. Finished about midnight."

"Okay." Liz noted the times in her notebook. "And then what?"

Conor fixed his blue eyes on a spot above Vic's shoulder. "I went out."

The air felt charged. "Where did you go?" Vic tried to keep his question even, non-threatening.

"Just driving. I have trouble sleeping at night. I do it a lot."

"And where did you go?"

"Edgewood, Lincoln, Larimer. Eastern suburbs. I just drive."

Liz stopped writing, and Vic knew she was calculating travel time from the eastern edge of Pittsburgh to Mt. Washington, where Steven's body was discovered. Vic decided the times didn't match up, if Conor was actually telling the truth.

Liz eyed Conor. "Any way you can prove your location?" Vic knew she'd come to the same conclusion.

Conor shrugged. "I had my phone with me." His eyes hardened, and his voice turned direct. "You have my permission to pull my phone records. That should give you my rough location and the time stamps." He hesitated. "Also, about one-thirty, I stopped at a Sheetz near Squirrel Hill. Bought an iced tea. You should be able to place me there."

From the way Conor was talking, Vic knew Conor had grasped his predicament. He was looking for an alibi, but the more important point was that he was doing it as they talked. Vic remembered how planned Steven's murder was. That someone had arranged to meet Steven at a time and place where they would be undisturbed, and transported a weapon to that location. How they must have preplanned taking Steven's phone, wallet and laptop. Those actions didn't square with Conor formulating his alibi now, as he spoke. Whoever murdered Steven would have already worked out an alibi. Would have trotted it out in front of them now as a done deal.

"We'll check all of it." Liz tapped her ballpoint pen on her notebook. "Anything else you want to tell us about being out last night? When did you get home?"

"About two. Phone records should give you an idea of that."

"Assuming you were the one with your phone."

Anger flickered in Conor's eyes at Liz's last statement. "Get serious. I gave my phone to someone and paid them to drive it around the city? C'mon. If I set out to meet Steven isn't the smarter thing to leave the phone here? Say I was home all night? Make you prove I wasn't? Instead of telling you I was out?"

"We get your point," Vic said quickly. "But you know as well as I do we have to look at every possibility." He gently rapped a knuckle on the table top. "Since you're being helpful, do you mind if we take a look in the car you drove last night?"

Conor considered him for a moment. "Sure. Why not?"

No one moved for a moment, until Vic stood. Liz did as well, pocketing her notebook.

Conor seemed to unwind himself from his chair. "It's in the garage." He led them through an archway into the kitchen, grabbed keys from a hook by the back door and went down the outside steps to the driveway. Conor lifted the garage door himself.

Parked in the narrow single-car garage was a reasonably new Ford sedan, the trunk facing them. Vic heard the click of Liz photographing the license plate number. Conor asked them to step aside, and with a bit of shimmying along the wall, got behind the wheel and reversed the car into the driveway.

Conor retreated to the small back porch of the house and watched as Liz took the passenger side of the four-door sedan. Vic started on the driver's side. Liz found a bag resembling an old-fashioned gym bag in the foot well of the passenger seat. Inside was only two well-used cans of red spray paint and a large rag smeared with the same color paint.

The trunk produced a small plastic crate containing rags and car cleansers to use at a car wash.

They finished, and without a word, Conor got back into the car and parked it inside the garage. He joined Vic and Liz on the driveway, the wind gone and the cool of the day settling on all of them.

"Satisfied?" Conor asked.

"It's a start." Vic glanced at Liz and she gave the smallest of shrugs. He thanked Conor, and soon, he and Liz were back in their own unmarked car.

"What was that about?" Liz clicked her seatbelt into place. "Searching his car doesn't do anything. We need the crime scene guys for that."

Vic started the car. "I was more interested to see if he would agree to it. He was figuring out his alibi as he talked. Steven's murder was well-planned. Someone who preplans would have planned their alibi."

"Unless he's trying to double-fake you."

Vic controlled a smile. "Really? We arrest a lot of people who are that smart?"

"Yeah. Probably not," Liz conceded.

"And the other thing, he said he drove a lot late at night. That he often took the car out for a drive, for his insomnia. I wanted to see the mileage on the car."

"And?"

"More than one hundred thousand miles on it. The car can't be more than six years old. He does drive it a lot."

Vic reached the end of the block and slowed for a stop sign.

Liz gave out a long breath. "And he really did seem shocked when we told him Steven was dead. Man, this case is going great so far, isn't it?"

Chapter Fifteen

Vic and Liz stopped for an early lunch at a sandwich shop in the Strip District, and Vic called the Kitterys. They agreed to meet an hour later.

The Kittery's house sat almost alone in a small cul-de-sac in Swissvale, a bluff-top community of narrow, upright houses that lay between the city's eastern Parkway and the town of Braddock. It crossed Vic's mind that Conor Byrne had driven in the same general area the night Steven was stabbed, but on the northern side of the Parkway East. Like the other houses in the neighborhood, the Kittery home was an upright brick building with two windows overlooking the front porch, below a peaked roof. A single American-built car sat in the short driveway, blocking the garage door. He and Liz got out. It was only as they approached the steps to the front porch that Vic saw red scrawls on the garage door. He glanced at Liz to see if she had noticed it.

Liz was already squinting at the words. "What the hell is that?"

"Friendly neighbors?"

Vic pressed the doorbell, listening to the tones being absorbed by the silence inside the house. He was taken with a surge of panic and fought it down. He didn't want to do this interview. He knew the personal memories it would dredge up, how hard this was going to be.

"Want me to take the lead?"

Vic looked at Liz. She was standing to one side, facing him. He couldn't read the message in her eyes, but he knew she understood his turmoil.

"Sure. I took the last one. Even it up."

"Right." Somehow, Liz kept any insinuation out of the word, and Vic was grateful.

A narrow window ran alongside the front door, and Vic saw Jake Kittery approach. His face was vacant, as if he'd taken a hard jab to the temple.

Jake opened the door without a word and ignored their greetings. He motioned them to his left, into a living room that ran the depth of the house. A far doorway looked as if it opened into the kitchen.

Ellie Kittery waited for them at one end of a long couch. She looked small and exhausted, her face pale. She barely registered their arrival. Vic and Liz chose armchairs facing the couch. Jake sat next to his wife.

"Thank you for seeing us." Liz's tone was brisk but understated.

"Where are you with this?" Jake asked.

"We're just getting started." Liz straightened her back, choosing to sit on the edge of her chair. "There are two things you might be able to provide us that would help a great deal. The first is a list of Steven's friends, the second is an accounting of Steven's day two days ago. The day it happened."

Ellie flinched at the mention of Steven's name. Vic slipped out his notebook and pen.

"Have you arrested Conor Byrne?" Jake's voice was loud in the hushed atmosphere.

Liz turned to Jake. "Mr. Kittery, please bear with us. There is a process we need to follow, and it's designed to minimize mistakes and wasted time. We'll get to Conor Byrne in due time."

Vic liked Liz's response. If they admitted they had already talked to Conor Byrne, and not arrested him, he guessed the interview would unravel quickly.

Jake drew himself upright on the couch. "I'm trying to save you time as well. Where there's smoke, there's fire. And I'm tired of him being protected."

The anger in Jake's voice sounded unemotional and disconnected, somehow.

"Mr. Kittery, I promise you we will thoroughly investigate Mr. Byrne. But right now, I'd appreciate it if you could provide a list of Steven's friends.

In our experience, with someone of Steven's age, friends are usually the best source of information."

Jake closed and opened his eyes, as if he was rebooting himself. Slowly, giving Vic time to write them down, he listed four names. Vic asked for a brief background on each person.

As he finished his notes, Vic thought back to the apartment and Steven's office, to the only photograph he'd found. "Mr. Kittery," Vic asked. "There is a photograph in Steven's office of Steven at graduation. I believe his MBA graduation. He's with someone else. Is that one of the names here?"

Jake hesitated.

"No," breathed Ellie, speaking for the first time. "You said the photograph in his office, right?"

"Yes." Vic watched Ellie close her eyes and gather strength.

When Ellie opened them, they were sharp. "That's Brandon. Brandon Ellis. They were at Pitt together."

Jake, Vic noted, looked surprised.

"Brandon helped us get the non-profit started." Jake looked at Ellie. "I didn't realize they were friends, really. I mean, I remember meeting him at graduation. But I thought that was about business. Brandon was always talking about how to make money. He never seemed like a guy Steven would take to a Steelers game."

Ellie gave a small shrug, as if she was too tired to argue.

Vic wrote down the name. "When you say he helped get your non-profit started, what do you mean?"

Jake punched his thigh lightly with a large fist. "Brandon handles the link between us and the medical insurance companies downtown. He helped us get the grants to get up and running, and those came through the same insurance companies. I think Stevie told him about my union contacts, which helped me get the job."

Vic carefully put a star next to Brandon's name.

"How about a girlfriend?" Liz looked from Jake to Ellie.

Jake waved a hand enthusiastically. "He dates a lot. Hasn't settled down yet." His lips tightened as he realized his words and attitude were out of time and place. "You get what I mean."

Ellie cocked her head but didn't say anything.

Vic waited, knowing Liz had seen Ellie's reaction and was waiting as well.

Jake seemed momentarily confused by the silence. He looked at Ellie. "Just dating sometimes, nothing serious, right?"

Ellie took a slow breath. "I don't know. He never said anything, but the last couple of months. It's just…" She fell silent.

"Perhaps there was someone?" Liz prompted.

Ellie gazed at Liz. "Just a feeling. If I asked directly, he'd clam up. So instead I'd ask him about his weekends, to see if anything fell out. He'd always say he "didn't do much," but lately, the way he said it sounded satisfied." Tears welled in her eyes. "Like he was happy. It was the kind of reaction a girl might give him."

Jake frowned at her. Ellie lifted both of her arms slightly and looked at Jake, as if she was apologizing. "I didn't think it was worth bringing up. It was just a feeling."

Jake shook his head. "No, that's okay." He turned to Vic and Liz. "He never said anything to me at work."

"Was he friendly with anyone at your offices? Regularly go to lunch together, that kind of thing?" Vic asked.

"Jake shook his head. "No, it isn't that kind of place. It was just Stevie, me and Edna full-time. The others are doctors or nurse practitioners, and they volunteer and only work maybe three-or-four-hour shifts. Plus, they spend most of their time making house calls. They only come in to talk about scheduling."

Vic remembered the large whiteboard inside TU Health.

"Okay." Liz turned to a fresh sheet in her notebook. "And Steven's activities that day? Just do the best you can."

Jake ran through Steven's day, explaining that Steven spent the afternoon working up a draft of the monthly financial report. Neither Ellie nor Jake knew Steven's plans for dinner or that evening.

"He just started doing that report a few months ago," Jake added. "I guess he wanted to get a look at how each month was shaping up."

"Monthly?" Liz asked. "Usually non-profits keep administrative requirements low, to save money."

"Stevie was always precise about everything. The report didn't surprise me. He even sent me something about it in an email at the end of that day. Stopped by my office and mentioned it. But that's all normal work stuff."

Vic considered the back and forth. "Is there a lot of cash flow every month? I mean, money in and expenses out?"

Jake shook his head. "The money is from Medicare and Medicaid to pay for the services our doctors perform for patients. Expenses are pretty fixed, those are mainly our salaries and utilities. We used grant money to buy the building right at the start, so there's no rent."

"And Steven managed all that?"

"Yes. I wouldn't know where to start." Jake glanced at Ellie. "Stevie was on top of all that."

"Huh." Vic wasn't sure what else to say.

"Well, thank you." Liz glanced at Vic with a question, but he shook his head. "We'll have more questions, but this will get us started. We'll talk to Steven's friends. I'm sure we'll get back to you with questions. Liz stood up, and Vic followed.

"By the way," Vic said before they reached the front door. "So far, we haven't been able to find Steven's laptop or phone. You wouldn't have any idea where they might be, would you?"

Ellie and Jake exchanged glances before Jake answered. "No. He didn't leave them with us."

Liz continued for the front door, but Vic hung back. The vacant look had returned to Ellie's eyes, and Jake looked distracted. "If you don't mind me asking." Vic waited as Jake refocused. "We noticed some writing on your garage door. It looks fresh."

Jake's eyes clouded. "I told you. Conor Byrne. He does this to us. Every few months."

"Why would he do that?" Liz held the doorknob, but didn't turn it.

Jake looked from Vic to Liz. "He thinks I'm responsible for the death of his son."

Of all the possible answers, that wasn't the one Vic expected. "Why does he think that?"

Jake shook his head slowly. His voice dimmed. "There was a union march years ago. Big one. His son was part of a group of officers who thought the marchers were getting out of hand, so they tried to break us up. It turned into a fight, although it didn't last long. Somehow, his son was hit on the head, and a few hours later, he collapsed."

"But how does that connect to you?" Vic was perplexed. He'd worked security on marches at the beginning of his career and understood the confusion and panic on both sides when police and demonstrators clashed. Finding one person to blame in those situations was almost impossible.

"Our union was in the middle of it. I was the shop steward. Head of our local. He blames me."

Vic thought of the two cans of red spray paint they'd found in Conor's car. "When was your door spray painted?"

"The night Stevie left us." Ellie made the comment so softly, Vic almost missed it.

"You can be sure we'll talk to Conner Byrne." Vic knew Liz was trying to sound reassuring and was sure she also remembered the cans of spray paint in Conor's car.

"Talk? No." Jake spat out the last word, his eyes flashing. "You need to arrest him for killing our son."

Chapter Sixteen

Vic and Liz drove in silence for a time, Vic turning either right or left as they exited the warren of residential streets to the main roads.

Liz turned her face from the side window. "There's more going on with Conor Byrne than we thought."

"He lied to us about where he was. Although I guess I wouldn't expect him to say his alibi was spray painting graffiti on the garage door of Steven's parents while Steven was being murdered on Mt. Washington."

"Even if he was making up the alibi as we talked." Liz glanced at him. "I thought about that, and I agree with you. Anyone who planned that murder would have a prepared alibi."

Vic relived the Kittery interview in his mind. "So maybe Steven did have a girlfriend."

"If he did, one of his friends will know who she is. Or he is. When we get back, I'll put Craig on tracking down the names they gave us."

"We lose him for a day soon, don't forget. Detective exam."

Liz smiled and shook her head. "I'd be shocked if he doesn't ace it."

"Same here, but you never know."

Vic guided the car onto the Parkway East, headed back to Pittsburgh. As they drove, Vic struggled to get the Kittery interview out of his mind. Ellie's blank look stuck with him, along with Jake's repeated loss of focus. He remembered how they reacted to one another on the couch, recognizing the unspoken communication of married couples. He and Anne lost that ability after Dannie disappeared. Many who lost a child did, but not for the reasons Vic first thought. He knew, now, that as Dannie grew, he and Anne had automatically structured their lives for Dannie's benefit. Organized themselves to meet Dannie's schedule, developed an entire way of communicating that protected their own unity. When Dannie was lost, he and Anne had rejected that entire way of living. It was just too painful for them to act and communicate as if Dannie was alive. To survive as a couple, they had to start over.

Ellie and Jake faced that same paralysis. And he knew how difficult that would be.

He slid the car into a parking space, and he and Liz returned to their desks in silence. Craig sat hunched over his computer monitor.

Craig looked up as they settled behind their desks. "Hey, I've got the incline security footage. Looking at it now."

"Anything?"

"I've got Steven going up. That was about 11:15. Still working on the rest."

Liz leaned back in her chair. "Did he have his laptop with him?"

"Not sure, but he did have a shoulder bag big enough to hold it."

Vic tried to concentrate on his emails, twice reading the final report from the Fire and Rescue team. They'd come up blank. No phone, laptop, or wallet. He was sure the crime scene investigators hadn't found a shoulder bag, but he reread the inventory list just to be sure.

It was another hour before Craig sat back. "I don't know," he said out loud.

Vic and Liz moved near Craig's desk.

"What *do* you have?" Liz asked.

Craig manipulated some windows, and a video popped up on the screen. "Here's Steven on his way up. See the shoulder strap? The laptop could be in that bag. Okay, that's eleven fifteen."

Craig moved to another window, pulling up a series of screen captures. "These are all the trips made by the incline, either up or down, after that. There isn't much. Only couples or maybe one or two unconnected people for each trip. Steven doesn't go down again, obviously."

One after another, Craig pulled up each screen capture. As always, Vic silently swore at the grainy texture and the way the placement of the camera created angles that made facial features hard to identify.

"That's it," Craig said after two more screen captures.

Vic blinked and looked around the offices. Outside, the sun had set, and the early darkness of autumn was settling against the windows. "Just pull up the last three trips down the incline before they closed."

Craig shifted windows around, and soon, three images were lined up on the screen. Craig expanded them as much as he could. Vic stared at each in order, but his eye slid back to the next-to-last trip. Two figures sitting in different parts of the incline car, clearly not people who knew one another. It was the woman farthest from the camera.

Vic pointed at the screen capture. "Make that one bigger."

Craig closed the other two windows and made the remaining window slightly larger until it was on the edge of blurring.

Excitement flickered in Vic's chest. "There." He pointed at the woman farthest from the camera, her face partially turned to the window." He glanced at Liz. "Does she look familiar to you?"

Liz frowned. "The hair, that straight cut at earlobe height. I've seen it."

"Right," Vic breathed. "Ms. Mercedes, from TU Health. The woman who left while we were there?"

Liz bent closer. "Maybe. Not one hundred percent."

"But close." Vic knew it wasn't a good view. He turned to Craig. "Pull everything you have on her. Let's see if we can get a better look."

Craig squinted at the screen. "Yeah. And see there? Looks like she has a black strap over her shoulder. Like the one Steven had when he rode up the incline."

"She does," Liz breathed softly.

"We need the list of doctors, soon as we can get it."

"There's one other thing," Liz said gently. "Looking at her, and I'm just saying, but she's about the same age as Steven."

Chapter Seventeen

Carty Swain felt the New Orleans night part around him, the humidity so thick he was tempted to use his arm as a bowsprit. He walked easily along the sidewalk, dressed in blue jeans, a long-sleeved black T-shirt, and a navy trucker's cap. A small navy blue backpack hung over one shoulder.

"Here comes the blue-man," he mused to himself, striding toward the garage next to the house where Liz and Demond Timmons once lived. "The Blue-Man Group, blue boy, baby-blue, Mr. blue balls." He grinned at the riff, letting it calm his nerves. Breaking into the garage was a risk—he couldn't talk his way out of it if he was caught.

He'd postponed a day, just to reduce the possibility that someone might have seen him driving by the apartment building. Now it was three-thirty in the morning, his car was parked in the lot of a doctor's office two blocks away, and his only real goal was not to get caught.

He turned up the driveway of the house next to the Victorian, swung behind it, and crossed the back yard. As his internet search had promised, the back yards of the two houses conjoined, and the side door to the garage appeared ahead, it's white paint a smudge in the darkness.

He checked the back windows of the Victorian were dark. Even better, none were open. Along the foundation, three air conditioning units sat in a neat row, fans whirring in two of them. That was a good sign. The apartment residents were asleep and cocooned in cool air and white noise.

He was out of practice, but still picked the deadbolt on the garage's side door in less than two minutes. Even his sweaty hands inside his blue latex gloves didn't slow him up. "Boss blue, blue thunder, all blue but no blues for me," he breathed, slipping into the garage's stuffy darkness. He closed the door and inhaled the musty interior.

Working by feel, he slid off his backpack, unzipped it, and found his penlight. His back to the window inset in the door, flashlight pointed at the floor, he followed the contours of the building until he understood the layout. Someone had separated the car bays into three free-standing storage areas using chain-link fencing and two-by-fours. Only the garage door closest to the side door was still functional. A long two-by-four was nailed over the second door and against the doorway frame to keep it closed.

Holding the flashlight low, Carty checked the chain link gates to the storage areas. The center one had a large number two painted on a board above the padlock. The bay was about half full with cardboard boxes and a dusty table and chairs.

That bay was for the second-floor apartment Demond and Liz once lived in, but Carty knew the contents wouldn't help him. Liz would have emptied the bay when she moved out. If the doubloons were there, she would have found them.

He looked up and risked a quick flash of the penlight at the ceiling. Just joists, and far above, the peaked roof. No attic.

Carty moved to the rear of the garage, brushing at the sweat trickling down his cheek. A workbench ran along half of the back wall, the top littered with small, sagging cardboard boxes of nails and dusty plumbing and electrical equipment. A pegboard for tools was centered on the wall above the bench, a narrow shelf just below it. Rusty-lidded jars jammed with screws, nails, and hooks glinted as he swung the penlight the length of the shelf. Carty stared at the workbench, then checked underneath. A larger shelf ran underneath the workbench, holding a row of old, partially rusty metal toolboxes. Carefully, one at a time, Carty removed each box, placed it on the benchtop, and looked inside. Most were empty, except for one containing carpet-laying tools and another filled with painting equipment.

He replaced them. Next to the workbench were free-standing grey metal utility shelves, holding half-empty paint cans, solvents, and empty coffee cans stuffed with used paintbrushes. Carty stared at them, his excitement ebbing away. Like the shack, this was turning into a bust. It looked like this trip would only result in crossing one more possible hiding place off his list.

A nudge of one of the paint cans produced a sloshing sound. He breathed out in frustration, but stopped himself. "Okay. I'm here now. Do this right. You don't want to find out later you *blue* it."

He smiled, picked up the next can in line, and gave it a shake. Sloshing sounds. He moved to the next. He continued like that, working across each shelf and down to the next, until only a few cans remained.

The next one he picked up rewarded him with a clunk. He weighed the can in his hands, placed it on the workbench, and used a screwdriver from the pegboard to pry off the lid.

With a trill of excitement, he removed what was inside. In his hand lay a snub-nosed .38 revolver slotted into a black ankle holster.

He recognized it, even after all these years. A Smith and Wesson, the crack on one side of the grip. The familiar ankle holster. This was Demond Timmons' back-up, and if needed, his throw-away.

Carty placed the gun on the bench and checked the last two paint cans. More sloshing. He went back to the snub-nosed and poked it with his finger. "Well, now," he said softly.

He knew the revolver's history. He and Demond, not long after they started as partners, were on night patrol in the Garden District when they spotted two wiry Black teenagers. From the boy's clothing and how they studied each house, he and Demond knew the boys were looking for a robbery target. They decided to ID the kids and warn them off, and Demond, who was driving, squelched the siren and lights. But the kids ran. Fast. Faster than he and Demond could chase them down on foot. Demond had directed their cruiser down an alley in a half-hearted attempt at pursuit, but stopped almost immediately. He'd got out, and when he returned, held the gun in his hands. One of the teenagers either lost it from his pocket, or purposely dropped it.

The serial numbers were filed off. An unmarked gun.

Demond had cleaned up the revolver, tested it at the range, and carried it from then on. Just not on that night they went to the shack. Their rubber waders didn't allow room for an ankle holster.

Not that it would have mattered.

Carty turned the gun in one hand, shining the pencil light on it. He felt good. The gun told him something important. Demond had kept secrets from Liz. Liz would never have approved of an unregistered gun, or carrying a throw-away. She wasn't built that way. In response, Demond had chosen to keep it a secret.

That meant chances were good Demond didn't tell Liz about the doubloons. His boss, Vargas, was wrong.

What he needed from Liz was a different kind of information. Where Demond liked to spend his time on a day off. Any special places he liked to go. Because Demond would hide the doubloons somewhere familiar.

Carty slid the revolver and holster into his backpack. It could be useful. He clicked off the penlight and added it to the bag as well.

"We're getting there," he thought to himself as he let himself out of the garage and closed the door behind him. He smiled as he started across the back yards.

But a deeper problem drove his smile away. So far, he'd only eliminated possible hiding places. To continue the search, he needed to contact Liz Timmons without her knowing it was him, without her even sensing his existence. Only then might she let something slip, perhaps repeat a few words Demond said the night before he died.

It was a long shot, and risky. The choice was whether to keep searching, or return to Costa Rica and Vargas.

He'd argued this out with himself many times. If he returned to Costa Rica it would be his entire life. He and Vargas, sitting on patios, and sipping whisky. Every day and night the same.

But he knew it in his heart. Working for Vargas wasn't enough. There had to be more for him.

He sighed. The Devon Blair part of his identity pulled him toward Costa Rica and Vargas. That name created a safe haven. But Carty Swain wasn't dead. And Carty Swain wanted to finish what started in that Route 90 shack. Wanted the type of life the doubloons promised.

He reached his car and slung his backpack onto the back seat. Slid behind the wheel and started the engine.

He knew one person who could help him. Who might approach Liz and ask the questions. He just needed a scenario that made sense.

She worked for his security team in Costa Rica. She was poised, quick-thinking, and had worked undercover before.

Carty thought about it and liked the idea. Because in addition to being talented and clever, she was young and good-looking. And suppose, just suppose, she liked the idea of gold doubloons and a new life.

Carty swung his car into the road and turned toward his hotel.

"This could be the start of something bluetiful," he said out loud to the windshield, the smile returning to his face.

Chapter Eighteen

Vic rose at dawn and spent thirty minutes on the heavy bag in his basement, then shook out a skip rope and flipped it over his head so it rested against his heels. The night before he'd reviewed all of the forensic and autopsy results, and now he emptied his mind, swung the rope over his head, and settled into a rhythm. He focused on that, letting the facts he'd reviewed the night before percolate. After ten minutes, breathing hard, he stopped hopping and let the rope slap against his feet. His hands ached from the bag workout, but in a way he liked and made him think he had done well. He put away the skip-rope and walked about the basement until his breathing slowed, dabbing at the sweat on his face with a workout towel.

Anne was in the kitchen when he came upstairs, Lettie at the table, eating an Eggo drenched in syrup.

"You're all sweaty, Papa." Lettie frowned at him, a forkful of Eggo suspended on the way to her mouth, syrup dripping onto her plate.

"I love that," Anne said, stepping away from the toaster. She reached up, kissed Vic on the mouth, and turned back to Lettie.

Lettie's eyes widened in disgust. "Ewww."

Vic considered wrapping Anne in a bear hug, but his T-shirt was soaked with sweat and Anne already wore her work clothes. "You don't know what you're missing," he said to Lettie.

Lettie gave a theatrical sigh and stuffed the forkful of Eggo into her mouth.

Anne laughed lightly and stepped back to the toaster.

"My turn to take Lettie to school?" Vic asked, studying the refrigerator schedule.

"If you have time."

"I do. Just let me shower."

Thirty minutes later, Vic helped Lettie out of her car seat and watched her head into her kindergarten classroom before turning his car toward Braddock and TU Health.

The night before, Craig had emailed Edna and asked her for a list of the doctors who volunteered at TU Health. He didn't want to wait, and wanted to name the doctor they'd spotted on the incline. He thought that showing up in person would produce the list faster than Edna taking her time to email it. He also wanted to talk to Edna. In his experience, people who worked administrative jobs for businesses knew the most about what happened at a business.

The traffic was light, and Vic arrived at TU Health only a few minutes after they opened. The parking lot was almost full, the silver Mercedes not among the parked cars.

Inside, four people were clustered around the large whiteboard, discussing what appeared to be a schedule of house calls. When Vic entered, their conversation faltered and retook once the side glances in Vic's direction stopped. Edna sat by herself in the center of the room, her head bowed to her computer screen. Jake's office, and Steven's, were empty, shadowy reminders of what the non-profit faced.

Vic stopped beside Edna's desk. "Hi, Edna, remember me? I thought I'd stop down and collect those names we asked for."

Edna looked him up and down. "I told that kid who works with you I'd email them to you."

Vic held her gaze. "Edna, waiting around won't get it done. Those names are important."

Edna gestured at the cluster of people in front of the whiteboard. "Half of them are right there; talk to them now."

Around the whiteboard, the conversation stopped.

Vic lowered his voice. "Not the way we work. But I will do this. If half are over there, I'll collect their names and contact information myself while you list out everyone who isn't here now. That splits the work, and then I'll be out of your hair."

She studied him for a few moments. "They've got enough to worry about. Give me a few minutes."

"Thank you."

Edna straightened each of the framed photographs on her desk with minute precision, and bent to her computer monitor again.

Vic turned to the group around the whiteboard, and as if by agreement, they scattered to different desks and started gathering laptops, purses, and shrugging into coats. Vic turned back to Edna. "Are they going out?"

"They've got house calls to make."

Vic took out his ID wallet and held it up. "Excuse me, everyone." He introduced himself, and explained they would all soon be contacted by someone on his team. He glanced at each person in turn. "I realize this is a difficult situation, but we would appreciate your cooperation. We'll need to ask everyone some questions."

"Is there any news? Any progress?" This came from a short, stocky woman with a matter-of-fact demeanor and a small knapsack over one shoulder. In her other hand, she held, somehow inappropriately, a Hello Kitty lunch box.

"No news yet, beyond the specifics of Steven's death and the circumstances around that."

A couple of people glanced at one another, but no one said anything. Vic thanked them, and they scurried out of the office. He understood their feeling. They were volunteers and hadn't expected anything like this. But it also told him they weren't very close. Even the tone of the woman who asked the question sounded like she wanted the investigation to be over. It made him think of another possibility. He turned back to Edna.

"I was wondering…" He waited for Edna to stop typing into her computer. She looked at him with brittle patience.

"That group was mostly doctors, right?"

"One is a nurse practitioner, yes."

"Do you get a lot of turn-over with them, or do they work with you for extended periods?"

Edna sat back, watching him. Vic had the feeling he might have asked a question that was a live nerve within the organization.

"We get turnover." Edna's gravelly voice filled the now-empty office. "It's a constant problem. Most of these doctors are young, and their schedules change regularly. We have to compete with the hospitals and clinics where they work. And we don't pay them. The only thing we have going for us is the insurer gives them credit against their medical school debts for the hours they volunteer. Most of them owe several hundred thousand dollars. When they get enough credits, the insurer pays down a chunk of their principle."

Vic considered that. "So the insurer gives TU Health a grant to operate, and an incentive for the doctors to volunteer with you."

"Yes." Edna turned to the list of names on her computer screen.

Vic was interested, but unsure why. "What does the insurer get out of it?"

Edna shrugged, somehow keeping exasperation out of it. "Most of our patients have chronic injuries and diseases and need to be constantly monitored. If our doctors catch changes in their health early, the treatments don't cost as much. That saves the insurance company money."

"But aren't most of the patients on Medicare? Why would the insurance company pay for treatment?"

"Most are, but not all. And do you think Medicare pays for everything? Plus it keeps people out of hospital, better for everyone." Edna turned back to her computer screen. "Almost done. Just name and cell phone number, right?"

"Yes." Vic fell quiet. Something about Edna's description of the business didn't sound right to him, but he didn't know enough about medical care to tell. This happened a lot. When he became a detective, no one explained to him that he needed detailed knowledge of how industries worked. It was the only way he could ask the right questions.

Edna tapped a couple of keys and stood up. She brushed past him and went to a desk that held a large printer. She returned with a sheet of paper and held it out to him.

Vic accepted the paper and skimmed the names. "This Meera Basu. Was that the doctor who was here the first time we came?"

Edna frowned, thinking back. "Yes. From India. Bobbed black hair, cut in a line at the bottom of her ears. I haven't decided if I like the haircut or not. Drives a Mercedes."

"Thanks." Vic placed the paper on a nearby desk and used a pen to star Meera's name. He photographed the list and texted it to Liz and Craig. After their phone call the night before she was expecting it, and would start setting up interviews. Meera would be first.

"Thanks," Vic said to Edna. He folded the list and slid it into his jacket pocket.

Edna glanced toward Jake's darkened office. "Any idea when he'll be back?"

"I'd say that's up to him. People deal with this differently."

Vic saw something shift in Edna's eyes, darken, and he remembered their earlier visit when she stood in the doorway to Jake's office and helped Jake refocus, kept him moving toward what he had to do next. He remembered how she'd looked in that moment, as if she was pulling herself back from her own black pit, as much as she was helping Jake.

Edna lightly touched the two picture frames on her desk.

"Your grandchildren?" Vic asked.

"Yes. My daughter's children."

Vic caught the note of sadness in her voice. It was as if the two babies in the photographs should have been more. In that moment, Vic knew Edna had lost someone as well.

"Thanks again," Vic said gently, and let himself out of the empty and silent office.

Chapter Nineteen

Liz was on the telephone when Vic arrived at headquarters, and she nodded to him. As he slid out of his Carhartt jacket, he noted that Sandy Vrail's office light was on, and she was sitting ramrod stiff in front of her computer.

She wasn't supposed to start until Monday.

Craig's desk was empty. Test day.

As Vic settled behind his desk, Liz hung up and rolled over to him on her chair. "Got most of the doctor interviews set up. Meera Basu is first. I caught her on her way to clinic. She didn't like it. Kept saying she couldn't change patient appointments. I told her we'd walk into her damn clinic, in front of everyone, and drag her out if we had to. She got the message."

"Sounds good." Vic tilted his head in the direction of Sandy's office. "You saw that, right?"

Liz's face tightened. "Like I said. A go-getter. We're all screwed."

Vic fought down a smile. "Starting to look that way. And, I went through the coroner's report last night. Did you see the detail about the entry wound?"

"The upward angle or the length of the stab channel?"

"Both."

"Yes. Steven was standing in front of the killer, and whoever it was stabbed upwards under the rib cage."

"Right. Steven's body ended up so close to the rock that it looks like the killer was sitting on the rock, Steven standing over him. A stab like that needs power from your hips and legs, and if you're sitting, it's hard to get good thrust. Only way it works is if our killer has really good upper body strength."

Vic saw a flicker of annoyance in Liz's eyes.

She leaned toward him. "You're thinking women don't have that kind of strength?"

"Hadn't jumped all the way to that. Just made me want to see Meera Basu's shoulders."

"Don't write her off before we talk to her."

"Just something we need to keep in mind."

Liz's gaze was distant, and Vic knew she'd moved on. "It could also present a problem." Liz glanced at him. "If someone is standing over you when you're sitting, it's easy to feel threatened. Especially if you're arguing."

Vic followed Liz's line of thought. "You think when we catch the killer, they'll claim self-defense?"

"Maybe. Killer could say they were seated together on the rock, Steven gets angry, stands in front of them, and makes threats. Killer gets scared for their life, stabs Steven."

"And then left the scene with Steven's phone?"

"We can't prove that unless we find the phone. Any half-bright lawyer will say the killer left it behind, that someone must have come along afterwards, found the body, and stolen the phone."

Vic thought about that. Liz was right. "Then we need to find the phone."

"It'd be a plus." Liz looked at her watch and rose. "We need to go. I told Meera we'd be there by ten."

Vic rose, and they shrugged into their coats. He noticed Liz glance at his Carhartt jacket. She didn't say anything. Small steps, he thought.

The drive to Meera's clinic took them into Mt. Lebanon in the southern suburbs. The clinic was in a one-story red-brick building set behind a narrow parking lot between two small strip malls. Two Mt. Lebanon police cruisers sat in the parking lot.

Liz leaned forward in her seat. "Something's going on." She pointed toward the far end of the parking lot. "Meera's here."

Vic followed her gaze and spotted Meera's Mercedes sitting beside a

Lexus SUV and three smaller economy cars. Vic parked alongside one of the cruisers, and he and Liz crossed the parking lot to the front door.

They stepped into a carpeted waiting room large enough for ten wooden chairs. A uniformed Mt. Lebanon police officer raised the palm of a large hand toward them.

"Office is closed," the officer called.

Vic pulled out his ID, opened it, and held it up. "Allegheny County detectives. We have an appointment with Dr. Basu. What happened here?"

The officer squinted at Vic's ID and nodded to himself. "Stay right there."

He left the high-front receptionist's desk and stepped through the doorway leading into the back of the clinic. He spoke to someone, his eyes on Vic and Liz the entire time. When he returned he was followed by another officer in a white shirt. The man's shaved head caught the light from overhead.

"I'm Sergeant Jerving." He crossed to Vic to Liz and shook their hands, his blue eyes steady. "What brings you here? I know we didn't call you."

"We have an interview with Dr. Meera Basu. Case-related. What happened here?" Vic gestured to the offices.

"Break-in. We got the call this morning when the first nurse arrived."

"The security system didn't go off?"

"Yeah." Jerving's lips tightened into either a smile or a grimace. "Funny that. Looks like our break-in artist knew the code."

"That gives you something to go on." Only a current or former employee would know the security code, which reduced the suspect pool. Vic knew Jerving would be relieved about that.

"Yes, it does." Jerving studied Vic. "And what brings you here to interview Dr. Basu?"

"Murder case. The body on Mt. Washington? She may be a witness."

"I heard about that. She's in the back. We have everyone in a conference room." Jerving's voice trailed away, and Vic guessed Jerving was wondering if the break-in might be related to the murder.

Jerving refocused and waved at the waiting room. "You can talk in here. We had the office cancel this morning's appointments; you won't be disturbed."

"Works for us. Was anything stolen?"

The half-smile or half-grimace reappeared on Jerving's lips. "Not that we can identify. Looks more like they searched the offices of the two doctors. Made a mess, but that's it. We might find something yet."

Liz broke in. "Does the clinic have pharmaceuticals stored here? Opioids?"

"Nothing that requires a prescription." Jerving turned to the officer by the desk. "Can you bring out Dr. Basu?"

"The daughter, not the father?"

Jerving turned back to Vic. "The daughter, right?"

"Yes. She works with her father? I didn't know that."

"Yeah, it's his practice." Jerving motioned to the officer by the reception-ist's desk, and he disappeared into the back.

Vic let that information sink in. The case now involved two children working with their fathers. Steven and Meera. Coincidences always bothered him, but congruences didn't do much for him, either.

The officer returned, Meera in his wake and easily a head shorter than the officer's six-foot frame. Vic recognized the bobbed haircut and pooled, watchful brown eyes he'd seen at TU Health the first day they visited. Meera wore blue medical scrubs and white sneakers. Her eyes were red, her mouth set in a tight line.

"Dr. Meera Basu?" Vic held out his ID and introduced Liz. "Thanks for talking to us."

"Will this take long?"

Her voice had a sing-song quality, but Vic heard tiredness behind her words.

"As long as it takes. The more helpful you are, the faster we're done."

Before she could reply, a man appeared in the doorway with the same large and watchful eyes as Meera. He was only a few inches taller than Meera, and wore slacks and a shirt and tie, topped by a white doctor's coat. The end of the stethoscope around his neck was stuffed into the upper pocket of his jacket.

"What is this?" The man blustered. "Why do you want to talk to my daughter? We are in the middle of an emergency." The sing-song tones of his voice were more pronounced than Meera's.

Meera sank into one of the waiting-room chairs as if she couldn't take any more.

Her father looked from her to Vic and back, his eyes bright with anger.

Vic noted Liz had decided to let him sort out the older Dr. Basu. "Dr. Basu, I'm sorry, but we're investigating another case. Your daughter is a witness, and we need her statement."

"What case? That is impossible. My daughter is a good girl. She has no connection to anything disrespectful."

Vic thought of the shadowy face on the Duquesne Incline, not long before, or immediately after, Steven's death. It was possible Meera was more than a witness. He looked at Sergeant Jerving, who didn't quite suppress a smile. "Sarge, perhaps you could escort Dr. Basu back to the conference room?"

"No." The elder Basu pulled himself to his full height. "She is my daughter. I will stay here."

Vic fought down his irritation. "Dr. Basu, my apologies, but your daughter is an adult. Parental oversight is not required."

"She is my daughter. It is unseemly for her to be interviewed like this."

"FATHER."

The room fell silent. Everyone looked at Meera.

"Father." Meera moderated her tone. She rattled out several sentences in a language Vic didn't recognize or understand. "I wish to help these detectives," she added in English. "Please return to the conference room with Sergeant Jerving."

Vic watched the elder Basu's face veer between shock at the vehemence of his daughter's reaction and parental concern. He shifted from one foot to another.

"Father." Meera said the word softly, a plea this time.

"Very well." Meera's father hesitated. "I will be in the conference room. If these people say anything untoward," he shot Vic a nasty glance, "Call for me."

Meera blinked slowly, looking too tired to respond. Meera's father glared at Vic, glanced at Sergeant Jerving, and turned on his heel.

"Okay." Sergeant Jerving nodded to Vic, gestured at the officer to follow him, and left Vic and Liz with Meera.

For a few moments, no one spoke or moved, until Vic pulled two chairs away from the wall and placed them so Meera, Vic, and Liz sat at the points of a triangle, facing one another.

"Like I said..." Vic hesitated, thinking about the right approach. From the reaction of Meera's father, he knew Meera came from a close family and one with traditional views about their daughter. He tried again. "Dr. Basu, I appreciate you taking the time. We do have some very specific questions."

He waited for her reaction, but was rewarded only with a vague nod.

He chose to come at the interview sideways. "I'm afraid I didn't recognize that language you were speaking with your father. What was it?"

Meera raised her deep eyes to him. "Bengali. My parents grew up in Bengal, and my father's medical degree is from university there."

"And what brought him to Pittsburgh?" Liz fell into Vic's softer approach.

"He attended a medical college in Kolkata. When he graduated, they hired him to do research. He specializes in pancreatic and gallbladder treatments. After a few years, the University of Pittsburgh hired him to do research. That's how we came to Pittsburgh. I was very small at the time. When I was a teenager, he started this clinic; we specialize in internal medicine."

Meera took a deep breath and let it out slowly.

Vic thought she was starting to relax and pushed a bit more. "We have several questions. As I think my partner told you, we're investigating the death of Steven Kittery. That requires us to speak to all of the doctors who volunteer at TU Health. Did you know Steven Kittery?"

Meera didn't answer right away, and Vic had the sense she was gathering herself.

"Yes. Of course," she said, finally. "It was hard not to. It isn't a big place."

"How would you characterize that relationship?" Liz asked. "Were you business acquaintances, personal friends, anything more?"

Meera threw a glance in the direction of the door that led to the clinic, as if checking for eavesdroppers. When she spoke, her voice was lower. "Well, we knew each other through the non-profit, of course. We talked sometimes. I mean, we were colleagues, in that sense."

"Tell us about him," Liz asked.

"Oh. He, um, was funny. And he had this direct way about himself." A smile flickered over her lips, and her eyes sparked. "Not arrogant, but sure of what he wanted. He knew his own mind."

Both Vic and Liz waited. Meera bunched the pants fabric on her scrubs in her fists. "He was kind. That's unusual in men that age." The last words came out in a sob.

Vic knew Meera wasn't fighting tiredness, but grief. "Did he ever say anything to you that made you think he might be in danger? Did anything ever happen that, looking back now, you see was a warning?"

Again, the darting look at the doorway. "I can't say there was."

There was something in Meera's choice of words. A message.

Vic leaned toward her. "Okay," Vic lowered his voice to match hers. "Let's not mess around. We don't have time for it. We want to find Steven's killer. On the night Steven was killed, we have you on security tape going up in the Duquesne Incline and returning on one of the last trips that night. You knew Steven much better than you are saying, and I bet when we get his cell phone data, we're going to find lots of texts and calls between you two. You need to come clean right now."

Meera's chin quivered. She raised her eyes to Vic, fighting tears. She opened her mouth to talk and failed. Tried again. "If my parents find out I was dating a white person, they will be very angry. It is forbidden. They might disown me."

"That may be true. But we need a statement from you. We need to know the extent of your relationship with Steven and what you talked about on Mount Washington that night. And we need to know if he gave you anything. Right now, as far as we know, you're the last person to see Steven alive. That makes you our lead suspect. That's much worse than what your parents might do."

Meera struggled upright in her chair and wiped tears from her cheeks. It was odd, but Vic thought she looked relieved.

"I know." She produced a tissue from one of the two patch pockets on the front of her scrubs and blew her nose, so daintily Vic was impressed. She dabbed her eyes dry, and the tissue disappeared into the other patch pocket, and Vic saw she had a system. One pocket for clean tissues, the other for used.

Meera took a breath. "Yes. We've been dating for several months." She kept her voice low, her eyes watching the doorway into the clinic. "My parents don't know."

Vic watched Meera's face carefully. "And what happened the night he was murdered?"

Meera tightened. "We'd agreed to meet on Mt. Washington by the Duquesne Incline. He said he had something important to tell me. So I said yes."

"Did you have any idea what he wanted to talk to you about?" Vic had his own notebook out, but had yet to take any notes beyond writing down the date, location, and Meera's name.

"I thought...I thought it might be about us." Tears welled in Meera's eyes again. "I guess I wanted it to be about that. I asked him, of course, but he said he'd tell me when I got there. But I should have known something was wrong. He didn't joke about it, normally he would. Tease me a little. But he was very serious. So I drove there and went up the incline."

"Did you take anything with you?" Liz had her head down and was writing. The question was nonchalant, and Vic admired everything about it. The delivery, the topic, and the built-in trap.

Meera frowned. "No. Just me."

Liz looked up. "You weren't carrying anything?"

"Well, my purse."

"Hand-held or shoulder bag?"

Meera frowned, realizing that something specific was behind Liz's questions. "Shoulder bag."

Vic thought of the grainy security footage. It did show a shoulder strap of some kind over Meera's shoulder. They'd thought it might be a bag holding

Steven's laptop, and now they couldn't be sure.

Vic decided to save the laptop question for last. "And when you met Steven, what did he want to talk to you about? Just tell me about meeting him, in your own words."

"Well, that's the thing. Nothing really. He met me by the statues up there, of George Washington? We walked down that path that goes to the left and sat on one of the rocks. He was in a good mood. I asked him what he wanted to talk about, and he said not to worry. It was going to work itself out. That was the wording he used. He said it would work itself out. So we sat and talked, and looked at the city." Her voice trailed off, her gaze inward.

Vic had the sense she was reliving that night. He waited, giving her time, wanting her to continue the story in her own way.

Meera blinked. "And that was kind of it. I mean, it was romantic for a little while." Her cheeks colored as her gaze darted to the doorway again. "And then he told me I should go. That the incline was going to close soon, and he would text me."

Liz stared at her. "You didn't wonder why he was staying up there by himself?"

"I asked him, and he said he was parked nearby. He walked me back to the incline and made sure I got on okay."

"And that was it?" Vic watched her as well.

"Yes. Although I did think one thing was weird."

Again, Vic and Liz waited.

"That he walked me to the incline. Steven was very…" Meera hesitated, searching for the right word. "Thoughtful. In a kind of old-fashioned protective way. I guess I was surprised that if he was parked up there, that he didn't drive me down the hill and make sure I got to my car okay. That would have been more like him."

Actually, Vic thought, it was significant. He didn't look at Liz, afraid he might give something away. They'd found Steven's car in the parking lot at the bottom of the incline. Logically, he should have ridden the incline down with her to get to his car. So he'd needed to stay on Mt. Washington longer. To meet someone?

"Did Steven get a phone call while you were together?" Liz tapped her pen against her notebook. Vic knew she was thinking along the same lines he was.

"No."

Vic pushed the oddity of how Steven and Meera parted from his mind. "There is one specific thing we need to ask you."

Meera looked at him expectantly.

"We haven't found Steven's laptop or cell phone. I guess the first question is whether he had either or both of those with him when you met."

"Oh." Meera hesitated for a moment. "I didn't see his cell phone, but he must have had it. I texted him when I got to the Incline and he texted back where to meet at the top. I don't know why he would have his laptop with him. That doesn't make sense, does it?"

Vic watched her. "I guess I need a yes or no. Did he have a laptop with him?"

Meera licked her lower lip, just a flicker of her tongue. "No."

"Aren't you finished yet? This is taking too long."

Vic looked toward the sound of the voice. The elder Dr. Basu started across the room, his footsteps heavy and final. "This is finished. My daughter has done nothing wrong. She isn't involved in anything illegal. You must go. We need to prepare the clinic for patients." He stopped next to Meera and dropped a hand protectively on her shoulder.

"I have one more question." Liz stared at Dr. Basu, challenging him to stop her. Vic saw she had turned her head slightly, so the scarring from the burns she received in a house fire several years earlier were obvious.

Dr. Basu opened his mouth to argue and thought better of it. "One more, and that is all."

Liz gave him a smile that would scare a shark. She turned to Meera. "How did you get involved with TU Health? I mean the volunteering."

"I told her that was a bad idea," the elder Basu said quickly. Everyone ignored him.

Meera blinked. "I wanted to do some volunteer work." She waved her hand at the clinic around her. "Forgive me, Father, but we only serve a certain kind of people here. I wanted to help people who are less fortunate." She glanced at Vic and stayed quiet.

Dr. Basu puffed out his chest. "This is a very good practice. Important patients. Good people. What is wrong with our practice? It is safe, very different than that place you volunteered."

Vic knew Meera had stopped talking because she expected her father to interject, and he tamped down a smile. She knew how to manage him.

Meera waited while her father took an indignant breath, then continued, staring directly at Vic. "I also had school loans to pay. I heard about a nonprofit that matches doctors with volunteer organizations. It's an App for your phone. Each time you volunteer, you fill out a short form on the app, and you build up credits to help pay off your loans. They have all kinds of volunteer organizations to match with. I chose TU Health."

"What is the name of the App?"

"WholePatient."

Vic wrote down the name.

"And now you are finished," Meera's father almost barked at them. Vic looked up and saw Sergeant Jerving in the doorway, a sheepish look on his face.

Vic pushed back his chair and stood. Liz did the same.

Vic looked at Meera. "We'll need to talk to you again."

"That isn't necessary," her father shot back. But Meera just meekly nodded her head.

Vic crossed to Sergeant Jerving. "Thanks for your help. And when you have a final report on the break-in, do you think you could share it? I'm interested."

The sergeant smiled easily. "I thought you might be."

Chapter Twenty

J ake Kittery slid into Ellie's car and turned the key. Ellie had taken
a day off work, and Jake had spent the morning talking to a funeral
home and arranging a cemetery plot. He felt inside out. He and Ellie
had never discussed burial options, and when Jake asked her if she wanted
to be buried as a family, Ellie gasped and threw her coffee mug at him,
then staggered upstairs. He'd sat in the kitchen, smelling the spilled coffee,
listening to the silence of the house.

Jake had known a decision still had to be made, so he'd instructed the
cemetery to reserve three adjoining plots, swept up the broken mug and
wiped the coffee off the wall and floor. Revolted by the silence of the house,
he'd taken the car keys and left.

He'd stopped at a diner in Swissvale, but was only able to down a few
forkfuls of a cooked breakfast. He boxed the remains.

Now, sitting in the car with the box in the passenger footwell, he thought
about what to do. He couldn't bring himself to go back to the house. Not
yet. He kept thinking about the two detectives from the day before and
how they'd sat in his living room calmly asking questions. He'd wanted to
scream at them, to shake energy into them. Make them pace the floor as
they asked questions, have them run out of the door to chase down Stevie's
killer.

But they'd left as pleasant as you please, and he'd heard nothing since. He
didn't even know if they were actually working on Stevie's case.

That thought kindled in his stomach and took flame.

Without thinking, he reversed Ellie's car out of its parking spot and nosed west. Fifteen minutes later, he slowed to a stop on Mt. Washington, next to the bronze statues of George Washington and an Indian. The area was deserted, except for some yellow crime scene tape attached to the sidewalk railing. He turned the car around, found a parking space on the opposite side of the road, and walked to the statues. He stared down the footpath at the large stones where Stevie's body was found. Indecipherable traffic noises floated over the bluff-top on the wind, mixing with the rustle of the crime scene tape. A train whistle-wailed through the long river valley like some wounded ancient.

He turned and stared at the city. This was the last thing Stevie saw, he thought. The night sky spread above him, the buildings topped by glowing business names, the flickering of lights as cars crossed the bridges. His chest and lungs stoked hotter.

He couldn't bring himself to walk down the path, or even look that way again. He returned to the car and sat for a time behind the wheel.

Half an hour later, he stopped in front of his house. As he walked to the door his eyes lingered on the crude message spray-painted in red on the garage door. He felt no need to clean it away.

Inside, the house was still silent, the door to his bedroom closed. Jake checked inside. The curtains were drawn. In the gloom, Ellie lay under the duvet, her chest slowly rising and falling. He closed the door to let her sleep.

He entered the bedroom they used for storage and went straight to the filing cabinet. A quick search brought him the thick documents from the last court case Conor Byrne had brought against him. He placed the files on some storage boxes and removed the paperwork. It took him less than a minute to find the address he wanted. He wrote the location on a sheet from a yellow Post-It note, folded the paper, and slid it into his shirt pocket.

It was a relief to leave the house, to have something to do. No definite plan yet, but a direction.

It took Jake thirty minutes to find the address, a single house on a tree-lined street. He parked in front of a house with a For Sale sign and a shaggy front lawn. He lowered the driver's seat and settled back.

As he waited, he found his mind didn't wander. It reminded him of his first job. Eighteen years old and watching molten steel from a converter furnace being formed into glowing slabs, blooms and billets. Formed. That raging heat hardening into something real.

He needed this.

Hours passed, but Jake barely noticed. He noted the infrequency of cars driving the road, the UPS truck that appeared and disappeared. And finally, a car pulled into the driveway of the house he was watching.

A tall, lanky man with black hair got out from behind the steering wheel. The man opened the trunk, retrieved two plastic shopping bags, locked the car, and carried the bags toward the house.

Conor Byrne, in the flesh.

"Got you, you son of a bitch," Jake breathed to himself.

Chapter Twenty-One

Carty Swain stood at the window of his fifth-story hotel room, staring down into the parking lot, the desk telephone pressed to his ear.

"I don't understand," Isabella repeated.

"I need some help with a project. Here in the U.S."

"We have no bank branches in the U.S. Why must I go there?"

He'd expected her to be suspicious, but her last few minutes of resistance meant she was worried about something deeper. Isabella worked for him; he'd plucked her out of the bank's finance department three years earlier. But the only people who knew she was part of the security department were Carty, her department head, and Vargas, the bank owner. It was no accident the head of the finance department also happened to be Vargas' nephew.

"I understand this sounds unusual, Isabella." Carty hesitated. Carty had dropped Isabella into three different departments where executives were suspected of embezzlement or fraud, with the cover story that she was there to help improve profitability. In fact, each time, she'd used her finance skills to prove or disprove embezzlement, and each time, she'd been perfect. That was exactly why he wanted her now. He decided to come clean. "Look, this is a personal project for me. Vargas gave me a month in the U.S. to sort it out. He'll agree to your coming. I only need you here for a few days, at most a week."

A pause. He heard dishes clatter through the phone and knew she was at a coffee shop somewhere. It was how they normally communicated. He'd sent a text asking her to take the call, and Isabella, assuming it was a normal assignment, had left the bank for a coffee shop so she wouldn't be overheard. They only met in person under controlled circumstances.

"Where would I stay?"

Carty finally understood what was worrying her. Carty had chosen her for the job instead of a young man in her department for a reason he thought he'd kept hidden. Isabella was almost thirty, pretty, her dark eyes full of fun, with a figure she worked hard to camouflage. He'd seen it immediately through the baggy business jacket and buttoned-up blouse during her interview. And now he was asking her to join him in the U.S. for a week, alone.

Women, he thought, always spotted a man's attraction. Despite his careful attempts not to give himself away, she must have recognized his interest.

He squeezed the phone. "We'll work the usual way. You go in alone; our main contact will be by phone and text. You choose your hotel."

"Can you tell me more about what I have to do? Since this isn't for the bank." She let the last statement hang in the air, but Carty knew she was interested. At the very least, it meant a free trip to the U.S. But he was beginning to like the idea of having Isabella out of Costa Rica and nearby. Perhaps he could get her into some clothes that showed off her figure, rather than hid it.

That idea warmed him.

"It's an interview," he said quickly, pulling himself back to the present. "We can work on this, but my idea is that you present yourself as a private detective, ask a series of questions—I'll help you with the wording—and you track what the target says. I'll create a backstory for you. You may need a second meeting, but if we're lucky, only the one."

"That's different from what I normally do. Usually, when I go into a branch or office, I'm working my finance job. I know what I'm doing. Then I just look around and see what is out of place or wrong."

"Right." Carty kept his voice calm. Neutral. "But this is what we do in security. We interview people to get information. Remember, after you spot something wrong on the job, I come in and interview the people involved.

Find out who's stealing. This is your chance to practice interviewing. It'll add to your skills."

"I can see that." She fell silent, and Carty imagined her sitting on a sun-dappled sidewalk outside a café in San Jose, an espresso in front of her. He missed the Costa Rican city, he realized slowly.

"Okay," she said, finally.

Carty knew she'd agree in the end. He was her boss, even if they limited their interactions to keep her undercover role a secret. Plus, he'd taken her to Vargas to present her findings after her last two jobs. He knew it would impress her. Access to the chairman and owner of a company always made people willing to help.

"Well," Isabella continued, "If this is something personal for you, perhaps I'll learn more about you."

Carty managed to get the phone away from his face so she didn't hear his intake of breath. That last sentence was a message, pure and simple. A vision of Isabella in frilly underwear leaped into his brain, overwhelming the prior one of her wearing figure-friendly clothes. He moved the phone back. "Ah, it'll be fun and good for your career. Can you get up here in a couple of days?"

"Yes. I think so."

"Okay. Come to New Orleans. I'll text you details. We'll need two days to prep, and then we'll fly separately to Pittsburgh. That's in Pennsylvania in the north. I'll cover you while you do the interview, and we'll come back here afterwards. Debrief and then you head home. Good?"

He was purposefully vague about the return to New Orleans. He fought down his excitement. He needed something out of that interview with Liz Timmons. A place, perhaps, or a name. But if they came up empty, a few days with Isabella in his bed would compensate.

"I'm looking forward to it," Isabella answered. She hung up.

Carty ended the call and looked down at the parking lot, smiling. He wasn't sure what warmed Isabella toward him, but it had occurred to him more than once that their relationship—the secret phone calls and texts, the illicit meetings—was a lot like having an affair. He wondered if she felt the same way and had simply decided to make it official.

One way or another, the trip was looking up.

Chapter Twenty-Two

Vic and Liz didn't speak for the first few minutes after they left Dr. Basu's clinic. Liz drove, frowning, her fingers tapping the steering wheel. Vic stared out of the side window, watching the Tudor-style houses and tended lawns slide by. He and Anne could never afford to live in Mt. Lebanon, and yet somehow, the conformity of what he saw meant he didn't mind.

"You believe her?" Liz asked, as they sat waiting for a traffic light to change.

"You mean about the laptop?"

"Right. She might have a reason to be lying." The light changed, and Liz eased the car forward. "I do believe she'd fallen for Steven Kittery."

"I believe that. Yes." Vic shifted in his seat. "There's two things I can take away from that interview." Vic paused, rearranging his thoughts, knowing the sequence of events mattered. "First, Steven asked Meera to meet him on Mt. Washington so he could tell her something, but when she got there, Steven said things had worked themselves out. Something happened between the time they talked and the time she arrived."

"I thought the same thing. Either a phone call or he met someone. We need his phone records. What's the second?"

"He lied to Meera. He said his car was on Mt. Washington. We know it was in the parking lot at the bottom of the incline."

"Right."

Vic slid his thumb under the seatbelt, pulled the shoulder strap away from his body, and let it snap back into place. "The only explanation about where the car was parked is that he planned to meet someone after Meera. He needed a way to stay on top of Mt. Washington without making her suspicious. Which also means he didn't want Meera to know about the meeting. He was keeping secrets."

Liz halted at another traffic light. "I could not live in this place. Start, stop. Start, stop."

"I guess living in Sewickley is easier?"

"Yeah. One light. It's like living in Dodge City after the Civil War. If I follow what you're saying, you think someone called Steven or talked to him just before Meera got there, and they decided to meet up later."

"Seems logical."

"Or that's what Meera wants us to think."

Vic sighed to himself. "There's also that. She's clearly smart enough to give us the right pieces to come up with the wrong conclusion."

They lapsed into silence.

As Liz pulled away from the traffic light, she added, "We need a timeline, and we need Steven's phone records."

"We need Craig chasing the carrier." Vic watched more Tudor-style houses slide by, these smaller and mostly red brick. "How about Conor Byrne? Could he have met Steven there?"

"How would he know Steven was on Mt. Washington? Where to find him?"

"Phone records," Vic said softly, more to himself.

They drove in silence a few minutes longer, Vic feeling as if the case was impenetrable. He knew it wasn't; they just didn't have enough to work with yet.

"I guess one of us has to ask the question." Liz glanced at him. "How about Jake Kittery? He could have known where to find Steven, and we never asked where he was the night it happened."

Vic knew from Liz's tone she didn't believe her own words. The grief in both parents was palpable and real. Vic's phone rang before he could reply.

"Craig?" he asked after looking at the caller ID. "How'd the detective's exam go?"

"It was fine. No trick questions."

Vic thought Craig sounded confident. "Unless they were really good trick questions."

"Nah. It went pretty much how I expected. Where are you guys?"

"Leaving the interview with Meera Basu. I think we have another doctor in about an hour." He glanced at Liz to check his statement, and she nodded.

"You might want to skip that one."

Vic tightened. "What happened?"

"Remember you asked me to talk to Ashley, the sales rep at Steven Kittery's condo? Get the security footage from the stairwells?"

"Did she send it over?"

"Not yet, but she left me a message while I was taking the test. Someone broke into Steven Kittery's apartment last night. Busted the door. A neighbor told her about it this morning."

Vic sat back, his pulse quickening. "We'll head over there now. Can you call Ashley and tell her we're coming?"

"Sure. Want me to take the doctor interview?"

Liz stopped the car at yet another traffic light.

"Yes. Liz will text you the contact details. And Craig, get after the cell phone carrier. We need Steven's records."

Vic hung up and looked at Liz. She was watching him, waiting. "Someone broke into Steven Kittery's condo last night."

Liz smiled. "I wonder if that was before or after they broke into Dr. Basu's office?"

"Yep, way too coincidental."

"So we aren't the only ones looking for something."

Vic nodded. "And I bet we're all looking for Steven's laptop."

Liz accelerated the car on the green light. "And how would they know Meera might have it? Whoever it was must have seen Meera and Steven together on Mt. Washington."

"That's one possibility, but there's another." Vic glanced at Liz. "If they didn't see Meera and Steven together on Mt. Washington, they absolutely knew Meera and Steven were seeing each other. But they kept their relationship low-key. None of the parents knew. So it had to be someone very close to them. A friend. Someone their own age."

"Starts to smell like a break."

"Well, it's something. Head over to Steven's apartment. I'll get Forrest over there to run the scene. Maybe we get lucky with fingerprints."

The traffic ahead of them opened up, the road now four lanes. The car's acceleration made Vic feel better. But the question about Steven's car still nagged at him. The incline closed shortly after Meera took the ride down. Steven had no easy way to get back to his car and would have known that. And yet, it was important enough for him to lie to Meera.

"We're missing something," he said out loud.

"No shit." Liz guided the car onto an entry ramp just before the tunnels under Mt. Washington.

"We're just walking around the edge of this thing. What ties Meera and Steven together? I mean, the central link?"

"Sex?" Liz's voice was at once dry and droll.

Vic nodded, but he knew that wasn't it. He breathed in and out slowly. He hated when this happened. Usually, it meant something was right in front of them, about to poke them in the eye.

Chapter Twenty-Three

As Liz pulled into a parking spot outside Steven's condominium building, Ashley skipped out of her office and waited for them to exit the car, a frown on her face.

"I called you as soon as the neighbor told me about it," she said breathlessly, as Vic straightened and closed the car door. "Then I went up to check."

"Thanks, appreciate that." Vic smiled at her, hoping it might give her a chance to get her breath back.

"Should I have called 911? Got regular police over here?"

"No need." Liz spoke with the tone she used when she was trying to confuse suspects with kindness.

"Oh good!" Ashley let out a long breath. "I've just never had to do this kind of thing before."

"You're doing great," Vic said quickly. "Can we go up?"

"Absolutely." Ashley darted for the front doors of the apartment building, remembered her sales office, went back, and fumbled with a large ring of keys before locking the office door. She led them to the elevator.

As they waited to reach the correct floor, Vic explained a forensics expert would arrive soon, to dust the door for fingerprints. "And I think you told Detective Luntz that you have security footage of the stairwells?"

"Who?" Ashley looked confused.

"Yes, who?" added Liz. She had a small smile, which Vic knew was Liz kidding him about calling Craig a detective before his exam results were posted.

"Craig," Vic corrected himself.

"Oh." Ashley reddened slightly. "I sent him the video from the night you wanted." She frowned, realization dawning. "You want it from last night, too?"

"Exactly," Liz answered.

The elevator doors opened, and Ashley led them along the hall to the front door of the apartment. The door was closed, the frame around the lock damaged.

"Small crowbar?" Liz posited, staring at the damage.

"Wouldn't need a big one." Vic turned to Ashley. "Was it found like this, or open?"

"It was ajar." Ashley pointed down the hall toward another door. "That's the neighbor. They said the door was open a little bit; that's why they noticed it."

"And who shut it?"

"I did." Ashley looked at Vic shyly. "I knew from TV I shouldn't touch the handle, so I did this." Ashley dropped into a squat, dug two fingers into the carpet at the base of the door, and pushed the door open using two fingers on the underside of the door.

As soon as the door separated from the frame, it swung all the way open. Ashley straightened up. "Shazam!" She grinned.

Vic smiled at Ashley's infectious enthusiasm. "Okay," he said. "That'll work." He glanced at Liz, to see her shaking her head in disbelief. He turned to Ashley, searching his pockets for latex gloves. "Maybe you could wait out here; we'll take a quick look around."

"Sure."

Outfitted in paper booties and latex gloves, Liz examined the floor just inside the door before leading Vic inside the apartment. Vic turned back to the doorway. "Ashley, now that I'm thinking about it, could you pull that security footage from last night now? I'd appreciate it. We can take it with us when we go."

"Sure thing. Just stop by my office when you're done."

Vic looked around. The living room looked unchanged from the first day they visited the apartment, as did the kitchen. They walked along the hall.

File folders littered the floor of the study, the box that originally housed them on its side. Mixed among them were books pulled from the bookcase, the largest ones splayed open as if someone flipped through the pages. But it was the corner of the room that caught Vic's eye. A large triangle of carpet was pulled back like a giant pointy tongue.

"What the hell? Liz asked.

They both crossed to the corner and looked down. Someone had cut a rectangle out of the exposed carpet pad, down to the plywood subfloor.

"You know what that looks like?" Vic asked.

"The size of the hole?"

"Yep." Vic bent over and gave the flap of carpet a tug, but it refused to easily come away from the walls.

"The hole is about the size of a laptop."

Vic straightened. "That's what I'm thinking."

"Which explains how we missed it the first time." Liz clucked her tongue. "Makes me wonder why he wanted to hide it."

"Now that's a good question."

Without discussing it, they parted, and each circled the perimeter of the room in a different direction and met at the door. Vic raised his eyebrows, but Liz shook her head. He led her to the bedroom.

The dresser drawers were piled on the bed, the drawer contents on the carpet. The mattress was askew on the box spring, as if someone had lifted the mattress to look underneath.

"Someone looking for documents," Liz said quietly.

Vic thought about the rifling of the books, the upended files, and the mattress. "That works for me. And with the missing laptop, perhaps it's a printout they want. Or Steven's hard copy back-up."

"Or maybe just making sure there isn't one. And no one keeps hard copy back-up anymore."

Vic ignored the dig. "Lines up too conveniently with Dr. Basu's break-in. And it means there's one other place they need to look."

Liz frowned, and Vic saw her following his logic. "Steven's office at TU Health?"

"Exactly." Vic slid out his phone and, after a quick search, found Edna's number. He dialed.

"TU Health." Edna's raspy voice was hurried.

"Edna? This is Detective Lenoski."

"You don't need more crap from me, do you? I have a million things to do."

"No, I just want to ask you something. Is Steven's office okay?"

"What do you mean, okay?"

"Has anyone been in it? Is it messed up in any way? Anything missing or out of place?"

Silence. Vic knew Edna was debating whether to ask more questions, but she thought better of it. "Just a sec."

As Vic waited, Liz walked the perimeter of the bedroom, studying the contents of the chest of drawers.

"Looks same as always," Edna reported back.

"Okay. There's been a couple of break-ins, we think someone is looking for documents Steven had, or someone thought he had. Do you have an alarm system for the office?"

"Sure."

"When you leave for the day, make sure it's turned on. Okay? And absolutely do this. Change the code before you activate it."

"I always turn it on."

"Just be extra careful today."

"I always am."

"Edna, just change the code. Thanks." He hung up.

"You two yinzers." Liz held up two fingers, one crossed over the other. "Like this."

Vic slid his phone back into his pocket. "Don't get me started."

He turned, and Liz followed him back to the living room. Vic stopped and looked around. Something about the space bothered him, but he couldn't say what it was. He looked at Liz. "Ideas?"

"Yeah. We got too hung up on Meera."

"She told us quite a bit."

"Right." Liz shifted on her feet. "Which is my point. Steven's mother gave us the name Brandon Ellis. The kid who graduated with Steven. We need to talk to him. And if someone tossed this place and the Basu practice for documents, we need to figure out what documents."

Vic considered her words. "Makes sense. We can let Craig finish the doctor interviews. I doubt they'll be very helpful, but we need to do them. Okay." He looked about the apartment, trying to understand what bothered him.

"Something up?"

Vic glanced at Liz. She was watching him.

"I don't know. Something feels off. Or different."

"So, talk it out."

Vic looked at her. Liz rarely said anything like that to him. She always stuck to facts, forensics reports, and interviews.

"We've got nothing to lose at this point." It was as if Liz could read his mind.

"I can't put my finger on it." Vic stared at the gleaming kitchen cabinets, the stainless-steel appliances, and how the walls reflected white in the sunlight. Now that he was considering it all, drinking it in, something shifted inside him, tiring him.

"I don't know."

Liz stayed quiet, standing a few feet away, watching him.

"No." Vic felt himself frown. "It's like this case is bringing back stuff I can't forget. It's making me see how much things have changed. Maybe it's got something to do with how we started. George Washington and Guyasuta, then seeing Braddock. It reminded me of the mill and river towns I grew up in. And then somehow we're in here." He waved his hand at the apartment around them. "Big windows and sunlight. Shiny appliances. Huge TVs. All that time, Jake Kittery fought for fair wages, marched, and stood in picket lines for mill workers, and the only thing he has left now is trying to give those union guys a peaceful death. And all the kids lost along the way. Jake's son, my Dannie, and I think Edna lost a child as well." Vic breathed, half shocked at the words coming out of him, but he couldn't stop himself. "For what? Bright empty places like this that don't even feel real?"

He didn't stop talking as much as ran out of things to say. He couldn't meet Liz's eyes.

"No one knows how any of this will go." Liz's tone was gentle.

Somewhere deep, anger flared, and Vic let it rise. He looked at Liz. "And you're okay with that? When Demond disappeared, what did you think? Did you accept it? I know you, Liz. You never did. You can't even talk about it."

The corners of Liz's mouth set, and her eyes darkened. "I can talk about it. You want to hear? Sure. Demond never came home the night after the levees broke. The truth is, nothing has changed for me since that night. I still dream about it. Wind coming and going, ragged, rain hitting the windows hard, like gravel. No phone, no cell. I'd sent Jayvon north to my aunt. I was alone. I had no way to tell either of them I was okay, make sure they were. Completely alone. Then I worked all the next day, doing whatever I could, still no word. Sleeping in the break room, and the sergeant waking me at four the next the morning. To tell me what? They found Demond's cruiser half in the water, trunk open. Demond gone. Carty Swain, his partner, gone. Where? Leaving me what? Air?"

As Liz talked, her posture gave way. Her breathing turned shallow. "Do I feel like shit's changed? Not at all. Two years of searching and waiting after that storm. Looking for any witness who saw them. Their bodies to show up. Nothing. But I've got Jayvon, I have to take care of him. Find a way to give him a chance. You know what happens to Black boys who grow up poor without fathers? So, I took the detective test. Just me. Did everything I could to keep Jayvon on track. I never had a chance to say goodbye to Demond. Never had time to get used to being without him. So, for me, nothing's ever felt like it changed. I'm still back there on the night the levees broke. When everything broke. And I can't ever forget. Ever."

Neither spoke. Vic's anger was gone. Liz looked wrung out, lips apart, breathing quickly.

"Excuse me?"

A voice from the hallway.

CHAPTER TWENTY-THREE

Vic gathered himself and turned to the front door.

"It's Ashley. I'm in the hall. I have the footage from the security tape."

"We'll be right there." Vic turned to Liz. She was staring out of the window, her back to him.

He didn't know what to say. He watched Liz draw herself upright. Take a deep breath.

"You ready?" Vic didn't like how gruff his voice sounded.

For a few seconds Liz was silent, then she turned to him. "Look at us. Everything changes, nothing changes. It's all different, it's all the same. But that isn't the point. Our shit doesn't matter. This apartment doesn't matter." Her eyes cleared. "What matters is that for Steven to get stabbed, something did change. Either with Steven or the person who stabbed him. Because, suddenly, Steven was a problem, and killing him was the only solution. Let's go figure out what changed for Steven. The stuff you and I can't forget? We worry about that shit later. We owe that to Steven."

Vic absorbed her words. "And the people most likely to tell us what changed for Steven are his closest friends."

"Should be. That's why I texted Craig to set up a meeting for us with Brandon. And we need to push Meera some more."

Vic walked to the door and opened it, holding it so Liz could go into the hall. They avoided looking at each other.

In the hallway, Ashley smiled and held out a thumb drive like a trophy.

Chapter Twenty-Four

Vic and Liz were barely settled in their car before Vic's phone rang. Vic answered after a glance at the caller ID. "Craig?"

"Detective Lenoski, Liz texted me to set up a meet with Brandon Ellis. I tracked him down. He says he can meet you in about an hour. Coffee shop, if that works."

Vic tightened his lips. Craig still felt the need to be formal with him. "Sure. Text us the details." He started the car. "Anything else?"

"I'll send over Brandon's DMV photo so you can spot him. I also have two interviews with doctors set up. I'll do those this afternoon."

"Thanks." Vic thought about what else they needed. "Craig, I know I asked, but any news from the phone carrier? We need Steven Kittery's phone records."

"Not yet."

Half an hour later, Liz and Vic took seats in a chain coffee shop in the Lawrenceville area of Pittsburgh, the shop set among early 1900s red-brick buildings retrofitted as restaurants, boutiques, and art galleries. They sipped coffee and waited, both in seats that overlooked the front door. Vic compared Brandon's DMV photo to the graduation photo from Steven's office. In the DMV photograph, Brandon wasn't smiling, and a haughtiness was unmistakable in his eyes.

Brandon was five minutes late. He pushed through the front door easily, his brown eyes and black hair projecting more haughtiness than the DMV photo. He filled the room, taller and huskier than Vic expected. It was evident his five o'clock shadow wasn't about to wait that long. He looked at the tables, adjusting a sleek grey shirt. The white soles of his black shoes gleamed underneath designer jeans. Vic was reminded of Steven Kittery's shoes.

Vic accepted the fact he was officially not up-to-date on men's styles and waved. Brandon crossed to their table, his gait smooth. Vic and Liz rose to meet him, but Brandon gave them a dazzling white smile and spoke first. "If you don't mind, can I grab a cup of coffee?"

"Sure." Vic gestured at the coffee bar.

Liz sat down without saying anything, and Vic joined her. "Salesman." She said the word like a curse.

"He's got a pair of shoulders on him. Bigger than Meera's."

Liz shot him a look of disgust, and they waited in silence until Brandon returned.

All electricity and action, Brandon slid into the chair directly across from Vic. "Thanks." Brandon looked at Vic and Liz, in turn, holding eye contact. "Been a long day so far. I need the pick-me-up."

"What do you do?" Liz's smile suggested Brandon couldn't possibly say anything interesting or right.

"Oh, I run a start-up. Tech. Streamlining the stuff that's been badly done in the past. Nobody knew how to do it right before us."

"Of course, they couldn't." Liz's tone betrayed no sarcasm.

"You got that right. We're automating medical record-keeping. End-to-end processing. Silver bullet kind of service. Franchising has to be next."

Vic was bemused by how Liz allowed Brandon to rattle off so many cliches without revealing any information. "Excuse me," Vic interrupted. "This is interesting, but we're investigating the death of Steven Kittery. Maybe we could start there?"

Brandon sat upright, suddenly serious. "Sure. Got off track. It's just that our tech is so good, I can't help talking about it."

Vic waved a hand in dismissal. "We need some background. How you met Steven, how friendly you were, right from the beginning until now."

Someone called Brandon's name. He raised a finger for Vic to wait, hopped up, and walked to the coffee bar. He returned with a coffee cup and wooden stirrer. Settled in his seat, Vic and Liz waited while he stirred his coffee and snapped the lid back into place.

"So, how do you know Steven?" Liz prompted.

Brandon folded the paper the stirrer came in and placed the wet end on the paper, holding it off the table. "Sure. We, uh, met in classes at Pitt. Undergraduate. We were both taking accounting. We hung out some. Partied." He gave a brief smile. "Then we ended up in the same MBA class. Pitt again. Got to be better friends. That was serious. Steven had it going. Smart. Worked hard." He grinned again.

Vic thought that for a long-time friend, Brandon was surprisingly buoyant in the face of Steven's death. "And how often did you see each other since? I mean outside work."

"Oh, maybe once every couple of weeks. We text a few times a week."

"So you would consider yourselves to be good friends?" Liz asked the question gently, but Vic knew she was circling Brandon, looking for an opening. A way to get him off balance.

"I guess so."

Liz leaned forward. "Okay, Brandon. When was the last time you saw Steven?"

"Oh, we texted at the beginning of last week. Talked about going out for drinks this weekend. Never finalized anything."

"Anyone else you guys meet up with?"

"Um, not really."

"Meera Basu?"

"Oh, forgot about her." Brandon sipped his coffee and sat back, looking bored. "Yeah. She showed up once or twice."

"Dr. Basu." Liz stressed the word doctor. "Steven and Dr. Basu were an item. You didn't know that?"

Vic knew Liz was annoyed at the dismissive way Brandon mentioned Meera. She'd found her opening.

Brandon gave a lopsided smile that Vic thought looked defensive. The hey-it's-just-me-the-good-guy smile. "Yes. I knew that. They've been dating for a while."

Liz glared at Brandon. He kept his eyes on his coffee.

Vic leaned forward and put his forearms on the table. "You said you and Steven texted last week, but the question was when did you last *see* him." He let his statement hang in the air.

"Sorry, oh, maybe early the week before?"

Vic thought Brandon's comments were too flip. He glanced at Liz.

"The next point is whether you've seen any change in him over the last few weeks. Was he suddenly worried about anything, or anyone?"

"Oh, not that he said to me. He was normal. Like always."

Again, Vic thought Brandon's answer was a shade too quick, but not obviously so. It could just be nervousness at having to answer the questions.

"Any ideas why he'd be on Mt. Washington late at night? Is there a place up there you go regularly?"

Brandon made a show of thinking about the question. "Yeah. That's Meera. Steven lives on the east side of Pittsburgh, Meera the south. Mt. Washington was a good midway point. Meera has problems getting out of her house; she has to sneak out sometimes. She can't drive far because she can't be away for long. Her dad gets suspicious. I guess he's very Indian. Old school."

Vic thought back to the way Meera's father behaved when they interviewed Meera, and agreed with Brandon. "I see that. Where did they go, when they met up there?"

Brandon picked up the coffee stirrer and tapped the wet end on the table. "You know the restaurants that line the bluff, right? Overlooking the city? They used to go to the bars inside those places. But they didn't really drink. After college, Steve cut way back, and Meera is a two-sip drinker."

"Okay." Vic thought back through their previous interviews. "Steven's parents said you helped found the non-profit where Steven worked. How did that come about?"

Brandon's face hardened just slightly. "Don't know why that matters."

Vic waited for Liz to weigh in, and she did. Sharply. "We don't know what's important yet. So, we ask questions. And are you really telling me that you didn't notice a change in Steven's behavior over the last couple of weeks?"

Brandon looked in Liz's direction, but Vic noted that he avoided eye contact. "I told you. We don't see each other much. I didn't pick up anything from his texts. And we were planning to go out for drinks. That's normal behavior, not abnormal."

Vic didn't like the contradictions in what Brandon was telling them. He'd said he and Steven were planning to have drinks, only to follow the comment with the statement Steven didn't drink much anymore. Brandon said he and Steven were friends, yet now claimed they rarely saw each other. Brandon helped get TU Health off the ground, yet had no interest in talking about it.

"Okay." Vic swirled the last of the coffee in his cup. "Sorry, but I'd like to know how you helped the Kittery's set up TU Health." He held up a hand. "Maybe it isn't relevant, I get that, but humor me. I'm interested. How did you get into a position to help them?"

Brandon gave Vic a look that seemed to say, okay, you want it? I'll give it to you. He sipped more coffee. "After I got my MBA, I got a job with a health insurer here in town. The biggest one, you can guess the name. I was in finance, but they pulled me into this big review about how to reduce the cost of chronically ill patients. Bunch of consultants were brought in. The problem is that chronically ill patients often skip appointments because they can't get to a clinic or their doctor. It's too difficult, or family members aren't able to take them. If they skip, they miss treatments, their health deteriorates, and when they finally go to a doctor, it costs more for them to recover. Even with Medicare and Medicaid, the insurer ends up paying more. The consultants suggested setting up in-home care. The idea was to improve in-home care so treatments don't get missed. Then the insurer avoids the huge cost that comes later if they miss treatments."

Brandon broke off talking and lifted his coffee cup, holding it mid-way to his mouth. His description was fluid and practiced, a salesman's patter, and Vic could see he was comfortable again.

"From there, it was easy." Brandon lowered his paper cup and leaned closer, as if he was passing along a secret. "The insurer I worked for lobbied the state for some grants to start non-profits to provide in-home treatments.

I wrote the business model for them. Volunteer doctors, that kind of thing. Steve got all that. He'd even written about an idea like that in business school. I knew his Dad was a labor organizer, and union workers was one of our target groups. So I talked to Steve and his dad, and boom, I made it happen. And once we got TU Health off the ground, I knew we could target other groups. Repeat the structure. That's when I realized we needed an App everyone could use. So I started my own company to make that happen." Brandon grinned.

Vic was impressed that Brandon's smile was as much smug as superior.

"And it's working?" Liz sounded skeptical.

"Yeah. The start was slow. The insurer had to market to the chronically ill folks, but we used Steven's dad in the marketing materials. Put his picture on everything. They trust him. Then it was just a matter of getting doctors to take part."

"And how does that work?" Liz watched Brandon carefully.

"Oh, the insurer incentivizes the doctors. They set up some kind of credit program to help them pay off med school debt if they volunteer."

Vic remembered Meera saying the same thing. He also remembered Edna's comment about it being hard to keep doctors volunteering.

Vic sipped his coffee, letting Liz run with the questions.

Liz tapped her pen on her notebook. "What are the names of Steven's other friends?"

Brandon looked at Liz, just briefly. "Beats me. If we met up it was just him and me. Meera showed up once or twice. That was it."

"Okay." Vic watched Brandon carefully. "And we have to ask. Where were you last Wednesday night, from eleven at night until one?"

Brandon looked upward slightly, his fingers tapping on the desk top. "Wednesday. Oh, with my mother. She's in an independent living place near Sewickley. I stay over every Wednesday. Have dinner with her, we watch a movie or something, then I sleep there and go to work the next day. Just easier than going back to my apartment."

"You're talking about the Masonic Village in Sewickley?" Liz watched him carefully.

"Yeah, you know it? Great place."

"So I've heard," Liz said slowly.

"What was the movie?" Vic asked.

Brandon sat back, making a show of remembering. "I forget. Something with Helen Mirren. Spy story. My mother likes her. Bruce Willis was in it. We streamed it."

Vic watched Liz write down the details, but he already knew the name of the movie. "Okay, Mr. Ellis. We appreciate you taking the time." He stood, and Brandon and Liz did as well. They shook hands, and Vic and Liz watched Brandon jauntily disappear through the door.

They sat down, and neither said anything for several seconds.

"Well?" Vic asked, still watching the door.

"He had all the answers," Liz breathed. "And he was very pleased with himself that he did."

"Yeah," Vic said slowly. "That bothered me as well."

Chapter Twenty-Five

J ake Kittery eased the driver's seat of his car upright and rubbed his eyes. Conor Byrne's house was just another looming structure among the evening shadows. He knew he needed to go home and check on Ellie. A streetlight flickered on at the end of Conor's street.

He was surprised none of the neighbors had called the police about him. Granted, on both days, he'd parked in the same spot outside the house that was for sale, but still. A man just sitting in his car for hours on end?

Conor hadn't spotted him, he knew that. Conor would have called his friends at the Bureau of Police to roust him.

And he'd learned a few things. Conor liked to stay at home. He'd followed Conor on only two forays. One to a supermarket and the second to a church. But not the church itself. He'd watched Conor take the door to a side building. When he didn't come out, Jake followed Conor to the door and studied a schedule locked inside a glass-covered bulletin board.

Conor, apparently, attended Alcoholics Anonymous meetings.

Jake started the car and checked the mirrors, deciding to exit the block at the opposite end from Conor's house.

No point alerting Conor to the fact he was here.

He doubted he would return to his stake-out. The telephone call from the Coroner's office an hour before had decided that. The waiting period was over. Steven's body was being released to the funeral home Jake had designated.

That was another reason to speak to Ellie. They needed to schedule a memorial service. A burial.

He breathed heavily. He wasn't sure Ellie was up to it, but he was. Watching Conor's house had cleared his head, and oddly, allowed the reality to sink in. He believed he could soldier through what happened next. Get himself ready for the days after Stevie was buried. For what he planned to do next.

"Maybe you believe in an eye for an eye," Jake said out loud to the interior of his car, to Conor. "But I'm going to take your entire fucking head."

It was a relief to say the words. He pulled the car from the curb and into a U-turn. He jockeyed through the intersection at the end of the block, Conor's house slipping from view. Around him, small, dingy houses with high peaked roofs crowded the road, like the anger bubbling just under his skin.

First, he needed to talk to Ellie, to properly bury their son.

Then Conor would get what he deserved.

Chapter Twenty-Six

Vic sat at his desk, wanting to leave for home, but knowing they needed a breakthrough in Steven's murder. Instinctively, he knew they were taking too long to find a prime suspect.

On his computer screen, he opened the file containing the security footage Ashley had provided. Liz had offered to do the review, but he'd suggested that she research Brandon Ellis. Brandon's charisma and arrogance bothered him, as did Brandon's self-serving answers to their questions. Vic knew Liz was better at online research, so the task logically fell to her.

Craig, who would normally review security footage, was out of the mix until he finished interviewing the TU Health doctors.

So the task fell to him.

He'd called Anne and warned her he would be late. Her response was easy and unconcerned, but she warned him about the following evening, when he would need to babysit Lettie.

Vic glanced around the office floor. It was dark outside, the few people working reflected in the window glass.

He turned back to the security footage. Ashley had provided data from five cameras. A static one in the lobby, one camera each just inside the lobby entrance to the south and north stairwells, and two elevator cameras. He clicked on the footage to the southern stairwell and began to watch.

An hour later, his vision was bleary. While the cameras were motion-activated and few people used the stairs—or at least entered the stairwell on the first floor—one overachieving young man spent forty minutes running the stairs in workout shorts and a T-shirt. Every few minutes, he descended to the first floor, touched the door, pivoted, and headed back up the stairs.

It made Vic tired just watching him. Vic had run enough stairs while training for boxing matches and remembered the aching knees and quads. He wondered why the young man was doing the training.

But the motion-activated feature did reduce the sheer bulk of footage he needed to watch, and in just over ninety minutes, Vic switched to the north stairwell. Those stairs received even less use.

The time stamp on the footage read two-ten in the morning when a figure slid past the camera and glided up the stairs. Vic sat upright. This man was tall and wore a baseball cap over a dark nylon windbreaker and blue jeans. A small, dark-colored backpack was strapped to his back. Something in his gait sounded an alarm in Vic's mind.

He reran the footage where the man was in-frame.

Nothing jumped out at him, beyond that little jolt of recognition.

Vic knew he had to be careful, because he wanted and needed to find something. That jolt might easily be wishful thinking. Still, he jotted down the time stamp.

Thirty minutes later, the man reappeared, coming down the stairs. He kept his face lowered, the bill of his baseball hat blocking his face. Vic noted the time stamp when the man was in frame and reran the section again, frame by frame. It was impossible to make an identification.

Vic switched to the lobby footage and found the time episode when the man crossed the lobby to enter the northern stairwell. He found him, but the man kept his face averted, his features blocked by the bill of his cap.

This, Vic knew, was the flaw in how the cameras were set up. If someone knew the camera locations they could avoid the lobby camera, then take the elevator to Steven's apartment. Even if the lobby or elevator cameras identified them, they could exit the elevator on the second floor and take the stairs to Steven's fourth-floor apartment without being recorded in the stairwell. Any competent lawyer could argue the person never visited Steven's fourth-floor apartment. He sensed the cameras were a marketing ploy to claim the building was safe, more than an actual deterrent.

Vic fast-forwarded to the time stamp when the man should be crossing the lobby as he left the north stairwell to exit the building.

Vic found him, walking swiftly toward the front door; his back was to the camera. Vic huffed in frustration.

Vic watched as the man reached for the door handle, just as the doors burst inward. The man hopped back, pulling his hand to safety. Two young men stumbled into the lobby, laughing and obviously drunk. One of the young men swept toward the elevators, but the other stopped. He seemed to realize the three men almost collided. Vic watched him mouth something to the man from the stairwell. Vic imagined the young man's slurred apology and watched as the man from the stairwell waved his hand as if to say the near miss was nothing, everything was fine.

The young man misinterpreted the waved hand and grabbed it, pumped it up and down in a handshake of peace-making, as he swung the man from the stairwell around.

Vic saw the taller man's lips move under his baseball cap, even though he couldn't see more than the man's chin and mouth. The young man dropped the man's hand and raised his arms as if a gun was pointed at him. He stepped back.

The man from the stairwell glanced up, pivoted, and disappeared through the front doors. The drunk man dropped his left arm and straightened his right arm in front of him, middle finger extended, and jerked his hand upward at what had to be the disappearing back of the man from the stairwell. Laughing, he turned for his friend and the elevator.

Vic paused the footage and reversed it, frame by frame, looking for the moment when the man in the baseball cap glanced up. He couldn't resist, Vic guessed. He needed to know if he was in the camera's field of view.

Vic paused the footage at the right moment and let out a sharp breath. In grainy black and white, Conor Byrne stared at him from the screen.

"Well," Vic said softly to the screen. "That certainly puts you in the frame, my friend."

Chapter Twenty-Seven

The next morning was a Saturday, but Vic called in Liz and Craig. He pulled up the security footage from the condominium and showed it to them on his computer screen. He paused on the moment Conor glanced at the camera.

"He knew where the camera was," Liz said over his shoulder. "He kept his head down when he went in and in the stairwells. It's the whole reason he's wearing a baseball cap."

"Right. He planned the whole thing and almost got away with it." Vic tapped his index finger on his mouse. "Just bad luck he ran into a couple of drunks. When that kid swung him around, he needed to orient himself to the camera. Couldn't help himself. Knowing where the cameras were actually tripped him up."

"Doesn't that mean we'll be able to find him somewhere else on the footage? Maybe a day or two earlier?" Craig asked.

Vic craned around to look at Craig, who was standing over his other shoulder. "You mean spot when he did reconnaissance?"

"Right."

"It's a good point, but let's save that for when we need it." Vic turned to his computer screen. "Unfortunately, all the footage shows is that he knew where the cameras were, entered and left via the lobby, and took the northern stairwell somewhere. We have no proof where he went. We all know he went to Steven's apartment, but we have no way to prove it."

"So we talk to him." Liz shifted next to Vic so they could see each other. "Ask him. See how nervous he gets."

"Maybe he lets something slip." Craig crossed to his desk, sat and rotated his chair to face them.

"No matter what, we need to talk to him." Vic had mulled this problem most of the night and decided there was only one thing to do. "In fact, I think we try and rattle him. He's a retired cop, he knows how we work. If we show up at his house and have a sit down, he'll just spin a story about why he was there. I think we take it up a notch. Have uniforms pick him up and bring him here. Let him stew in the interview room for a few hours, and then go in and threaten to charge him with Steven's murder. He might give us the breaking and entering to stay clear of the murder charge."

"Unless he did kill Steven." Liz crossed to her desk chair and sat, facing him. "I guess professional courtesy is out the window."

"I can't figure out another way to do it. I think we have to hit him hard." Vic stared at Liz. She was frowning at her lap, working through the problem.

Liz looked up. "If we want to threaten him with a murder charge, we need something that puts him near Mt. Washington. Or suggests we can place him there. Right now, his alibi for that night is pretty good. We know he stopped to get gas and buy a drink, where he was, and we're pretty sure he graffitied the Kittery's garage door about the time Steven was murdered. Hard to put him on the other side of town on Mt. Washington."

"How about the tunnels?" Craig glanced from Vic to Liz.

"What do you mean?" Vic wasn't sure where Craig was headed.

"The tunnels. We know where he lives. The only way to get from there to Mt. Washington is through the Squirrel Hill Tunnels, it's either that or add forty-five minutes to the trip, and drive through downtown Pittsburgh or circle through the south hills. The tunnel authority runs footage of the vehicles in the tunnel, and they're easy to work with. They'll give it to us. If we spot him driving through the tunnel headed toward Mt. Washington, and the time is right, it's leverage."

Vic stared at Craig. Out of the corner of his eye, he saw Liz give a faint smile. "Good point," Vic said. "Get onto the tunnel authority."

"And we bring Conor in before we look at the footage from the tunnel, or after?"

"No. Bring him in right now. I want him to know we're onto him. He knows the apartment building camera caught him, and I want him to start worrying about how quickly we're moving. Just one more thing to rattle him. And during the interview, we can drop the idea that if he went through the tunnels, we'll soon know about that, too."

"Okay. And you want uniforms to pick him up?" Liz watched him intently.

"Yep. Suspicion of breaking and entering and interfering in a murder case. I want to talk to him this afternoon."

"Okay. I'll keep researching Brandon Ellis."

Craig grinned. "I'll get on the phone to the tunnel authority."

"Good." Vic picked up his phone and dialed the desk sergeant. He explained what he wanted and hung up. His guess was that Conor would try to talk them in circles. Conor couldn't escape the fact that he was in Steven's condominium building two nights earlier, but unless they got lucky with a fingerprint on the doorknob or inside Steven's apartment, he'd know they couldn't place him in the apartment.

Vic turned back to his computer screen and stopped. Frowned. He looked at Liz. "Hey, remember when we searched Conor's car?"

Liz nodded.

"We found that bag with the red spray paint inside, right?"

"Right."

"I just remembered. There was a box of latex gloves in the bag as well. I guess to keep paint off his hands when he was spraying."

Liz stared back at him. She sat back suddenly. "Or fingerprints off a doorknob or inside an apartment."

"Right."

Liz pursed her lips in disgust. "This case is like the case that couldn't. We don't get any breaks."

"Well, let's shake him up, see what falls out." Vic knew that was about the best they could hope for. Sometimes, people just needed a push to open up. It had happened before. He doubted Conor was one of those people.

A little after ten o'clock, Vic got the call saying Conor was waiting in one of the interview rooms. Vic asked about Conor's reaction when he was picked up.

"Officers said he shrugged and got his coat. Talked football on the way here."

"Lucky us," Vic said. "Thanks."

Vic found the video stream from the interview room. Conor was stretched out in his chair, long legs sticking out from under the table, hands behind his head. His eyes were closed, a small smile on his face. Vic decided to wait until two o'clock. With that smile, Conor needed four hours. Maybe by then, he would be angry.

At one-thirty, Vic skimmed the online newspapers and news sites, looking for any stories on their case. Nothing so far, beyond the facts of the body being discovered. He did find Steven Kittery's obituary. He read slowly, searching for anything he didn't know. Apart from Steven's school and work history, there was little to tell, beyond the obvious grief of his parents. At the bottom was the announcement of a memorial service, to be held the next day. On impulse, Vic printed out the story. When he returned from the printer, he nodded to Liz and looked at Craig, who was gazing at his computer screen.

"Too soon?" he asked Craig. Craig toggled a switch and sat back. "I just got the tunnel footage half an hour ago. I have to run it in slow motion. I need a few hours."

"Better to go slow and not make a mistake. Take your time."

Vic waited for Liz to join him, and at two o'clock, they finally entered the interview room.

Conor was folded over the table, head on his arms. When Vic pulled his own chair out he purposely banged the leg of the table hard to wake Conor up.

Conor straightened up groggily, blinking his eyes. "Oh, look who decided to make time in their busy day."

Vic arranged himself on his chair and dropped a closed file folder on the table. He stared at Conor for a few moments, then instructed Conor they were recording the session and identified the day, time, and who was in the room. Finished, he said, "Yes, our day is busy, and you're the asshole making it that way."

"Oh, please. Your problem is you can't figure out who killed Steven Kittery. I'm a sideshow. That's why you left me in here so long."

Liz cut him off. "And why did we bring you in here to begin with?"

"You'll have to tell me." Conor smiled, his blue eyes sharp.

Vic knew Conor had expected the question, and he decided to avoid a charade. "You know as well as we do. We have you on breaking and entering."

Conor raised his eyebrows. "Can you prove it?"

Vic opened the file and removed a printout of one frame from the security footage. "Here you are in the apartment building lobby." He explained the exhibit for the recording. "Do you deny it's you?"

Conor squinted at the paper. "I can see why you'd be confused."

"Cut the crap. That's you. Or give me an alibi."

"I was at home?" For the recording, Conor emphasized he was asking a question.

"You aren't sure? You're asking a question? Are you saying you were at home or asking a question about it?" Vic waited, watching Conor. Vic was genuinely interested to see if Conor would lie.

Conor finally broke the silence. "Let me explain something to you. Even if you place me in the lobby, you can't prove I was the one who broke into Kittery's apartment. I'm in the lobby, maybe the stairwells. Hey, I was interested in buying a condo in that building, wanted to take a look around at night. See how safe it was." Conor smiled, his face smug.

Vic avoided looking at Liz. Conor had just swung and missed, and Vic suspected he didn't even know it. "Okay, so if we ask the salesperson for the building, she'll remember you asking for information and maybe a tour of an apartment? Is that right?"

Conor blinked.

"What is that person's name? The salesperson?" Vic looked at Liz. "Do you remember?"

Liz shook her head slowly. "Damn, I don't remember." She looked at Conor. "Do you remember the salesperson's name?"

Vic saw a slight shift in Conor's face. "I did online research," he said quickly. "Internet these days. They have everything."

"And if I told you we have your fingerprints inside the apartment that was broken into?" Vic cocked his head and smiled.

Conor crossed his arms. "Impossible."

"That's a big word," Vic said lightly. "The kind of word people use when they know something. Exactly why would you think it was 'impossible' we might find your fingerprints?"

"Couldn't have happened."

Vic waited, watching Conor. The silence widened. Conor's answer was strike three, Conor's third mistake. He decided to push. "But then again, maybe we can forgive and forget. All we'd ask is that you give us the laptop and document you found in the apartment. We know you were looking for them, we just don't know why. See? I'm being honest with you. Telling us what we do and don't know. And now it's your turn. Hand them over and we'll give you a ride home. Make it easy on yourself."

"You don't know what you're talking about." Conor unfolded his arms, looked unsure for a moment, and refolded them.

Vic turned to Liz. "You know what's interesting? I mean apart from all the mistakes Conor, here, has made as we talk?"

"What would that be?" Liz playacted as if she really was interested in Vic's question.

"The reason why Conor wanted to search Steven Kittery's apartment." Vic turned back to Conor. "Oh, and that was the first mistake you made, Conor. I never said Steven's apartment was broken into, or was even in that building. You did. Now, how did you know that? I checked the media sites before I came in here, and there's no news report on the break-in at Steven's apartment. But you already knew whose apartment was broken into."

Conor blinked.

Vic didn't give him time to respond. "I mean, the only people who know about the break-in are Liz and me, Steven's neighbor, who discovered it, and the sales rep at Steven's condo building. Her name is Ashley, by the way. That was your second mistake. She's the one whose name you couldn't remember. And you can be damn sure we'll ask her if you came in asking about a condo."

Conor opened his mouth to speak, and Vic held up a hand. "I'm not done. Your third mistake. Why you were so sure that we wouldn't find your fingerprints inside the apartment. I've got a pretty good idea why. When we searched your car, we found red spray paint. And with it, a box of latex gloves. You latexed up before you went into the apartment. No fingerprints. But this is all secondary. It's the document that interests me. And why the hell would you be looking for a document inside Steven's apartment? What would he have that was so critical to you that you would take that kind of risk?"

Vic opened the folder and took out the printout of the obituary. He spun it around so Conor could read it and tapped it with his finger. "Is it in here? The reason you wanted to search his condo?"

Conor dropped his arms and leaned forward. He quickly scanned the obituary and sat back. After a moment, he crossed his arms over his chest. His bravado was gone. He frowned. "We're done. Nothing more until I have a lawyer."

"Just be careful about which one you pick," Vic said slowly. "We're looking at footage of the cars going through the tunnels the night Steven was murdered. Are we going to find your car headed toward Mt. Washington? Because if we do, things will get bad for you."

"You know where I was that night," Conor hissed, his blue eyes hooded. "I already told you. I was out driving. I stopped for gas. You can put me on the other side of town."

"No," Vic shot back. "You only told us that part. Not all of it. If that's all you did, then you had time to get to Mt. Washington. It was tight, but you could do it. By driving through the tunnels."

Conor straightened. "Lawyer. My phone call." His voice was strangled, mouth tight.

"The laptop, the document," Vic answered. "Take the get-out-of-jail-free card. Unless we spot your car in the tunnels, and then it's lights out."

CHAPTER TWENTY-SEVEN

Vic rose, and Liz followed suit. Vic stared at Conor. "Still want a lawyer?"

"Yep. And where the hell is my professional courtesy?"

Vic stared at him. "Wow. Just wow. We'll send in a phone." Vic started for the door as Liz announced the interview was suspended.

Chapter Twenty-Eight

The next morning, as Vic cooked pancakes for Anne and Lettie, he relived the interview with Conor. It had gone about as well as he could hope. He knew he'd gotten under Conor's skin, enough for Conor to demand a lawyer, but two questions still lingered from the interview.

He took bacon out of the oven, arranged it on three plates, and placed a plate of stacked pancakes on the kitchen table. He called to Anne and Lettie.

Lettie streaked into the kitchen and clambered onto her chair. The sprint was her default pace, now, and Vic wasn't sure when she developed that gear. Anne followed at a more sedate walk.

"You got back later than I expected last night," Anne said.

"I had a guy in an interview room, and it took forever for his lawyer to show up. And then the lawyer sprung the guy in about five minutes. It was a lot of sitting around."

He didn't mention that he and Liz had strung out the release paperwork and then stood in the lobby smirking at Conor as he left with his lawyer. Just a little low-key harassment.

"Well, I wasn't about to wait up."

"Not a problem." Vic sat and served up pancakes to Lettie, who was already chewing on a rasher of bacon.

"This is the Kittery murder?" Anne asked.

"Yes. The memorial service is in a couple of hours, and I want to go. Just see who shows up."

"How about the interview? Did you get anything out of it?"

Lettie dumped enough syrup on her pancakes to float an armada. Anne grabbed the plate away from her, rose, and placed the pancakes on another plate. She returned the new plate to a pouting Lettie.

"Two things I can't quite figure out; they came out before he asked for his lawyer and clammed up."

Anne raised an eyebrow.

As they ate, Vic explained Conor's feud with the Kitterys, and Conor's decision to break into Steven Kittery's apartment. "We think he was looking for a document, but right now, he's not talking."

Anne chewed for a few moments and swallowed. "If Steven had a document Conor wanted, then he and Conor must have been in touch. It's the only way Conor would know about the document and why it was important enough to risk breaking into the apartment."

Vic felt like a fool. Anne was right. And if Conor and Steven had communicated, somewhere an email or text string could be found. At the very least the record of a phone call.

"Good point." Vic made a mental note to have Craig chase Steven's cell phone carrier again. "The other thing is just as weird."

"And that is?" Anne put down her fork, dipped her paper napkin quickly in her water glass, and wiped a spot of syrup from Lettie's T-shirt.

"We're going through footage of the tunnels, looking for his car. If we find it, which I doubt we will, then he could be the killer. But he also has an alibi. About the time of the murder, he was putting graffiti on a garage door. But he won't use that alibi. He just doesn't mention it."

"That's more complicated." Anne balled up the wet napkin and put it on her empty plate.

"I don't get that one either." Vic scraped the last of the syrup off his plate and licked it off his fork.

"Have you ever had anything like that before? Someone not protecting themselves?"

Vic shook his head. "Nope. Completely new."

Anne frowned and fell silent, thinking. "I've got nothing on that," she said. "I'd think most people would want to prove their innocence."

"Normally, they do."

From the corner of his eye, Vic saw Lettie sneak another rasher of bacon. She kept it under the table, pretending she hadn't done anything. Vic looked at her. "If you want more bacon, put it on your plate and eat it properly."

Lettie flushed and tossed the bacon onto her plate. Anne stared at Vic, her eyes saying 'can you believe it?'

"Okay," Vic said slowly. "I need to get ready for the memorial service. "Thanks for suggesting Conor and Steven were in touch. I might be able to use that."

"What would you do without me?" Anne smiled at him.

Vic stared at her. "You already know how I'd do without you, and it isn't well. I think I proved that."

Anne stared at him. "All the more reason to get home at a decent hour."

Chapter Twenty-Nine

Vic turned his car uphill from Braddock's main street and climbed a block above the looming Greek Catholic church where Steven's memorial service was to be held. He parked and walked back down the hill under low, flat, and gray clouds. The air carried a stubborn chill and a vague mill-smell of carbon. Below him, the steel mill and mostly empty cross streets where TU Health was located lay beside one another on the river flats.

Opposite the church, two historical markers sat inside an area of scraggly and wind-blown grass. A small fence, perhaps eight inches high, surrounded the grass. Vic stopped to read the plaques, vaguely aware of cars parking along the street and a slow stream of people into the church.

The first recorded that Braddock's namesake, the British General Braddock, was defeated by French and Indian forces nearby in 1755. It was the first time George Washington—who took command of the British forces after Braddock was shot—and Guyasuta faced one another as enemies. The second memorialized the Whiskey Rebellion of 1791, and a crucial gathering of six thousand rebels at nearby Braddock's field. How Washington handled the uprising was a test of Washington's presidency and the country's fragile unity.

Absently, Vic checked the road and saw Meera Basu park her silver Mercedes against the curb near the Church's front door. She hurried inside, her face drawn. Vic followed, choosing a pew several rows behind the gathering of mourners clustered at the front of the church.

Vic counted fifty-seven people. On the far side of the church, a grouping of elderly men whispered to one another in the cool, still air. He wondered how many once worked the area mills. Jake and Ellie Kittery sat in the front row to the right of the aisle, Edna a few feet away. Arrayed in the pews behind them were younger and middle-aged people with small children. Vic guessed they were Steven's relatives. Meera sat next to the center aisle, near two people Vic recognized as volunteer doctors for TU Health. She sat stiffly, her tan raincoat pulled tightly around herself.

An organ began a slow hymn, and some of the elderly men swayed to the music.

Vic was struck by two intertwined emotions. Loss, as the service reminded him of the one held for Dannie, his own daughter, entwined with the bitterness he'd felt at Anne's insistence at having the service only seven months after Dannie disappeared.

But a softer, warmer memory followed, brought on by the high-pitched ceiling and slow-moving air, the heavy wood carvings, and the embroidery of the altar cloths.

His mother, holding his hand, when he was perhaps six or seven. A finger to her lips to remind him to stay quiet as the priest sang, his words soaring and falling.

Vic pushed his memories away and studied each person, noticing with a slight charge that Brandon Ellis wasn't attending. Brandon had called himself Steven's friend, and yet he was a no-show.

They reached the halfway point of the ceremony, and Jake read a passage from the bible, struggling to get the words out. As he sat down, the music swelled.

Meera rose. For a moment Vic thought she planned to walk to the front of the church and speak, but she spun on her toes and hurried down the aisle to the front door, her jacket held tight about her, her face pale and strained.

As she left, the music softened, and one of Steven's relatives stood up to make his way to the pulpit for a reading. As he climbed the steps, the front doors clunked. Vic glanced at the rear of the church, expecting to see Meera returning.

Conor Byrne walked a few steps down the aisle and slid into a nearby pew. He wore a black suit, white shirt, and black silk tie.

Vic couldn't believe Jake invited him and turned to the front of the church to see if Jake noticed Conor's entrance. But Jake was faced forward, his attention on the pulpit.

Vic felt a slow burn rise. He was the one who showed Conor the obituary, with the memorial service time and place listed at the bottom. Conor must have remembered it and chosen to insert himself into the Kittery's grief. He found it disgusting.

Jake would react badly to Conor's appearance; Vic was sure about it.

The reading ended, and the strains of a hymn rose to the high ceiling. The priest followed it with a homily and a short memorial of Steven. Another hymn was sung, the attendees joining in ragged chorus, until the priest gave a final prayer and thanked everyone for attending.

People shifted and stood. Jake and Ellie rose, hugged, and Jake shook hands with two men in the pew behind him. His eyes crossed to the group of elderly men, who were now sliding baseball caps onto their heads and nodding to one another, their wives and other family members holding their arms to steady them. Jake's gaze stopped at Vic, momentarily, but he showed no recognition. Jake continued his sweep of the church and spotted Conor.

His face shifted from shock to anger in a split second. As Vic expected, Jake immediately moved for the center aisle. Vic rose and turned to Conor. To his surprise, Conor was slumped in his pew. He looked drained and tired. Pale.

As Vic hurried to Conor, he tossed a glance at Jake and saw the hard set to Jake's mouth, the glare in his eyes as he walked toward them.

Vic reached Conor first. "Have some respect," Vic hissed. "Leave the family alone. Get going before Jake gets here."

Conor didn't react for a moment, then looked at him. "You don't get much right, do you?"

Vic slid his hand under Conor's arm and lifted, urging him to stand. Vic knew he only had seconds before Jake reached them. "I don't? And you coming here right now was the right thing? Get your ass up."

Conor allowed himself to be pulled upright. "You don't understand. You can't. I want to pay my respects."

Vic tightened his hold on Conor's arm and force-marched him to the church doors. He glanced over his shoulder. Jake was fifteen feet away, still coming, his face red and wracked in anger.

Vic pushed Conor through the church doors and spun around to Jake. "Leave it."

"That son of a bitch," Jake breathed, moving as if he would break through the doors.

Vic stood his ground, blocking the doors, and Jake pulled up in front of him. Vic placed his hand flat on Jake's chest and stepped inches away for him. "Think of your family. Not the time or place. I'll get him out of here."

"That son of a bitch," Jake repeated. Vehemence flattened his words.

"Let me take care of this, Jake. Don't get in the middle of it. Don't do anything stupid." Vic turned his hand and grabbed a fistful of Jake's shirt and tie, and rested his forearm across Jake's chest, in case Jake tried to sidestep him.

Something flared in Jake's eyes. "He killed my son."

"If he's the one, he'll go to jail. Do you understand? Let us handle it. Let me handle him right now."

Jake swallowed two deep breaths, his chest heaving against Vic's arm and fist. Behind them, people were stopping, staring, watching the stand-off, the crowd gathering.

Vic searched Jake's eyes, but Jake was no longer there. "Jake. You've got a burial service to attend, right?" Without letting go of Jake's shirt, Vic shook his arm once, trying to bring Jake back. "Jake. Go and bury your son. I'll take care of Conor."

Jake blinked, as if he was having trouble absorbing the words.

Edna elbowed through the crowd to Jake's side. "Jake. Listen to me. We have the burial service."

Finally, Vic saw something flicker in Jake's eyes. Jake was back. Just.

"Do what Edna says, Jake. Family first. Wait here. I'll make Conor leave."

Edna's head snapped to Vic as soon as he said Conor's name. "He came here?" she hissed.

"And he's leaving. Jake, I'm going to let go of you. Do you understand? Let me do this."

Ellie appeared beside Jake, on the opposite side from Edna. Vic glanced at her. "Do you have him?"

Ellie grabbed Jake's arm and nodded. Vic took a short breath and let go of Jake's shirt.

For a second, no one moved. Vic counted the next few seconds in his head, holding Jake's gaze, and saw nothing in Jake's eyes that said he might try something. Ellie and Edna each hung from one of Jake's arms. Vic reached behind him, found the door handle, and backed through the door, closing it behind him.

He glanced around. Conor was standing on the opposite side of the road, in front of the historical plaques, staring down at Braddock and the mill. Vic crossed the road.

"Hey," Vic shouted at he approached Conor.

Conor ignored him.

With both hands, Vic jammed Conor hard on his chest, sending him over the low railing protecting the historical plaques and flat onto the scraggly grass.

Conor rolled and jumped to his feet. "What the hell?"

"That's your professional courtesy. I stopped you from getting your ass kicked. Now get into your car and get the hell out of here."

Conor's face twisted in anger. "I don't have to do shit. You assaulted me."

"I stumbled on the curb. It happens."

"Bullshit. You're pissed about yesterday. Because you don't have squat on me."

"I'm pissed you showed up here. That's harassment." Vic glanced around. "Where's your car?" He spotted Conor's Ford a block farther up the street. He pointed at it. "Get going."

Conor didn't move; he stared at Vic, his blue eyes flinty.

Vic didn't understand him. "What are you doing, Conor? Do you even know? You might think you're a tough guy, but I can tell you right now Jake Kittery would kick your ass if I didn't stop him. You'd be fighting Kittery, with all his anger and grief. No one wins that fight. He's convinced you killed Steven. And you just show up? How did you think he'd react to you here?" Vic glanced at the church entrance. They were taking too long. Several of the elderly men were outside the church now. Vic realized their red caps marked them all as Vietnam veterans.

Conor glanced at the church doors. Vic saw something come over him. Conor brushed at his knees, took two steps, cleared the rail, and stood on the sidewalk again. He stared at Vic. "I told you, I wanted to pay my respects. I said that from the start. What Jake and I have, that's between us. His son had nothing to do with it."

"Yeah. And horses don't shit. Now, understand something. I'll keep doing my job until you're either cleared or in jail. Get used to the idea. Now go."

Conor studied him. "You're getting yourself in a hole, Lenoski. You keep doing it, and I'll bury you."

Vic returned his stare. "Stop boring me. Go."

Conor shifted on his feet and turned, finally. Hiked toward his car.

Vic watched Conor reach the next intersection and continue across. As Vic returned to the church, Jake came through the doors, Edna and Ellie glued to his sides. The elderly men grouped around them like a phalanx.

"He's gone," Vic said quickly. He turned to check that was actually true, that Conor hadn't turned around. He was just in time to see Conor duck into the driver's seat of his Ford.

When he turned back, Jake was staring at him. "Why isn't that asshole in jail?"

"If the evidence takes us there, he will be."

Jake slowly shook his head in a show of disbelief. "Cops," was all he said. With Edna and Ellie beside him, he turned downhill, to the driveway that led behind the church to the parking lot.

Vic watched him go and turned to check on Conor again. His car was gone, and Vic was glad Conor hadn't decided to drive by the church as he left. He took a deep breath. It had felt pretty good to push Conor over the railing.

Vic started up the sidewalk, headed to his car. As he passed the spot where Meera's Mercedes was originally parked, he noticed a dark spot in the gutter. He looked at it.

Someone had thrown up. Recently.

Breathing through his mouth to avoid the smell, he continued to his car.

Chapter Thirty

Carty Swain waited in the windowless conference room, a floor below grade, the air conditioning pumping relentlessly through the ceiling vents. His arms were littered with goosebumps, and the doubloon felt cold against his chest. Isabella had texted him the night before, telling him she had checked into his hotel. He'd suggested meeting in the conference room, knowing it would keep him from being seen in public. His real reason was that he didn't want to invite her to his room. Not yet. He wanted to stay professional at first and see how she reacted, so she gained confidence and relaxed her guard.

Isabella swept into the room exactly on time. She wore a clinging yellow halter dress, her black hair in a ponytail, deep brown eyes flashing. Carty had to fight down a charge of excitement. She'd never worn a dress so tight to her figure or bared her shoulders to him. She sat down with a flourish and placed a matching yellow clasp bag on the table in front of her.

She smiled. "It's so cold in here."

"Sorry. It's freezing, but there's no thermostat. I could call housekeeping and see if they can turn it off for a while?"

Isabella tilted her head, her eyes bright. "Will this take long?

He shrugged. "Half an hour?"

She waved a hand. "Let's get started, then. Perhaps it will turn off by itself."

"Right. I said on the phone we'd need two days of prep. I'll give you the background now, tomorrow we can practice and role play. Does that work? Tomorrow will be longer, so I'll talk to housekeeping about the air conditioning."

She nodded. "Good."

Carty paused, gathering himself. The backstory he'd created was truthful and a lie, but it had to sound authentic. That was the acid test. "Okay," he said carefully. "You'll be a private investigator, hired by the nephew of a man named Carty Swain."

Isabella frowned. "Carty Swain?" She repeated the name. "It doesn't sound real."

Carty smiled, enjoying the humor of the moment. For as long as Isabella had known him, he'd used the name Devon Blair. "Actually, Carty Swain was a real person. He was a New Orleans police officer and the partner of another police officer, Demond Timmons. Demond and Carty went missing during Hurricane Katrina. You'll be interviewing Demond's widow, Liz Timmons. Liz knows the name Carty Swain, and that will make her want to talk to you. She'll want to know if you know anything about what happened to her husband."

"Okay." Isabella shrugged slightly, as if her bare shoulders were getting cold.

From the periphery of his eyes Carty saw it was more than that. Her nipples were pushing against the fabric of her halter dress. Carty kept his eyes on her face, keenly aware of something else. She was making no move to hide the effect of the cold air. She hadn't crossed her arms over her chest. This was a stunning distance from the usual camouflage of baggy clothes.

"Right," Carty continued, "The idea is this. You will approach Liz Timmons as a private investigator from Dallas. You'll say that Carty Swain's nephew hired your company. The hook is this. On the last night of the hurricane, Carty telephoned his nephew and said that Demond had hidden something for Carty. Carty told his nephew it was important, and he wanted his nephew to have it. The idea was that Carty was worried his apartment would flood, so Carty and Demond took the item somewhere to hide it, somewhere Demond knew. Somewhere safe."

"Wouldn't the nephew have searched for this earlier?" Isabella's eyes were bright, as if the story entranced her.

145

"You can say the nephew thought whatever was hidden would turn up at some point. However, in the years since the hurricane, he's started to think that perhaps he should look for it. On the off chance it can be found."

Isabella blinked. "And the nephew doesn't know what the item might be?"

"No. All you want from Liz are her thoughts on anywhere Demond might have hidden something important. On the night of the hurricane, where could he have gone? Somewhere within the city of New Orleans, but safe from the rising waters. You just want to hear any suggestions she might have."

Carty struggled to hold Isabella's gaze. "Does that sound workable?"

Isabella nodded. "It sounds workable. I just think she will be skeptical."

"Of course, she will. She's a police detective."

Concern and a shade of fear crossed Isabella's face.

Carty held up his hand. "How you present your questions is the key. It's why we need to role-play tomorrow. For instance, it would help if you let her know—without being obvious about it—that you are skeptical about the story yourself. That you think it's unlikely anything is hidden, but since your client hired you, you're going through the motions. And that really you don't expect to find anything. Your tone in how you do the interview will matter. You'll want to give your questions some lightness."

She nodded slowly. "Okay, I can see that. And what is it that was hidden?"

Carty shrugged. "You don't know. Neither does the nephew. Again, it's the possible location that matters. And honestly, if Timmons can't think of somewhere, it's over."

"And what is the name of the nephew?"

"Client confidentiality. You can't tell her."

"And what about the detective agency? Won't she see through that?"

Carty reached into his briefcase and removed his laptop, glad for the distraction from Isabella's chest. He lifted the lid and hit the start button, glad the screen hid everything below Isabella's neck. Once the computer booted up, he did a quick search and turned the screen around so she could see it.

"I had a fake website set up, and I'll have business cards for you tomorrow.

If she calls the number, it's linked to a burner phone that my secretary will answer. She'll handle it. Hopefully, we won't need more than that. If she starts looking for business records we're finished, we can't fake those. But with luck, we'll be gone by then."

"Sounds complete."

"Best we can do on short notice. So, do you think you can handle it?"

Isabella smiled at him over the laptop's screen. "I do. What time tomorrow?"

"Let's start at ten."

Isabella rose from her chair, showing her entire body. Carty forced himself not to gape.

Isabella picked up her clutch and held it at her side. "Then, if you don't mind, I'm going to explore New Orleans."

"Great. Have fun."

Isabella blinked and hesitated. "See you tomorrow." She turned and let herself out of the conference room.

Carty thought her reply was too high and bright. She'd expected him to suggest they go together. The door to the room clomped shut. Perfect, he thought, get her wondering why he wasn't attracted to her.

It would make her try harder to get his attention.

He rose from his chair and snapped down the lid to his laptop, that last vision of her standing on the other side of the table, dress tight to her curves, the effect of the cold air on her, all of it lingering in his mind. Miss Vision in Yellow, he thought, but his thoughts veered to her body. "Her royal pokiness," he grinned to himself. He thought about how the two straps holding up the top of her dress met in a bow at the back of her neck. A bow that just needed a single tug.

After returning his laptop to his briefcase, he did a little hip shake to arrange himself comfortably, and straightened the front of his pants before leaving the room.

Chapter Thirty-One

Vic arrived at work Monday morning wondering how Sandy Vrail would organize her first day. All he hoped was that she would trust her detectives to do their jobs.

When he reached his desk, he spotted Sandy in her office, her back plumb-line straight even as she typed on her keyboard. He slid out of his sportscoat and hung it on a hangar on the wall of his cube.

"You back to the sportscoat?"

Vic turned to see Liz hanging up her leather jacket. Beyond her, Craig was already hunched over his computer screen.

"Too warm today," Vic said.

"Or you wanted to look good for the new teacher?" Liz gave him a knowing smile.

"Didn't think about it." Vic waited for what was coming. Liz could smell him lying from another state.

Instead, Liz cocked her head toward the rest of the floor and full complement of day shift detectives. "Everyone wants to look good for the new teach."

Vic smiled as he opened his email account. At the top of the list was an introductory email from Sandy, explaining she was calling a short all-hands meeting at the start of each of the day's shifts, followed by one-on-one meetings with each detective team or pairing. A schedule of one-on-one meetings was listed, and Vic saw that he, Liz, and Craig were first on the list.

He looked up and saw the same email open on Liz's computer. Liz caught his eye and shook her head in disgust. He knew what bothered her. He'd sent Liz and Craig a long text about the church service the evening before, but didn't have Craig's update on the doctor interviews and Liz's research results on Brandon Ellis. With the all-hands meeting only five minutes away and being first on the interview list, they didn't have time to update each other. They would need to wing it when they met Sandy.

Irritated, Vic looked toward the break room, thinking he might get coffee before the meetings started. So many people were jammed in the doorway, and inside the room, it looked like a rave.

Sandy marched out of her office, holding a sleek black travel mug. She stopped in the center of the room, placed the mug on a nearby desk, and checked her watch. As usual, Sandy's hair was pulled tight into a bun at the back of her head, not a hair out of place. Her uniform looked immaculate. Vic didn't see any jewelry on her at all.

Sandy glanced at the doors leading onto the floor and frowned.

"Here we go," Liz whispered. She rose, and Vic and Craig followed her. Liz grabbed the chair to an empty desk, and Vic and Craig stood behind her, waiting as the other detectives gathered, dragging over chairs and everyone settling into a semi-circle in front of Sandy.

Sandy looked from face to face. Vic counted seven detectives and another five in support staff.

Sandy checked her watch again, a sleek Apple watch, Vic noticed, and took a quick sip from her travel mug. The conversations in the room limped into silence.

Sandy hesitated and glanced at the doors again. Vic realized she was expecting someone.

Something flickered in Sandy's eyes, a decision, and she faced the group. "Thank you for taking the time." She hesitated, and when she started to speak again, Vic had the feeling she'd made a specific attempt to soften her tone. "As you will all know, my name is Sandy Vrail. I'm your new commander."

The doors to the floor opened and the district attorney, Hana Richards, entered the room, followed by the doughy form of Lester Canvin, the

County Executive. Lester looked harried, and the flush on his face matched his red hair. Apparently, keeping up with Hana was a struggle for him.

Hana crossed to Sandy and spoke to her softly. Sandy nodded. Lester looked around the room, a vague look of surprise on his face, and Vic wondered if it was the first time he'd visited the floor.

Hana turned to Lester and raised her eyebrows.

"Yes," blustered Lester. He pulled himself upright, spread his feet, and looked about the gathering. "For those of you who don't know me, I'm Lester Canvin, your duly-elected County Executive." He stopped, as if expecting laughter or applause. He got none. The detectives spread around the room stared.

"So much for introductions." Lester waved a hand. "Well, I suppose it is exactly the time for introductions." Lester launched into a description of the Allegheny County police that was both disjointed and rambling. He finished with several positive statements about the future of the force and its leadership in county law enforcement, adding that today marked a new era and a new opportunity. He stopped talking. It took everyone a moment to realize Lester expected applause, and it took a few seconds for some uneven clapping to start. It died almost immediately.

Lester introduced Hana, and she received genuine applause. Lester, Vic thought, didn't look happy about that.

Hana's introduction of Sandy was succinct, precise, and explanatory. Hana ran through Sandy's background as an Army brat, her rise to Major in the Military Police, and her responsibility as Commander of the Military Police at Fort Bragg. Vic sensed that Hana glossed over Sandy's one-year stint with the Connecticut State Police as she transitioned out of the military, although as commander of Troop H, she oversaw the Hartford area, including Bradley International Airport, which meant she would have liaised with Customs and Border Protection and the DEA.

When Hana asked the detectives to welcome Sandy, the applause was strong and prolonged. Sandy was unproven to everyone in the room, but there was no mistaking her credentials. Lester stared over everyone's heads, applauding gingerly, as if his hands hurt. He seemed a bit put out, Vic thought.

Sandy's speech was mercifully short. She promised to support the detectives and staff and lead by example. She was complimentary about the detectives and the force and said she hoped to live up to their standard of excellence. Vic thought she did a good job balancing humility and respect with a no-nonsense demeanor.

Vic noticed Hana listening intently as Sandy spoke, and it crossed his mind the speech sounded very close to the kind of speech Hana would give. He wondered if Hana's publicity team had given Sandy some help.

The applause, when Sandy finished, was again sharp and sustained. As it died away, Sandy encouraged everyone to get back to work. The crowd dispersed slowly, returning to their desks. Hana and Sandy spoke to each other for a few moments, and Lester started around the room, shaking hands with anyone he could and laughing loudly sometimes. Vic, Liz, and Craig had a few minutes before their meeting with Sandy, so they returned to their desks. Vic was about to sit down when Hana motioned to him and pointed at the doors to the department.

Vic slid on his sportscoat. Hana turned and left the floor. Understanding that Hana might not want people to see them talking, Vic turned to Liz. "Be right back. How long until we meet with Sandy?"

Liz, distracted by an email, glanced at her watch and held up five fingers. "Be back then."

Vic slid out of the doors. Hana was holding the elevator door open for him, and he hurried into it.

"Sorry about this," Hana said quietly, as the elevator descended to the ground floor.

"What's up?"

Hana held up a finger for him to wait. Off the lobby was a small cafeteria, and Hana led him inside. They took a table in the back corner.

Hana smiled at him, but it was a tight, serious smile. "I have to get back, so I'll make this quick."

"I have to meet Sandy in a few minutes, so quick is good."

Hana hesitated, gathering her thoughts. "You know, when I first told you about hiring Sandy, I wasn't very forthcoming about her."

Vic shrugged. "Your prerogative."

Hana tapped a perfectly manicured finger on the table top. "I'd like you to be aware of something, and I'd rather it stays between us."

Vic was taken several years back, to the first time he and Hana met alone. It was in the coffee shop of the downtown William Penn hotel, and he'd used very similar wording to her as he asked her a favor. "I think I owe you that."

"Good." Hana's dark eyes searched his face. "Obviously, Sandy has all the credentials to be a very good commander."

"Sounds that way."

"Right, but I can't say her transition out of the Army has been clean."

Vic remembered his first meeting with Sandy on Mt. Washington, and the way she seemed to expect a salute and fought her own urge to give one. "I can see that. She's been Army her entire life."

"Right. And her year with the Connecticut State Police was a mess. That's how I was able to get her. It's why she only lasted a year. She's still learning that Army procedures are not civil ones. She needs to learn how to manage people, not just order them around, and that how we work isn't as buttoned down and square-cornered as the military."

"We still have a command structure here."

"Right, but not like the Army. We talked about that a lot when I interviewed her. The way she managed led to a lot of pushback from her troopers and the detectives in Connecticut and she spent most of the year in the dog house with her boss. She knew she wasn't going to last and put out her resume. That's how I found her. But I also talked to the Hartford DA, a professional courtesy call, and he filled me in. I asked Sandy about it, and I thought she was very honest. She's done some soul-searching about herself and is aware she has to adapt her management techniques to a civilian force. That said, I need to know if that is actually happening. Can you help me with that?"

Vic hesitated. Hana was asking him to spy on his boss, and he didn't like the idea. At all.

Hana studied him. "I know what it sounds like. I understand that runs against who you are. Hear me out. I'm not asking for meetings in parking garages and dead drops. All I'd like is a heads-up if your department starts to fail. If Sandy loses the trust of the detectives. Think of yourself as an early warning system. Maybe one of those tsunami ocean buoys. I can't afford to have a breakdown within this department again. Can you do that?"

Vic thought about it. Hana's last hire as commander, Jon Lee, had leaked case information to the press as he angled for Hana's job. After he was fired, Jon had sued the DA's office twice. Hana had come out on top, but the time and stress of it affected everyone.

"Sure." Vic didn't like the word when he spoke it, but he understood what Hana needed.

Hana stared at him for a few seconds. "Good. To repeat, we only need to talk about this again if something really goes south. I'll assume no news is good news if I don't hear from you."

"Okay."

Hana glanced at her watch and stood. "I think we both have places to be."

Vic rose. "I know I do."

They crossed into the lobby, just as Lester walked out of the elevator. He joined them, and Hana introduced Vic.

"I've heard about you," Lester said when they finished shaking hands. "Bureau of Police, and now over here. You did a good job with the murder of the symphony director."

Vic thanked him. Lester glanced at Hana. "Car's waiting."

"Right behind you, I just need a last word." Hana shifted so she was standing closer to Vic.

Lester thanked Vic for his service and headed for the front doors. Hana let him get a few steps away before she turned to him. "Last thing." She smiled, her eyes flashing. "Craig Luntz, the one you brought onto your team?"

"Sure. He's been doing well."

"I'll say. Best score on the detective's exam. He's officially bona fide. Sandy will tell him sometime in the next couple of days, once the paperwork comes through."

Vic couldn't get the smile off his face. "Good to hear."

Hana punched him lightly on the bicep. "Keep it up, Vic. Thanks."

Chapter Thirty-Two

Vic reentered the detectives' floor to see Liz and Craig following Sandy toward a conference room. He fell in behind.

Sandy sat at the head, and Vic chose not to take the opposite end. He sat across from Liz and Craig.

Sandy looked at Vic. "The Mt. Washington case. Where are we?"

Hana's words echoed in Vic's ears and he decided on tact. "Um, unfortunately, we haven't had a chance to review the work we did individually over the weekend, but I can summarize where we are to date. Then we can round robin at the end to add what we learned this weekend."

Sandy's eyes hardened, and her lips parted as if she was about to say something, but she seemed to catch herself. "Let's give it a try."

As succinctly as he could, Vic summarized their progress to date. He outlined the results of the forensics reports, the timeline, their research, and the events of the last few days.

"Do you have a suspect? This Conor Byrne?" Sandy's question was sharp. "I'm sorry," she added, "I realize it's early yet, who would you list as persons of interest? Do you have a priority order for them?"

Vic noted how Sandy moderated her tone after her apology. She really is trying, he thought. He folded his hands in front of him. "I think there are three. Top of the list, as you said, is Conor Byrne. He's been feuding with the Kittery family for thirty years. He showed up at the Kittery memorial service, and I had to run him off before Jake Kittery assaulted him. As I mentioned, we can probably make a B&E case against him, but I'd like to know what the heck he was searching for in Steven Kittery's apartment."

Sandy nodded, hurrying him along.

"Then we have two people with a lot of open questions around them. Meera Basu, Steven Kittery's girlfriend, or whatever it's called these days, and Brandon Ellis, Steven's friend, who clearly tried hard not to answer some of our questions."

"Something else."

Everyone turned to look at Craig.

Craig smiled a bit sheepishly, looking at Vic. "Sorry, like Detective Lenoski said, we haven't had time to update each other yet, but I did learn something else over the weekend." He looked at Sandy. "I interviewed all the doctors who volunteer at TU Health. I confirmed they all use a telephone application called WholePatient. It's how they schedule their house calls and maintain patient charts. I researched it, and it turns out Brandon Ellis' tech company runs it."

Vic looked at Liz. "Brandon never mentioned that when we talked to him. He just said he runs a high-tech company that sells an app."

Liz nodded. "Oh, there's more." She looked at Sandy. "I was doing background on Brandon Ellis this weekend. I found the app, but I didn't know the doctors all were required to use it. I also found that apart from TU Health, Brandon's a board member for three other non-profits." Liz ticked them off by holding up a finger for each. "Veterans Health, Firefighters Health, and a new organization that's just getting started, BlueLine Health. That's for police officers."

Vic saw the connection immediately. "All groups whose retirees have higher levels of health problems."

"He just needs Lumberjack Health, and he's got all the dangerous professions." Craig grinned at Vic, but suddenly remembered who was in the meeting. He turned serious and looked at the table-top, a slight flush on his cheeks.

"That might be next," Liz breathed, covering for Craig.

At the head of the table, Sandy shifted in her seat. "How does the app make money?"

Vic kicked himself. Sandy had asked the next logical question faster than he'd thought of it.

Craig looked up, eager to redeem himself. "I know the app charges the doctors a fee to sign up, but it isn't much. I can take a look. It might be through a grant, same way the non-profits started. Let me work that."

Sandy nodded, sat back, and looked at Vic. "Does any of that change your angle of attack?"

"It does." Vic thought for a moment. "We need to talk to Brandon. He didn't bother to mention any of this." He turned to Craig. "Where are you reviewing the tunnel footage? That will help us either clear Conor Byrne or move him to official suspect."

"I need a few more hours. End of day today. And I finally got the data from Steven's cell phone this morning. I need to go through that."

"Okay, then I think next we visit Meera Basu." Vic looked at Liz to see if she agreed. She nodded. "She's been pretty helpful, and she might be able to explain this WholePatient app. That might give us more information for our next Brandon Ellis interview. Ask him why he forgot to mention the app and why he's on the boards of these other non-profits. There's something holding all of this together."

"Good," Sandy said. She looked around the room. "I'd like an update tomorrow, midday. Dismissed." Sandy's cheeks flushed just slightly. "I'm sorry." She half smiled. "Old habits. Thank you, everyone. Vic, could you stay a moment?"

Craig and Liz rose and left the room. When the door clicked shut behind them, Sandy pressed her palms together and looked at Vic, her blue eyes clear. "You have a good team. You work naturally together."

"Liz and I have been partners off and on for more than ten years."

"It shows." Sandy interlocked her fingers. "I saw Hana Richards wanted to talk to you."

Vic tightened and didn't say anything.

"When I interviewed, she talked about you quite a bit. More than the other detectives. She told me about your cases. Especially the murder of the symphony director. It's an impressive record."

Vic nodded, trying to figure out where the conversation was going.

"What I took from the way she talked about you is that she trusts you."

"I think it's fair to say we trust each other," Vic said slowly.

"Right. And my guess is that when she talked to you today, it was about me."

Vic searched for something to say, but Sandy held up her hand. "No need to tell me about that conversation, Vic. Believe me, I'm the first one to say I didn't handle my first year out of the Army well. I still struggle with it. Army habits are ingrained. However, I will say this. My goal is to transition to civilian life and make a career. So, all I would ask is that if you see me getting out of line, don't complain to your team or other detectives, come to me first. Can you do that?"

Vic studied her for a few seconds. He liked how honest she was being with him and knew she didn't want grousing to start in the department. "I can. But I'm not the diplomatic type, and I really don't like politics."

"I thought so, given that you didn't apply for my position. Did you consider it?"

Vic felt himself reach safe ground. "I did. But the fact is, like I said, I'm not much on diplomacy and politics. I feel like you need both in your job. I like working out what happened after a crime. That's what I do best."

"Good. And I don't know if Hana mentioned it, but we'll need to do something for Craig when his promotion is official. It should be in the next couple of days." She smiled, and it was as if something fell away from her. Vic was surprised at her warmth. "And he got the top score."

Vic grinned at her. "Well, we don't need to tell him that part. It might go to his head. But he is turning into a sharp detective."

"Good. I'll let you know when he's official, and we can tell him. And keep in mind what I said about me." She rose and left the room, her back straight.

Vic was glad to see this other side of Sandy. It also made sense that talking about Craig would bring it out; he had that effect on everyone.

Chapter Thirty-Three

J ake Kittery paced his living room, his chest tight. Ellie was back upstairs, although during breakfast, she'd announced she would return to work in a couple of days. She still sounded exhausted when she talked, and Jake hoped working would bring color back to her face.

In the kitchen, their tiny countertop television clattered on with a talk show about politics. Jake too preoccupied to understand the gist or the details.

He sat at the kitchen table, the constriction in his chest unabated. Conor Byrne. He couldn't believe Byrne came to the memorial service. It felt like a desecration, as if something pure they'd done for Stevie was fouled. Breathing carefully, he tried to moderate the pressure in his chest, the feeling that he was rising out of himself.

He rose, crossed into the living room and stopped, knowing he couldn't stay in the house, couldn't keep pacing about. He needed to do something.

He went upstairs and found Ellie stretched on the bed, swamped by the duvet. He took his wallet and car keys from the dresser, still unsure what to do. Downstairs, he continued into the basement and garage. Ellie's car sat in its space. He opened the garage door, pulled the car into the driveway, and parked.

Inside the garage, he paced about, looking at the shelves. His eye fell on his square gun case, neatly tucked on the shelf under his workbench. He stared at it for a time, thinking about the weapon inside. When he last cleaned and oiled it.

He shifted his gaze. Stevie's baseball bats stood in a corner. He counted four of them, the remains of Stevie's high school varsity career. His chest still aching, he knew what to do. Visit the batting cages, as he used to do with Stevie in little league and pony league. Get a swing going. Tire himself out.

Jake placed two of the bats in the trunk of the car, and after texting Ellie his plan, slid behind the wheel. He faced the open garage door for several seconds, doing absolutely nothing. His gaze was drawn to the gun case. As he stared at it, a certainty settled through him.

Jake shook his head, hit the button to close the garage door, started the car, and backed down the driveway and into the street.

As he pulled away, he glanced back at the door to make sure it was closed. *Dam commie pinko*, the door said to him, in bloody, red-streaked paint.

Right then, the truth of what he needed to do hit him like an air blast into a steel furnace. The constriction in his chest tightened and released. He felt lighter, and utterly focused.

Chapter Thirty-Four

"I wasn't going to say anything in front of our new commander," Liz said quietly from the passenger seat as Vic drove toward the Basu's house, "But why are we visiting Meera again?"

"I want to ask her if she uses the WholePatient app. How it works, that kind of thing. Figured that information might be useful before we shake Brandon's tree."

Liz didn't bother to hide her skepticism. "I guess so."

Vic didn't mention Meera leaving the memorial service early and the vomit in the gutter beside her empty parking space. Perhaps she was just overwhelmed by Steven's death and the service. It was possible. But he wanted to bring it around in the conversation with Meera. Exactly how, he didn't know.

Vic spotted Meera's car in the driveway as he pulled their unmarked cruiser to a stop in front of the Basu house. Vic and Liz climbed out and started up the walk. They were halfway there when the front door opened, and Meera appeared, dragging a large rolling suitcase behind her. She banged it down the two steps leading to the front door; her head twisted around as she talked to someone inside the house.

Dr. Basu chased his daughter through the doorway. "Stop!" he shouted.

Meera put her head down and pulled the roller case hard onto the grass, veering toward her car.

"You will not leave this house," Meera's father shouted. He caught up to Meera and clamped a hand on an unused suitcase handle, stopping Meera in her tracks. They pulled in opposite directions. "You have already disgraced this house. You cannot make it worse. A single woman cannot live alone." His voice was shrill.

Meera let go of her suitcase, and Meera's father, without Meera's counterpull, stumbled back and sat hard on the grass, the suitcase tangled in his legs. He shoved it aside and scrambled up.

"This is unseemly," he sputtered.

Vic wasn't sure if he meant his fall, or Meera leaving.

Meera grabbed the suitcase handle and straightened. "I'm going," she hissed, "I will not live here. Not a single minute longer." She turned as she spoke and saw Vic and Liz for the first time. Her mouth opened in surprise.

Vic stared. Meera's face was wet, the left side of her face swollen and red. A bruise was blossoming next to her eye socket.

"What the hell?" Liz asked.

"No. You will stay here," roared Meera's father. "I will not let you go."

Vic stepped closer to them. Meera had been struck several times; he was sure of it. "Meera," he said quickly. "Can we help you with anything?"

Meera's father turned to Vic, seeing him for the first time, and held up a palm. "This is a family problem. You will not get involved."

Vic stepped closer to him. "If you're the one who hit her, I'm involved."

The older man's eyes flashed. "She has dishonored this house. Our family. She cannot make it worse by living alone. A woman her age cannot do that." He pointed in Meera's direction to make his point. "She must live with her parents until she marries, and then she moves into her husband's house."

"She's an adult by every definition there is." Vic locked his gaze on Meera's father. He decided to take a guess. "And if she's pregnant, it's absolutely up to her where she lives."

Meera's father spun toward Meera. "You told the police? You took this outside the family?" He stepped toward her and raised his hand to slap her.

Vic jumped behind him, grabbed the father's raised hand by the wrist, and windmilled the arm down and up against the father's back. Pushed up. As Meera's father brayed in pain, Vic clamped his other arm around the father's shoulder and chest.

"That's attempted assault."

In his peripheral vision, Vic saw a middle-aged woman in a sari at the front door, a phone to her ear.

Liz stepped next to Meera, talking softly to her.

"She has insulted her family," rasped the father. "Insulted me. And sleeping with a white boy..." Meera's father shifted as best he could in Vic's grip to face Meera. His voice notched higher in anger. "Do you think I don't know about your trips to meet him? Sneaking out of the house and going to Mt. Washington? I followed you and saw you with him. After I forbade you to see him. Many times."

"That's enough," Vic shouted in the father's ear. But the words sizzled in his mind. He glanced at Meera's suitcase and made up his mind. He swung the father around and forced-marched him to their car. Bent him facedown over the hood. "Don't move." He leaned closer as Meera's father squirmed. "Did you follow your daughter to Mt. Washington last week?"

"I had to know what she was doing. She was betraying me," he huffed.

Liz appeared beside him. "What are you doing?"

Vic grabbed the father's other wrist and pulled both together. "Cuff him," he said to Liz.

Liz squinted at him, but slid out her handcuffs and clicked them on the father's wrists.

"Wait. Why?" shouted Meera's father, as Vic stepped back and pulled the father upright.

"Open the back door," Vic said to Liz.

Liz did so, and Vic spun the father around, controlling him with one hand on the links connecting the handcuffs and another on his collar. He spoke directly into the father's ear. "I'm detaining you on suspicion of the murder of Steven Kittery. Now get in the back seat of the car."

Meera's father twisted his face around to see Vic, eyes wide, shock written across his face. "What? You are arresting me?"

Vic propelled him in front of the open car door. He took a moment to check Dr. Basu's pockets with his free hand and asked about a weapon, but Dr. Basso didn't even have a wallet. "Get in the back seat. Watch your head."

"But..."

"But nothing. Are you resisting me?"

Meera's father sagged and twisted to align himself with the door opening. Vic pushed and let go of the handcuffs, and Dr. Basu lowered himself into the seat and rolled to his right to get his legs inside the car. Vic slammed the back door behind him.

He turned to Liz. "How's Meera?"

Liz stared at him for several seconds. "What are you doing? You don't have enough to arrest him."

Vic took her elbow and steered her away from the car. "I'm not. I said I'm detaining him. I didn't Miranda him. All I want is for you to help Meera pack and get out of here. As soon as she's gone, I'll let him go. But you heard it. He followed Meera last week. He'd going to need an alibi for the night Steven was killed. If he doesn't have one, maybe I will arrest him. He's pissed me off enough. But right now, I want Meera out of here. At the very least, we can charge him with assault."

Liz smiled as understanding dawned. "I'll talk to Meera. How'd you know she was pregnant? Steven Kittery's kid?"

"Has to be Kittery's. But help her, then ask. I didn't know if she was pregnant. She left the memorial service looking ragged and threw up outside, but she could have just been worked up by the service. I was guessing."

Liz's smile broadened. "You got it." She turned and started for Meera, who was standing beside her car, eyes wide.

Vic looked at the front door, at the middle-aged woman. She was sitting on the top step, legs drawn up and chin on her knees, arms holding her legs against her. She was weeping. A moment later, Meera swept past her and into the house, followed by Liz.

Vic took a deep breath. He knew what he'd done was on the edge of being legal, but it felt right. He looked into the back seat of the unmarked car. Meera's father had dragged himself partially upright and was staring over the back seat and through the windshield. Vic wasn't sure, but the way his mouth was open and he was huffing in breaths, it looked like he might be crying.

He wondered what Meera's pregnancy would mean to the Kitterys. He knew what it meant to Anne and himself, the day he discovered Lettie.

More than that, what it meant every day afterwards.

He took a deep breath, and as he did, a police cruiser took the turn at the end of the street and drifted up behind his unmarked car. Meera's mother leaped from the front step and ran toward it, her orange sari fluttering behind her.

Vic checked the driver and recognized Sergeant Jerving's shaved head. Meera's mother reached the car and called to Jerving through the closed driver's side window. Jerving glanced at her, and although the Sergeant tried to hide his facial expression, Vic saw enough. This wasn't the first time Sergeant Jerving had run into Meera's mother.

Meera reappeared at the front door of the house, lugging a second, smaller suitcase. Liz followed, her arms filled with sheets, a pillow, and a comforter. Meera's mother was so intent on Sergeant Jerving, bouncing from one foot to the other, that she didn't notice when Meera popped the back of her car and loaded the suitcases.

Jerving carefully opened the driver's side door to his cruiser so he didn't hit Meera's mother, and stepped out. The mother's words were a constant stream, but nonsensical. Vic realized her English wasn't as good as her husband's and daughter's.

Meera disappeared inside the house, followed by Liz.

Jerving said some words to Meera's mother to calm her and walked over to Vic. Vic extended his hand. They shook without speaking, and Jerving looked into the back of Vic's unmarked cruiser. His jaw muscles clenched and released.

"You've arrested Dr. Basu?"

"Detained him."

Meera's mother, who had fallen silent while they talked, started again, telling Jerving to release her husband.

Jerving turned to her and held up his hands. "Please, Mrs. Basu, I need to understand what is going on. Could you wait by my car?"

"I want you to release my husband."

"I can't do that, Mrs. Basu. He was detained by the Allegheny County police, not our force. We're different police forces."

Meera's mother looked from Jerving to Vic and back again, her face twisted in confusion.

"Please, Mrs. Basu," repeated Jerving. I need a minute to talk to Detective..." he glanced at Vic, obviously embarrassed.

"Lenoski," supplied Vic. He turned to Meera's mother. "Just give me a minute to explain to Sergeant Jerving what is going on, and he can fill you in."

Meera's mother fell silent. Jerving nodded encouragingly to her, and she retreated a few steps, her face clouded.

Jerving turned to Vic and waited. Just then, Meera came back through the front door, lugging a cardboard box.

Vic nodded in her direction. "See her face? When we pulled up, she and her father came out of the house arguing. I think he's struck her several times. She wants to move out, he doesn't want her to. At the same time, Dr. Basu, the father, admitted following his daughter to Mt. Washington last week, the night Steven Kittery was killed. I have to consider him a suspect until he gives a statement. So I detained him to give his daughter time to leave the premises. Then I'll see if I need to arrest him."

Jerving nodded. "Okay. Thanks." Jerving glanced at Meera's mother and leaned closer to Vic, softening his tone. "Not the first time we've been called here. The father has a temper, but I think the Missus winds him up. It takes two." He straightened, turned to Meera's mother, and led her away from Vic's unmarked cruiser. He started an explanation, and Vic noticed Jerving had the sense to position Meera's mother so that her back was to the house, to keep her unaware of what Meera was doing.

Meera appeared through the front door, a bundle of coats in her arms. Liz followed, lugging a pile of doctor's scrubs. They both dumped the clothing in the back of the car and Vic saw Liz say something to Meera, then write on the back of a business card and give it to Meera. Moments later, Meera backed down the driveway.

Her mother heard the engine, turned, and saw Meera leaving. She ran toward the car, but Liz stepped in front of her. Meera, brushing a tear away with the back of her hand, wheeled the car into the road and drove away.

The only sound was a muffled sob from Meera's mother, her hands clamped over her cheeks.

Liz crossed to Vic. "Okay."

Vic took a deep breath, let it out, and crossed to the unmarked cruiser. He opened the back door and leaned into the opening. "Dr. Basu. I need to know what you were doing last Tuesday night. You said you followed your daughter to Mt. Washington."

Dr. Basu just looked ahead. "Yes," he said finally. "She said she was going to the supermarket, but I knew she was going to visit that boy."

Vic resisted reminding Dr. Basu "that boy" was now dead. "And?" was all he said.

Dr. Basu rocked slightly. Vic knew how uncomfortable it was to sit in the back of a cruiser handcuffed, but he didn't really care.

"She went up the incline. I didn't know what to do. If I parked and followed her, she might see me. So I came home."

"And what time did you get home?"

"Midnight, I think."

Vic closed the door and crossed to Meera's mother. "Mrs. Basu, I'm Detective Lenoski of the Allegheny County Police. I have an important question to ask, and I think you can answer it. Were you home last Tuesday night?"

She wouldn't look at him, but Vic saw from her eyes that she was thinking through the question. "Yes," she said finally.

"And did your daughter go out?"

"Yes, my husband was angry about it." She raised her head and looked at him. "So was I. We knew she was going to meet that boy. She thought she was being clever, but we saw through it."

"Okay, and what did you husband do when Meera went out?"

She took a breath and let it out. "He followed her. He wanted to catch her with that boy. Stop it."

"And did he, catch that boy?"

She cut a look at her husband. "No. He is useless. He said Meera parked, and he didn't know what to do."

"But he must have done *something*. What was it?"

"He came home."

Vic saw the annoyance written on her face. He was aware of how Liz had drifted closer to overhear the conversation, while Sergeant Jerving kept his distance.

"And what time did he arrive home?"

Meera's mother puffed out her cheeks as she thought. "He was back about eleven-thirty. I remember, because I usually go to bed at ten o'clock, but I stayed up. I was worried and kept checking the time."

"Thank you, Mrs. Basu. In the next day or two, we'll need an official statement about that. Someone will contact you."

He started to turn away but stopped. "I'm sorry, Mrs. Basu. Did you ever meet Steven Kittery?"

She adjusted her sari. "Who?"

"Steven Kittery, the man your daughter was seeing."

She nodded slowly. "So that's his name."

"Yes. And have you ever met him?"

The repeated question seemed to surprise her. "Of course not. He isn't the type of person Meera can bring home to meet us. It wouldn't be proper."

Her words were so dismissive they left Vic cold.

Chapter Thirty-Five

C arty Swain felt the slight downward trajectory of the passenger plane's flight path. From his aisle seat, he checked the front of the plane. Isabella sat in the third row, a window seat, and he couldn't see her. They'd acted as if they didn't know each other when they boarded the plane, a standard precaution, but the forced separation was starting to bother him. She'd worn tight jeans and an embroidered peasant top onto the plane, and somehow, the simple clothing was more attractive than he'd expected.

One thing at a time, he told himself. Do the interview, then do Isabella. He grinned inwardly at the tightness that thought produced in his crotch.

He glanced along his row and through the window. They were low enough to be underneath the cover of grey clouds. He glimpsed a tight collection of skyscrapers hemmed in by two rivers combining into a Y. Hills rolled away into the distance, covered by rumpled tree-tops.

Already, he didn't like the outside light. It was dull, greyish, unlike the promising orange brightness of Costa Rica. Two nights, he thought to himself. That's all. Then, back to New Orleans.

And with luck, a fortune. Or not.

Either way, Isabella. She was his trophy and his consolation.

He checked his phone. They were low enough now that his phone was updating. He spotted a text from Luis Vargas, his friend, and owner of the bank where he worked.

Devon, the text read. Carty wondered if he would ever tell Vargas his real name. He doubted it. He read on: *I hope your trip is going well. I did talk to*

169

Isabella the other night. She was looking forward to the trip. Good luck with your search, my friend. Luis.

Something tingled in the back of Carty's brain. He reread the message. Vargas, he knew, was terrible at subterfuge. He was too used to the protection of his money to bother with deceit. Carty learned that the night he spirited Vargas' mistress through the back door of his house. He was the one who spotted the bra on the stairs and pocketed it, just as Vargas' wife entered.

From then on, he'd handled all of Luis' visits to his mistresses, as well as the limousine and apartment arrangements needed to keep Luis' wife in the dark. Lately, Carty had even become the cupid killer, as he'd nicknamed himself. When Luis grew tired of one of his girlfriends, now it was Carty who showed up with a gift bag containing a diamond bauble, and the news the woman had two months to find somewhere new to live. Unless she was willing to start paying rent.

Oh, and that Luis would no longer be visiting.

Carty reread the text, thinking about Luis' laziness about hiding his actions.

It was two words: 'night' and 'search.' Why did Luis think he was searching for something?

He decided that Luis' use of the word 'night' was simply a reaction to the time of day when he and Isabella talked. And the word 'search?' Most likely a guess.

Still. He didn't like how his senses tingled. He wasn't even sure why Luis would send the text to begin with. It felt superfluous.

With a bump, the plane touched down, and the engines roared into reverse. The plane's forward motion slowed.

Stay tight, Carty told himself. Isabella can make contact with Liz Timmons tonight, and, with luck, get an in-person meeting for tomorrow. It was time to hear what Liz Timmons had to say.

He closed his eyes as the airplane taxied toward the terminal. It's been so long to get here, he thought. And now it's so close.

But go carefully. One step at a time.

Chapter Thirty-Six

It took another hour for Vic and Liz to get Dr. Basu out of the back of the cruiser, out of the handcuffs, and into the house to make a statement. Sergeant Jerving left as soon as Dr. Basu was inside his house.

Vic and Liz drove back to Pittsburgh in silence, until Liz looked over at him. "Did you get a close look at Meera's face?"

"No. But I saw enough."

"Open hand, from the look of it. The bruises setting up looked like fingertips. Very small fingertips."

Vic glanced at her. "You think the mother? Not the father?"

"I asked Meera, but she wasn't saying."

"Always seems to go that way." Vic couldn't count the times he'd made a domestic call, only to find the wife or girlfriend didn't want to press charges, despite the beating she'd received. It always depressed him.

As he turned into the entrance to their headquarters building, Liz asked, "Are you okay with Dr. Basu's alibi?"

"I think so. The statements made by him and his wife fit together pretty well. Oh," Vic added, wanting to cheer himself up. "Don't tell Craig, but he passed his test. Hana said he had the best score."

"Of course he did." Liz smiled. "But let's definitely not tell him that. Let him think he's got work to make up."

Vic parked and turned off the car. "That's our job. Beat 'em up every chance we get."

"You know it. When will he be told?"

"Next couple of days. Paperwork has to clear. Sandy Vrail will do it. I think she wants to start off her job with good news for someone. I would."

As Vic and Liz reached their desks Craig waved to them.

They crowded around his desk, and Craig pointed to his screen. "I've been through the text messages and emails from the day Steven died. Nothing setting up the meeting on Mt. Washington. There is a text exchange between him and Meera agreeing to meet, and that is day of. The exchange starts at nine o'clock. Meera says she can't get out of her house until after ten."

Liz looked at Vic. "That's when the mother said she usually goes to bed. Meera was hoping to sneak out after her parents were asleep."

Vic thought about that. "I wonder how long the parents were on to her and Steven?"

"Had to be awhile. We need a list of questions for Meera's father. Have him come in." Liz studied him, her brown eyes patient.

Vic knew Liz wanted another shot at Meera's father, that she wasn't satisfied that Meera's parents were innocent. He wondered if her opinion might have more to do with how Meera's parents treated their daughter.

"We can get him in here tomorrow." Vic turned to Craig. "Any luck getting us some time with Brandon?"

"Yes." Craig sat back. "Early this afternoon." Craig smiled as if he was a cat who'd just swallowed a bird.

"What?" Liz stared at him with a frown.

"He wants to meet at his lawyer's office. A conference room. A lawyer hanging on every word he says, I bet."

Now, it was Liz's turn to smile. She looked at Vic. "Well, now. Nothing says innocent like wanting a lawyer present."

Vic shook his head. "Yeah, but it doesn't help. We want Brandon to clarify things, and that's the last thing lawyers want. They like generalities. Lots of interpretations. As few words spoken as possible."

"Chase me into the roundhouse, buddy. You'll never corner me there." Liz crossed her arms.

"Exactly." Vic sat at his desk. "What time?" he called to Craig.

"Right after lunch. One."

"And where are you on the tunnel video footage? Anything on Conor's car coming or going?" Vic knew he was pushing Craig, but Craig didn't look annoyed.

"Sorry, I switched to Steven's phone data when it came in. But I did look at the routes Conor might take going home from spray-painting the Kittery's garage. Found a couple of convenience stores he might have passed and got their footage from that night. That might be better. If Conor isn't on the tunnel footage and shows up on the convenience store cameras, he definitely went home. No way he went to Mt. Washington."

Liz sat at her own desk. "How'd you get the convenience store footage so fast?"

"When I was working Tech, I got to know the guy at the convenience store chain who does the maintenance on the cameras for the whole chain. I called him, and he contacted the two stores and had them send the footage to him. He sent it to me."

"Nicely done." Vic was impressed. Without knowing who to call, he would have stopped by the stores. He guessed they would have requested a warrant, and getting the footage would have become a three-day process. Basically, Craig had made a phone call.

"Does your guy have any parking tickets he needs fixed?" Liz called to Craig.

Craig looked at her and was suddenly sheepish. "His girlfriend likes the symphony. I talked to Eileen, and she's going to comp him a couple of tickets."

Vic laughed. "Good thing your girlfriend plays violin for the Symphony."

Craig reddened slightly. "It has its perks."

Chapter Thirty-Seven

Brandon's lawyer worked for Jones Flaherty, a firm Vic knew for its work with Pittsburgh's major corporations. As Vic and Liz entered the soaring lobby and crossed the granite floor, he wondered how good their lawyers might be at criminal law. Their usual meat was business law. They passed between two groupings of leather armchairs clustered on thick Oriental rugs and stopped at the dark wood of the high-fronted receptionist's desk.

"How may I help?" asked the immaculately-dressed and coiffed receptionist.

Vic found himself vaguely annoyed at the rich atmosphere of the lobby and the receptionist's oily smoothness. Instead of asking for the lawyer they were supposed to meet, he showed the receptionists his ID and told her they had an appointment.

The receptionist didn't blink. "With whom are you meeting?"

"Feel better about yourself?" Liz whispered, and gave the receptionist the name of Brandon's lawyer.

"Of course." The receptionist gave Liz a long smile, picked up her telephone, and tapped in four digits. She spoke briefly and returned her phone to its cradle. "Fifth floor. The elevator is behind me. And if you don't mind, could you put these on?"

She held out two adhesive-backed paper tags with the word Visitor emblazoned on the front.

Vic took his, peeled off the label, and stuck it to his shirt where his sportscoat would hide it. Liz affixed hers to the front of her leather jacket.

Together, they circled the desk and entered an elevator that opened the moment they pushed the call button.

As they whirred upward, Liz glanced at Vic's sportscoat where it hid his Visitor tag. "Day got you worn down a bit?"

"This place bugs me, for some reason."

"It's never the place. It's the people in it."

Now, it was Vic's turn to glance at Liz. Normally, she wasn't so philosophical. "Something on *your* mind?"

"Nothing you haven't heard before. Be careful with this kid. Yeah, he forgot to mention some things to us, and yeah, it's weird he wants a lawyer already, but apart from that we got nothing on him."

The doors shushed open to a young woman in a navy blue suit and cream blouse. She spotted the Visitor tag on Liz's chest. "You are the detectives, Mr. Lenoski and Ms. Timmons?"

"We are." Vic waited until Liz stepped out of the elevator and followed her, coming up the rear as the young woman led them into a small glass conference room with a round table. Brandon waited there, next to a middle-aged woman who stood. She, too, wore a navy blue suit, but Vic knew from the cut and material that it cost much more than the young woman's attire.

"I'm Tori Hart." She stepped around the table and gave Vic a brisk handshake that was cool and firm. Vic mumbled his name. She repeated the greeting with Liz, who spoke much more clearly. Tori returned to her seat and waved at the two remaining chairs.

Vic watched Brandon as the introductions unfolded. He'd adopted a stern, protective posture. Vic wasn't sure what to make of it.

Vic and Liz took their seats, barely touching their chair, before Tori launched into a monologue. "I'm a partner at Jones Flaherty. We represent Brandon's company in a variety of ways, usually for intellectual property." She took a moment to establish eye contact with both Liz and Vic. "When Brandon called me, I thought it best to sit in, assess the situation, and afterwards, make a decision about the kind of legal representation Brandon might require." She paused a beat. "If any."

Vic looked at Brandon. "Hi, Brandon; good to see you again." He waited.

Brandon realized from the silence he was expected to speak. "Detectives." He didn't quite keep the annoyance out of his voice.

Vic turned to Tori. "So you are just assessing. You aren't actually Brendan's legal representation right now."

Tori didn't miss a beat. "For now, I am his legal representation. Are you playing at technicalities, Detective Lenoski?"

Vic liked her. She might not be used to criminal law, but she was certainly used to holding her own over a conference table. "I'm just making sure I understand the situation here, Counsel."

Tori gave the slightest of nods. "And now it's clear. Let's proceed."

Vic turned to Brandon. "The last time we met, we asked a series of questions about how you knew the deceased, Steven Kittery, your relationship to him, and your involvement in TU Health."

Brandon looked bored. "Is there a question in there?"

"Did it sound like there was? I was just setting the groundwork so your counsel is up to date. In case you haven't told her everything." Vic glanced at Tori, and she gave a tiny, prim nod.

"So. The reason we're here today. It may come as a surprise to you, but after we last talked, we continued to investigate the case. In the course of that investigation, we discovered some things we'd like you to clarify, given your previous statements."

Tori broke Vic's patter. "I would appreciate it if you explained both what was said in the past meeting and the new information. Needless to say, I wasn't in the last meeting and have no notes or a transcript."

Vic liked Tori a bit more. Her request was practical, but it also slowed him down. She was making sure Vic wasn't going to steamroll Brandon.

Vic nodded at her. "So, we'd like to focus on a couple of things we've discovered. First, your company has created an app called WholePatient. It's the app used by doctors to help organize their volunteer activities."

"Well, yeah."

"Even the doctors who volunteer at TU Health."

"Sure. Right."

Vic watched Brandon. He'd come across as expansive and helpful the first time they met, even though he'd avoided mentioning how his app was used by the non-profits. Now, his answers were only one or two words long. Tori had clearly told him to say as little as possible, as expected. "And, in addition to that, you sit on the board of several other charities, involved in much the same type of activity as TU Health. They are Veterans Health, Firefighters Health, and possibly Blue Line Health.

"Sure."

"I'm not sure how any of this is relevant," Tori said quietly.

"I'm not sure it is. I think our question is why Brandon didn't mention how involved he is in the support of TU Health. He acted as if he had some minor involvement in its start-up, when in truth, his app controls when and where the doctors volunteer for TU Health and several other non-profits that offer the same kind of medical care."

Tori stared at Vic, then slowly opened her hands in a 'what of it?' gesture.

"It puts him right in the center of the case," Liz explained. "And he clearly didn't want us to know that when we first spoke to him."

"Well, that's a bit of a stretch." Tori looked at both Vic and Liz. "I think that's enough. There is no possible criminal activity in what you have described. You simply sound miffed that, in your view, and I stress the point, that in your view, Brandon wasn't as forthcoming as you would have liked in your first interview. But as I said, that hardly speaks to criminal behavior. I'm inclined to think that right now, you are wasting my client's time. And mine."

"Are we, though?" Vic studied Brandon. "That's not all that Brandon downplayed. He pretended to forget the victim had a girlfriend, who also happens to be a doctor who volunteers at TU Health."

"You are speculating, detective. How could you possibly know that my client *pretended* to forget about the girlfriend. Again, I don't see the relevance."

Vic turned to Tori. He was starting to accept that Tori wasn't about to let them have any kind of meaningful discussion with Brandon. "Well, when we pressed your client, he suddenly remembered quite a bit about

Steven's girlfriend. Even that her father disapproved of her dating Steven Kittery. In fact, that was why your client believed Steven was found on Mt. Washington. It was a convenient place for Steven and his girlfriend to meet."

Tori's eyes flashed. "Detective Lenoski, again, how is this relevant?"

Vic smiled at her, but watched Brandon out of the corner of his eye. He needed a way to get under Brandon's skin, and suddenly he had it. "Well, perhaps you are right. Although, on the night Steven was murdered, the father of Steven's girlfriend followed her. He wanted to confront the couple about their relationship. Put an end to it. But what he saw on Mt. Washington after his daughter left was quite different."

Brandon didn't flinch, but he also was so motionless his heart might have stopped. He didn't even blink.

As lies went, Vic knew he could have done better. And he knew he'd made a mistake. Before tossing out a lie like that, he should have stress-tested Brandon's alibi.

Tori frowned and glanced at Brandon.

That, Vic knew, was a rookie mistake on Tori's part. Any decent criminal lawyer would have instinctively counterattacked his statement to cover their client's reaction.

Tori blinked and recovered. "I don't know what that means, detective. What are you saying exactly?"

"Your alibi for that night," started Liz, looking at Brandon, but Vic put a hand on her arm to stop her.

Liz turned to him, a question in her eyes. Vic willed her to stop talking, and she did.

Vic turned back to Tori, determined to brazen it out. "Just what I said. We were quite surprised by what he saw. And we'll be back to discuss exactly that." He rose from his chair.

Liz automatically rose as well. Tori stood, but Vic could tell she was split on what to do.

Vic put his arm out to Brandon. "Until next time."

Brandon shivered back to life. He stared at Vic's hand, pointedly leaned back, and put his hands in his pockets. He stayed seated.

Vic smiled at Brandon and turned his hand to Tori. She took it and gave him a brief handshake, her eyes boring into Vic's.

"Do take good care of your client, counselor. He needs it."

"These are just insinuations, detective."

Tori was recovering fast, and Vic knew they needed to leave.

"Are they?" He left the room, Liz on his heels. At the elevator, neither said anything until they were headed back to the lobby.

"What the hell was that?" Liz asked.

Vic raised a hand. "What did you think of Brandon's reaction when I said Meera's dad had seen what happened on Mt. Washington?"

"He looked like if he moved, he might shit his pants."

"Right."

"But he gave us an alibi. It sounded good. He spent the night at his mother's. At the Masonic in Sewickley. The care facility," Liz added.

"Yes. And I should have checked that before pretending Meera's dad saw what happened to Steven. But I needed to shake Brandon up. Tori wasn't going to let us get anywhere near him, and Tori was right. Just because Brandon didn't mention the phone app and his board seats doesn't mean anything. So I tossed a hand grenade."

"Never gets boring with you," Liz said, looking straight ahead. "Still not sure if that's good or bad."

The elevator doors whirred open, and Vic followed Liz through the lobby. They walked in silence down the street to the parking garage and got into the car.

As they pulled out of the garage and into traffic, Liz turned to him. "Let me check out Brandon's alibi. His mother lives in Sewickley. I can stop by on my way home and talk to her."

Vic was about to agree when Liz's phone rang. She took the call and, beyond one or two words of agreement, said little. She finished the call with "Text me the number."

"Something up?" Vic asked, when she finished the call.

"Craig. I had a call from some PI who wants to meet me. I need to call them."

"So go ahead."

Liz slowly shook her head, her gaze inward. "When we get back." She said it more to herself than to Vic.

At headquarters, they parked and got out of the car. Liz held up her cell phone. Vic nodded and set off across the parking lot. When he reached the entrance, he turned back and looked across the lot. Liz stood by the car, one hand on the trunk, eyes blazing at the sky, her other hand pushing her phone hard against her ear as if the words she heard were an echo from past years, fading faster the more she tried to decipher them.

Chapter Thirty-Eight

J ake Kittery roused himself. He was at his kitchen table, his windbreaker thrown across the back of the chair next to him, the top of his plaid shirt unbuttoned. He'd slid down in the kitchen chair, legs splayed in front of him, one arm tossed across the table top.

He blinked, rousing himself, and looked around. Ellie lay on the living room couch. Her eyes were closed, but she didn't seem to be sleeping. They'd returned from the workshop that made gravestones, after finally picking the stone for Stevie's grave. Somehow, before the funeral, they hadn't had the strength to make the trip.

Stevie was laid to rest, but Jake knew one last thing needed to be done. Stevie wouldn't rest peacefully until Jake was finished.

Conor Byrne's indistinct face floated through his mind, his blue eyes bright.

Slowly, Jake stood. He trudged upstairs to their bedroom and slowly, numbly, peeled off his plaid shirt and chinos. Stepped into jeans and tugged on a flannel shirt. Strung a plain brown leather belt through his belt loops. He rummaged in the back of his closet until he found his Red Wing steel-toed work boots. He hadn't worn them in years, but he was going to work now and needed to be prepared. To be ready.

Downstairs, he knelt on the floor beside Ellie.

"Elle," he whispered, using his pet name for her.

She stirred and drowsily opened her eyes.

"I'm going out. Need to do something."

"What?" Her blue eyes scanned his face.

"You know what."

She breathed in lightly, struggling to focus on him. "No, I don't."

Jake wondered if she had taken more of the sedatives the doctor had given her. "I need to put this right. What happened to Stevie."

Ellie blinked, staring at him. "What do you mean?"

Jake found he didn't want to have this discussion. He was too tired; he didn't want to be talked out of it. "I'm just going to talk to Conor. Make him stop."

Ellie's eyes flickered as she struggled to concentrate. "You don't have to. Not today."

"It has to be today. And Ellie, I'm sorry for everything I've put you through. I should have stopped this years ago."

"Oh God, it's all right. It doesn't matter."

"But it does."

Ellie stretched her arms around his neck and pulled him close, cheek to cheek. "It's okay."

"I love you, Elle."

She shifted and kissed him before letting him go. From the coolness of his cheek, Jake knew she was crying. That with her kiss, she'd tasted the salt of her own tears.

Her eyes were dull. "When will you be back?"

"Soon."

"Okay."

Jake kissed her on the forehead, rose, and squeezed her hand. He turned for the door to the basement and garage. As he opened it, Ellie called after him, "When will you be back?"

Jake hesitated. "Soon." He started down the steps and shut the door to the basement so he couldn't hear her reply.

In the garage, Jake squeezed along the front of the car and found the gun case on its shelf under the workbench. He unlocked it and removed the Colt .45 his father had bought after mustering out of the army. The same weapon his father carried when he was stationed in Korea. After his father died, it came to Jake. Jake had planned to give it to Stevie. Jake checked the chamber was empty and inserted the magazine.

As he carried it to his car, he felt himself separate and rise above himself, watching himself move. He watched as he opened the garage door and slid into the car. It was only as he started the slow reverse to the road that he rejoined himself.

After closing the garage door, he backed into the road and nosed the car forward, the red-painted words on the garage door imprinted in his vision.

He hated that the last words he'd spoken to Ellie were a lie. But she was too perceptive and, despite the grief, would have realized what he really planned to do. He couldn't risk that.

He glanced at the Colt lying on the passenger seat.

The truth was, what he planned to do, there was no coming back from it. He would never see Ellie again, and he knew it.

But the man who murdered Stevie would be dead. He wanted to drive up to Mt. Washington and see the place where Stevie died. See what Stevie last saw. And then he would visit Conor, and put everything right.

Chapter Thirty-Nine

As Vic reached his desk, he received a text from Liz, saying she was leaving for the day and she would call on Brandon's mother and confirm Brandon's alibi on the way home. Vic checked the time on his phone. Liz was right; they were almost finished for the day. But he couldn't shake the notion that Liz's decision to leave had something to do with her phone call.

Craig was hunched over his computer, and Vic stopped by his desk. "Spotted Conor's car on any of the camera footage?"

Craig sat back and rubbed his eyes. "Working on it now. Almost there. I need another half hour to be sure."

Vic thanked him and continued to Sandy's office. She was reading something on her monitor when he arrived at the door, but stopped and waved him inside.

"Something new?" she asked.

"Yes and no. I think by tomorrow, we'll have a lot more clarity. We visited Brandon Ellis today, and he insisted on having a lawyer present."

Sandy raised an eyebrow.

"Yes. We thought the same thing. We just wanted some clarity from our last interview, and he went full battle stations on us. So there's that. Plus, by tomorrow we should know about Conor Byrne, if he's in the frame or out. And we have a new person we need to check. The father of the victim's girlfriend, Meera Basu. Her father followed Meera to Mt. Washington to confront Steven and Meera. He was against their relationship, but says he came home without seeing Steven. His wife confirms that, but we need to be sure. It looks like Dr. Basu, or his wife, can get a little free with their fists. We visited Meera today, and she had bruises on her face."

Sandy was silent for a few seconds, thinking. She looked up. "You think this Dr. Basu was so against Meera's relationship with our victim that he would kill Steven?"

Vic heard the skepticism in her voice. "Agree, it's a stretch, but there's a motivating factor." He picked his words carefully. "Meera's pregnant with Steven's child. That might be enough to send Dr. Basu over the edge. The question is, when did he find out Meera was pregnant? If it was before he followed Meera to Mt. Washington, then he's more of a suspect. If he found out after Steven died, then less so."

"That works." Sandy gave him a small smile, but Vic had the feeling she was forcing it.

"So right now," Vic continued, "Liz is on her way to stress-test Brandon's alibi, Craig is checking camera footage on Conor Byrne, and I'm headed home. I have to pick up my granddaughter at daycare tonight."

Now Sandy's smile looked authentic. "You being a grandfather always surprises me."

"Me too." Vic turned away so Sandy couldn't see his face. Lettie was a joy, but how she came into being was a shadow that walked next to him every day. He trudged back up the aisle to Craig.

"Craig," he called as he passed, "As soon as you get the footage sorted, call me, okay? I need to know if Conor is in or out."

"Got it." Craig gave a thumbs up without looking up from his monitor.

* * *

Vic slid his car into the rush hour traffic, creeping down the hill toward Pittsburgh. He did have to pick up Lettie at daycare, but he had plenty of time to do that. In truth, he wanted to think. Something was going on with Brandon, but he couldn't make out what. Tori, Brandon's lawyer, was right. On the surface, Brandon was simply a guy on the board of several non-profits who also provided a way for the non-profits to coordinate their activities. How any of that translated into a motive to kill Steven Kittery was beyond him. He just couldn't see anything there.

He exited the tunnels and turned onto the parkway, headed east. As the traffic piled up, he exited at Oakland and took the Boulevard of the Allies, cutting through Schenley Park, to avoid the daily pile-up of traffic leading into the Squirrel Hill tunnels.

His phone rang, and he accepted the call, putting it on speaker.

"Detective Lenoski?" asked Craig.

"Craig, will you just call me Vic?" As he spoke, Vic realized that Sandy hadn't said anything about Craig's promotion to detective.

"Yes sir, sorry."

Vic looked helplessly at the sky. Maybe Craig's promotion would shake the formality out of him. "What's up?"

"I'm through the camera footage about Conor Byrne. I've got nothing of his car going through the Squirrel Hill tunnels, and I have his car twice on footage from convenience stores near his house. Add that to the gas station stop he made, and there is no way he was on Mt. Washington when Steven Kittery was killed. Didn't happen. He just spray-painted the Kittery garage and drove home. No doubt about it."

"Okay." In one way, Vic was glad that put Conor behind them, although he still wanted to know why Conor broke into Steven's apartment. Perhaps robbery could get that out of him. "Thanks, Craig. Good work."

"Sure thing…Vic." Vic's name sounded unnatural when Craig used it.

It was everything Vic could do not to check the sky again. "See you tomorrow."

Vic ended the call and thought about where that put them. Now, the only real suspect was Meera Basu's father, unless Liz discovered a crack in Brandon's alibi. He sighed and slowed at a red light.

His phone rang again, but the caller ID only showed a number, no name. He hesitated, but took the call.

"Detective Lenoski?"

It was a woman's voice that Vic didn't recognize right away. "Yes?"

"This is Dr. Meera Basu. Detective Timmons gave me her business card, and she wrote your number on the back. She didn't answer her phone, so I thought I should call you."

"Sure. What can I do for you?"

"Um, I'm not sure if this is important?"

Vic eased his car forward on the green light. "Well, you called me. Try it out."

"Yes, you see, I'm at the Kittery's home? I wanted to talk to Steven's parents, Mr. and Mrs. Kittery?"

"Yes."

"I, um, I wanted to tell them that I'm pregnant. I thought they should know."

"Okay." Vic wondered how that would go over with the Kitterys. He hoped it was well.

"But, when I got here, only Steven's mother was here. So we talked, and now she's very worked up."

"Well, it would be a surprise. I think it would be a lot to hear right now." Vic remembered his own reaction when he found out he had a granddaughter. He'd almost been in shock for the first few hours.

"No, not that. I told her, and she was happy about the baby. The problem is that Jake isn't here, so she called him, she wanted him to know. But he isn't answering. And suddenly, she got very agitated. She keeps saying she has to stop him. She ran in and out of the garage twice."

Vic frowned. "What do you mean?"

"She keeps saying he went out wearing his work boots. That he only wears them when he has a job to do."

"Okay."

"And she says he took his gun."

Vic turned cold. "Meera, where did he go? Who is he going to see?"

"Someone named Conor something or other. Does that mean anything to you?'

187

Chapter Forty

J ake Kittery turned onto Conor Byrne's street, still thinking about Mt. Washington. He'd parked and walked past the statues of George Washington and Guyasuta, down the path to the place where they'd found Stevie's body. He didn't know the exact location, but he could guess.

He'd found the large rock mentioned in the police report, turned, and looked down at the city. All of it was there. The rivers, joining at the tip of Pittsburgh's arrowhead to form the Ohio River. The Ohio snaking away to the west, toward the Gulf of Mexico. The buildings and stadiums scattered across the river flats on the far side of the Ohio River. To the east, over a high ridge, stood the tip of the gothic tower of the University of Pittsburgh.

It all looked ridiculous to him. For his entire life, he'd told himself he would work toward making this city a place for everyone who worked here. He'd wanted every single person to feel all of it belonged to them. His weight shifted, and he had to step sideways to keep his balance. The wind pushed at him. Now, he knew none of that was true. He'd worked for one person only: Stevie. So Stevie could walk between those distant buildings. Ride the incline to this spot. Feel the pride of belonging here.

And somehow, after leaving Mt. Washington and a drive he couldn't even remember, he was here. Conor Byrne's house.

He pulled to the curb one house down from Conor's house and turned off the ignition. His ringtone shrilled. He glanced at his phone. Ellie, calling again. He picked up the phone from the passenger seat and switched it to silent mode. Swiped away the call.

Conor Byrne's car was in his driveway. He was home.

He picked up his father's Colt from the passenger seat, pointed it into the passenger footwell, and pulled back the slide. Heard a round chamber.

He had the odd feeling he needed a plan. Did he, though? Somehow, he knew there was something he wanted to say to Conor. He hesitated, then decided it would come to him in the moment, or not, he didn't care. There was only one thing he needed to do.

He let a breath trail away. His phone vibrated, and he glanced at the screen. Allegheny County Police, showed on the caller ID. He frowned. Lenoski? He hesitated, staring at the screen, then opened the door and got out. He left the phone ringing on the seat.

Chapter Forty-One

Vic heard his call to Conor go to voice mail. He ended the call with his thumb and called Liz, holding the phone and steering wheel at the same time as his call rang through. No answer. He gauged the traffic at the intersection ahead and tossed the phone on the passenger seat. Held his car horn as an intersection loomed. He'd already flipped on his brights.

He weaved through the intersection, grabbed his phone as the road ahead straightened, and speed-dialed Craig.

Craig answered on the second ring. "Vic? What's up?"

"I just found out that Jake is armed and headed to see Conor Byrne."

"He thinks Conor killed his son?"

"Yes." Vic fought a surge of adrenaline. "And Conor's been goading him. He showed up at the memorial service. I tried calling Jake, and I'm headed to Conor's house now." Vic swung around a slow-moving Honda.

"I can get a unit out there," Craig said.

"Do it. I'm maybe two minutes away. Make it a wellness call, but warn them one party is armed. And call Sandy, tell her the situation."

"I can call Conor. Warn him. We have his details."

Vic laid on his horn and shot through a stop sign. He tried to think. "Conor was a cop. He'll have a gun. If we warn him, he might start shooting when Jake knocks on the door."

"Jake might start shooting before he knocks on the door."

Vic gritted his teeth at the difficulty of the decision. Most likely, either option was wrong. "Okay. Call Conor, tell him to lock all his doors, stay

190

away from windows, and only answer the door for me. Do you understand?"

"Got it." The call went dead.

Vic rounded a corner and jammed on his brakes. Traffic stretched back from a red light. He checked the oncoming lane of traffic, held down his horn, swung into the oncoming lane, and gunned past the line of cars. He two-tapped the brakes at the intersection, and seeing a break in traffic, gunned through the red light.

Chapter Forty-Two

Jake Kittery cut across the front lawn of Conor's next-door neighbor, his Colt against his thigh. He swung into the gap between the two houses, circled to the rear of Conor's house, and took the wooden steps to the back door, treading lightly. The top half of the door was glass and covered inside by a sheer curtain. Standing to one side of the door, Jake looked through the window and saw Conor's hazy form standing in the kitchen, his phone to his ear.

Jake tried the doorknob and found the door unlocked. With a quick motion, he swung open the door, stepped inside, and leveled his Colt at Conor.

Conor, his phone pressed to his ear, stared at him, frowned, and said into the phone, "He's here already, inside my kitchen."

"Hang up." Jake gestured with the Colt.

"You heard the man," Conor said into the phone. He carefully lowered the phone to his side.

"I said hang up." Jake stared at Conor. "Now."

Conor raised the phone, swiped at it with his free hand, and held up the screen for Jake to see. He placed the phone on a small breakfast table. "There you go. Now what?"

Jake hesitated. He was disembodied again, somewhere up by the ceiling, watching the scene. He sensed it had something to do with being here, inside Conor's house. He'd known Conor for so long, had sat across from him in so many lawyer's offices and conference rooms, even stared at him from the stand in courtrooms. Yet he knew absolutely nothing about the man personally. He wanted to look around the kitchen, trail through the house, and see how Conor lived. Understand him better.

"Living room," was all Jake could muster.

Conor shrugged and started to turn.

"No." Jake was himself again, the part that looked at them from above gone. Conor turned back, and Jake waved the Colt. "Back it up. Face me."

Conor kept his arms partially raised and backed through a doorway to Jake's right. Jake followed. Conor led him through a dining room and into a living room at the front of the house.

"Sit." Jake used the Colt to point at an armchair.

Conor sat and folded his hands in his lap.

Jake felt himself separating again, part of him swirling toward the ceiling, looking down at the department store furniture. The dust on the side tables. Distractedly, he wondered why most of the tables were empty. Had they once held things, but someone had taken them away?

Again,' Jake was at a loss for what to say.

Conor slapped his thighs. "What do you want? Tell me." His voice was gruff, almost guttural.

"We'll get to it," Jake heard himself say.

Conor stared at him. "Why the hell wait? I'm ready. I've been ready."

"You don't tell me what to do. You haven't earned it."

"Christ. You aren't a talker, are you? Whatever you're going to do, just get on with it."

The part of Jake floating near the ceiling retracted back inside him. Coiled like a fist. "You don't tell me what to do." The force of his words surprised him, and even Conor sank deeper into his chair.

Jake wanted to say something to Conor, but the words wouldn't come. "You killed Stevie. You did it," was all he could say.

"No. I didn't." Something like anger entered Conor's eyes. "That night, I spray-painted your garage door. I wasn't anywhere near Mt. Washington. I know you won't believe me, but it's true."

"You took him." Again, Jake felt part of himself rise away. His words slid away with that other part of himself.

Conor's eyes were alight. "I lost my son too. I know how it feels. Sure, I went after you. You stopped me from finding out what happened. How exactly my son died." Conor opened and closed his mouth, gasped a breath that was mostly a sob. "You're just starting to understand what happens when you lose your kid, aren't you? How it feels. What it does to you. To your family."

Jake saw them both from somewhere near the ceiling. Registered how the arm that held his gun shook. Saw the way Conor pressed himself into his chair, as if he wanted to push back through it.

Conor's head tilted forward. Jake saw the movement from above at the same moment he saw the pleading in Conor's eyes. Their startling blue color.

"I know how it feels." Conor's voice was throaty. "Exactly how it feels. And I would never put you through it. I wouldn't put your wife through it. I wouldn't put anyone through it. I just want to know what happened to my son. How he died. I want to be sure of it. That's all I've ever wanted. Believe anything you want, but believe that."

Jake couldn't stand it. The way he was torn in two. How part of him floated along the ceiling, looking down on them both.

"Listen to me." Conor leaned forward at the waist. "It never goes away. Wanting to know. Missing him. Aching for him. Killing me won't help you. The fact is, you'd be doing me a favor. It would set me free. Let me see my son again. So make up your damn mind. Shoot me or walk out."

Jake felt the pull of Conor's words, their seduction. Knew he couldn't live like this. Ever.

Jake fired. Once, twice, three times. Sank to his knees. He couldn't hear anything. See anything.

He sobbed in a breath. Let it go, and with it went everything that made him.

Chapter Forty-Three

Vic steered into Conor's street too fast and almost sideswiped a parked car. He gunned down the street to Conor's house, spotting Jake's car as he shot by. No cruiser, or uniformed officers yet.

He swerved into Conor's driveway, his rear tire bouncing over the curb. He killed the ignition, grabbed his Glock from the center console, holstered it, opened the door and swung his legs from the car. Halfway across the front yard, he heard a shot, followed immediately by two more. Vic broke into a run, took the steps to the porch two at a time—and without breaking stride—lowered his right shoulder and slammed into the front door

The door crashed open, and Vic stumbled inside, landing on his knees. He rose, unholstered his Glock, and threw himself against the wall next to the opening into the living room. He pushed the barrel of his Glock around the corner and followed it with a quick look.

Jake was on his knees in the center of the living room, back stiff and arms at his sides. Conor kneeled in front of him, his arms encircling Jake in a hug. Vic couldn't comprehend the scene. They weren't fighting or grappling. They were just kneeling there, holding one another. Conor twisted his face toward Vic and gave a single head nod, as if saying they were okay. A Colt lay on the floor next to Jake's right side.

Vic swung around the wall, his Glock trained on Jake. He hooked the Colt away with his foot and kicked it over by an armchair. He looked around, wondering where the spent rounds went. Plaster dust on the floor near the dining room entry made him look up. Three holes in the ceiling formed a triangle.

Vic turned back to see Jake shudder and, slowly, Conor and Jake disentangled themselves. Jake wiped at a tear. Blue and red light washed the front window. Conor helped Jake stand up and led him to the couch. Conor sat opposite him. Vic looked at them, Glock loose in his hand.

"What happened?"

Conor nodded at the holes in the ceiling. "Jake was pissed at my ceiling." It was a joke, but Conor was too emptied out to make it sound funny.

Vic stared at Conor, angered at how he never answered a question. Even now. He took some satisfaction in that Conor looked as white as milk, and his hands shook, then chastised himself for the thought.

Voices from the front door called out and Vic held out his ID and identified himself to the uniformed officers. He asked them to take possession of the Colt and move Conor into the kitchen. He then squatted in front of Jake. "How about you? How are you doing?"

Jake's eyes were dull. His lips parted, but he said nothing. He nodded slowly.

"You need to understand something," Vic said slowly. "Conor had nothing to do with Steven's death. We proved it conclusively just now. We have him on video footage near here at the time Steven was killed on Mt. Washington. Do you understand? Conor didn't kill Steven."

For a few breaths, Jake didn't respond, and then he nodded.

Vic glanced at the ceiling. "And what happened up there?"

Jake opened his mouth as if he was going to speak and closed it. Seemed to consider his words. "I, I felt like I was in two places. Up there watching and down here."

"Okay."

"I needed that to stop."

"And what did you do?"

"Shot at myself up there."

Vic didn't know where to start with that explanation. At the same time, it made a weird kind of sense.

"And you're doing better now?"

Jake looked up and met Vic's gaze. "Yeah."

"Okay." Vic looked at the officer standing in the entry to the living room. "Can you watch him?" Vic nodded at Jake.

The officer replied he would. Vic rose. "Jake, do you have any weapons on you? Another gun or a knife?"

Jake slowly shook his head.

"I need you to say it out loud."

Jake met his gaze again and blinked. He seemed more aware of his surroundings. "No. Nothing. I just had my Dad's Colt."

"Okay, then. I'm going to talk to Conor. Can you stay here with this officer?"

Jake glanced at the patrolman. "Sure."

Vic crossed into the kitchen. Conor was sitting at the small table, the officer by the back door.

Conor looked up. "Couldn't get here a bit earlier?"

"Quit complaining. We tried to warn you."

"Yeah. Big help. I got the call right as he walked in the door."

"Conor," Vic took a quick breath to control his anger. "We know for a fact you didn't kill Steven Kittery, okay? We figured that out in the last hour. So can we cut the bullshit?"

Conor shrugged as if he was disgusted.

Vic heard voices at the front door, and a moment later, Sandy Vrail walked into the kitchen. Vic almost didn't recognize her. Her hair was halfway down her back, her head covered by a blue bandana. Her blue jeans, and white t-shirt were paint-spattered, a smear of blue paint on one cheek. Her Glock was holstered to her hip, and she wore her badge on a chain around her neck. Vic liked how she looked. It was natural.

"Craig called me," Sandy said, and stopped just inside the kitchen. She looked at Conor. "Glad to see you in one piece, Mr. Byrne."

Conor pointed at Sandy and said to Vic, "See, a little sympathy for my situation. You could learn something."

Vic laughed. "Commander Vrail means that if you're still walking around, we have less paperwork to do."

Conor looked at the ceiling. "Lenoski, you can be a dick sometimes, you know that?"

"Don't give me that. You know how much time my team put into making sure you're innocent? Three straight days. But you just had to show up at Steven's memorial service. And you still won't tell me why you broke into Steven Kittery's apartment. You want sympathy? Earn it. And what about that stupid message you left on the Kittery's garage door? You don't even know how to spell the word damn?"

Conor swung his face at Vic, eyes angry. "That was a joke, genius. Dam as in stop something or hold the pinkos back. It's a pun on the swear word damn."

"And about as funny as black mold."

"Okay, you two." Sandy Vrail moved a couple of steps closer to Conor, and Vic could have sworn he saw the trace of a smile on her lips. "Mr. Byrne, answer me this. Do you want to press charges against Jake Kittery? We'll arrest him for discharging his weapon, but you need to press charges to make it all stick."

Conor frowned. For a few seconds, he stared at the door before turning to Sandy. "Tell him if he agrees to come over here and fix my ceiling, I'll forget about it. Honestly, I don't even care if he fired his weapon."

Sandy glanced at Vic, and he knew she didn't like the idea of Jake coming back to Conor's house. He thought about what he'd seen when he first looked into the living room. "I'll explain later," Vic said to Sandy, "But I think that could work."

Sandy's mouth tightened. Vic could see she *really* didn't like the idea of Jake and Conor getting together again.

"Why don't we talk to Jake?" Vic nodded into the living room.

Her mouth still tight, Sandy nodded. Vic went back into the living room. Jake still sat on the couch, but he was leaning back now, staring at the holes in the ceiling. Vic stopped in front of him.

"Jake, have you talked to your wife in the last hour?"

Jake looked at him. "No, why?"

"Do you have your phone? I think you need to."

"My phone's in my car." His eyes turned inward, remembering. "Yeah, she was calling me."

Vic took out his phone and scrolled through his notes until he found Ellie's number. He dialed and held out his phone to Jake.

"What's this about?" Jake took the phone.

"Just talk to her. She has something to tell you."

Vic and Sandy watched as Jake talked into the phone. For a time, he listened and then said, "Dr. Basu? Who volunteers for us?"

Seconds later Jake sank deeper into the couch, shock on his face.

What followed was a back and forth, Jake's voice high, until Jake touched the screen to end the call. Dazed, he held out the phone to Vic.

"Okay," Vic said. "That was why she was calling you. Gramps."

Jake nodded slowly and looked up.

"And here's the other thing." Vic pointed at the holes in the ceiling. "We're going to charge you for that, but I don't think it will amount to anything. Conor won't press charges if you agree to come over and fix the holes in his ceiling. Is that acceptable to you?"

Conor and the police officer from the kitchen appeared in the hall. Everyone watched Jake, who took a moment to digest what Vic had just said. Vic actually wasn't sure they could arrest Jake. If he remembered, the law had to do with firing into a residential structure, not firing within one. But he thought Jake might need the wake-up call of the arrest process.

"Sure," Jake said after a moment. He stood and looked at Conor. "Yeah, I can do that."

Conor nodded. "And I'll fix your garage door."

The two men stared at each other for several long seconds. Vic thought they looked as if they were in agreement about something, as if they understood one another.

"Right." Vic looked from one to the other. "Jake, you can go with these officers. I'll tell Ellie where you are and that your car is here."

"Sure."

Vic thought Jake still sounded dumbfounded, which was understandable.

Vic gestured to the uniformed officers. One of them handcuffed Jake, and the other placed the Colt in an evidence bag. They escorted Jake out of the house.

Everyone watched them go, before Conor turned to Vic. "Give me a second." He disappeared into the kitchen.

Vic heard a cabinet door thump, and Conor returned. He held out a silver laptop to Vic. "Found this in Steven Kittery's apartment. It was under the carpet in a corner of his office."

Vic stared at him for a moment, before digging through his pocket for a latex glove. He found one, put it on, and used that hand to accept the laptop. "And why did you take this?"

Conor shrugged. "I was looking for a document. After the union march, when my son was killed. Jake's union held a membership meeting the next day to talk through what happened. They always took minutes at those meetings, but when my lawyers asked for the minutes in discovery, Jake's local suddenly couldn't find them. We got a warrant and searched the local and the Kittery's house, but that was a bunch of nothing. Made me wonder if Jake gave the minutes to his son to keep. And when I heard his apartment was empty. It seemed like the right time."

Vic hefted the laptop. "Okay."

"The thing's password protected. I couldn't get in anyway."

Vic nodded slowly, aware of Sandy standing beside him. He sensed her tightness and knew what she was thinking. This was beyond breaking and entering. Conor had obstructed their investigation.

"We'll get back to you." Vic turned to Sandy and saw the set to her mouth. She didn't move.

"Commander?" Vic said gently.

Sandy blinked at Conor. "You'll be hearing from us, Mr. Byrne." She pivoted and marched toward the front door.

Vic looked at Conor. "This is it? This is everything?"

Conor nodded. "Yes. I just wanted the meeting minutes."

Vic followed Sandy outside. She was standing near Vic's car.

"Vic," Sandy said as he approached. "That's obstruction. And breaking and entering. You need to arrest him."

"You're right." Vic crossed to his car and opened the trunk. He found an evidence bag and slid the laptop inside. He placed the computer on the floor of the trunk and closed the lid. When he looked, Sandy was staring at him, waiting.

Vic took a careful breath. "Sure. We can charge Conor with those things, we can. I'm just not sure what good it would do."

"He broke the law. Twice. If he tried to access the laptop there's more charges."

"Yes. But he ended the feud with Jake. You heard that yourself. Plus, Liz and I missed the computer when we searched the apartment. We didn't search that carefully, but still. The fact is, Conor did us a favor by handing it over. I feel like that evens things out."

Sandy stared at him for a time. "You know, Vic, I was trained to do everything by the book, and I always insisted on it from my investigators. That meant I knew what kind of detectives they were, what kind of police they were. Sticking by the book is clean. It works."

"I agree. Sometimes you have to be that way. But say we charge Conor right now, drag him into jail. My question is the same. What good does it do? He only broke those laws because of his son's death. He did it out of anguish. But when I got here Conor and Jake were on the floor, hugging. Now that's a good thing. It's why I'm not worried about Jake coming here to fix the ceiling. Conor and Jake made peace today, in their own weird way. And did you hear what he said about the message he left on Jake's garage door? He put a joke in it. Only bored people do that. I think Conor's anger with Jake has run out; he's just doing stuff out of habit. And now? I bet they end up helping each other. They both lost sons; they're living through the same thing. I guess I just don't see the point of throwing Conor in jail. I'd rather just charge him with something like vandalism and make him pay to fix the door to Steven's apartment."

Sandy stared at him for at least thirty seconds. Vic could see the internal battle she was having. Finally, she said, "Vic, look, I know what I know. Doing things by the book, insisting on that, makes us all a certain kind of police officer. What you're describing, what kind of police officer does that make you?"

"The old-fashioned kind."

Sandy shook her head, her lips pursed. "I don't even know what that means." She fell silent.

Vic looked around, at the houses lined up along the street, at the low grey sky. It was quiet here, and he ached to hear the shift whistle of his childhood. The message that his father was coming home.

"It's up to you," Vic said, finally. "I'll do what you want."

She stared at him. "I know it's up to me. Remember that." She took a breath. "But I'll sleep on it." She turned to walk away but didn't move. Turned back. "That said, I'm starting to realize I'm not in the Army anymore." Then she did leave, her back straight and shoulders square, crossing to a small black pick-up truck. Reaching it, she opened the driver's-side door and, standing in the gap between the door and the cab, tugged off her blue bandana. She shook her hair free, climbed into the cab, and drove away without looking back.

Chapter Forty-Four

Vic arrived at work the next morning at seven. The night before, he'd picked up Lettie from kindergarten and cooked dinner, without mentioning to Anne how tight the timing was after his detour to Conor Byrne's house.

The thought of Liz nagged at him. She hadn't replied to his telephone call the night before, so she wasn't up-to-date about Jake and Conor. And Vic wanted to know about Liz's interview with Brandon's mother. It was unusual for her not to call. He tried to ignore his concern as he placed the evidence bag containing Steven's laptop on Craig's desk.

That morning, he'd risen early and worked out on his heavy bag, and his knuckles were stiff as he typed his computer password. He found an email from Liz waiting for him. She said she had a personal matter to attend to and would arrive mid-morning. That terse note was followed by a summary of her meeting with Brandon's mother.

Liz confirmed Brandon's alibi, down to the movie Brandon and his mother watched. But Vic felt a quickening as he continued to read. Brandon's mother also reported that she'd been unusually tired and couldn't remember going to bed. She'd slept through the night and didn't wake until the morning, when Brandon made breakfast for her.

Liz also pointed out that Brandon could have left the apartment after his mother went to bed, reached Mt. Washington by midnight, met Steven, and returned to the apartment. And her last two sentences gave him pause. In the first, Liz told him she'd made an excuse to look through the mother's bathroom medicine cabinet and found prescription sleeping pills. The second line, a question, was two underlined words: "Mother drugged?"

Vic sat back. There was no way to know, but the alibi had holes.

Sandy arrived as Vic finished reading. She nodded to him and swept past on her way to her office. As she entered her office, Vic noted her hair was pulled back in a loose ponytail. The tight bun had disappeared.

Craig arrived at seven-thirty, ten minutes after Sandy arrived. He stripped off his sportscoat, turned to Vic, and pointed at the laptop, his eyebrows raised in a question.

"Steven's laptop. Conor Byrne gave it to me last night. It's password protected, but maybe if you call Edna at TU Health, she might have the password. She's the secretary?"

Still standing, Craig powered up his computer and bent over to check the case file. Moments later, he was on the telephone to Edna.

When he hung up, Craig flashed Vic a smile and a thumbs up. "Got it. I'll copy the hard drive and send it down for physical processing." He dug into his drawer and found latex gloves to open the computer.

Vic took out a pad of paper and tore out two sheets. One he headed with the name Brandon Ellis, the other Dr. Basu (father). Those were their two best suspects, and Vic had woken up in the middle of the night, keenly aware that neither of them had a strong reason to kill Steven. At least that he knew about. He'd promised himself he would write down everything they had on each person and see where it went from there.

He worked at the sheets for a few minutes, but his mind kept slipping back to Liz. What was the meeting she had to attend? The last time Liz went to a meeting outside work, it was with the FBI, and they'd been fishing for information about Vic.

Hopefully, that wasn't starting again.

Chapter Forty-Five

Carty Swain pushed his earbud deeper into his ear and asked Isabella to test her microphone one last time. He knew he sounded like a rookie but couldn't resist. All the years to reach this point had caught up with him. And Isabella had specifically told him twice that she taped the tiny microphone between her breasts.

His imagination was a galloping elephant.

Isabella throatily whispered, "Check, one, two."

"Copy. Got it. Over." Carty swallowed and straightened his baseball cap and sunglasses. He was parked three cars down from the coffee shop where Isabella and Liz Timmons had agreed to meet. He'd been impressed when he listened to the recording of Isabella's set-up call to Liz. Isabella had been confident and matter-of-fact, and her story about being a PI and working for Carty Swain's nephew had clearly affected Liz. He hadn't heard a single hitch in Isabella's voice. He knew Liz would be suspicious, but nothing about Isabella's call sounded false.

They also had a secret weapon. He guessed Liz would be so desperate for Isabella's investigation to be genuine—to have any chance of discovering something new about Carty and her husband—that she would discount any lingering suspicions about the meeting.

He drummed his fingers on the lever of the parking brake, checked the door to the coffee shop and then his mirrors, in case Liz approached from behind.

He spotted Liz with his next glance at the coffee shop. He recognized her immediately. Her hair was more closely cropped to her head than last he'd seen her, but her determined walk and rigid posture were the same. Her purse was clamped under her right arm, the strap over her right shoulder. She wore black khakis and a white blouse under a short leather jacket. Carty shifted down in his seat, watching, his heart pounding.

"After all these years," he whispered to himself.

With a sharp pull to open the door, Liz disappeared inside the coffee shop.

"She hasn't changed," Carty breathed to himself. "Still got a stick up her ass."

His earbud scattered to life, fragments of words swanning out of the background noise. "Are you sure you don't want anything?" Isabella's voice was suddenly so clear Carty blinked.

"I'm fine. I had coffee on the way here."

"Okay." Isabella hesitated, and Carty knew she'd expected Liz to order coffee.

"C'mon," he willed Isabella, careful to not press the transmit button on his radio.

Isabella gathered herself immediately. "Well, I apologize for this sudden call."

"Not a problem. I'd like to see your ID. Your Texas PI license?"

Carty sighed. There it was, Liz's constant and petty demand for honesty, just as he remembered from her marriage to Demond. Carty spoke softly to Demond, "I did you a favor, my friend." He counted ten seconds.

"Okay." Liz's voice, louder now. Carty guessed Liz had inspected the fake ID, accepted it, and sat down. He'd worried that Liz might be suspicious of how new the ID looked, given that he'd only received it from his contact in Texas two days earlier.

Carty fought down his excitement. They were over one more hurdle.

"I know I explained why I'm here," Isabella started, "but let me walk you through it again."

As she spoke, Carty thought Isabella sounded confident and sure of the details. Isabella mentioned the phone call to Carty's nephew the night before Carty and Demond disappeared, the mysterious explanation about

Demond helping Carty hide something that was promised to the nephew.

"And the nephew's name again?" interrupted Liz.

"I'm afraid he doesn't want his name to be repeated. We signed a confidentiality agreement."

Silence. Carty wiped at a bead of sweat. He'd considered using his nephew's name, but it would be too easy for Liz to track him down and discover the truth. He couldn't risk it. The silence widened.

Carty cursed the windshield, the car windows, the roof.

"Although," Isabella said carefully, "He did say that if anything comes of this conversation, he'd be glad to meet you in person."

Carty held his breath. Isabella was off-script. They hadn't role-played this. But at the same time, he saw the beauty of what she suggested. How it could string Liz along.

"That could work." Liz's words were just as carefully considered as Isabella's, and Carty knew this was a moment when Liz overrode her caution. That her need to discover something about Demond, and that night, was pulling at her.

"Good. Then do you have any ideas? My own instinct was they may have hidden whatever it was at your house, but I'm guessing you went through everything before you moved."

"I did. If anything was hidden in that apartment, I would have found it."

"Not so," Carty thought to himself, thinking of the .38 in the paint can.

"And you have no idea what was hidden?" The skepticism in Liz's voice oozed into Carty's earphones. "I mean, talk about a load of crap. After twenty years, this nephew of Carty decides now is the right time to go looking for something; he has no idea what, claiming that Carty said it belonged to him." The white noise of the coffee shop filled Carty's ear. "And you agreed to go along with it."

"Well, my company did." Carty heard a laugh underlying Isabella's words. She was agreeing with Liz, letting Liz know that she, too, saw the absurdity of it. "But then again," Isabella said, her words turning earnest. "This was my first chance to travel for work. Take on a case that involved several states. If I can make something out of this, it will help me at work. It's tough to get ahead with all the men in the office."

Carty had to smile. Isabella was off-script again, and she was perfect. Playing to Liz's understanding of how difficult it was for a young woman to advance in an office overrun with men. Silently asking for help.

Liz didn't immediately answer, and Carty wished he was in the coffee shop, that he could see the expression on Liz's face.

"So…" Isabella's voice dropped to just above a whisper. "Do you think you can help me?"

Carty grinned. A personal appeal. Nicely done, he thought.

Again white noise, this time broken by two sharp bangs that Carty recognized as someone rapping an espresso machine portafilter to empty the grounds.

"There is," Liz said slowly, "a place owned by Dee's cousin."

Carty felt a twist as he heard Liz use Demond's nickname. He'd heard Liz call Demond that years ago, but somehow, at the time, Carty had felt it too personal to adopt himself.

"Yes?"

"It was in Bywater, in the part that didn't really flood. Back then Dee's cousin lived in a small house he got from his parents."

Carty closed his eyes. Of course. He hadn't thought to check on Demond's family when he was reviewing real estate holdings. Not that it would have helped. He didn't know their surnames.

"Is that close to the area they patrolled?"

"Close enough. And if it was the night before the levees broke, first responder vehicles could move around."

"So they could have driven there."

"It's possible."

"And who owns the property now?" Carty heard a note of excitement in Isabella's voice, as if Liz had given her a Christmas present.

"I'm pretty sure it's still in the cousin's family." Liz's voice sounded distant, as if she was thinking.

"What's the address?"

"At'ta girl," Carty breathed to himself.

CHAPTER FORTY-FIVE

Silence for a beat. "I can call around. Find out who lives there now."

"That would be so helpful."

Carty slammed his hand on the dashboard. It wasn't helpful at all. This was Liz being suspicious. As cagey as always. They needed the address.

"What do you plan to do, once you know the location?" Liz's voice was tight. Considering.

"I would imagine I'll go and visit. If you let them known I'm coming, that would be perfect."

Isabella was off script again, but Carty liked the way she kept it personal and enlisted Liz to help solve the problem. It was a good technique.

Another pause, this one longer, before Carty heard Liz's words in his earpiece. "I can do you one better. We'll go together."

Chapter Forty-Six

Jake Kittery walked through the front doors of the county jail and stopped on the sidewalk. The brightness made him squint. He took a deep breath, clearing the musk smell of the jail out of his nostrils, his eye skimming the dozen people sitting along the low brick wall edging the walk. Someone rose to greet him.

Edna. She raised her arm.

Vaguely, Jake wondered why Ellie hadn't come to pick him up.

"Yeah, I know," Edna called as she crossed to him. "I ain't Ellie."

"That's okay. Good to see you, though."

Edna shrugged. "She was planning to come, but Dr. Basu called her this morning. Meera's got some doctor's appointment, and Ellie wanted to go with her. It's about Stevie's baby. Ellie asked me to pick you up."

"Yeah," Jake repeated, still struggling to grasp the significance of Meera Basu needing to visit a doctor. Ellie had clearly adapted faster than him. He was glad suddenly that Ellie had a reason to leave the house, that she wanted to get out and be helpful. He didn't mind at all that she chose the doctor's appointment over picking him up.

From jail.

Edna nodded at the county jail as if she knew what he was thinking. "Still like the old days?" She gestured for him to follow her and headed toward a car park.

Jake followed, thinking about her comment. With this, he'd been arrested, what, four times? The middle two were for union protests, and he still remembered the camaraderie of the men arrested and the burning feeling of righteousness that carried them through the night or two before their release. The first time he'd been seventeen, caught by the local police for spray-painting anti-company slurs on a concrete bridge abutment. That was a different story.

"Here we are." Edna beeped open the doors to a small Ford. Jake slid into the passenger seat.

Edna arranged herself behind the wheel and, once they were clear of the lot, glanced at him. "So you went after Conor Byrne, huh?"

Those few minutes in Conor's house returned to Jake in a rush. The way he'd felt split in two, Conor goading him. "Yeah, I suppose I did."

"Well, he's an asshole, but I'm glad you didn't shoot him. I feel like you still have things to do."

Jake didn't answer. He wasn't sure he did have anything to do anymore. It was Stevie who had convinced him to open TU Health. Stevie, who helped him transform the Whiskey Rebellion into their offices. Stevie again, who ran the administration and maintained the liaison with the local health insurer. He was simply there because the union members trusted him. He was the key that turned the lock. It was Stevie who built the door, pointed out the lock, opened the door after he unlocked it, and led the way through. He didn't know what he could possibly do now. He didn't have the skills to actually run the non-profit.

"Ellie told me about Dr. Basu," Edna continued, her eyes on the road. "Grandchildren are a blessing."

"That was a surprise," was all Jake could get out.

"You'll love it." Edna eased the car onto the parkway, headed toward Braddock.

Jake guessed he would. But what rose in Jake's mind was the way Conor grabbed him after he fired at the ceiling and dropped his pistol. That floating sensation of looking down from the ceiling was gone. Conor's weight had tethered him to the ground.

The other thing he appreciated was Vic Lenoski's patient explanations afterward. He realized how alike that was to his first arrest for spray painting the bridge abutment. Lenoski reminded Jake of that first police chief. He couldn't remember the man's name, just the chief's presence. Solid. Unhurried. Serious. The kind of guy who stood with his legs slightly spread and moved in a way that kept everything in front of him. In those days, each Pittsburgh locality had its own police force, linked to the industry in each of the local towns. Places like Homestead, Braddock, West Mifflin, Allegheny City, McKees Rocks. In time, those towns melded into Pittsburgh's identity. But the cops on those local forces had to depend on themselves and handle crimes the way they thought best. That responsibility gave the chiefs a kind of gravity, and Vic had it.

Vic was old-school, and Jake liked it.

"Are you okay?"

Jake glanced at Edna, in time to see her turn her head back to the road ahead.

"Yeah. Sorry. A lot to process the last few days."

"Yes. And you should know that Vic Lenoski character found Stevie's laptop. I got a call about it this morning. I think they're going through it now."

"Good." Jake's mind flickered back to a moment late in the afternoon of the day Stevie died. Stevie, leaning against the door frame to Jake's office, frowning, asking if he talked to someone regularly. Who had he asked about?

Edna slowed with the traffic entering the Squirrel Hill tunnels.

Jake remembered. It was Brandon Ellis. Stevie asked if he talked to Brandon Ellis at all. The tunnel closed around them; the daylight snuffed out.

Jake remembered responding, saying he didn't talk to Brandon. Hardly ever.

At the time, Jake had thought the question odd, but forgotten about it. He realized now he'd thought about the question the wrong way and shouldn't have discarded the memory so quickly. He should have noted the frown on Stevie's face. Wondered why Stevie asked the question in the first place. He shook his head to clear his mind. How had he not read the concern on Stevie's face? What else had he missed?

Chapter Forty-Seven

C arty Swain's mind swirled as he drove back to the hotel. He should have anticipated Liz wanting to accompany Isabella to New Orleans. It made sense. Isabella's cover story smelled worse than a slaughterhouse, and even Liz's need to discover absolutely anything about Demond's death couldn't make her believe it.

Common sense dictated accompanying Isabella to New Orleans.

Carty smiled at the windshield. Still. Having Liz with them in New Orleans was doable. Isabella could handle Liz. And if they actually found the doubloons, well then, he would simply step in. Send Isabella outside. Send Liz to meet Demond.

What had Luis called doubloons? A flood of blood. The bloodletting of the gold being plundered. The spilled blood of slaves forced to cast the coins. The bloodthirsty pirates and their cutlasses hacking at the Spanish and Portuguese sailors transporting them. That flood just didn't stop. Even today. First Demond. Next it would be Liz, if needed.

He knew it would be.

"A flood of blood to wash away the crud. With only the doubloons to judge." Carty smiled again as he pulled into the hotel parking lot. Their hotel was located halfway between Pittsburgh and the city's airport, on a ridge of land topped by a series of conjoined strip malls. He stepped out of the car into a buffeting wind under a blue sky littered with flat grey clouds.

Inside his hotel suite, he made coffee and paced the floor. The television was on, but he didn't see or hear it. He was so close. He fingered the doubloon on his necklace. Felt its weight. Finally, a soft knock from the

213

hall.

Carty opened the door and stepped aside for Isabella. She slid by him, trailing warmth and a scent of spice.

He closed the door.

Isabella stood in the section of his suite with the couch, coffee table, and armchair. For a moment, they both just looked at one another, Carty straining not to let his eyes roam over her body. The king-size bed to his right loomed into his peripheral vision.

Carty realized Isabella looked worried. "Well done." He forced a smile. "I heard everything. That bit about not giving up the nephew's name but telling Liz she could meet him later was genius. And playing the card about being a woman in a man's world? She bought it. She *wants* to help you."

"But she also wants to come to New Orleans with me. I didn't know what to say. How will that work?"

Carty waved his hand. "Let me worry about that." Carty searched his thoughts. "Look. Your instinct was right. The most important thing right now is to keep stringing her along. Make sure she gives us access to her cousin's house. And keep in mind, if you don't find anything, it's job done. You both go your separate ways. If you do find something, I'll find a way to handle things."

"Can't you tell me what we're supposed to find? I felt like a fool talking to her."

Carty hesitated. Should he tell her? "I'm not sure myself." He grinned, but he knew it was feeble. She didn't believe him: he could see it.

"Why are we doing this?" Her eyes flashed. "What's the point of going to all this trouble?"

A cold anger settled over Carty, the same sober rage he'd felt in that tiny shack all those years ago. He reheard Demond telling him he planned to return the collection. "Something was taken from me, years ago." His words sounded flat, even to his own ears. "Her husband took it. I want it back."

"If it was taken from you, why don't you just ask her for it? Why the tricks?"

They stared at one another, the anger pulsing in Carty's temples. The television rumbled in the background. Isabella lowered her head.

"I'm sorry if I overstepped," she whispered, looking at Carty's feet.

Carty realized his expression scared her. He tried to compose his face.

Isabella peeked up at him. "I asked Liz when she wanted to go, and she checked her phone. She suggested we fly tomorrow. We have to switch planes, so we'll get there late. We can visit the house the next morning."

"Okay, good." Carty tried to soften the words.

Isabella raised her head. She looked at him frankly and suddenly ran her hands around her waist, untucking her blouse. As soon as it was loose, she undid the button at her chest.

For a mad second, Carty thought she was getting undressed. His anger evaporated with his breath, and his skin warmed.

"Sorry." Isabella blushed slightly and stopped unbuttoning.

Carty was about to tell her to keep going, when she reached inside her blouse toward the small of her back, and with a grimace, tugged.

She removed her hand carefully, holding the small, black box of the transmitter. The strips of medical tape she'd used to affix it to the small of her back trailed like streamers. With her other hand, she followed the wire leading from the transmitter to the microphone, tracing it toward her breasts. Carty glimpsed the flat plank of her belly as her arm lifted the front edge of her blouse.

She fumbled in her cleavage, holding his gaze. A moment later, the hand under her shirt appeared, holding the microphone and the strip of tape she'd used to affix it to her skin. With quick movements, she wrapped the wire around the box, stepped close to him, and held out the mechanism.

Carty automatically took it. The transmitter and microphone were warm from her body heat. He took a shallow breath. She was right there, in front of him, shirt untucked and half unbuttoned. Her cleavage beckoned.

Carty was about to reach for her when she floated back, just out of reach. She rebuttoned her blouse and, with quick hand movements, tucked it back into her jeans.

Carty's mouth was dry. "Okay," he managed to squeak out.

Isabella cocked her head. "Okay," she parroted, with a small smile, her brown eyes deep and innocent. She slipped around him and reached the door. "So we stick to the protocol? We stay apart in case anyone is watching. Act as if we don't know each other on the airplane."

"Right." Carty's mind failed to produce a thought. "Wait." He bore down, thinking. "You should keep this. We'll need it when you go into the house." He held out the transmitter.

Isabella lifted the mechanism from Carty's hand and, in almost the same movement, slipped out of the suite. The door clumped shut.

Carty blinked and looked at his hand. Without the warm transmitter, his palm felt plundered. He tried to understand what just happened.

Isabella had no need to remove the transmitter in front of him. Unless she wanted him to see her almost undressing. Her blouse gaping open.

That was a good sign, he thought.

But he couldn't shake the idea she had done it to change the balance between them. To somehow put herself on equal footing with him. That her actions were planned.

Carty shook his head, trying to clear his mind. Maybe that was it. She wanted to confuse him.

But why?

He took a couple of deep breaths, waiting for his thoughts to settle. For his body to relax.

Another thought came to him. There was no way he could get on an airplane with Liz. He couldn't risk being seen by her. He needed to get to New Orleans ahead of Liz and Isabella.

Chapter Forty-Eight

Vic and Craig were at their desks. Vic had taken over reviewing the data sent from Steven's phone carrier, while Craig reviewed the files from Steven's computer. After two hours, Vic had little substantive to show for his efforts. He sat back and rubbed his eyes. "I'm not finding much," Vic called to Craig. "Not on the night of."

"Did you see his calendar?"

"Yeah. Day of, he met with someone called Oskar Glimt at three."

Craig straightened from his computer screen and rubbed his neck. "Right, and the day after he was killed, did you see who he planned to meet?"

Vic sifted through the data until he found the calendar. "Day after," Vic said slowly, as he read. "Two-thirty, Paul Drum."

Craig leaned toward Vic. "I looked up Oskar Glimt. Guess what, he's the CEO of Firefighters Health."

"The non-profit like TU Health, but for retired firefighters."

"Right, then I looked up the Drum guy. He's the CEO of Veterans Health."

"So Steven was calling around the CEOs of his sister non-profits."

"Right."

Vic thought about that. "Since they do the same kinds of things, maybe they meet regularly?"

"I've got two years of calendar from his computer. Never had a one-on-one meeting with either of them before."

"Then we need to interview them." Vic realized Oskar Glimt was one of the last people to see Steven alive. "We do Glimt in person. Drum never met with Steven; we can do that over the phone." He glanced at Liz's desk. Still empty. He picked up his phone and saw a new text message. He opened it, read the note, and turned to Craig. "Okay, as soon as you finish your first cut, let's go talk to Glimt."

Craig studied Liz's empty desk. "Liz isn't coming in?"

Vic held up his phone. "Just got a text. Apparently, she's decided to take three days off."

"Huh."

Surprise was written across Craig's face as he turned back to his computer. Vic knew they were both thinking the same thing. Liz never took time off in the middle of cases. But Liz also hadn't recently mentioned Levon Grace, her live-in boyfriend. Vic wondered if Levon was the reason for the vacation.

He couldn't help himself. He called Levon, but his call went directly to voice mail, and he left a message. It felt like he was going behind Liz's back, but he knew Liz wasn't about to explain her personal life to him.

"How are we doing?"

Vic looked up in surprise. Sandy Vrail stood next to his desk. He hadn't heard her arrive, and he made a mental note to stay more alert.

"We finally got Steven's phone data." Vic straightened in his chair. "Turns out Steven was visiting the CEOs of TU Health's sister non-profits. He doesn't normally do that, and he met with one of them the day he died. That's our next interview. I want to ask him about their conversation."

"Good." Sandy spread her feet and folded her arms, clearly searching for the best way to change topics. "Vic, I talked to one of the prosecutors in the DA's office. If Conor Byrne doesn't want to press charges against Jake Kittery, the prosecutor doesn't see the need to force it. No harm, no foul, as he put it."

Vic was careful to keep his voice neutral. "Okay. And I got an email this morning. Jake Kittery was released. I'm guessing he's home by now."

"Good." Sandy gave him a wry smile. "This old-fashioned policing thing takes some getting used to."

Vic shrugged. "I'm still not used to it either. Not sure I ever will be."

Sandy smiled, nodded her thanks, and walked toward another detective sitting at a nearby desk. Vic watched, and chuckled at the way the detective jumped when Sandy stole up behind him. "She does that on purpose," he thought to himself.

"I'm good to go," Craig called to him.

Vic turned to him. "Find anything?"

"Bits and pieces, but nothing that obviously links together. It might help me to talk to this Glimt guy."

* * *

Once Vic and Craig were on the slow, downhill drive to the Fort Pitt tunnels, Vic glanced at Craig. "What were the bits and pieces you found?"

Craig was silent for several seconds. "There was one thing that struck me as weird. I just don't know what to make of it."

"And?"

"It was an email exchange with the health insurer TU Health works with, the one that gave them the grants to help get them started?"

Vic waited.

"So, the first email in the string came from the health insurer, from a couple of executives there. One is in charge of community relations, the other something to do with elderly care. Anyway, they sent a certificate, saying TU Health's growth has surpassed a certain level and continues to grow, and it thanked them for their hard work."

"Okay. That doesn't sound bad." Vic wasn't sure why Craig was being so tentative.

"But here's the thing. Steven emailed back, saying there had to be some kind of mistake. Steven said their growth was pretty much flat the last five months, that they were talking to unions to try and line up more retirees for doctor visits."

"How did the guys at the insurer respond?"

"They got into this back and forth with Steven about it. Turns out what they meant by growth was the volume of Medicare chargebacks. The insurer even sent over some Excel files they said showed how TU Health's chargebacks had increased. But Steven kept insisting there was a mistake, that he also tracked their chargeback numbers, and his own numbers didn't show that kind of growth."

Vic checked the navigation on his phone. Oskar Glimt's offices at Firefighters Health were in the eastern end of the Strip District. He negotiated a turn onto Smallman Street, driving past the newly renovated Terminal building toward Glimt's offices.

"How did they leave it?"

"It wasn't resolved. Steven said he would do more research." Craig grinned. "I mean, the two executives at the insurer thought they were doing something nice for TU Health, and they got it thrown back in their faces. They were polite about it, but I could tell they thought Steven was being a jerk. It was just a certificate of appreciation. Nothing that called for a reaction that strong from Steven."

Vic thought about Jake Kittery and his stoic honesty. The way he wouldn't back down from his crusade to improve the lives of union workers. "Steven sounds a bit like his dad."

"Maybe. So that exchange was weird, but I have nothing to connect it to."

"But if both sides are sure of their numbers, something is going on." Vic didn't say what he was actually thinking. That mismatched numbers might mean Medicare fraud. "Let's see what Glimt has to say."

The Firefighters Health address was a two-story brick building shoe-horned between two warehouses. Vic parked on the street and, together, they passed a grubby wall plaque proclaiming Firefighters Health and entered the offices.

The layout of the ground floor was similar to TU Health, with eight second-hand desks pushed together in a central bullpen area, surrounded by several offices and a glass-walled conference room. A large whiteboard covered the left-hand wall. Two people sat at the desks, and neither raised their eyes to Vic.

"Can I help you?"

Vic turned to a young woman seated in an alcove just inside the door. With a quick shake of her head, she moved long black bangs out of her eyelashes. Her steady brown eyes reminded Vic of an owl. Vic guessed she was in her mid-twenties, and watched her gaze settle with interest on Craig.

"Sure." Vic showed her his ID and asked for Oskar Glimt.

The young woman blinked at Vic's credentials. "Oh. Just a moment." She rose and hurried toward one of the offices against the outside wall, her shoulder-length black hair swaying behind her. She knocked on the door jamb and disappeared inside.

Vic studied the writing on the whiteboard. He couldn't make out the handwritten abbreviations and time stamps. After a moment, he decided the left-hand column, which held a long list of five-digit numbers, must be the identity numbers of particular patients. The abbreviations had to be treatments or procedures. It all looked clinical and impersonal. A thicket of numbers instead of the mud flats of people's lives.

The young woman reappeared through the office door and crossed to them. "Mr. Glimt will see you now. Can you follow me?"

Vic thanked her, noting the small smile she gave Craig as she turned to lead them. Vic was amused at the unnecessary formality. The offices were small enough that they didn't need the receptionist to lead the way to Glimt's office.

Oskar Glimt was waiting for them, standing behind a desk cluttered with files and stacks of paper. Vic counted three different takeout coffee cups on the desk top.

A short, sturdy man with wavy brown hair, Oskar's shirt strained to stay buttoned over a muscular chest.

Oskar introduced himself, and asked, "Is this about Steven Kittery? I was wondering when you would stop by." Glimt's sharply defined eyes skimmed from Vic to Craig and back. He waved at two chairs facing his desk.

"Thanks," Vic answered, and introduced Craig and himself. "We had some trouble tracking down Steven's computer, so it took a few days to find his schedule and what he was doing in the days before his death."

"Horrible thing." Glimt shook his head and clucked softly as he sat down. "I met him several times. Our non-profits do similar things, did you know?"

"That's what we understand. And we also understand you met with Steven the day he died."

"I did." Glimt slumped just slightly in his seat. He took a raspy breath. "He came here. He'd called kind of suddenly, and I had to fit him in. I couldn't take the time to meet him somewhere else."

"Okay. We were wondering what you talked about?"

"Oh, the usual things. How well we were doing, number of clients. That kind of thing."

Vic thought Glimt's answer was oddly passive. He noticed Craig staring at a whiteboard on the side wall. Vic followed Craig's gaze but couldn't make any sense of the boxes with lines between them and various acronyms scrawled in a slanting, hurried hand. It vaguely reminded Vic of a flow chart, but the spaghetti collection of lines was too much to follow.

"I'm sorry," Vic said, pulling his attention back to Glimt. "Could you be a bit more specific about what Steven wanted? It's important."

"Oh, right. Sorry." Glimt lifted one of the coffee cups, realized it was empty, and tried a different one. Same result. He put it back down and didn't try the third. Vic noted that he also didn't throw the empty ones away.

"You see," Glimt said slowly, "We regularly worry that we have enough clients. And there's the whole problem with finding doctors to volunteer. The turnover with doctors is really difficult to manage. We talked about that."

Vic leaned forward. "And did Steven ask about Medicare chargebacks?"

Glimt blinked. "It came up. It always does. But I don't remember anything specific."

Craig turned from the whiteboard and stared at Glimt. "We discovered that TU Health works pretty closely with one of the local health insurers. How about you? Who do you work with?"

"Oh. The same one as TU Health. We all do."

"And does the health insurer track your Medicare charges and payments?" Vic watched Glimt carefully. From his conversation with Craig, Vic knew the answer to the question, but he was interested in Glimt's reaction.

"I don't really pay attention. But we all use the same app. I bet the insurer can see our charge rate, number of charges, that kind of thing." A satisfied smile flickered across Glimt's face, but quickly gave way to a frown. "But the insurer doesn't know the name of the patient. We use a code to protect the patient. We keep everyone's medical records private. The insurer should only look at metadata, but my guess is they can determine the individuals."

Vic waved his hand. "We aren't worried about anyone's privacy being violated."

Glimt sat back, visibly relieved. "Then how else can I help you?"

Vic thought about Glimt's question. "How did you leave it with Steven? Did you make plans to do anything during his visit?"

"He said he was touching base with Paul Drum, who runs Veterans Health. Paul has a much larger organization. There's a lot of veterans in Western Pennsylvania. Steven said he'd circle back to me."

"How about Brandon Ellis? Did he say he was going to talk to him? You all use the app created by Brandon, right?"

Glimt blinked again. "I can't remember Steven saying he was going to meet with Brandon."

As Vic sat back, unsure what to ask next, Craig spoke up. "I have a question." Craig glanced at Vic, silently asking for a go-ahead to speak. Vic gave him a short nod.

"I'm just wondering, do you track your Medicare chargebacks?"

"Oh, sure. We all do. We do a monthly report. We keep all the chargeback codes in a spreadsheet and generate reports from that."

Something clicked in Vic's mind. "Do you know if Steven did that?"

"I would guess so." Glimt shrugged, disinterested.

Vic pressed on the point. "So Steven would have a good picture of how many Medicare chargebacks TU Health made, month to month??

"I would think so."

All three of them were silent for a few moments. "Okay," Vic said finally. "Did he say anything you thought was unusual?"

Glimt shook his head slowly. "Not that I remember."

"And what was his attitude? Did he seem upset in any way? Worried?"

Glimt thought for a few seconds. "I'd say he was focused. The other times I met him were cocktail things, and it was a different environment. But this time, he seemed more serious." Glimt smiled. "What do the psychologists call it? Task-oriented? But I just don't know in relation to what."

"Thanks." Vic rose, but hesitated. He felt he was missing something, that he had one more question to ask. Craig rose as well. Vic thanked Glimt and gave him a business card.

As he reached the door, Vic remembered what he wanted to ask. He stopped and turned back to Glimt, who was standing behind his desk, to see them out. "One last thing. Did you tell anyone about your meeting with Steven?"

Glimt frowned in concentration. "No, I don't think so. I was just waiting for him to get back to me after he talked to Paul Drum." Glimt shrugged apologetically.

"Good, thanks." Vic stepped aside so Craig could leave the office first and followed him out to the car.

Chapter Forty-Nine

"What do you think?" Vic asked Craig, once they were in the car. "Glimt didn't have a lot to offer?"

Vic nodded. "Agree. He made it sound as if Steven was there to review their usual problems. But did you notice what he said at the end?"

"That he was waiting for Steven to get back to him?"

"Right. But he knew Steven was trying to get to the bottom of something. Yet he came across as uninterested in what it was. Which is odd." Vic started the car and pulled into traffic. "I keep going back to that certificate the insurer sent Steven. How he knew the certificate was wrong. Maybe Steven was just worried TU Health was doing their chargebacks wrong."

"And the insurer had the right numbers? So he decided to visit all the non-profits and see how each reported, so he could spot the problem?"

Craig, Vic thought, was one of the brightest detectives he'd ever worked with. "Right. He knows how TU Health tracks and reports chargebacks, and his next step is to see how Firefighters and Veterans Health do it. How long ago did he get the email from the insurer about being awarded the certificate?"

"Beginning of the week he died. He argued with them, then went to meet Glimt and set up an appointment for Drum. Died that night. He was moving fast."

"Right." Vic slowed to a stop at a red light. "That's important." Vic felt his own pulse quicken. "Why did he move so fast if he thought TU Health was doing their reporting wrong? And he argued with the health insurer. That means he thought that TU Health's numbers were correct. He believed in them."

The light turned green, and Vic accelerated. He glanced at Craig. "One reason he might have moved fast is if Steven suspected Medicare fraud. Then he'd be worried about his father. If fraud was discovered, the finger would point at Jake Kittery, right? He needed to protect his father."

Craig tapped the dashboard. "Is Medicare fraud common?"

Vic sorted through what he remembered about it from a seminar. "The two most common are charging Medicare for services you didn't perform, or upcharging. That's when you do a procedure for a client but report to Medicare you did a different service with a higher repayment rate. If a doctor is cheating the system, they often do both kinds. The fraud is in the billions of dollars every year."

"Okay." Craig sounded shocked.

Vic realized he'd sped up the car in excitement. This was the first sense of a motivation that might lead to Steven's murder. He eased off the gas, but his muscles still tingled. "How about this? Maybe Steven was ahead of us. Maybe he already believed some kind of Medicare fraud was happening, and he was trying to figure out *how*. He knew TU Health wasn't doing it, yet the insurer they all used was seeing higher chargeback rates. He gets worried his Dad might take the fall for it, so he figures out who is behind the fraud, confronts them, and gets murdered for it."

"And Brandon Ellis is right in the middle of it." Craig drummed his hands on the dashboard. "All the non-profits use his app, so it's likely the fraud happens within Brandon's app. We need to follow in Steven's footsteps. Duplicate his investigation."

"Right." Instead of taking the ramp to the Fort Pitt bridge and their offices, Vic took the ramp that veered east. "For starters, you call the insurer downtown and get the reimbursement numbers they're using for TU Health. Get as many months as you can. Right now, we go to TU Health itself and get copies of their monthly report of reimbursements. We compare them. If they're different, and they will be, we figure out how."

"Got it." Craig grinned at the windshield.

Vic smiled at Craig's enthusiasm. Liz was different. If she was sitting in Craig's place her thinking would have been as acute as Craig's, but her attitude would have been taciturn and angry.

As he merged onto the parkway headed east, it made him wonder again why Liz had taken vacation days.

Chapter Fifty

Jake Kittery stood in the middle of his office at TU Health, unable to move. Instead of taking him home, Edna had driven to Braddock and told him to catch up on work until Ellie picked him up. Among the desks that made up the bullpen, Edna sat with her head down, reading emails. To his right, outside the glass of his office wall, Steven's office sat in darkness, leering at him like the black of an empty eye socket. He wanted to look at it but couldn't. Water gurgled in the heating pipes. He and Edna were alone. His stomach sank as if he was on a tightrope halfway between skyscrapers.

He forced himself to move forward.

He reached his desk, sat, and powered up his computer. He was aware of each breath he took. He glanced at Edna, and, using her as his guide, opened his emails. More than fifty were unread. He skimmed the subject lines and senders. Most were from acquaintances, the subject lines referring to Stevie. He couldn't stand to open them. He scrolled down. His eye fell on a previously read email from Stevie, the last one he'd sent. Jake clicked on it.

The message was terse. "Take a look. Need to discuss." A file was attached. Jake remembered the email. He'd opened it and looked at it, but it didn't mean anything to him at the time. Out of idle curiosity, he clicked on the attachment.

His computer screen fluttered, and a spreadsheet opened. Jake stared at the column headers, then skimmed the rows and column totals.

For several seconds nothing gelled, and then he understood what he was looking at. What he didn't understand was the significance. He checked for more spreadsheet tabs and ran his cursor over the columns, but the file was a single spreadsheet without any embedded explanations or descriptions. According to the headline, the numbers were TU Health's Medicare chargeback totals by month since the beginning of the year, compared to what the insurance company identified they processed. Only one of the monthly totals matched. The chargebacks in the insurance company column were significantly higher, three times higher, in some cases, than what TU Health posted.

Jake wondered how he'd missed the obvious discrepancy when he first opened the attachment. But he did now. This was Stevie's territory, and he let Stevie handle it. If there were problems, he waited for Stevie to tell him. And now, Jake realized, Stevie was telling him there was a problem.

Movement caught his eye, and he looked toward the front door. Vic Lenoski crossed the bullpen toward Edna, trailed by a younger man. He watched Vic and Edna exchange words before Edna rose and crossed to his office door.

"I got this Lenoski character," Edna said from the doorway.

"I see that."

"He wants to know if we do a report every month on our Medicare chargebacks. He's wondering if he can see it."

Jake glanced at the file on his computer screen. This wasn't a coincidence. He hit the print command on his computer. "I'm printing it now. Give it to them."

Edna gave him a long look. "Okay." She sounded skeptical but turned and headed to the communal printer.

Jake rose and approached Vic, who turned to face him directly, his face tense.

Jake stopped a few feet away from him. He nodded at Vic's wide-legged, defensive stance. "This isn't Conor's house. But I guess I deserve that."

They eyed one another for a few moments. "Well, at least no one innocent got hurt," Vic said finally.

"Lucky us."

Vic gestured toward the younger man. "This is Craig Luntz. He put in about twenty hours watching video and proved—without a doubt—Conor wasn't on Mt. Washington that night. I said to you the first time I talked to you, let us handle this. We know what we're doing."

"Right. And you've lost a kid, so you know how it feels."

Vic's face hardened. Craig's eyes widened, and he shifted back a half step. Jake had the feeling he'd stepped on a landmine, and any shift in weight meant an explosion. He froze, confused.

Edna arrived from the printer and offered Jake the printed report.

Jake took the report slowly, looking for a way to change the subject. "I guess I did learn," Jake said carefully, "That Conor Byrne isn't such a dick. He even offered to come clean my garage door."

Slowly, Vic's posture relaxed. "You might find you guys have more in common than you thought."

"We'll see." Jake hefted the report. "You were asking about Medicare chargebacks?"

"Yes." It was Craig Luntz who spoke, as if he also wanted to smooth over the moment. "We discovered Steven was interested in them right before he died. Made us wonder about it."

For the first time since he met Vic, Jake had the sense that Vic and this kid might be making progress finding his son's killer. They'd actually discovered Stevie's concerns about the chargebacks without his help. He held out the report. "Well, I just found this. I didn't understand it at the time. It's a comparison of what we submitted for Medicare chargebacks, and the chargebacks the insurer actually filed with Medicare."

"And there's a discrepancy?" Vic didn't sound surprised.

Jake held out the report. "See for yourself. Comparison since the beginning of the year. Stevie put this together."

Vic took the report, glanced at it, and handed it to Craig, who stared at it greedily.

Vic's face relaxed. "Did Steven say anything to you about it?"

"No. He just sent it to me and asked me to take a look."

Craig looked up from the report. "These numbers don't match. At all. The insurer is submitting two to three times higher charges to Medicare than you filed with the insurer. When did Steven send this to you?"

"The day he died." Jake heard his voice crack on the last word, and for a second, everyone was quiet, as if they wanted to be sure he held it together.

"Anything different in his behavior that day?" Vic's voice sounded kind.

"No." Jake snapped off the word as a thought came to him. "Wait." He let the memory surface. "Steven left early that day. He planned to meet someone and stopped by my office. Leaned on the door frame."

Jake hesitated at the memory, aware of Vic waiting, not pushing. "He asked me," Jake said slowly, reliving the moment, the last words his son said to him, "He asked me if I talked to Brandon Ellis regularly." Jake gestured at the report in Craig's hand. "He'd emailed me the report right before that. And the question about Brandon Ellis was the last thing he said to me."

Vic nodded slowly. "Was it now."

Jake saw something shift in Vic. It was as if Vic had pushed aside a branch and spotted a blood trail. The set of his face was different.

Jake recognized the look taking form on Vic's features. He'd seen it among his own union members when—late in contract negotiations—it was clear the company executives were on the ropes, their resolve weakening. It was the look that appeared when someone knew they were going to win.

"You think Stevie's death had something to do with these chargebacks," Jake said.

Vic hesitated. "Well, it's a damn interesting thing to look at," he said, finally.

Chapter Fifty-One

At headquarters, Vic and Craig went straight to the conference room and the whiteboard. Vic used the blue marker to draw a horizontal line. On the starting point, he wrote the day and time of the email from the insurance company that notified Trade Unions Health of their award for growing Medicare chargebacks. At the endpoint, he wrote the day and time of the scheduled meeting with Paul Drum of Veterans Health. Two inches before that endpoint, he notched a horizontal line and wrote "SK Murdered."

Vic turned to Craig. "Okay, first, we fill in this timeline. Everything Steven did, who he talked to, emailed, texted, called, and met with, starting with the moment he got that email from the insurance company. Then, we write down how the Medicare chargebacks work. Everyone involved, how they were filed, everything."

"Yep." Craig was still standing, shifting from one foot to another. For the next fifteen minutes, they discussed everything they could remember about Steven's last three days, adding each item to the line in chronological order.

Out of things to add, they fell silent. They stared at the whiteboard, now a jumbled mass of notes connected to the horizontal line by vertical lines of varying lengths.

"We need to double-check Steven's phone records." Vic looked at Craig. "He had a number of text messages with Meera. I didn't pay that much attention to them because I figured it was just boyfriend and girlfriend stuff." He gestured at the whiteboard. "Knowing this, we need to read through them carefully."

"Right." Craig frowned. "So let's get at how the Medicare chargebacks worked. The administrative part of it."

"Explain that to me," said a voice from the back of the room.

Vic and Craig spun around. Sandy Vrail stood just inside the door to the conference room, a patient look on her face. Her hair was loose but tucked behind her ears. Again, Vic hadn't heard her arrive. He glanced at her feet. Sneakers. Of course, Vic thought to himself.

Vic gestured at the whiteboard. "I think we've landed on motive for Steven's death." He explained the discrepancy in Medicare chargebacks, and how the email from the insurance company started Steven investigating them.

Sandy listened intently, nodding sometimes.

"I like it," Sandy said when Vic finished. "Money is a good motive. So is, wanting to keep the money you stole and stay out of jail. If someone knew Steven was on to them, murder might be the right solution. I agree with Craig. You need to get the administrative side of the chargebacks clarified." Sandy cocked her head, her eyes bright with a memory. "A few years ago, we caught a guy doing something similar, except in his case, he was double-ordering parts for the base motor pool. Not the military vehicles, but the ones used around base. We figured he was selling the extra parts off-base. But he was good with the paperwork, and we couldn't figure out how he was doing it."

Vic waited, interested.

"So we got him another way." Sandy paused, making Vic think she'd told the story before. "We followed the money. If he sold the parts for cash, where was it? So we looked for cash."

Craig let out a breath. "Oh yeah. That has to be why Steven was so surprised by the certificate from the insurer. I bet he was monitoring the Medicare chargebacks for TU Health, and the payments they got from Medicare and insurer matched what they charged Medicare."

Vic caught Craig's line of thinking. "So Steven understood the money flow. And if he knew that, he'd know that somewhere between TU Health and the insurance company, someone was adding fake Medicare charges, then skimming off the payments for the fake charges before the money got back to TU Health."

"Right." Sandy smiled at them. "So the question should be how does TU Health's financial system work? What's the billing and payment flow? All this is done electronically, right?"

"Right." Craig's eyes lit up. "And it's through the app they use to schedule the doctors."

Vic turned to Craig. "I thought that was just used to schedule doctor visits?"

"No, I played around with it. The doctors also use the app to write a summary of their patient visits and enter the Medicare chargeback codes. And there's a desktop version, too. But there was a tab I couldn't access called Financials, which I bet is reserved for only approved users, and they can see the cash flow through that."

Vic felt a quickening inside him. "And Brandon Ellis runs the app." He glanced at Sandy. "That's the WholePatient App. The first time we talked to Brandon, he didn't tell us about it. As if he didn't want to call attention to it."

Craig nodded vigorously. "Right."

"Brandon's in the middle of this, no matter how you cut it." Vic glanced at the whiteboard and turned back to Craig. "Tell you what. Let's call Meera Basu. Ask her how she uses the app, what data she puts into it. Just to confirm. We can ask her if she can access the financial section."

"Sure." Craig hesitated, frowning.

Vic stared at him. "What?"

"The interview with Oskar Glimt." Craig glanced at the whiteboard as if he was steadying himself. "Glimt told us that Fireman's Health and Veterans Health also use the software. If that's true, Brandon's app manages the Medicare chargebacks and the money flow to *all* the non-profits."

"There's the nexus." Sandy smiled.

Craig looked down, a small patch of color on his cheeks. "I'll see if I can reach Meera to confirm that." Craig glanced at Vic and left the room.

When the door clicked shut, neither Sandy nor Vic said anything for a few moments. Sandy studied the whiteboard.

"You're making good progress," she said, finally. "I can see why you like Craig."

"Getting there. He just needs the right credentials."

"Well, he's got them now." Sandy turned to him. "I was going to make the announcement about his promotion today, but I thought I would wait until Liz got back."

"Thanks." Vic was surprised at how proud he felt for Craig. "And one other thing." He searched for the right way to raise the topic. "It's unusual for Liz to take off like this. I mean, completely out of character. Did she say anything to you?"

"Only an apologetic email saying she had some personal business that couldn't wait. She just needed a few days."

Vic stared at her. "She was apologetic?"

Sandy started to smile and stopped. "That's out of character too?"

"It's more unusual than taking personal days in the middle of a murder case. I don't mean it in a bad way. It's just how she is." Vic felt a distinct unease.

"I didn't think of it that way, but I don't know Liz as well as you."

Vic pushed away the thought but couldn't get rid of it entirely. He gestured at the whiteboard. "Anything I can explain?"

Sandy asked two more questions, and as Vic finished responding, Craig shot back into the room, his excitement contagious.

"I talked to Meera," Craig said breathlessly, almost interrupting them. "And yes, she confirmed they use the app to record the Medicare chargebacks. They do it as part of writing up their patient notes. She was told it saved the non-profit from the paperwork. And she can't access the financials tab."

Vic saw the method unfold in front of him. "So, as doctor visits are added to the app, Brandon Ellis adds false chargeback codes. When the repayments arrive, he siphons off the income from the false chargebacks and forwards the rest of the cash to the non-profit. The non-profits don't see anything wrong and are repaid exactly for the charges they made."

Sandy nodded. "Impressive, really. And since it's an app, he could automate the whole process. Write an algorithm to handle it. How much are we talking about?"

Vic walked up to the whiteboard. "The report Jake Kittery gave us showed the insurer's Medicare chargebacks compared to what Trade Unions Health actually charged." Vic wrote "$500K" on the whiteboard and turned around.

"Good money if you can get it." Sandy grinned.

"And there's more to it." Craig glanced at Vic. "Sorry, Vic, I didn't get a chance to mention this. But there's a pattern to Steven's report. There was a small overcharge to Medicare in January, nothing in February, and then the chargebacks almost doubled each month from there. I think someone tested the system in January, waited through February to see if anyone noticed or said anything, and then ramped up the fake chargebacks each month after that."

Vic hid a smile. "Right. Then repeat the process with two more non-profits, and you get to real money. That pattern also explains why all this surfaced now. I bet the fake chargeback scheme started this January."

Vic turned and stared at the whiteboard. "The monkey wrench was the certificate the insurance company sent Steven for the increasing Medicare chargebacks. Steven might never have noticed any overcharges otherwise. Steven starts asking questions, and Brandon has to find a way to keep him quiet." Vic looked at them both. "Should be easy enough to prove, we just need the financial records for Brandon's company. There will be cash no one can explain, or inflated revenue numbers." Vic frowned. "But there is one problem. How did Brandon find out Steven was on to him? Oskar Glimt said he didn't tell anyone Steven was looking into the overcharges."

"Maybe the insurance company told Brandon." Craig went to the whiteboard and wrote the name of the insurance company. "Maybe after that email exchange between Steven and the executives at the insurance company, one of them talked to Brandon to see if he knew why Steven was arguing so much. They would know Brandon's app was the focal point of all this."

Vic nodded. "Good. Call them, and I'll run down Drum, the CEO of

Veterans Health. Steven was scheduled to talk to him but never made it. Maybe Steven said something to Drum on the phone, and Drum passed it along to Brandon. And then we drag Brandon in here on his ear."

Sandy held up a hand. "Not so fast. This is way out of our comfort zone. We need help. We need techs to spot the algorithm in the code that runs the app, and we need forensic accountants to find the defrauded cash. That'll take time. We need the FBI."

Vic opened his mouth to argue but saw the sense in what Sandy was saying. He'd already met with Brandon's lawyer, and he was absolutely sure Brandon wasn't going to confess to killing Steven or defrauding Medicare. His lawyer was too smart to let him.

Vic felt the case slipping away from him. "If the FBI steps in, they'll prosecute. We won't get a shot at Brandon."

Sandy settled her gaze on him. "What matters the most? Jailing Brandon or us having jurisdiction? We don't have the right resources. The FBI does. They do investigations like this all the time. I'll call them as soon as we're done here."

Vic knew she was right, but he still didn't like it. "And what if Brandon gets wind the FBI is investigating? Takes off?"

Sandy was quiet for several seconds. "That's on them, not us."

Vic watched her. "And you're okay with that?"

"It's the right call, Vic. You need to live with that."

Chapter Fifty-Two

Carty Swain woke to the changing sounds of the aircraft engines as the airplane settled into its final approach into New Orleans. After Isabella left his hotel room, he'd headed straight for the airport and found a discount airline that flew direct to New Orleans. Luck still with him, he'd been able to purchase a seat. He'd fallen asleep almost immediately. Now he wiped his lips and looked around the airplane.

As he'd waited to board, Isabella had texted him to say that she and Liz had reserved seats for the next morning, flying through Charlotte. Carty was too annoyed to respond. This close to ending things, he wanted the pieces to fall into place faster. He wanted to know. Had the doubloons been sitting in an empty house for all these years?

He was also unsettled by Isabella. The meeting in his hotel room had unnerved him. Isabella was too confident, her movements almost choreographed and practiced. He didn't know what to make of it.

He took a deep breath. "Around the bend to the end," he told himself. He was close. He couldn't stop now.

Chapter Fifty-Three

Vic woke before dawn the next morning and stared at the ceiling, listening to Anne's gentle breaths. Sandy had emailed the evening before to say she wanted him in a mid-morning meeting with the FBI. It was the official handover of all the evidence he, Craig, and Liz had collected.

He considered skipping the meeting and letting the FBI figure it out for themselves. He rose and swung his legs over the edge of the bed and stared at his white feet. The thought was petty, and as he'd known the day before, Sandy was right. To prove Medicare fraud, they needed FBI resources.

With a sigh, he rose and went into the bathroom to shower. Later, downstairs, he toasted two slices of wheat bread, slathered them with butter, and ate standing over the sink.

He couldn't get Liz out of his mind. Her behavior was so different than anything he was used to. He glanced at the clock on the microwave and thought about calling her but decided not to. It would only anger her. Instead, he drank water and placed the glass in the sink, listening to Anne and Lettie moving about upstairs. Before he could stop himself, he collected his service weapon from the locked drawer in the hall table and closed the front door behind him. Once he was driving, he called and apologized to Anne for leaving early.

The meeting with the FBI lasted through lunch, Vic's thoughts never straying far from Liz. But the meeting went better than Vic expected. Three FBI agents arrived, took Vic's investigation seriously, and, to Vic's surprise, promised to only focus on Brandon Ellis' app and the financial side of his business. Vic and his team retained the murder investigation. By the end of the meeting, Craig and the youngest member of the FBI team were huddled over a computer, and Sandy left the meeting without giving Vic an "I told you so" look.

When the FBI were finished, Vic followed them out of the building and slid into his car, Liz forefront in his mind.

Thirty-five minutes later, north of the city, he exited Ohio River Boulevard, and cruised the treelined streets of Sewickley. He'd only been to Liz's house one other time, but he found it easily. It was a small house with a smaller yard, shoehorned among others on a street shrunk by curbside parking.

Vic parked in the first space he found and returned to Liz's house. He climbed the steps to the front porch and rang the doorbell, wondering exactly how Liz would react to his arrival. He knew the chance of her being glad to see him was, at best, fifty-fifty.

For several moments nothing happened, and then the door swung open. Vic blinked. "Dr. Meera Basu?"

Meera stared up at him. She wore a thick, white terry-cloth robe. "Detective Lenoski?"

"Yes. Um, I was expecting Liz. Detective Timmons."

Meera flashed a smile, enjoying Vic's surprise at finding Meera in Liz's house. "I apologize, she isn't here."

"But you are." Vic was unsure what to do. He noticed the bruises on her face had yellowed and were fading.

"I am." They stared at one another for a few seconds, until Meera stepped aside, and gestured him inside. "You should come in. Liz is out of town, but she left something for you. She said it's for you only, although she thought you wouldn't show up for several days."

Meera closed the front door and led him into the kitchen. A mug of tea sat on the small table. Vic glanced around. The kitchen was uncluttered and clean, with no sign of breakfast preparation.

Meera followed his gaze. "I was feeling a bit nauseous this morning. I got as far as tea." She gestured toward the mug.

"No problem. I'm just surprised to see you here."

Meera considered him. "Well, you will remember that I had to leave my father's."

"I remember."

"Liz offered me a room here until I can find a place of my own. She said she raised a child by herself, so she knows the difficulties. She was..." Meera glanced at the ceiling, "Very direct about it."

And this, Vic thought, was Liz in a nutshell. Big-hearted enough to open her house, hard-headed enough not to give Meera a choice. "She raised her son alone. Jayvon is his name. He's in college now. She did a good job. It's hard by yourself."

Meera nodded. "Right now, I'm just glad for the room."

Vic wondered where Levon fit in. Levon had lived with Liz for several years, but he seemed to have disappeared. "You said Liz went out of town. Where did she go?"

"New Orleans."

Vic stared at her, struggling to get his head around Meera's answer. "Did Levon go with her?"

Meera blinked. "Who?"

"Doesn't matter. You said she left something for me?"

Meera turned and went to a cupboard. She opened it, removed a white envelope and handed it to him. "Liz said she would be back tomorrow night. She said if she wasn't, that you would come here sometime after that. She told me to give it to you then. It all sounded mysterious. I guess you're just getting it a few days early."

"That's okay." Vic tapped the envelope against his hand. The envelope was sealed, his name written in Liz's tight hand across the front. He noticed Liz hadn't written his title, only his name. It made the letter more personal, and he wondered at the reason.

"Okay, well, thank you, Meera. I'll get going." He turned and started for the door, Meera following.

When he stepped onto the porch, Meera stood at the open door, holding the doorknob.

"Detective Lenoski?"

Vic turned back to her.

"I wanted to thank you for what you did at my parent's house. I knew you weren't really arresting my father. But it was very helpful."

Vic considered her. "And I'm glad you went to Steven's parents and told them about the baby. You didn't have to do that."

"When I called you, I was worried I was getting Steven's father arrested."

Vic smiled. "No, that was on him. But no one got hurt. And I think Steven's mother will want to help you, like Liz."

"She'd never met me, but she seemed happy at the news."

"It's probably exactly what she needs right now."

Vic started to turn away from her.

"Wait."

Vic stopped his turn and waited.

Meera stared at the ground. "Is there any news? I mean, about what happened to Steven? Are you making progress?"

Vic noted the way Meera phrased her questions, avoiding the word murder. "We think so," he said carefully, the long meeting with the FBI fresh in his mind.

Meera looked up, her eyes pleading.

Vic felt she was owed more than platitudes. "Yes, we've been interviewing, and we've found what might be the reason Steven was attacked. It makes one person a very good suspect."

Meera frowned. "Good. I was worried what happened was random and might never be solved. I couldn't think of anyone close to Steven who might want to kill him. Like any of the doctors or Brandon."

Vic stared at her, absorbing her words, his heart thumping. "Just out of interest, what makes you say that about Brandon Ellis?"

"Oh, he's all talk. He likes to make out that he came up with the idea of the non-profits to serve groups like unions and firefighters, but the whole thing was Steven's idea. He wrote a paper about it for one of his MBA classes. He showed it to me one time." She smiled. "He only got a B. The professor didn't like that you couldn't get rich off the idea. But Steven didn't care about that. In the paper, Steven even suggested using an app to centralize the bookkeeping across the non-profits. He had the whole business model worked out."

"Then how did Brandon get involved?"

"Well, Steven and Brandon were friends in graduate school. They both got jobs at the insurance company. Steven told Brandon about the idea when he wrote the paper. Brandon liked it and started talking to the insurance company executives about it. He convinced them it could work and secured funding to get the non-profits off the ground. That's what he's good at. Convincing people to do things. You need that, but I don't think Brandon's ever had an original thought beyond how great he is."

Vic wasn't sure what to do with Meera's opinion. "That's useful," he said, thinking through Meera's words. "Wait, so how did Oskar Glimt and Paul Drum get involved?"

"I think Paul Drum was the first hire. Oskar came afterwards. Oskar used to hang out with Steven sometimes."

Vic tamped down his surprise. Oskar hadn't said anything about being friendly with Steven. He'd actually left Vic with the opposite impression. "Really? Did they meet in graduate school as well?"

"No, I think Oskar was at CMU. Studied multimedia or something. He wanted to go to Hollywood, make documentaries, I think."

"But he ended up running Firefighters Health."

"I guess so. I don't know how all that worked."

Vic filed away the information about Oskar. "Thanks for your thoughts, Meera. Anyway, we have a way to go. But we're making progress, and we've brought in some added resources to help us. I know it's frustrating, but sometimes it takes longer than you expect."

"Sure, I understand." Meera nodded at the letter. "You should check that."

Vic held up the letter in thanks, nodded, and headed for his car.

Behind the steering wheel, he tore off one end of the envelope and shook the contents onto the passenger seat. A single sheet of paper dropped in his lap. Vic unfolded it to find a handwritten letter, dated that morning.

Vic,

If you're reading this, something went wrong. Here's the background: I was contacted by a private detective from Texas. Her details are below. She claims to be working for the nephew of Carty Swain, my husband's patrol partner. Carty disappeared the same night as Demond, during Katrina. The PI has some stupid story about Carty calling his nephew the afternoon before he disappeared, and telling the nephew he and Demond hid something for him. According to the PI, the nephew is only now chasing this down, and was wondering if there was anywhere Demond might have hidden something for Carty. It's all a croc of shit and about as believable as the Texas PI ID she showed me when we met. But something is happening, and if I can learn something about Carty, then I might get closer to what happened to Demond. I have to go along with it. Normally I would tell the PI to screw off. So I'm taking the PI to a house that belongs to my sister-in-law's husband. The address is below. It's the only place I can think of that Demond might hide something for Carty. The building was damaged during Katrina, and no one has lived there since. I'm flying down there today and will take the PI to the house tomorrow morning. I'm doing this slow so I can protect myself. I've got some strings I can pull. But, if you're reading this, something screwed up. You'll be able to figure out what.

Liz

PS Yes, I asked Meera to stay at my house. Do you have a problem with that?

Vic studied the name of the PI and the house address and the name of the homeowner appended to the bottom of the sheet. They meant nothing to him. He breathed, trying to loosen the tension he'd built up reading the letter. She was right. The PI's story was ridiculous, but he understood why she needed to play it out. He looked at the windshield. He couldn't see why Liz might be in danger, but the entire scenario was so weird he couldn't count it out.

He took a breath and let it out slowly. He knew what he had to do.

He called Liz, but she didn't pick up. He left a message telling her to call him. He suspected she wouldn't. This was a personal quest for Liz, and she never talked about her past. Even to him. As long as he'd known her, when it came to her life before Pittsburgh, she was a shut book.

Vic placed the letter on the passenger seat and photographed it with his camera. He attached the photograph to a text addressed to Sandy and added three short sentences:

See the letter from Liz. Need to go to New Orleans and give her back-up. Return in a day or two.

He hit send and researched flights. He found a direct flight leaving in two hours, but it was full. The best he could do was a flight leaving for Charlotte in four hours, with a five-hour layover and an arrival in New Orleans well after midnight.

His phone dinged. Sandy's text asked if he had called Liz. He responded yes, but she wasn't picking up. Her reply was to take the days if he needed them.

He booked the flight and called Anne, explained the situation, and she told him to get on the next airplane. Vic started his car, knowing he had just about enough time to go home and grab an overnight bag. He accelerated as he left Sewickley, glad to be moving.

Chapter Fifty-Four

The first leg of Vic's flight was uneventful, and they arrived in Charlotte on time. During the layover, Vic wandered the halls of the airport, bought an overpriced sandwich, and hoped his checked bag would make the connection. If it didn't, his weapon would be lost with his clean underwear. Outside, the darkness was complete. Some months earlier, at Jimmy Pronghorn's suggestion, he'd bought a poetry book by Gary Snyder. He tried to read, but the metaphor or allegory—he wasn't sure which—about axe handles escaped him. He gave up.

He'd sent Liz at least two text messages since he arrived in Charlotte and received no answer. Despite everything he knew about Liz's personality, her lack of response annoyed him. It seemed over the top.

The trip then unraveled. First, an announcement about a mechanical check on the airplane. A half-hour delay. An hour later, he noticed that his departure time, without any accompanying announcement, showed a two-hour delay. Fifteen minutes later, an announcement confirmed the fact, eliciting a collective groan from everyone seated at the gate.

It was four in the morning when they finally boarded, and another forty-five minutes before the airplane lifted off. After their arrival in New Orleans, Vic waited another forty-five minutes until it was clear his checked bag hadn't made the trip. He filled out the required forms and wasted another thirty minutes renting a car from a young man with multiple ear and nose studs, who was as functional in his job as a stoned clerk at a twenty-four-hour convenience store.

When Vic pulled into morning traffic, it was six-forty-five in the morning.

Liz still hadn't responded to his texts, even the passive-aggressive one he'd sent saying he'd landed in New Orleans and was 'coming to find her.' He was sweaty, red-eyed, and needed a shave. His mouth tasted of raw garlic.

He wanted to punch the person behind the serene GPS voice who directed him, relentlessly, into specific highway lanes.

On the radio, Arlo Guthrie started singing about riding on the City of New Orleans.

Vic lowered the window and spit.

Chapter Fifty-Five

Carty Swain woke with a start at dawn. He was wide awake in an instant, staring at a bright red bar of sunlight lying across the hotel window. Today was the end of his journey. Or perhaps the start of a new one. The feeling was electric to him.

He showered and dressed, glancing at the clock every few minutes. He checked the revolver he'd found in Demond's storage area. He'd changed the bullets, careful to wipe each one to remove fingerprints. The gun went into a small duffel with his electronic equipment and earpiece. In the lobby, he grabbed a Granola bar and a cup of coffee from the breakfast area on the way to his car. Isabella and Liz would head to the building Liz said was the most likely hiding place, and Carty wanted to be near their hotel when they left. Isabella had set up her Google Maps so Carty could follow her movements and location, but an innate fear of losing them made him want to be close from the start.

It was the best they could do, given that Liz had refused to give Isabella the house address. Carty had warned Isabella not to press it. He hoped that Isabella set up her microphone correctly so he could listen to their conversation.

Despite what he thought was a good view of the parking lot exit from Isabella's hotel, the traffic was busy enough that he didn't see Liz and Isabella leave their hotel at seven-thirty. Fortunately, he checked his phone a few minutes after their planned departure time and saw her icon moving east on Route 10, headed away from the airport. With a stifled curse, he pushed his car into gear and followed.

As he drove, he told himself this was a better situation. When he was this far back, Liz couldn't see he was following. He kept Isabella's icon on the map equidistant to the blue dot representing his own movement.

They drove for more than forty minutes, heading south off Route 10, and gradually, Carty guessed where they were headed. They cut through the lower ninth ward, one of the areas worst affected by Katrina's flooding, and turned south. Liz led them through a warren of streets, some with houses boarded up or condemned until they entered Holy Cross, a neighborhood on the southern tip of the lower ninth ward. The area had flooded during Katrina, but not with the same devastating consequences.

Carty slowed. Isabella's icon on the map had stopped. The houses in this area were small, many sitting on blocks, surrounded by postage-stamp yards that showed no signs of landscaping. The buildings were a mix, some painted and well-kept, others boarded up with flapping plastic covering holes in walls and roofs.

A block from Isabella's icon, Carty parked and studied the block ahead. A few seconds later, he spotted the tail of Isabella's rental car sticking out from a parking space alongside a tiny, white shotgun shack with boarded-up windows and an overgrown yard. A ragged chain-link fence surrounded the house. No one moved on the street; a blue, cloudless sky hovered overhead.

"Dammit," Carty breathed to himself. He couldn't see any real cover, and he needed to be within twenty yards to pick up Isabella's microphone. Finally, taking the risk, he cruised just past the house and parked on the far side of a large, half-dead tree. He hoped the tree trunk was wide enough to block the sight lines from the house.

He plugged in his earpiece and fiddled with his receiver. Isabella's voice leapt into his ear. "This place belongs to your sister-in-law?"

"Yes, Demond's sister. She and her husband. They never moved back in after Katrina. The plan was always to fix it up and sell it, but they never got around to it."

Carty nodded to himself. That explained why he hadn't found the listing during his property search. Demond's sister probably took her husband's name when she married. It then occurred to him he hadn't known Demond had a sister. He'd never mentioned it.

He'd never asked, either.

"Sister shmister," he said softly to himself.

"Wouldn't your sister-in-law have known if your husband hid something here?"

Carty smiled. Isabella didn't miss a trick.

"Not if they hid it the day Katrina hit. They'd evacuated."

Carty thought that Liz's speech had slowed and taken on more of a southern lilt, as if her return to New Orleans had drawn her into a past life.

"And you have no idea what Carty's nephew thinks is hidden here?" Liz's tone had a needling, skeptical tone to it.

"None." Isabella sounded dispirited. "And this place has been cleaned out. Closets, dressers, everything. It won't take long to search."

"There is one place."

Carty heard footsteps. "Up there." Liz's voice sounded distant. "See that? It's the attic access. No one goes up there. The access and the attic are too small."

"How do we even get up there?" Isabella still sounded as if she'd lost hope.

"Out back. There's a storage shed. There used to be a wooden ladder there."

For the next two minutes, neither Isabella nor Liz spoke. Carty heard the slam of a door, and a little later a scraping sound as if something was being dragged across a floor.

Liz's voice broke the silence. "There's a trick to this. You use the ladder to push the panel out of the way, then climb the ladder and push the panel far enough aside to get up in there."

Scraping sounds and a thud. "Oh, that worked perfectly!" Isabella was excited again. Carty breathed a sigh of relief.

"I'll take a look." Liz's voice.

Carty waited, resisting the impulse to text Isabella. As he weighed his phone in his hand, it vibrated. A text from Isabella. "Liz in attic, only possible place," was the note.

Carty shifted in his seat. They were so close. To what? The entire collection? Nothing?

Static cackled in his earphone, a couple of words he couldn't make out in the middle of it. Liz and Isabella talking urgently to each other in mumbles.

"What is it?" Isabella's voice suddenly, very clear.

Liz's voice, garbled. Carty guessed she was still in the attic, talking through the opening in the ceiling.

"I can take it so you can come down." Isabella again.

Something, thought Carty.

More scraping sounds and several heavy breaths from Isabella. A clunk. Silence, a creak, and silence again.

"It's an old ammo box." Liz's voice, clear as a bell. She must have descended the ladder. "It's a World War Two type. Demond's grandfather served."

Carty pictured the box. Green metal, handle on the top, latch closure. About twice the size of a ream of paper sitting on one side.

"It was near the opening, between a couple of joists."

"Can we open it?" Isabella, excitement in her voice.

"Sure." A loud snap. Carty guessed a spring-loaded latch.

Liz's voice again. "Christ. Gold coins."

"Doubloons," echoed Isabella.

The awe and surprise in both of their voices was palpable.

Carty squeezed the doubloon around his neck with his fingers for luck and pulled Demond's revolver from his duffel. He slid out of the car, gulping a breath, his stomach tight. This was it. Liz couldn't walk out of the house. She would claim the coins, refuse to give them up. He was sure of it. As Carty topped the last step to the door, what Isabella said pricked him. She'd known the coins were doubloons. How? He pushed it from his mind.

Carty turned the door handle and stepped into a hallway. Stale air of a house rarely used. A vague smell of mildew. He tugged out his earpiece. Liz and Isabella were talking at the end of the hall.

Speed, thought Carty. Not the time to worry about the floor squeaking. He hurried down the hall, past several doors shut or ajar, and into what was left of the kitchen.

Isabella and Liz were squatting on the floor, staring into an open green

251

metal box. Something glinted inside. Liz looked up sharply and shot upright, frowning, her lips twisted. "You," she managed to say, the word sounded strangled by disbelief. Her eyes went to the gun in Carty's hand.

"It had to be you," Carty crooned in his best Frank Sinatra impression.

"Where's Demond?" Her words were hoarse, but anger sparked in her eyes.

Isabella, squatting between them, rose slowly and daintily stepped to one side. She seemed to understand this was between Carty and Liz. That whatever it was ran much deeper than coins.

"Where's Demond?" Liz barked the words and stepped toward him. Carty raised the revolver, stopping her.

"As dead as Katrina." Even through the intensity of the moment, Carty heard poetry in his words. Appreciated himself for saying them.

"And you lived." She spat the words, glanced at the coins, and drilled her gaze into him. "Over this?"

"That's on you." Carty made a dismissive motion with his free hand. "You kept telling him to be honest. To do the right thing. You should have let him be himself. Demond always had secrets." He hoisted the gun. "Like this gun. Stolen. He kept it for a throwaway."

Liz stood straighter. "But you're the one holding it. You're the one blaming me. For what? And where is Demond?"

"I'm so sorry to interrupt."

The voice came from the hallway, and everyone froze. Carty recognized the self-satisfied tone, the oily diction. He stepped sideways to see the entrance from the hall, his gun still pointed at Liz. Luis Manuel Arias Vargas entered the kitchen, a large silver handgun pointed directly at Carty.

Carty couldn't fathom how his boss got from Costa Rica to this hovel.

"Luis," whispered Isabella.

"My dear," Vargas replied to Isabella. "It is such a pleasure to see you. I have truly missed you."

It was everything Carty could do not to vomit. There it was. Luis and Isabella. The times he'd taken Isabella to meet Luis. The willingness of Luis to approve Isabella's trip to the U.S. Isabella's new confidence in herself, in her sexuality.

It was like looking at a favorite painting for the thousandth time and suddenly seeing the horror the painter actually wanted you to see.

"You," he managed to say to Isabella.

"Me," Isabella replied and shrugged. She shifted so Carty could see her face. Her eyes gleamed, but the look was pure disgust. "Do you think you were the only one following me on Google Maps? That I couldn't tell what you were planning for me?" Her features hardened.

Carty knew in that second Isabella detested him.

"Come now, Isabella." Luis's smile was glued in place. "We have better things to do than settle old scores. Why don't you take those doubloons to the car. You know what to do. I will resolve things here."

Isabella squatted and flipped the lid of the metal box back into place. Snapped the latch. She needed both hands to lift the box from the ground, and she struggled with the weight as she walked.

"Be careful," Isabella said, as she passed Luis.

"Of course. And I will see you later, my love," called Luis, as Isabella disappeared into the hall.

Carty tried to settle his racing heart. He knew there was only one outcome. He had to stall. "How did you know?"

Luis considered his question. "I suppose I owe you an explanation. It was almost too easy. You showed me your doubloon, the one you claimed your father gave you? But you didn't know where he got it. As I said at the time, that is impossible. Not with a coin like that."

Carty remembered them sitting on the country club veranda, the taste of the cigar in his mouth, the glaze of the whiskey they'd drunk. "But connecting it to me here?"

Luis shrugged. "I knew about the collection lost during Katrina. I told you about it at the time. I searched, and what did I find? Photographs of two police officers who disappeared during the storm. I looked at those photographs. A Black man and a white one, and the white man looked like my new head of security, Devon Blair. But in that photograph, his name was Carty Swain."

Luis paused and considered Liz. Carty knew he was trying to work out why Liz was there. Carty knew he only had a few seconds. He had to act. His revolver was still pointed at Liz, but he shifted slightly, trying to shorten the distance the gun would need to travel to point at Luis. He sensed Liz had also moved, closer to the back door.

Luis shrugged and turned his attention back to Carty. "Why does a man change his name and move to a foreign country when he is a lost hero? The answer is simple. He is running from something. Also, if you had the coins, you would not need to work for me. So, when Isabella told me you wanted her help in New Orleans, and by then, Isabella and I were already, shall I say, allies? I knew you were on the trail of the collection."

Luis' toothy smile evolved into a somehow elegant snarl. "But that is a collection I would like to have. So what shall we do?"

Carty focused on what he had to say, to keep his voice even. "Perhaps we could start with this?" Slowly, he reached inside his shirt and tugged out his doubloon, holding it so Vargas could see it. He flipped the chain over his head, letting the coin and chain sit in the palm of his free hand. This had worked once before. He remembered the wind howling around the shack. Demond, watching him from a few feet away.

Vargas' gaze snapped onto the gold.

"Take a closer look. You've got all of them now." Carty tossed the coin lazily toward Vargas in a high arch.

Chapter Fifty-Six

Vic wanted a bottle of water but wasn't about to waste the time needed to buy one. He didn't know when Liz would arrive at the address she'd provided in her letter, but he guessed he was late already. It was unlikely Liz, or her fake PI would linger over breakfast and run a couple of errands on the way. He simply drove as fast as he could.

The street that matched the house address, when Vic found it, ran in a perfectly straight line for multiple blocks, something unusual for anyone from Pittsburgh. Reading house numbers, Vic slowed, noting the tail of a newer car sticking out of a gravel parking space alongside the house with the correct number. As he did, a dark-haired young woman exited the door from the house, lugging a green metal box with both hands. She struggled under the weight, the box bumping the front of her thighs, and lowered it to the ground next to the car's passenger door.

Everything about her and what she was doing looked out of place. She was too well-dressed for the neighborhood, too pretty, the car too new and shiny. As Vic slid past, he also didn't like the newer model Range Rover parked across the street. Vic pulled to the curb ahead of a car just beyond a large tree and cut the engine. He slid out of the car and returned to the house.

The young woman was in the process of walking around the back of her car toward the driver's door. The box was nowhere to be seen, and Vic assumed it was already inside the car.

"Hey," Vic called to her.

The woman stutter-stepped but kept walking.

"I'm talking to you." Vic used his command voice and she stopped, her hand on the driver's side door.

"I'm looking for Liz Timmons." Vic kept his voice sharp, giving himself time to approach her.

"I don't know who you're talking about."

Her words were rushed and scared, a poor lie.

"Sure you do. You're Isabella, the bullshit private investigator."

Isabella's face flushed. Vic reached the car trunk and patted the driver's side rear corner.

"I don't know what you're talking about." Isabella yanked on the door handle, opening the door and keeping it between them. A gunshot echoed from the house, then another. Vic spun and ran for the front door. He was up the three steps and onto the small porch in a moment. He hesitated by the front door and reached for his weapon, knowing as he made the movement he didn't have it. It was inside his lost suitcase. A door slammed, and Vic looked to his right. From the house across the street, a squat Black man with a barrel chest, blue jeans, and a white shirt jumped the patio steps and ran toward him. The front door beside Vic started to open. Vic settled back against the wall of the house. A man backed through the doorway, closing the door behind him. Vic registered the man held a weapon in his left hand. As the man turned toward him, Vic separated from the wall of the house, planted his right foot, and used the turn of his hips to punch the man—just behind the point of the chin—with a right cross.

The man went down like a bowling pin, his body rigid. The gun skittered away, and Vic kicked it off the porch.

"Police! Don't move. Show me your hands."

The stocky Black man from across the street was halfway up the front walk, training a weapon on him. A badge dangled on a chain from his neck.

"Shots fired," Vic called to him. "I'm a police officer. My partner, Liz Timmons, is inside."

An engine roared, and Isabella, tires spitting gravel, slew backwards into the street, the car bouncing over the curb.

"Hey," shouted the police officer. He swung his gun from Vic and raced toward the car as it shuddered to a stop in the road. Dust from the parking space swirled over the trunk the moment Isabella shifted the transmission. The tires squealed, but Isabella wrestled the car forward and roared down the street.

The police officer, distracted, stopped in the middle of the road and stared after it. Vic stepped over the stiff body on the ground and backheeled it enough to open the front door. He darted into a dank hallway that led straight to the back of the house.

"Liz," he shouted.

"In here."

Vic strode down the hallway into the kitchen. Liz rose from a squat next to the wall, staring at a man on the ground. Blood leaked from two holes in his chest.

Vic thought Liz looked lost. "What happened?"

Liz frowned at him. "What the hell are you doing here?" She crossed to the man and checked his pulse. Her mouth tightened.

"I came to help you."

Liz stood and gestured at the body. "Great timing."

Vic stared at the prone man's white shirt. "Who's that?"

The police officer stepped into the room from the hall, pointing his gun at Vic. "I told you to hold."

Liz looked from one to the other. "Cleets. This is my partner from Pittsburgh. He's a cop. He thinks he's helping me."

"Oh." Cleets lowered his weapon.

Liz gestured at Cleets. "Vic, this is Cleets, Sergeant Otis Leclair to you. My brother-in-law. His wife owns this piece of crap house."

Vic recognized the name from the bottom of Liz's letter. He was about to reach out his hand, but something flared in Liz's eyes. "Where the hell is the girl? Isabella?"

Vic knew Liz's look. He let Cleets answer her question.

Cleets cleared his throat. "Uh, she got away."

Liz gave him a look that would have withered a Sequoia. "And the other guy? I think his name is Vargas."

"Handcuffed. To the front porch."

"Well, that's something." Liz let out a long breath.

Vic gestured at the man lying on the floor. "Again. Who's that?"

Liz stared at the body for several seconds before answering. "Demond's old partner. Carty Swain. He and Demond went missing during Katrina. Turns out Carty ran to Costa Rica. Worked for the Vargas person outside."

"You okay?" Vic watched her.

Liz raised her eyes to him. She looked lost. "How'd you catch Vargas?"

"I was trying to corner Isabella at her car when I heard shots. I went to the front door, and Vargas came out. I, um, punched him." Vic avoided Liz's eyes.

"Where's your gun?"

"Airline lost my luggage."

"And you?" Liz looked at Cleets. "I thought you put video in here. How come you were late?"

Cleets also avoided Liz's eyes. "The video set-up was glitchy. Kept freezing. I heard the shots."

Liz raised her eyes to the ceiling for several seconds before turning to Vic. "That's your question, Vic? Am I okay? Well, let's see, I had to dive out the back door so I didn't get shot, because my brother-in-law can't figure out how to plug in a video jack. You show up and punch a guy because you lost your gun at the airport. You had to *punch* a guy. Carty is dead, so I can't find out what happened to Demond. And both of you, both of you, let the Chiquita, Isabella, get away with a fortune in gold coins. Does it sound like I'm okay?"

Cleets straightened up. "We'll catch her."

Liz looked from Cleets to Vic in disgust. "And it's men who insist on running the world."

Vic frowned. "Wait. Gold coins?"

Chapter Fifty-Seven

The third time Vic finished giving his statement to a New Orleans PD detective, it was almost three in the afternoon. He was tired and felt grimy. Cleets had promised to move them through the procedures following the shooting quickly. To Vic, it was anything but. At three-thirty, Vic was led from his interrogation room to a conference room. Liz waited inside, the first time he'd seen her since they'd been in the kitchen with Carty's body.

Liz was talking to a man in his fifties, heavy set, with thinning sandy hair plastered to his pink scalp. His white uniform shirt was pressed into knife-edge creases. He looked overfed and sure of his position. Despite that, he rose when Vic entered.

Liz waved a hand at the man. "Vic, this is Deputy Chief Jeremiah Goodwin."

"Call me Jerry," the man said. He turned to Liz. "That's all I get?"

Liz looked annoyed. "Jerry was my first commander when I made detective."

"Damn right." Jerry's blue eyes twinkled as he gazed at Vic. "You got to jackhammer concrete to get anything out of her. Ever had better luck?"

Vic liked Jerry right away. "Not much."

Jerry waved Vic to a seat. Jerry sat as well, settling in, a man used to command. "We're cutting you two free. We've got Vargas, that's a start, and maybe he can lead us to Isabella."

"She got away clean?" Vic was surprised. As the police had arrived, he'd asked Liz where Isabella might go, and she'd said that both the rental car and hotel were in Isabella's name. She should have been easy to track down.

Jerry interlocked his hands on the tabletop. "She was smart enough not to go back to her hotel, and we found the car abandoned near the train station. Four trains left in the window of time when she would have been there; we have people meeting each train at their first stop."

Vic thought about it. "How did you find her car so quickly?"

Jerry tapped his nose in a knowing way. "She was in such a hurry she parked beside a fire hydrant. Boutique owner called it in. She hates when people park there."

Vic thought about that. "Actually, I bet Isabella parked there on purpose. It's a head fake. She wanted you to find the car quickly. She knew if you did, you'd guess she took the train. Better move would be to check for stores selling luggage within a couple of blocks of the car. I saw her carrying the coins out of the house, and they were too heavy for her. She needs an easier way to transport them. I bet she left the car where you'd find it, bought a roller case from a nearby store, and took public transport somewhere else. Like the bus station. Find the store and you can get a description of the bag and what time she bought it. Track her from there."

Jerry stared at Vic, his blue eyes unblinking. After several seconds, he turned to Liz. "This Yankee might be okay."

Liz let out a slow breath. "He has his moments. Just not today."

Vic realized he had about thirty questions to ask Jerry about Liz.

Liz cut him off before he could start. "Good catching up, Jerry, but we have to go. We have a flight back to Pittsburgh in a couple of hours."

Surprised, Vic looked at Liz. She ignored him, still talking to Jerry. "I booked us both on a flight leaving at six. Direct. No need to be here anymore."

"We'll pump Vargas for everything he knows about Carty," Jerry told her. "Maybe that will lead to something about Demond." He paused, watching Liz. Vic saw affection in his eyes. "I haven't forgotten about Demond," Jerry added gently.

Liz rose. "Thanks, Jerry."

They all rose.

"I'll have someone run you both out to the airport," Jerry said.

From the way he said it, Vic knew Jerry wanted to add something, but it took him a moment to work around to it.

"Liz, next time you have something like this, call me. I can bring in the cavalry for you."

Liz looked like she was about to say something sharp, but Vic saw her relent. "Thanks, but I'm hoping this does it."

"You like Pittsburgh, then?" Jerry looked like a concerned parent.

Liz took a moment to respond. "It's been good to me."

"I'm glad. Now, let's get you two to the airport. Vic, you give me your keys, and I'll have someone return your rental car for you."

* * *

Liz was silent for the first part of the drive, saying nothing as the car swung by her hotel and she collected her luggage. She just stared out of the side window and ignored the young, unformed officer at the wheel.

Vic thought about the right way to start a conversation. As he did, his phone beeped, and he checked his messages.

"Look at that," he said. "Airline found my bag."

Vic typed a response telling the airline he was on his way and would recover the bag within the hour.

"Sorry about Carty," Vic said finally, choosing that as his opening.

Liz was silent for a time, watching the city outside the window. Then, still staring through the glass, she said, "Carty always was an asshole."

"Right. But now you'll never know what really happened to Demond."

Liz turned to him. "Carty always thought he was clever, but he was an open book. I can pretty much figure it out."

"And?"

Liz took in a breath and let it out. "Carty always looked for the easy way. I got into arguments with Demond about it because Carty was a bad influence."

"Okay."

261

"I don't know how the two of them got the coins, but I know Demond, and I can kind of figure it from that." She stared ahead. "Somehow, Demond had the coins. I'm guessing Demond decided to turn them in, but Carty found out about them and wanted to split them, or take all of them. They argued, and Carty killed Demond. That's a small fortune in gold. But somehow, Demond had hidden the coins, and Carty didn't know where. So he's got Demond's body and no coins. It would be easy to make a body disappear in the middle of Katrina. Then Carty ran to Costa Rica, and all these years later, came up with this ridiculous plan to find the coins."

"And somehow, Vargas figured out the coins were out there and worked with Isabella to let Carty find them. All the while planning to steal the coins from Carty."

"Right. Turns out Vargas was tracking Isabella on Google Maps. Jerry found a text from Isabella on Vargas' phone, telling him when I found the coins. She must have texted when I was climbing out of the attic."

"So Carty walks in on you to collect the coins, and gets double-crossed by Isabella and Vargas."

"Looks that way. Carty made the first move on Vargas, and Vargas had no choice but to shoot. But honestly, I don't know how Vargas gets out of there without shooting Carty. Carty knew that, and he acted first."

"Vargas would have shot you as well."

"Well, that's why Cleets was there. I told you in the letter I had a string to pull."

Vic realized Liz had known all along the trip was a trap but was still willing to risk her life to find out what happened to Demond.

The airport terminal loomed ahead. "Okay," Vic said slowly. "Let's get home, and when you're ready, we'll solve Steven Kittery's death. Go after Brandon Ellis."

Liz was about to say something, but Vic's phone rang. Vic glanced at the caller ID. "Speaking of," he said to Liz.

He answered the call.

"Vic? Sandy Vrail here. Where are you?"

"Just getting to the airport. Liz and I are flying back tonight. We'll be at work tomorrow."

"Good. Something for you to chew on?"

"Yes?" Vic wondered what was happening now.

"We have another murder related to your case. Craig is processing the scene now."

Vic had a cold thought of Jake Kittery and Conor Byrne. "Who?"

"Brandon Ellis. Stabbed, same MO as Steven Kittery. Your vacation is over."

Chapter Fifty-Eight

Vic hung up and turned to Liz.

Liz met his gaze. "You look like someone just slapped you."

"Pretty much. That was Sandy. Brandon Ellis is dead. Stabbed like Steven Kittery."

"We just lost our lead suspect. This day keeps getting better and better." Liz shook her head, frowning.

Vic took a heavy breath. "We missed something."

"No, we didn't miss anything."

"Then what?" Vic settled back in the car seat and stared at the ceiling.

"Nuh-uh." Liz shook her head. "We've got all the pieces; we need to put them together differently."

The car stopped at the airport's curb. They stumbled out, Vic thinking that Liz looked as dazed as he felt. They hardly spoke three words as they collected Liz's overnight bag, recovered and rechecked Vic's bag, cleared TSA, and settled at their gate.

Vic gave up trying to reconnect the facts of the case. He was tired, hot, and needed to sleep. He turned to Liz. "So Meera is staying at your place."

Liz looked at him deadpan. "I was wondering when you'd get around to that."

"Just saying. I thought it was kind of you."

"Cut the crap, Vic, that isn't your question."

"Well, I also wondered about Levon. Couldn't help that."

Liz's eyes narrowed. "It's over." Her words were terse. "He's working for Washington full time. Started a few months ago. And before you ask, I'm fine with it."

"Doesn't sound like it."

"Yeah, well, wouldn't be the first time you got something wrong. And I'll also say this. He might be your friend, but Levon and me is none of your business."

"Right you are."

As he said the words, something tingled in Vic's brain. Something to do with Meera. Vic thought back. Meeting Meera at Liz's house. Their conversation. Something.

Nothing came to him. He was too tired, his brain lumpen. The tingle sputtered out, replaced by a numbness that their lead suspect was dead. He needed sleep and a fresh start tomorrow.

Chapter Fifty-Nine

D riving to work the next morning, Vic's mind alighted on his conversation with Meera. He remembered her comment now, the one he'd tried to tease through his exhaustion the night before.

At work, he kept Meera's words to himself through Craig's comprehensive description of the Brandon Ellis crime scene. Stabbed in his office two evenings earlier, Brandon was found by a staff member the next morning, at about the time Vic and Liz were standing in the kitchen of Cleet's empty house, staring at Carty's body.

For Vic, the numbness at losing Brandon as a suspect was now irritation. He felt as if someone had blocked him just as he stretched for a tackle. He kept pushing the feeling away, but it resurfaced, again and again, as if it enjoyed nagging him.

It took almost an hour for Craig, standing beside the whiteboard, to finish his report. He leaned heavily on the forensic evidence, or at least as much as was available at that time. Analysis of fingerprints found at the scene, any DNA, and the detritus collected from the carpet near the body was ongoing.

"And the person in the office with him wasn't an appointment?" Vic knew Craig had already explained this, but he wanted more color.

"Right. He had a six o'clock meeting with one of his managers. It was a performance review. I found the person's HR file on his desk. He sent an email at 9:50 p.m., so I'm thinking the attack came closer to ten o'clock."

"And the last inbound phone call to him?"

Craig leafed through his notes. "Nothing after the performance review meeting. We're still waiting for personal cell phone records."

Liz looked up from her notebook, pen in hand. "And the manager getting the review checks out?"

"Oh yeah." Craig's answer was confident. "I talked to her yesterday. She met Brandon, then went out drinking with friends. Got home after midnight. She's clear."

Liz tapped the end of her pen on the table. "Check everyone who called him during the day. Any one of them might have made an appointment to meet Brandon after hours."

Vic turned over Liz's statement in his mind. "Right, we need to do that, but the question to answer is this. Who would Brandon agree to meet in his office after hours? That's got to be someone he's close with personally, a girlfriend or something, or a very close business associate. You don't agree to meet joe schmo in your office at ten at night."

Liz turned to Vic. "If it's in his office, it's more likely a business associate."

Vic nodded. "And not someone who works for him. He's the boss and would tell his employees when to meet him. So who are we left with?"

Craig checked his notes. "From his schedule, we know Brandon had a conference call with the heads of the non-profits that afternoon. Oskar Glimt and Paul Drum. I guess Jake Kittery was on the call as well."

Vic nodded. "Someone like that makes more sense. Or maybe someone from the insurance company that bankrolled the nonprofits?"

"If there's Medicare fraud and the insurance company is part of it, that fits." Liz turned to Craig. "Has the FBI found anything in Brandon's financials?"

Craig frowned. "See, that's the thing. Sandy got an update from them last night. First cut, the forensic accountant didn't find anything. Brandon looks clean. No secret accounts, money moving around, none of it."

Vic and Liz stared at Craig, neither speaking. Finally, Vic said slowly, "Craig, maybe you could have led with that? Are you saying the FBI thinks Brandon is clear of fraud?"

"Well, they're seeing evidence of double billing and upcharging, but the money from that didn't go to Brandon."

Vic leaned forward. "Then who got it? We're talking well over a million dollars."

Craig shrugged. "FBI doesn't know. Not yet, at least."

"But Brandon wrote the code that created the app." Liz stared from Craig to Vic.

Vic thought this was finally the time to relate his conversation with Meera to Liz and Craig. "Did he? I talked to Meera before I went to New Orleans. She thought that Brandon didn't kill Steven. She didn't believe he had it in him. She also thought the only thing he did well was connect people. If she's right, he's not the kind of guy who writes code."

Craig plopped into one of the seats around the conference table. "So, who created the app?"

Vic shrugged. "Maybe Meera knows? Steven might have said something to her."

Vic called Meera and left a voicemail. While they waited for a return call, Vic, Liz, and Craig discussed the possibility of the insurance company committing the fraud.

"It doesn't make sense," Craig finally pointed out. "If someone at the insurance company committed the fraud, they would never send Steven Kittery the certificate thanking TU Health for their higher volume of chargebacks. They'd do everything they could to keep things hidden."

Meera called back after an hour, and Vic put the call on the conference room's speakerphone.

"Sorry," Meera was quick to say. "I was seeing patients."

"Which clinic?" Vic asked, just to preface his real question.

"My father's."

Liz looked as surprised as Vic felt.

"I normally see patients here," Meera said quickly, understanding the reason for Vic's silence. "And my father called and apologized. A lot. He wants to support me having the baby."

"I think we're glad about that, Meera." Vic glanced at Liz, to make sure he wasn't speaking out of turn. "Also, we called with a question about the WholePatient app that TU Health and the other non-profits use. Do you know anything about it?" Vic held his breath.

"Not much." Meera sounded distracted. "I mean, I use it to book my appointments and do my post-appointment reports."

Liz leaned toward the phone. "And record your Medicare chargeback codes?"

"Sure, of course. That's part of the reporting process after seeing a patient."

Vic let out his breath. "Do you know who wrote the code for the app? Was that Brandon Ellis?"

Meera laughed, suddenly engaged in the conversation. "Oh my, no. Couldn't have been. He never wrote code." She hesitated. "But I don't remember Steven saying anything about who did, if that's what you mean." She sounded sad, suddenly. "It was just there when I started volunteering, so I used it."

Vic realized there was something they'd forgotten to ask Meera, but he couldn't pin down what it was.

Liz, still hunched toward the telephone, asked, "Do you remember seeing any copyright information on the app screens, anyone's name anywhere?"

The line was silent for several seconds. "No, sorry, not that I can remember."

Craig held up a piece of paper with five words scrawled on it. *I didn't see anything either.*

"And do you know how the non-profits handle their finances?" Vic closed his eyes, knowing the answer.

"No, sorry." Meera sounded tired.

Vic realized what they'd forgotten to ask Meera. "Meera, different subject, the night you went to visit Steven on Mt. Washington, how did you set up that meeting? I mean, communicate with Steven? We never found any text messages on Steven's phone about you two meeting up, and he had no incoming calls from you that day."

"Oh." Meera was silent for several seconds. "Right. I remember. You see, Steven and I tried to minimize text messages and calls because my father checked my phone. It wasn't worth the trouble if he found them. I left Steven a note. I did that a lot."

Vic saw Liz cock her head in surprise. "Wait," Vic said quickly. "Where did you leave it?"

"With Annie. You know, the receptionist at Firefighters Health? I was volunteering there that morning and called Steven to say hi. He said he was planning to visit Firefighters Health to speak to Oskar Glimt that afternoon. So I wrote a note telling Steven where to meet and the time. I asked Annie to give it to Steven when he arrived."

Liz was staring at the phone so hard Vic thought it might melt. "What was it, a folded piece of paper?" she asked.

"Oh, no. It was in an envelope."

Vic leaned forward. "So the note was in an envelope on Annie's desk. Did you seal the envelope?"

Again, several seconds of silence. "No. I don't think I did. Just folded the envelope flap inside." Silence widened. "So anyone could have read it." Her last sentence had the tone of a revelation.

Vic knew Meera understood the significance. That it was perhaps her note that led someone to Mt. Washington, knowing Steven would be there.

"Oh, no," Meera breathed through the phone.

Chapter Sixty

J ake Kittery sat in his office, staring at the spreadsheet on his computer screen. He'd opened the last email Stevie sent him, and, after rereading Stevie's short note several times, moved on to the spreadsheet. He reviewed the comparison of chargebacks listed by TU Health and the insurance company each month, considered the small overcharge in January, the lack of overcharges in February and the slow build during March and running through the year.

He knew what they meant. He'd been involved in something similar years ago, at a rolling mill near Aliquippa. With contract negotiation six months away, they'd instructed the workers to quietly run a one-month slow-down, then return to normal production. It was a chess move to see how the company executives reacted. The idea was to gain insight into the mindset of company executives as contract negotiations approached.

The executives did little more than inform the union of the slow-down and tack memos to the company bulletin boards noting the production drop-off. Believing the executives were running scared, the union agreed to enter the contract negotiations aggressively.

Jake's stomach turned. He remembered that first day of negotiations. The mill executives sitting in the motel conference room, window air conditioners thrumming in the background. Beads of water on the outside of the plastic water jugs. Management's negotiating team sitting in shirt sleeves and ties, their stares blank as the union president outlined the union's new contract demands.

When the union president finished and sat down, management's lead negotiator rose—and without breaking eye contact with the union president—told the union representatives that corporate had decided to close the mill. Effective in three months.

In that moment Jake learned that when you played a game, it didn't guarantee your opponent was playing the same game.

He pushed away the memory and stared at the numbers. No doubt about it. A test run in January, February a wait-and-see, then the gradual increase in overcharges.

Anger sifted through him. If he could see the pattern, Stevie certainly saw it. And someone had killed Stevie for it. He was sure. And those overcharges must be linked to the murder of Brandon Ellis.

He stared through the glass wall of his office. Edna sat at her desk in the center of the bullpen, hunched over her computer. One of the volunteer doctors was leaning back in their chair, staring at the ceiling, phone glued to one ear.

He needed a plan. He needed to find out what game everyone was playing.

The front door to their offices opened, and a tall, lean form stepped inside. Conor Byrne.

Jake stared at him, stunned. Conor looked around the bullpen, taking it in with a single swoop of his head. He turned in Jake's direction, and their gazes met through the glass of Jake's office. Conor started toward him.

Like a lineman coming out of their crouch, Edna stepped directly in front of Conor. Jake was surprised she didn't tackle him. He couldn't hear what Edna was saying but knew from Conor's expression it wasn't good. Jake rose and crossed to the door of his office.

"Edna," he called.

Edna shifted her body to see him but kept her wiry frame in front of Conor.

"It's okay," Jake called. "He can come through."

"I'll call the cops." Edna's voice was sharp, her cheeks splotched with color.

"I am the cops," Conor said.

Jake crossed the office and stared into Conor's gaunt face. "Not helpful."

He looked down at Edna. "It's okay. Seriously." He turned back to Conor. "What do you want?"

"Checking in on you." Conor shrugged. "Buddy of mine from the jail said you were out. Figured I'd make sure you're okay."

Jake considered him. Conor looked tired, the creases under his eyes deep and dark, and he'd missed a patch of stubble while shaving his neck. Jake realized that Conor didn't have an office to visit every day, as he did. In fact, Conor had nothing, beyond the fading belief Jake was somehow involved in the death of Conor Jr.

Even that seemed to have run its course.

"C'mon back." He gestured to his office. "Edna, we're good."

Edna glared at him as if she wanted to smack some sense into him. After a moment, she turned and looked up at Conor. "And you. I'll be watching you." She stepped out of Conor's way.

Jake led Conor into his office and waved at one of the chairs around the small conference table. He took another and waited as Conor looked around. He saw Conor study Stevie's darkened office for a few moments before turning to him.

"That's all this is?" Jake asked him. "You want to see how I'm doing?"

Conor shrugged. "Yeah. You were pretty worked up when you were at my house. Wanted to be sure you were back in the groove."

"Pretty much."

"And your wife is okay? Ellie?"

"She's taking it better than I thought. Turns out Stevie's girlfriend is pregnant. We just found out. It made a huge difference to her."

Conor's eyes warmed. "There's something. How about you? Excited about that?"

Jake spread his hands. "Sure. Of course. It's just a lot to take at the same time and a lot to work out."

Conor nodded but didn't speak. He seemed to be searching for something to say. "And everything else is good? As much as it can be?"

Jake watched Conor's face. Conor really was struggling to find words, he thought. The whole visit was odd. And then Jake thought that perhaps it

273

wasn't. That perhaps a different kind of game could be played.

"There is something," Jake said quietly. He locked eyes with Conor. "I think I know why Stevie was killed."

Conor tensed as if he was listening with his entire body. "Yeah? Tell me."

Jake did. He explained Stevie's last email to him and the spreadsheet. The planning behind the Medicare chargebacks. Stevie, lounging against his door jamb and asking him about Brandon Ellis, and how Brandon was now dead.

When he finished, Conor looked as tight as a tuning fork waiting to be tapped. He stared at Jake, eyes bright. "No shit."

"No shit," Jake repeated.

Conor watched him. "We need to get to the bottom of that."

Jake was suddenly grinning. In a rush, he said, "Yeah, we do."

Chapter Sixty-One

Vic glanced from Liz to Craig. "We agreed?"

Craig bobbed his head, grinning. Liz was slower to react, agreeing in a guarded, tired way. Vic had noticed her despondency earlier. He knew that finding Carty alive, then watching him die before she could ask about Demond, weighed on her. He knew Liz always believed she would discover what happened to Demond. She'd lost that hope, and accepting the fact would be hard.

"Are you up for this?" he asked Liz, measuring each word.

She shifted in her seat, considering his words. "Yeah," she said finally. She looked up and gazed directly at him. "First, we visit Oskar Glimt, then Paul Drum. Push hard. Do they have alibis for Brandon's time of death."

"And the money question?"

"Who the hell built the app they all use? Because just like amateur hour, we leaped to the conclusion that Brandon built the app and stole the money."

Vic watched her. "Unless you have a better idea?"

Liz sighed. "Not yet. This makes sense. It has to be one of them."

"Okay then." Vic turned to Craig. "While Liz and I do that, you dig up everything you can on Glimt and Drum. And keep on the FBI. In case they find out where the money went."

"Sure." Craig was grinning again, and Vic wondered if Sandy had told him about passing the detective's exam, rather than waiting until Liz was back. He seemed too happy somehow, or perhaps sitting next to Liz and her funk made him appear happier than he was.

Vic tapped the tabletop. "Let's get at it."

Chapter Sixty-Two

"What do we do first?" Conor stared at Jake.

Jake hadn't thought through that question yet, and he said so. He remembered the lack of fraudulent payments in February, the test to see if anyone noticed the January overcharges. It merged with the memory of the slow-down of production his union engineered for one month. How that failed to mean anything. "I think we go right up the gut at Oskar Glimt and Paul Drum. No games. I call them both, tell them someone is using our non-profit to hide Medicare chargebacks. Ask if anyone is doing that with their non-profits. Listen to what they say."

Conor leaned forward. "See how they react?"

"Exactly. Someone killed Stevie because he found out about the fraud. Now we know it can't be Brandon Ellis. If I say I know about the fraud as well, what are they going to do?"

"When do we start?"

Jake liked that Conor didn't say the obvious, that Jake was making himself bait. He lifted the handset from its cradle. "Right now. I'll call Glimt and Drum. Put it on speaker so you can listen. That'll get the word out."

Conor smiled. "Just don't tell them I'm listening in. Gives us an edge if they think only you know about this. You should say that. Make them think it's just you."

Jake shrugged. "Maybe, but the cops are down this road too. They wanted Stevie's report."

"Yeah, but they can't do what we're doing. I was a cop, remember? I know how they work. They have to build a case against someone. Do it by the book. We don't. We can drop a match on dry grass."

Jake weighed the phone receiver in his hand. He knew what Conor was saying was correct, but he liked Lenoski. "We might need to bring them in. We leave that door open." Jake said quietly.

Conor grinned wider, but Jake didn't see any humor in it. Conor waved his hand. "Sure. No problem. If the time is right."

Jake wondered what kind of deal he'd just made but punched in the telephone number for Oskar Glimt. He decided to go slowly and carefully with Conor, but he liked what they were about to do.

Chapter Sixty-Three

Vic and Liz didn't talk much as they drove toward the Strip District and Oskar Glimt's offices. Liz was still lost in thought, and Vic guessed it would be several days before she came out of it. For one brief moment, he wondered if he should suggest a few days of vacation. He decided that was asking to be punched.

"I haven't met this Glimt character," Liz said quietly, surprising him. She *was* thinking about the case.

"Nothing special with him from the last interview, although he acted like he didn't know Steven Kittery, when Meera said he and Steven were friends. Not sure what to do with that."

"What do we know about him?"

"Not much. Meera told me he was a CMU graduate, studied multimedia, whatever that is. She thought he wanted to make documentaries and was surprised he hadn't gone to Hollywood. How he ended up as the head of a non-profit we don't know. It's worth asking. Oh, and take a look at the whiteboard in his office. It looks like a bunch of flowcharts. Neither Craig nor I could figure it out."

Liz settled back into silence, staring out of the window.

Vic glanced at her. "Have you talked to your old commander in New Orleans? Did they catch Isabella?"

Liz huffed out a breath of disgust. "I forgot to tell you. Yeah, Jerry texted me. He wanted to thank you. You were right. There was a luggage store at the end of the block near where she left the car. She bought a roller bag. They have her on CCTV at the bus station. She bought tickets to Miami and Denver. Didn't show up in either place."

Vic smiled. "Those gold coins, what are they worth?"

"A few million. Jerry said the collection was reported missing right after Katrina. No leads since then."

"But the coins have to be difficult to cash out, right?"

"If she only cashes a few at a time, no. Even easier if she gets to Costa Rica. And she only needs to cash one right now to have enough money to run for a couple of months. And she's good-looking enough most guys will want to help her."

Vic guided the car through the narrow Strip District streets, angling toward Glimt's offices. He thought about Carty Swain and what made a man risk so much after he'd likely got away with murder and created a new life for himself.

"I would like to know what made Carty tick," Vic said quietly, as he searched for a parking spot.

"Unhappiness." Liz's voice was dry.

Vic parked and looked at her as he turned off the ignition. "That's it? He didn't like his job? He got away with murder, makes a new life for himself and then decides he's unhappy?"

"Demond's death doesn't figure into it." Liz unstrapped her seatbelt. "From the start Carty wanted to be rich. After Demond, Carty had to lie low. But knowing those coins were out there somewhere, it just made him unhappy. Greed does that to you, and he gave in to it. He got what he deserved."

As they approached the front doors of Firefighters Health, Vic thought about teasing Liz over her willingness to explain Carty using psychology and the snap judgment about his fate. She normally stuck to facts, which was the main reason he liked working with her. He turned in her direction, but the set of her face made him drop it.

Inside, Vic took in the two people lounging at desks in the bullpen and looked to his right, wondering if Annie, the receptionist, was there. She was. Vic caught a flicker of disappointment on her face, as if she'd expected Craig to be with him, not Liz.

"Hi," Vic said quickly. "Is Oskar around? We have a couple more questions for him."

"About Brandon Ellis?" Annie's dark eyes swelled with unhappiness, and Vic wondered if she looked for Brandon perhaps more than Craig.

"Among other things. Is he here?"

"No, sorry. He just went out."

"When will he be back?" Liz's voice was sharp.

"Um, I don't know. He didn't say." Annie shrugged apologetically.

Vic stepped closer to her desk. "Can you access his schedule?"

Concern clouded Annie's features. "Well, yes."

"Look," Vic said quickly. "We're not invading his privacy. We just need to track him down. It's important. We need to know where he is."

Annie considered Vic's words and pushed a strand of black hair behind her ear. "He doesn't have anything on his schedule until two. He just got a phone call and went out right after."

Liz shifted her hips and spread her feet. "Who called?"

And there was Liz, back to focusing on facts. Vic felt better for her.

Annie shifted in her chair. "Um, Jake Kittery, from TU Health? Do you know him?"

Something stirred in Vic, a warning, but he didn't know why.

"We know him." Liz sounded thoughtful, and Vic knew she was untangling the same question of why Jake called. "Can you call Oskar for us?"

"Sure." She dialed a number into her desk telephone, and flipped it to speaker. After four rings, the call went to voice mail. Vic leaned over, and at the prompt, left a message for Glimt asking him to call. When he finished giving Glimt his cell phone number, Annie hung up.

Vic looked at Liz.

"Best we can do," was all her expression said.

Vic turned to the receptionist. "Thanks. Could you write down Oskar's cell phone number for us? Then we'll get out of your hair."

Without a word, Annie wrote the number on a Post-it note and handed it to Vic.

As soon as the front door closed behind them, Liz looked at him. "Did that Kittery call give you a vibe? He said his son did all the work."

"It did, but we can worry about that later. Let's go find Paul Drum. See what he has to say."

Paul Drum's offices were in the East End of Pittsburgh, inside a renovated brick three-story house, the building itself surrounded by a warren of gentrified homes and updated storefronts. The change in the area always surprised Vic. Fifteen years earlier, as a beat cop, he'd patrolled the area for a time. Then, it was a patchwork of dive bars, homeless centers, low-level drug dealing, and boarded-up stores.

Oddly, litter still lingered in doorways and around the base of the saplings the city had planted as part of the revitalization effort.

The interior of the Veterans Health offices was a replica of Jake's and Oskar's offices: a central bullpen of desks surrounded by offices and a meeting room. A middle-aged woman sat at a desk near the door. She glanced up as they entered, and her look reminded Vic of Edna's protective attitude.

"Can I help you?" the woman asked, and Vic heard an echo of Sandy's clipped military delivery in her voice.

Vic introduced himself and Liz, showed his credentials, and asked for Paul Drum. The woman didn't introduce herself, but Vic noted her nameplate attached to the low wall of her cubicle. Marla Kriff.

"What is this about?" Marla asked.

"Medicare fraud." Liz said the words sharply, and Vic knew for certain she was tired of treading lightly.

Marla blinked. "Wait here." She rose and disappeared into an office along the back wall. A moment later, she appeared in the doorway and gestured for them to join her.

Paul Drum rose when they entered. He was in his early sixties, Vic guessed, six feet tall and wiry thin. The sides of his head were covered with close-cropped white hair, his face and the bald dome of his head deeply tanned. He radiated authority. A lifer in the Army, Vic thought, and the last guy you'd want for a drill instructor.

"Paul Drum," the man almost barked. "And you are?"

Vic again introduced himself and Liz and showed Drum his credentials. Drum waved to the two chairs facing his desk with a movement that looked suspiciously like a karate chop. Marla, Vic noted, adopted an at-ease stance near the door. Drum accepted Marla staying in the office without a word.

As soon as they were seated, Drum said, "Medicare fraud. Topic of the day. Had a call about that forty minutes ago."

"Let me guess," Vic responded. "Jake Kittery."

"The one and only. I've talked to his son a few times. This was the first time Jake called me directly."

"And what did he tell you?"

"That he suspects TU Health is a cut-out for Medicare fraud. He asked me if we'd spotted anything like that."

"And have you?" Liz asked.

"Absolutely not. We are ship-shape."

Vic corrected himself. Not Army, more likely Marines. "Did Jake explain how he discovered the fraud?"

"No."

"Okay," Vic didn't like delivering bad news, but he agreed with Liz that it was time to be direct. "Steven Kittery discovered it by accident. It's actually hard to spot. The cash TU Health received from Medicare matched their refund requests. You're probably the same. But someone added chargeback codes to TU Health's doctor reports *after* they submitted them, then skimmed off the additional refunds before the payments were returned. Someone could be exploiting you the same way."

Drum considered Vic's words and looked at Marla.

She gave a quick bob of her head. "I can check with the insurer."

"Give us a day or two," Drum added.

"Thanks, and what else did Jake Kittery say?"

"That he knows what is happening, and he's going to put a stop to it."

Vic hid his annoyance. His instinct in Oskar Glimt's office was correct. Jake had decided to find the murderer himself. Out of the corner of his eye Vic saw Liz glance at him, and knew she was concerned, too.

"You had a meeting scheduled with Steven Kittery for the day after he died. Did he tell you what he wanted to talk about?"

"What day was that?"

Vic told him, and Drum procured a pair of metal-framed glasses. He slid them on as he checked his computer. "Yes." Drum looked up and peeled off his glasses. "The meeting is on my schedule. The only note I made says 'cash flow.'

As Vic thought about that, he studied the wall behind Drum, with its framed photographs of uniformed men. A red Marine banner featured in one. Nearby, a large shadow box held military patches, a ribbon bar, and medal collection. Vic recognized a Purple heart. Hanging near them were two certificates, but all Vic could make out were the large initials BBBS, and something about fifteen years of volunteering. Vic recognized the type font, but couldn't remember the name of the organization.

"Nothing more specific?" Vic asked, turning his attention back to Drum.

"No. I've been in this job two years now, and he was one of the people who interviewed me for it. I liked him. Just a kid, obviously, but this whole thing was his idea. I mean, I'm sorry about Brandon, but I always thought Brandon was a bullshitter. Not to speak ill of the dead. That Kittery kid had brains."

As Drum talked, Vic's eyes drifted across Drum's desk. It was painstakingly neat, empty except for two small piles. One, some envelopes, was topped by a smooth, black volcanic rock. The second, a collection of files, was topped by, of all things, a bayonet.

Vic stared at the weapon, aware Drum had stopped talking. He pointed at the bayonet. "What's that?" He already knew but was interested in how Drum would respond to someone who seemed clueless.

"Bayonet." Drum held it up with a grin. "Maker of widows and spilled guts." Drum admired the length of it. "This is a World War II design, for the M1 Garand. Ten inches long. They shortened them for Vietnam and the M16. This one could do some damage." He placed it carefully back on the files and patted the handle. "You seriously don't know what it is?"

"I guess I do," Vic said, not wanting to lie. "But does anyone really use them in warfare today? I guess that's my question."

The skin around Drum's blue eyes tightened. "Bayonet Hill, Korea. America's last bayonet charge. 1951. The British pulled one off in Afghanistan in 2004. Sent the Taliban running. You charge the enemy with one of those on the end of your weapon, and their definition of you changes. You're not an infidel cake-eater anymore. You're balls-out screaming crazy. It's primal."

"And you're trained to use that thing?" Liz asked.

"All Marines are." He looked at Marla. "Were you?"

"No, sir." Marla glanced at Vic. "I was Army. We were issued bayonets, but they stayed in our barracks, and we weren't trained to use them. Maybe if I deployed to Afghanistan or Iraq we would have. I don't know."

Drum looked from Vic to Liz. "Are you asking about that bayonet for a reason?"

Vic shrugged. "You never know what can help." As he spoke, he tried to remember Steven's autopsy report, the length and width of the blade channel inside Steven's chest cavity. He couldn't remember, and he suddenly wanted to know. Exactly.

"Something else," Vic said quickly. "I'm assuming your doctors use the same app as the other two non-profits. Is that true?"

"WholePatient? We do."

"Do you know who wrote the code for it?"

Drum frowned and looked at Marla, who shrugged. "I don't think we do."

"It was already being used when you started?" Vic asked.

"Yes. Works well for us."

"And your financial transactions are managed by Brandon's company?"

"Exactly. Good cost-savings for us. Without it, we'd have to hire bookkeepers and billing admins."

"Okay." Vic tried to think of another question and only came up with one. "Your counterpart at Firefighter Health. Oskar Glimt. What's your relationship with him like?"

"We get along." Drum stared at him.

The way Drum said the words made Vic think that Drum and Glimt didn't get along at all.

"Doesn't sound like it," Liz said, again tromping on politeness to ask the question.

Drum turned to her, his face stern. "Are you saying you don't believe me?"

The thought that went through Vic's head was, "Here we go." But he decided to let it play out.

"I'm skeptical." Liz reflected Drum's stern look back at him. "It was the way you said it."

Drum and Liz stared at one another for a solid three seconds, before Vic broke in. "We need to get to the bottom of Steven's murder. Like I said earlier, you never know what can help. This isn't the time to worry about hurting people's feelings."

Drum's eyes slid to Vic. "Okay. It was early on, not long after I started. We were all getting used to the app, and we had one doctor who sometimes delayed recording his patient calls. Sometimes, if he waited a few days, it would slide into the next month. If that happened, we'd be forced to amend our monthly report. Guess what. Every time that happened, Glimt would call and give me shit about it. It was annoying, and he was a dick about it. We were all still learning the system."

Vic felt his face muscles tighten. "But how did Glimt know you'd amended your report?"

Drum shrugged. "Back then we sent our reports to each other. Steven, Glimt, and I. Like I said, we were all figuring it out. That's why it pissed me off. The insurance company submits our chargebacks to Medicare. If they called me to complain, that's fine. I just didn't feel like it was any of Glimt's business."

"This was what, eighteen months ago?"

"About."

Vic could think of several reasons why Glimt would be angry that Drum's reports needed adjusting. The main one was that updated reports might accidentally reveal added Medicare charges.

"Tell me something else," Vic said, still trying to understand the context of how the three non-profits worked together. "Did you all start working here at the same time? You must have known each other well."

Drum's blue eyes were steady. "No. Steven and Brandon started. Then I came in, and Glimt a little after that. Steven interviewed me. We have a board that oversees Brandon's business and the non-profits. Steven was on it, but he had a kind of operational control as well. Basically, nothing serious got done without Steven agreeing. Steven was just informal about it. Brandon talked big, but Steven called the shots." Drum held up his bayonet. "That's why I gave Steven one of these. He's the guy who really led the charge, and if you got something wrong, Steven was the guy could spill your guts."

Vic didn't remember seeing a bayonet listed in the crime scene inventory, nor seeing one in Steven's office. He saw Liz frown as well.

"He got the joke." Drum grinned, and it took Vic a second to understand what Drum meant.

"He understood why you gave it to him?"

Drum nodded. "Oh yeah."

Vic guessed it was more Steven appreciating someone understood his role in the organization, rather than recognizing a joke. He realized he was starting to like Drum. Compared to Glimt's vague and sculpted answers, Drum was direct and unabashed.

"Back to Glimt for a second. When did he join exactly?"

"Like I said, a couple of months after me. Steven came up with the idea for this organization, Brandon bought in, and they made Trade Unions Health the test case. When it worked, they started Firefighters Health and Veterans Health, and hired Glimt and me."

Liz leaned forward. "The app you all use, when did that launch?"

"Brandon put that online a few weeks before we started. They wanted to test that as well before they committed."

"And you really don't know who wrote the code for it? Even a company name?"

Drum leaned back. "You know, Steven or Brandon could have explained that. When I came on board it was our operating system, so we learned it and used it. Didn't really give it any more thought than that."

Vic studied the photographs and shadowbox on the wall behind Drum for a few seconds. "Last question from me." He glanced at Liz. "Did Oskar and Steven get along? We heard they were friends."

Drum cocked his head, and his eyes flitted to Marla. "You want to answer that?"

Marla drew up slightly, as if reflexively standing to attention. She caught herself and stopped. Vic had the sense that Marla and Sandy might get along very well. "I'm not sure of the details, sir."

Drum watched Marla for a moment, and Vic saw humor and fatherly affection flicker in his eyes. "Marla, we aren't in the military anymore. Just tell them what happened."

Marla gave a brisk nod. "We were at Mr. Ellis' business, he does a sort of summit meeting twice a year. At the last one, after a couple of hours, we'd taken a break. I went to the bathroom. I was going back to the conference room, and as I passed the men's room, I heard Mr. Glimt and Mr. Kittery arguing. I, um…" Marla flushed. "I stopped to listen."

"As we all would have," Drum said quickly.

"Well, it was just a few seconds, and the door was closed, but they were arguing."

Vic repressed a grin. "And the topic of the argument?"

"Apparently, it was about one of our doctors. A Dr. Basu? Mr. Glimt was telling Steven Kittery not to date her, because he was. Steven was saying she could date whoever she wanted."

Vic turned to Liz.

"Nope," Liz said quickly, "Meera never said anything to me about dating Glimt."

"And Meera still volunteers for Glimt." Vic turned to Drum. "You didn't happen to be in the bathroom, at the time?"

Drum gave Vic a mock stern look. "I'm a Marine, detective. We are taught to hold our water."

"Not sure that will always work out for you." Vic turned back to Marla. "Anything else?"

Marla shook her head. "No, I went back to the conference room." Marla pursed her lips. "I was a bit embarrassed at myself for listening."

Vic waved a hand. "How did the two of them appear when they came back to the conference room?"

"Steven Kittery was the same as always. Mr. Glimt was a little red in the face. And restless."

"Okay, thank you." Vic smiled at her. "That was helpful." He wasn't actually sure it was. Every time they lifted a stone, they found something new, and they still didn't know who had written the code for the app.

"Okay," Vic said slowly. He glanced at Liz, but she gave just the slightest shake of her head. "Mr. Drum," he glanced at Marla, "And Marla. Thanks for your time. This was very helpful."

Vic rose and held out a business card to Drum. "In case you think of anything else."

Drum rose and took the card. "Glad to help. Hopefully, the organization can get past all this. I feel like we're doing good work." He gestured at Marla. "And Marla will take a run at our records and see if there are any discrepancies on the Medicare chargebacks."

"One last thought," Vic said, as a question rose to him. "Do you collect bayonets? You have one here, you gave one to Steven Kittery."

Drum considered him. "I wouldn't call it a collection. Just five or six I picked up over the years. The best is a Russian World War Two spike bayonet for their Mosin-Nagant rifle. Now that's a weapon that'll pucker your balls." He glanced past Vic. "Sorry, Marla." He turned back to Vic. "Found it in an antique store when I was stationed in Germany."

Vic wasn't sure what a spike bayonet might be, but passed on asking, too amused that a former hard-charging Marine visited antique stores. "Thanks again."

He and Liz crossed the bullpen and went outside. Settled in the car, Vic waited before starting the engine.

"Yeah," Liz said into the quiet. "I'll ask Meera what the hell. She keeps forgetting to mention things."

"Yes, she does. Do you remember finding a bayonet in Steven's possession?"

"Nope. And I don't remember the length of the weapon that stabbed Steven. But it was long enough to run under his rib cage all the way to his heart."

"I'll take that one," Vic said slowly. "I'll check the coroner's report. But Steven might have kept it at home. I want to talk to Jake Kittery anyway. Tell him to stand down."

Liz turned to him. "You think he will?"

"Probably not." Vic let out a slow breath. "Call Craig and tell him to go through the financial records for Steven's business. They must have paid whoever built the app. Tell him to spot regular payments to any company that writes code or develops apps. The payments probably stopped not long after the app went live, or they shifted to a service kind of retainer. Tell him to ask the FBI to help."

Vic started the car.

As he pulled into traffic, Liz said slowly, "Finally feels like we're getting somewhere."

"Yeah," Vic replied. "And it's mostly to a place where I wish Meera would tell us everything. But what really pisses me off is Jake Kittery."

Chapter Sixty-Four

Conor Byrne rose from the conference table in Jake's office and stretched the small of his back. "If Drum or Glimt were guilty, I figured they would have done something by now."

Jake spread his hands. "Be patient. Most of negotiating labor agreements is waiting. Then out of nowhere, we'd get an answer from management, and it'd be a damn fire alarm."

Jake checked the office through the glass wall of his office. The desks were deserted, even Edna was at home. Dusk arched its back against the front window.

Conor worked his shoulders until he was satisfied. "We need to goose them."

"I only called them a few hours ago. Give it some time."

Conor's eyes flashed. "We need to get under their skin." He frowned, lost in thought, and snapped his fingers. "Got it. We go tonight."

"Meaning?"

Conor grinned and explained his plan. As he finished, Jake heard the front door clunk shut. He looked into the bullpen and saw Vic Lenoski's thick-shouldered bulk heading toward them.

"What the hell does he want?" As he finished the question, Conor pressed a finger to his lips, telling Jake to stay quiet about their conversation.

Vic reached the door to Jake's office and stepped inside. He studied Conor and Jake for a long moment. "Should have known I'd find you two together."

Jake thought he detected a note of indecision in Vic's tone. "Anything new in the case?"

Vic seemed to make a decision. "Let me put it this way." He glanced at Conor but focused on Jake. "Liz and I wanted to do two interviews today. You guys screwed that up. We got to Glimt's, and he wasn't there because he walked out of the office after you called. Still hasn't called me back. With Drum, we had to backtrack through your conversation with him. A waste of time. So hear me on this." Again, he looked from Conor to Jake, but slower this time. "Stop. Whatever you are doing, stop. This is no bullshit. It's our job to find out who killed Steven, and we will. We know how to do it, and Liz and I have done this before. A lot. Don't muddy the waters. More than that, it's dangerous. Someone out there has killed two people. They'll do it again in a heartbeat. We're trained for that. You're not." Vic pivoted and held his palm out to stop Conor from talking. "And don't you start. You've been retired for ten years. You're so out of practice I'm gonna call you Rusty. So. Again." He turned back to Jake. "Stop. Stop making phone calls. Stop playing junior detective. Leave this to us. Am I clear?"

Jake spread his hands. "I hear you." But he'd sat at enough negotiating tables and listened to enough executives to know when bullshit was being tossed at him. Vic's diatribe had the same hollowness. He wasn't sure why.

When Conor didn't say anything, Vic wheeled on him again. "Rusty? Am I clear?"

"Crystal."

Vic looked from one to the other, frowning.

Jake saw Vic wasn't convinced he'd warned them off. He waited.

"This is your only warning," Vic said finally. "Let us take care of this."

"You guys are the best at your job," Conor said brightly.

For a split-second, Jake thought Vic was going to take a swing at Conor.

Instead, Vic slowly pivoted to Conor. "Don't bullshit me. Just listen and do what I say."

Vic let out a slow breath and turned back to Jake. "One other thing. Drum says he gave Steven a bayonet as a joke. A real bayonet, and a crappy joke. But we didn't find that weapon on Mt. Washington, and we don't remember seeing it in Steven's office or apartment. Or his car. Any chance it's in your house?"

"I remember when he got it. We talked about it. After that, I don't know."

No one spoke for a few moments, and Vic turned without saying goodbye. Jake watched him weave between the desks to the front door. When the door clunked shut, Jake looked at Conor.

"Did you hear that?" Jake asked.

"Oh yeah, I did. You called Glimt, and he left the office."

"See? Patience." Jake sat back in his chair and smiled.

"We still good for tonight? I can stop by at 12:30. Go from there?"

Jake rocked forward and stood. "One hundred percent. See you then."

Together, they crossed the bullpen. Conor waited while Jake locked the front door, and together, they walked through the gathering darkness to their cars.

As he watched Conor pull into the road, Jake wondered about the real reason for Vic's visit. Vic had warned them off, but it was almost as if he didn't believe they would listen. Perhaps, he thought, the warning was just something Vic needed to do in case something went wrong later. That way, Vic could insist he'd warned them. That made more sense to him. But that was cover-your-ass behavior, and Vic didn't seem that type. He started the car and pulled out into the road.

Chapter Sixty-Five

Parked three-quarters of the way down the block, Vic watched Conor pull out, followed, thirty seconds later, by Jake. He started after Jake's car, and called Liz once he was moving.

"They gone?" She asked.

"Yep. I'm following Jake. They've got something planned."

"You couldn't warn them off?"

"I tried, but I knew when I walked in they'd been talking about something and weren't going to tell me what. I decided to let them play it out. I'll stay close. Those two are six inches away from being a damn comedy team, and they are going to get into trouble." Vic let out his anger in a breath. "How did your visit to Jake's house go?"

"No bayonet. Ellie let me look through Steven's old bedroom."

"Okay, Jake didn't know where it was either. I checked the autopsy report and talked to the medical examiner. Bayonet makes sense for the murder weapon. The stab track is long enough."

"Steven was stabbed with his own bayonet?"

"Maybe. At least we have a weapon to look for now." Vic accelerated to make the same green light as Jake. "From the last turn, looks like Jake is headed home. I'll follow him there. Call Craig and tell him he's got the overnight. I'll cover Jake until midnight, Craig can do midnight to six. You take it from there. Jake is not a guy to sit around and wait. Neither is Conor. Not where their sons are involved."

"I believe that."

"Right now, I'd like you to go home and ask Meera why the hell she forgot to mention she dated Glimt before Steven."

Liz laughed softly. "Oh yeah. That I will. See you in the morning."

Vic ended the call and watched the taillights of Jake's car slow-run a stop sign and take a right. He was sure Jake was headed home. He dropped back, just catching Jake's car at the far end of each block, making the turns that would take him home. Fifteen minutes later Vic slowed to a stop just before the turn into the cul-de-sac where Jake lived. He doused his lights and engine. Across the front yard of the corner house, Vic watched Jake lock his car and climb the steps to his house.

Vic called Anne, told her he would be late home and settled into the seat. "Alrighty then," he said to himself softly. "Let's see what you boys have in mind."

Chapter Sixty-Six

At eleven-forty-five, the high round lights of a Jeep appeared in Vic's mirror as Craig tucked his vehicle behind Vic's. The lights cut off, but the engine needed to wheeze itself to a stop. A moment later, Craig slid into the passenger seat and closed Vic's door softly.

Vic stared at him. "You're early."

Craig grinned. "I wanted to update you. Remember you asked me to look into Glimt's background?"

"I do." Vic tried not to smile at Craig's enthusiasm. He guessed some of the excitement would wring out of him in a couple of years.

"It's interesting, and there's a lot to unpack." Craig was grinning.

"Okay. Can you summarize? I haven't eaten dinner."

"Sure." Craig rocked slightly in his seat. "Glimt moved to Pittsburgh in seventh grade with his mother."

"No Dad?"

"Right, I guess the Dad left them when he was small. I figured out they were from New Jersey, near Philadelphia, and when I checked the New Jersey courts, I found a divorce petition his mother filed when Glimt was maybe four years old. Abandonment."

"The father took a runner."

"Looks like it. Anyway, his mother got a job in Philadelphia at Mellon Bank, and a few years later was transferred to Mellon's headquarters here in Pittsburgh. They lived in Squirrel Hill, and Glimt went to Taylor Alderdice."

Vic's heart thudded and he lost the thread of what Craig was saying. When his daughter, Dannie, disappeared, she was walking to that same

295

high school for classes. Just the name catapulted him back to the first days she was missing. A wave of emotion dragged him from shore. He held the steering wheel as if it was a life ring.

"You okay?"

Vic took a breath and kicked against his grief. "Yeah, sorry. I said I was hungry." Even to his own ears, the excuse sounded thin.

"Sure." Craig hesitated.

"Go on." Vic lifted his hand from the steering wheel and waved. He knew Craig was staring at him but couldn't look him in the eye.

"Okay. Um, here's the interesting thing. I checked Glimt's high school yearbook. He was in the computer club all four years."

Vic's mind focused, and he rode free of his emotions. He looked at Craig. "Really? Any idea what he did?"

"I have a call into the teacher who ran the club, but he hasn't called me back yet."

"If he doesn't call, first thing in the morning, go find him. I don't care that tomorrow is Saturday."

"Got it. Okay. After high school, Glimt went to Carnegie Mellon. It gets confusing here. Dr. Basu said he had a degree in Multimedia. There's no such thing. His degree is in Immersive Technologies in Arts and Culture. Basically, it means using immersive technology to tell stories. I bet that's why Dr. Basu thought he wanted to make documentaries. But here's the thing. He also had a minor—they call it a concentration— in Health Systems."

Vic stared at Craig. One side of Craig's face was bathed in streetlight, the other dark. "Does that mean he writes code?"

"Possibly."

"He wrote the app they all use?"

Craig shrugged. "Can't say for sure, but maybe."

"But we asked him who wrote it. He said he didn't know." Vic made a fist and bumped the heel of it on the steering wheel. "He lied."

"Again, possibly. Or maybe he worked for the company that produced it. You asked me to look for any payments Brandon might have made to a company to create the app. I'm still working on that, and so are the FBI."

"Right, keep doing that, but ask that teacher if Glimt did anything in the computer club that could have prepared him to code an app." Vic frowned. "Remember that chart in Glimt's office? We didn't know what it was. Could it have anything to do with how the app runs?"

Craig scratched his head. "A user flow diagram, maybe? I didn't think of that. Possibly, yes. I need to see it again."

"We can do that tomorrow. We need a long talk with Glimt, that's for sure." Vic glanced at Jake's house, alone in the cul-de-sac. The living room window threw light on the street. He glimpsed facts aligning. Meera Basu, choosing Steven over Glimt, Glimt wanting revenge for that. Perhaps having the training to code the app. His college study of health care systems. His disappearance after Jake called him. Vic checked his phone. No return call from Glimt.

"This is good, Craig," Vic said gently. "It might be enough to Miranda him tomorrow. If we can find him."

"I was thinking about that," Craig answered. "The amount of money that's already been taken in overcharges? I wonder if he decided to run."

Vic felt his mouth tighten at the thought. A memory of Isabella came to him, lugging her gold coins somewhere, maybe holed up in a motel, working out how to cross the border. "Take the money and run," Vic said quietly. "That is what people do."

Chapter Sixty-Seven

Vic was pulling into his driveway, take-out Chinese on the seat beside him, when his phone rang. He glanced at the dashboard clock. 12:35 a.m. Saturday morning was only thirty-five minutes old.

"Craig?" Vic asked, seeing the caller ID.

"Sorry. But Conor came over to Jake's house. They're getting into Conor's car."

Vic groaned inwardly. So much for dinner. "Follow them. Keep this line open and give me updates on where they're heading. I'll catch up to you."

"Yep."

"Try not to get made."

"Nobody on the roads and my Jeep has distinctive headlights. What could go wrong?"

Vic smiled. Craig was getting comfortable enough to be sarcastic. He placed the Chinese food in the passenger footwell. "Just do what you can and keep the line open."

"Sorry."

Vic thought Craig sounded distracted. "Quit apologizing. Just do the best you can and keep giving me updates. It's almost impossible to follow someone at this time of night."

Vic reversed out of the driveway and headed in the general direction of Jake's house, course-correcting each time Craig provided an update. He texted Anne as he drove, letting her know where he was.

Craig kept the line open, talking on speaker. About twenty minutes later,

Vic heard a muffled curse.

"Sorry," Craig breathed into the phone. "They gunned a yellow light, and I was the only other car on the road. I couldn't run the red. Too obvious."

"Where are you?"

"East Liberty, on Penn Avenue. Not far from the headquarters for Veterans Health."

Vic was nearby, having turned again and again with each of Craig's updates. "Don't worry about it. Park on Penn Avenue and watch the cross streets. It's straight and long there; you might get lucky and see them go through an intersection. I'm almost to you."

Four minutes later, Vic eased to a stop behind Craig's Jeep. He got out and walked up to the driver's side as Craig lowered his window.

"Anything?" Vic asked.

"Nope. Sorry again."

"Like I said. Quit apologizing. This is the job. At least, we know they were out. We can ask them why tomorrow."

"There!" Craig pointed so quickly he almost stoved his finger on the windshield.

Vic spun and spotted, five blocks away, the tail of Conor's car as it crossed Penn Avenue toward the center of Pittsburgh. Craig twisted his ignition key, and the Jeep groaned to a start.

"Wait." Vic stared along Penn Avenue, through the harsh white of the streetlights. The wind carried a plastic bag along the deserted road. The sky above was ink-black. "We won't catch them." Vic considered the cross-street Conor had used. A block beyond it, traffic lights changed and threw different colors onto the blacktop. "Tell you what. Let's take my car and look around. I bet they were down that particular road for a reason."

Craig shrugged and cut the ignition on his Jeep. The engine wheezed as it turned off. Vic returned to his car, Craig following.

Ten minutes later, Chinese food now on the floor behind the passenger seat, Vic started a grid search, first in the blocks below the street where they last saw Conor's car, and when that proved fruitless, on the blocks above it.

"There," called Craig, suddenly.

Vic slowed to a stop. This particular block was a row of small, two-story houses set ten feet back from the street with narrow footpaths between them. Despite the general shoehorning of one next to the other, the houses were well-kept and, for the most part, freshly painted.

Craig pointed at a house so freshly graffitied, that streaks of red paint from the word "killer" still glistened on the wall and front door.

"Son of a bitch," Vic said softly. "Let me guess who lives here."

Craig was already typing into his phone. "County real estate site," Craig said, half holding his breath. They both waited as the site loaded, and Craig typed in the address and ward.

"Paul Drum," Craig said finally.

"Paul Drum of Veterans Health. He's in for a surprise when he wakes up."

"What are Conor and Jake doing?"

Vic studied the scrawled letters. They looked exactly like the writing on Jake's garage door. "Goading them. First, Jake called them both and told them he was onto the Medicare fraud, and now this. They're trying to get one of them to make a move. Do something stupid. And I bet if they tagged Drum, they're headed to Glimt's house. Where does he live?"

Craig searched once again and named the address.

"Strip District," Vic said, hearing the street name. "Makes sense; his offices are nearby. Conor's car was headed in that direction. Must be those new condos behind the old terminal building."

"Check it out?"

"Yep. But take a couple of photos." Vic waited until Craig snapped pictures, then goosed the accelerator. "I'll drop you at your car and meet you there."

Twenty minutes later, Vic slid into Craig's Jeep half a block from Glimt's front door. Streetlights lit the street surface in individual pools, like a perforation line between the row houses on each side of the street. Every identical front door was separated by an identical garage door, mirrored on the opposite side of the street. This time, the word "killer" was scrawled across a garage door. Vic studied the writing and the house number.

"I guess they got the right door," Vic said. "Handwriting looks different on this one. I think Jake gave it a shot. Earning his bones with Conor."

CHAPTER SIXTY-SEVEN

Craig huffed a laugh and, without being asked, snapped a couple of photographs.

Vic shifted his legs. He was tired, the kind that seeps into bones. "They're like a couple of teenagers."

"Think it will work?"

Vic fought back a yawn. "Doesn't matter. For the next few days, we stick to them like glue, just in case Drum or Glimt gets pissed."

"Want to see if Glimt is home?"

Vic thought about that. It was a good question. "No," he said finally. "First, if he answers the door, we aren't ready for him. You need to talk to his high school teacher. Second, if we're here now, when he sees the graffiti, he'll think we should have stopped it. We don't need that problem." Vic rubbed his eyes. "Okay, no need for you to watch Jake the rest of the night. He's had his fun. I'll text Liz about tonight and tell her I sent you home. She can take over watching Jake at six. We'll work it out from there."

Craig nodded. Even in the poor light, he looked distant, as if something was on his mind.

"Something bothering you?" Vic asked.

Craig tilted his head, thinking. "Kind of. I just don't know what to do with it. It's out of context and doesn't fit anything else."

"I've told you before, it's the things that are different or aren't there that matter the most."

"Right, okay. When you and Liz were in New Orleans, I cleared the crime scene in Brandon's office."

"Yep. Sounded like you had it under control."

"Right, but Brandon's lawyer showed up. She is impressive. Confident. Put together."

Vic's exhaustion fell away. "I remember. Tori Hart? She ran interference the second time Liz and I talked to Brandon."

"That's her. She wanted access to some of Brandon's files and his laptop. I said no, and she went full-court press on me. But I'd already sent the laptop in for processing, so I had one of the uniforms escort her out."

"Good. So what's worrying you?"

"I looked her up. She isn't a criminal lawyer at all. Her main specialty is advising on IPOs. So I couldn't figure out why she was there and so anxious."

"She advises on taking companies public? She told us she did intellectual property."

"She does that as well. But she's known for taking companies public."

"But these organizations are non-profits."

"Brandon's company isn't."

Vic looked at Craig. "That's more than interesting." Vic closed his eyes to clear his thoughts. "You're right. I don't know how that fits in. But let me take that one. If Brandon wanted to take his company public, I know someone they would have approached for funding. I bet she also knows the lawyer. Let me talk to her."

"Okay."

Vic placed his hand on the door handle. "Go home and get some sleep. We need to be sharp in the next couple of days."

Chapter Sixty-Eight

It was one-thirty when Vic returned home. He stashed the Chinese take-out in the refrigerator untouched. He just wanted to sleep. He climbed the stairs, checked on Lettie, and tucked her blanket about her. Lightly kissed her cheek.

Anne stirred when he slid into bed. "Are you okay? I saw your text." Her voice was thick with sleep.

"No problems. Beyond the stupid stuff guys talk each other into doing."

Anne shifted closer to him, her body warm, and kissed his cheek. "I'm shocked," she whispered and burrowed back into her pillow.

Vic stared at the ceiling, his eyes adjusting to the dark. Now that he was in bed, he was wide awake. His mind shifted to Jake and Conor, then to Drum and Glimt. He tried to find a slot for Craig's information about the IPO. If Brandon was planning to take his company public, he didn't see how that connected to Steven's death. Steven identified fraud, but according to the FBI, Brandon was uninvolved. Of course he was. To pull off an IPO, the company's financials had to be squeaky clean. Brandon wouldn't consider an IPO if he was using the company to commit fraud. He clearly planned to make his money on the IPO. Vic steadied his breathing. He knew, at bottom, that he needed to understand more about IPOs to find a connection. He wanted to talk to Mary Monahan, the person he'd mentioned to Craig. She ran a venture capital fund that specialized in high-tech startups, and he guessed Mary already knew about Brandon's company. He checked his phone, charging beside the bed. It was two-thirty.

"Probably not the right time to call Mary," he thought to himself. He let out a slow breath and closed his eyes.

A shrill ringing ruptured Vic out of a full-body dream about hallways and doors that refused to open. He blinked, his senses reeling, struggling to realize the noise was actually his cell phone. He scrabbled for it and held it in front of his face. A number he didn't recognize, no name. The time was 5:45 A.M.

"Hello," he answered, his voice gruff.

"Vic? It's Jake Kittery."

Vic sat up and swung his feet to the floor. His mind felt like taffy. "What's happened?"

"I got an email. I thought you should know. Paul Drum wants to meet me at my office this morning. In an hour."

Vic tried to shrug off his sleepiness and had little luck.

"That's unexpected."

"Yeah, I thought so too."

"No." Vic finally blinked himself awake. "I mean, he probably hasn't stepped outside yet. Seen what you guys painted on his door."

Silence on the line. Vic waited.

"Look." Jake fell silent again, and Vic thought he heard a series of sounds, as if Jake was tapping the edge of a table. Perhaps working something out in his head. "Okay, look. We're closed Saturdays. If Drum comes over, he and I will be the only two people in the office. You warned me about that."

"You don't want to be alone with him or Glimt. And do you really want me to believe you didn't already call Conor?"

"Well, yeah, I did. He wanted to keep this between him and me. For some reason, he's not a fan of yours."

Vic had a vision of chasing Conor out of Steven's memorial service and shoving him into the base of Braddock's historical marker. If he was Conor, he wouldn't be a fan of Vic either. "I get why. Okay, I'll get to your offices. My partner will, too, but it'll take her longer. What did you and Conor work out?"

"He's going to hide in one of the offices and listen in. I'm going to set up my phone on speaker and hide it on my desk for him."

"Good. Include me on the call. I'll listen in as well. We need to hear what he says." Vic knew that anything overheard on the phone wouldn't be admissible in court, but he didn't care. He wanted Jake to be safe. If Drum said something that made him liable, he would get it out of him some other way.

"Sure."

"And something else. If anything gets weird and you want us to bust in, ask Drum how long he served in the Marines. I hear that, and we'll come right in."

"Got it."

Vic pinched the bridge of his nose between a finger and thumb. He knew he shouldn't mention this to Jake, but he wanted him prepared. "Something else, between you and me, the weapon used to murder Steven and Brandon was a long-bladed knife, like a bayonet. That's hard to conceal, so look for something he can use to carry it. If you see a briefcase, just comment how much you like it. Then I'll know he may be armed. If he pulls it, don't wait. Use the code phrase and we'll be in. Don't take any risks. None."

"Do you really think Drum could be the guy?"

Vic stood and sidled away from the bed, realizing too late that he may have woken Anne. "We don't know yet, but I don't want to take the chance. Let's hear what he has to say, okay?"

"I can do that."

"And tell Conor not to butt in. We just want to hear what Drum says when he thinks the two of you are alone."

Jake laughed easily. "Yeah, well, Conor. Do I need a safe word for him as well?"

When Vic ended the call, he turned to Anne. She was sitting up in the morning gloom.

"Sorry," Vic said. "I should have put it on vibrate."

She shook her head slowly. "Sounds serious."

"It might be. Might not. But I need to get going."

"Go." Anne smiled at him in the semi-darkness. "And try not to wake up Lettie on the way out." She snuggled down under the covers.

Vic used the closet light to find his clothes, dressed, and moments later was downstairs. He retrieved his Glock from the locked drawer in the front hall and moments later slid into his car. As he pulled into the street, he called Liz.

Liz answered on the second ring. "I thought you'd sleep in," Liz said without preamble, when she took the call.

"No such luck. Where are you?"

"Just got in the car to go watch Jake's house. I saw your text from last night."

"Skip that. Meet me at Jake's office, but park well down the street." Vic brought her up to date, telling her about his telephone call with Jake.

"Drum wants to meet? Would not have expected that. But I guess he knows how to use a bayonet. But if I'd stabbed two guys with a bayonet, would I use one as a paperweight?"

"I had the same thought. But then again, Glimt still hasn't returned my call. That's suspicious as hell."

"Which reminds me."

Liz fell silent, her voice replaced by the surge of a car engine.

"Sorry." Liz was back. "Speaking of Glimt, I asked Meera if she dated him. She rolled her eyes so hard I thought she might hurt her baby. She said Glimt asked her out a couple of times, she said no, but he kept trying, and she finally agreed to get coffee with him. I guess all he talked about was his Dad walking out and how he'd wanted to move to Hollywood after college, but didn't have the money. Total 'feel sorry for me' play. Disgusting. Then he tried to set up another date. She said no and quit volunteering at his non-profit. The only reason she was there the day Steven died was to cover for another doctor who called off last minute."

Vic stopped at a traffic light. "Then how did Glimt know Steven and Meera were dating? When Marla overheard the argument, she said Glimt was telling Steven not to date Meera anymore."

"I had the same thought. I asked Meera. She said she didn't know, but she and Steven talked about it after the bathroom argument Marla overheard. Meera thought Glimt might be stalking her."

CHAPTER SIXTY-EIGHT

"Glimt keeps digging himself into a deeper hole."

"Yeah, but it's all circumstantial." Liz fell silent for a few moments. "Okay, I'm on Route 279. Twenty minutes from Jake's offices."

"I'm almost there. Look for my car. I'll be a block down from Jakes offices toward the river."

"Got it."

Liz ended the call, and Vic glanced east. The horizon was milky white in a preamble of dawn.

Vic took the ramp that led into Braddock and turned right one block before the street where Jake's offices were located. He ran parallel to that street for two blocks and took two left turns. After the second, he pulled against the curb, doused his headlights, and cut the ignition.

About one hundred yards ahead, the brick two-story building that housed TU Health's offices poked upwards. Another hundred yards past that was the main road that ran through Braddock, with cars and trucks crossing through an intersection. Beyond that, the road rose steeply to the bluff that overlooked the town, the sky a red glow above. Vic checked his dashboard clock. Twenty more minutes until Jake's meeting.

Ten minutes later, a sedan pulled into the parking lot next to TU Health, and Jake let himself in through the front door, followed by Conor's lanky frame. They'd arrived in one car, and Vic liked that. Two cars in the parking lot might make Drum suspicious. The office lights blinked on. About three minutes later, Vic's phone rang.

"Can you hear me okay?" Jake asked, when Vic answered.

"Loud and clear. I'm here, too. Parked a block down from your building."

"Good. Conor is going to hide on the steps to the second floor. Turns out you can't hide in the offices. Too much glass."

Vic thought Jake sounded tight, perhaps a bit nervous. He didn't blame him. "Like I said, if Drum feels hinky in any way, ask him how long he served in the Marines. We'll be right there. Don't take any chances."

"Just need to warm up."

Vic thought he still sounded tight. "I can come in if you want. We can meet him together."

"No. Not my first negotiation. I'm fine." Something rustled. "I'm hiding the phone now, so better not talk. Just going to leave it on my desk with a piece of paper over it."

"Sounds good."

Vic turned up the volume on his own phone, hit mute, and placed it on the dashboard. He stared up the road, betting himself, that Drum would arrive at five minutes to seven. He was military and wouldn't be able to stop himself.

Sure enough, at six minutes to seven, an older, boxy Jeep Cherokee turned down the road and into the parking lot. From the phone, Vic heard Conor call to Jake, although he couldn't make out the words. Conor was playing lookout, Vic guessed.

A minute later, Drum appeared on the sidewalk, a briefcase in his right hand. Vic pursed his lips. Already, he didn't like it. He looked around to see if Liz was nearby and saw a pair of headlights slide to a stop behind him. Moments later, Liz slid into the passenger seat. She pointed at Vic's phone.

"It's on mute," Vic confirmed.

"Anything?"

"Drum just went inside. He's got a briefcase."

Liz fell silent and they both stared at the phone, willing it to life.

Chapter Sixty-Nine

J ake fought down a surge of nerves as he directed Drum toward his office. He made a point of gesturing Drum ahead of him to keep Drum in sight, but even that didn't relax him. Drum's rigid and square posture intimidated him, and he kept wondering what Drum's briefcase held. He was glad he'd worn his steel-toed boots. They were heavy, but he felt ready for what was coming.

Inside his office, Jake directed Drum to a chair facing his desk and settled into the facing seat, glad for the desk between them. Drum placed his briefcase between his feet.

Jake considered him. "This is pretty short notice. What can I do you for?"

Drum waved a hand. "I figured you for an early riser. No corporate ten-to-four bullshit for a guy who spent his life on shop floors."

Jake decided to wait. Contract negotiations had taught him patience and how silence could undermine people. Plus, the less said, the less your own words were used against you.

"To the point," Drum said, when Jake didn't respond. "I like that. Okay. First, I'm sorry about your son, Steven. I liked him. He was a stand-up guy. And smart. He built this organization. Made it successful."

"Thanks for that." Jake was surprised at the tightness of his throat. It would be like this from now on, he knew. Never sure if he could hold it together when Stevie's name came up. He was glad he and Drum weren't negotiating, although he suddenly had an odd feeling they actually were. It was something in Drum's tone.

But that sense was overwhelmed by another thought, the realization that

Drum, sitting right in front of him, might be the person who murdered Stevie. Stabbed him. Jake lost track of his thinking. He went numb, Drum's words arriving as if spoken from a distance.

"But what happened has turned everything into a shit show." Drum shifted in his seat, radiating intensity. "Steven passed away, Brandon Ellis dead. All the plans everyone made on hold."

Jake struggled to concentrate.

"Look." Drum leaned forward. "It's up to us to save this organization." Drum punched his right fist into the palm of his left hand. "Right now, it's just you, me and Glimt. We need to work together. Drag this organization out of the crapper."

Drum fell silent as if he expected Jake to say something. Jake found his voice. "I'm with you that things are a mess. What are you thinking?" Jake was sure of it now. This *was* some kind of negotiation.

A small smile appeared at the corner of Drum's lips. Jake thought it looked especially wolfish.

"That's what I like about you, Jake. Action-oriented. I say we divide and conquer. I see three problems. This bullshit about Medicare fraud, the IPO Brandon was planning, and personnel. We've lost some of our guys; it's time for others to step up."

Jake hadn't heard about any IPO and had only the thinnest idea what it might be. He decided to play dumb. "An IPO? I hadn't heard anything about that. I'm not even sure what it is."

Drum waived a hand in dismissal. "Brandon wanted to take his company public. Use the money he raised to open more non-profits around the country. Keep building the fee base for his WholePatient app."

"But we're non-profits. Based here."

"We are, but his company is for-profit. I think the app gave him the idea. What's the old line? You want to make money during a gold rush? Sell the miners pickaxes, food, and camping shit."

Jake felt out of his depth. He understood protecting his workers, the need to reinvest in a working company. But Drum was talking about what he always thought ran companies into the ground. He was sure of it. To him, as soon as business owners talked IPOs, buy-outs, mergers, or restructuring management, bad things happened to unions.

"We need to shelve this IPO crap." Drum stared at him his gaze unrelenting. "Brandon Ellis is gone, and yeah, that sucks. But we've got too much on our plate right now to worry about an IPO. I think we go to the board and tell them to stick it. Then we focus on what really matters."

"Which is?"

"Bury this Medicare fraud. I think it's bullshit. Smoke and mirrors. We checked our records. There's nothing like that going on with us. Look, I respect Steven. When your son said he found some kind of fraud, I believed him. But we looked hard. I think Steven actually spotted some kind of record-keeping snafu at the insurance company level."

Jake was overcome with a need to defend Stevie. "Stevie doesn't get stuff like that wrong. How about Glimt? Did he find anything with the Firefighters record-keeping?"

"Not that I know of. He's looking into it, but he's away this weekend. Camping or something. But I see where you're going. I suggest we leave the fraud question open, until Glimt reviews his own records. But, if he doesn't find anything, I suggest we shelve it. You included. If he spots something, then damn sure we red-flag it. Go to the authorities."

Something nagged at Jake. He couldn't quite put his finger on it. It had to do with Drum's certainty, how his words were almost a salesman's patter. And then he knew. Drum hadn't said anything about the graffiti written across his front door. He hadn't complained at all. He'd walked in and gone straight into his pitch.

"That gets us to the last thing." Drum lifted his briefcase to his lap.

"Uh oh," Jake said quickly. "You need something out of your briefcase? You got a presentation in there?"

Drum hesitated. He seemed surprised by the comment and looked at the battered leather briefcase in his lap. "You're right. I do have a short presentation, but you know what, I'm not going to use it." He returned the briefcase between his feet. "Let's just talk, you and me. Man to man."

"Okay. That's good." Through the glass wall of his office, Jake saw Conor's shadow on the carpet. "So, what is the last thing you wanted to talk about?"

"I said earlier. Personnel. I have some ideas about that."

Conor's shadow receded, and Jake waved at Drum to continue.

"I mentioned going to the board earlier."

"Right." Jake felt they were finally getting to the heart of it.

"When we do, I'll put myself forward as Brandon's replacement. We'll go to the board with a package. Show that we've put this fraud question behind us, that you and I and Glimt are united, all of us on the same page, and we can take it from here. Can I count on your support?"

Jake stared at him. Of all the reasons for Drum's visit, he hadn't expected this. But as Drum said the words, Jake felt his natural argumentativeness rising. Perhaps it was too many years of avoiding the first offer from people on the other side of the negotiating table. "I don't get it." Jake gathered his thoughts, "How are you going to dodge the IPO? I said I don't know much about that, and that's true, but I do know that just about any board will support an IPO. It's their chance to get rich. And the fraud isn't behind us. You said earlier Glimt hasn't checked his records. He might find it."

Drum looked unfazed. "Brandon was shooting for an IPO too soon. His company isn't anywhere close to being a unicorn. The board knows that. And sure. As I said before, if Glimt finds fraud, damn right we call in the authorities."

Jake considered Drum's words. He didn't have enough information about the inner workings of the board to know if Drum was speaking the truth. "Well, let's see what Glimt comes back with." Jake knew he sounded wishy-washy but wasn't sure what else to say.

"I need a bit more than that, compadre." Drum shifted in his seat.

"I don't think I can give you more than that. Not right now." Warm anger seeped into Jake's muscles. He hated being dictated to. He wasn't going to back down on what Stevie had found. "Look, you called me up out of nowhere and sprang this on me. Before I agree to anything I want to hear what Glimt says about fraud. And I'm going to figure out a way to have someone check what Stevie found."

"There's absolutely no need to bring anyone else in on this. You're wasting your time."

Jake barely noticed that Drum had lifted his briefcase onto his lap again. "What makes you so sure?"

"Common damn sense."

"I'd say the same thing about not committing. We don't know enough yet."

Drum rose, and Jake was suddenly keenly aware of the briefcase. Drum made no move to open it.

"We need to move fast." Drum sounded tight, as if he was reining in anger. "And you, me and Glimt need to stick together. I thought you'd understand that. Being a union guy."

The sarcasm in Drum's tone when he said the word 'union' brought Jake to his feet. "Call me when Glimt is done. We'll talk then. I didn't say no."

Drum stared at Jake for several seconds. "Well, don't say I didn't warn you. You had your chance."

"No, you tried to railroad me."

"If I'd tried to do that, you'd know it." Drum pivoted and left the office, moving quickly through the deserted bullpen to the front door.

Jake watched Drum let himself out and tried to relax enough to slow his heart. It didn't work. He gave up, slid his phone out from underneath the papers on his desk and held it against his ear. "You guys hear all that?"

Chapter Seventy

Vic glanced at Liz as Jake's question rose from the phone. Liz slowly shook her head in disgust, scrunching her features.

Vic tapped the mute button to open the call. "Yeah, we did."

"There's a guy who sees his chances," Liz added.

Vic watched the parking lot entrance, next to Jake's office building. Drum pulled into the road, a phone pressed to his ear, and turned right toward downtown Braddock. Something about the phone Drum was holding bothered Vic, but he didn't know what.

"He's gone," Vic said into his own phone.

"Glad to hear it." This was Conor's voice, growing louder as he spoke the sentence. "Guys like that, planning how to make money off people dying."

"And not wasting any time to do it." Liz followed her statement with a huffed breath of disgust.

"Okay, everyone." Vic lifted his phone from the dashboard. "The guy's an asshole. We get it. Jake, did you feel threatened at all? I was almost out of the car when you mentioned he'd raised his briefcase."

"No." Jake paused, clearly gathering his thoughts. "He's intense but not in a crazy way. But he's controlling. He expects me to go along with what he says. He makes you think what he says is going to happen, and you need to be on board."

Two blocks away, the taillights on Drum's car glowed as the car stopped at an intersection. Moments later, Drum turned left onto Braddock's main street.

"Didn't sound like you bought in," Vic said.

"No. I sat across the table from too many guys like that. You meet all types. Some guys try to bullshit you by talking fast so you're always off balance, but he's one of the good old boys who talk in deep voices and try to use the force of their voice to make you think it's their way only. But they're all the same bullshitters."

Vic smiled. The more he talked to Jake, the more he liked him. Vic's Glock pinched against his side, and without thinking, he slid it out of his holster and under the front seat.

"And he gave himself away," Jake added. "He never mentioned the graffiti on his door. Most people would be so pissed they would be ranting about it. I couldn't figure that out. Then I realized he wasn't going to talk about anything that made him look bad, and that meant he was after something. And sure enough, he was."

"Goes back to you saying he was disciplined," Conor interjected. "Drum had enough self-control not to mention the graffiti, so he could get after what he wanted."

"Yeah. Or the graffiti didn't bother him. I know some guys like that." Jake's tone was needling, and Vic knew the comment was directed at Conor.

"Yeah. I should have figured that out years ago," Conor replied, almost meekly.

"You sure-as-shit should have."

The call fell silent. Vic would have liked to see the expression on Jake's and Conor's faces as they finished hammering out their own history.

"Okay." Vic glanced at Liz with a quizzical expression, and she nodded. "Liz and I are calling it. Not sure how all this helps us. Anything else from you guys, or is that it?"

"That's it," Jake answered.

"Not completely," Liz interrupted. "Monday, we need to interview you guys. About last night."

Silence again, until Conor said slowly, "Let us know when you need us."

"We will." Vic touched his screen and ended the call. He looked at Liz. "Yeah, I guess we can't let the spray painting lie."

"Nope." Liz stared through the windshield. "There is one other thing."

315

Vic waited.

"I thought Drum sounded weirdly confident that Glimt wasn't going to find fraud. Drum sounded sure of it. That statement about we'll call the authorities if Glimt finds anything…that smelled."

"It did," Vic agreed. "He was too quick with it. He knew that's what Jake wanted to hear."

The door to Jake's office building opened. Conor and Jake stepped onto the sidewalk and stood facing one another, grinning about something. They looked relaxed, and after a few moments, shook hands. Conor started down the street, Vic guessed to where he had parked before meeting Jake. Jake went back inside.

"Best buddies," Liz breathed.

"That's better than what it was before. And Conor knows something about losing a son. It'll help Jake."

Liz stayed quiet for a few moments. "What do you think? Drum isn't our guy? That leaves Glimt. If we can find the kid."

"Yeah. Camping. Do you believe that?"

"He didn't seem the type, but you never know."

Vic thought about that. "You know what, give Glimt a call. Try him again."

"Okay."

"Wait a minute." Vic struggled to marshal his thoughts. "How did Drum know Glimt was camping?"

"Interesting question."

"Tell you what, why don't you call Marla, Drum's admin. Ask her if Drum and Glimt have talked recently. She'll know if Glimt called their offices or stopped by."

"Sure." Liz opened the car door and slid out. She bent down and looked inside the car, holding the door open. "By the way, I got a text from Chief Goodwin in New Orleans. They've come up empty on Isabella. She hasn't showed up anywhere. He thinks she's in the wind."

"She'll show up sometime." But Vic liked the idea of Isabella on her own, dragging along her very own roller bag of gold coins.

"I don't know about that." Liz smiled, and Vic knew she also liked the idea of Isabella being free. "She's smart. If she just turns in a couple of coins a year, she can live on a beach somewhere for a long time."

"As long as she doesn't get greedy."

Liz nodded. "There's that." She closed the door to Vic's car and headed for her own.

Chapter Seventy-One

Vic started his car and repeated Drum's route to Braddock's main street. Took the same left. He cruised through downtown Braddock, his mind nibbling at his last conversation with Liz. How Isabella might stay free if she wasn't greedy. It made him think of Drum's almost angry need to take over Brandon's job. How greed drove Carty Swain right out of a new—and safe—life in Costa Rica. Propelled him all the way back to New Orleans and his death. How it undid him.

Vic navigated his car along the two-way streets leading back to the parkway. He saw a parallel in Drum and Carty. The way greed guided them, smooth and clean.

Vic drifted through a green light. Smooth. That word. What had Drum said to Jake when he lifted the briefcase to his knees? He had a presentation. He didn't show it to Jake, but he said he had one. What if that was true? Suppose he did have a presentation? That meant preparation. Planning.

So Drum had planned this move for some time. He hadn't just come up with it when Brandon died.

This niggled at Vic. Had they looked at the evidence wrong? What did Liz say when they heard Brandon Ellis was dead? She said they had collected the evidence the right way. They just needed another way to look at it.

Vic slid through another intersection and thought about that. Their only approach to the evidence was to explain why fraud led to Steven's death. To find out who had the most to win or lose with Steven dead.

A red light brought Vic to a stop. He tapped the steering wheel absently. But what if the murders came about because they interfered with a larger

318

plan? What if they weren't just a knee-jerk reaction to Steven discovering the fraud?

The back of Vic's neck tingled. He grabbed his phone and called Craig, urging him to pick up.

On the third ring, he did.

"Craig," Vic said, before Craig could greet him. "Did you ever talk to that high school teacher of Glimt's? The one who ran the computer club, or whatever it was?"

"Yeah. He called me back this morning."

Vic heard the distant sound of a violin through the phone. "What did he say?"

"I asked him if Glimt could write computer code. If they did anything like that in the high school club. He said no, they mostly did robotics. They entered those events where robots fight each other?"

Vic felt the air leave him. He'd been sure Glimt was behind the app. "So we'd have to prove Glimt learned to write code at CMU."

"That would help. But I also pushed him on it, because I knew Glimt was our best suspect. I asked the teacher if he was sure. He thought about it, and then said the robots have to be programmed. Glimt did that. He got apologetic. He said he didn't think about it because the bot worked so well. He missed that Glimt must have programmed it perfectly."

"Does that translate to coding an app?"

In the background, the violin tempo sped up. Even with his adrenaline rising, Vic pictured Eileen Liang, Craig's girlfriend, bent over her instrument, her thin arm moving gracefully, the music pouring out of her. He felt like the music was moving him along as well.

Craig laughed. "I asked that exact same question. He said not really, they're different capabilities, but he also said people post bits of code for different programming functions so anyone can use them. Freeware. And that if Glimt programmed the bot, then he'd know where to find the code he might need. So yeah, he changed his opinion. He thought it's possible Glimt created an app. The app functionality actually isn't that complicated. He could have linked together a bunch of freeware and made it work."

"Damn. You didn't think to call me about this after you talked to this teacher?"

Craig was silent for a moment. "Um, I sent you a text. Right after."

"Oh." Vic felt foolish, but his mind was working too quickly to care. A horn blared, and Vic looked up. Green light. He glanced down the crossroad, spotted a parking space, and took a left. He pulled into the curb. "Sorry. I'm driving. Something else." He closed his eyes. Craig's discovery about freeware wasn't concrete proof. It was logical but had gaps. Just knowing where to find freeware didn't mean Glimt downloaded it or linked it together. "Another thing. You said his father died early, right?"

"Yes. Glimt's father disappeared not long after he was born. His mother filed for divorce a few years later. That was in the New Jersey legal documents."

"I'm asking because Glimt's mother might know if Glimt used freeware. Maybe she can fill in the gaps."

"Yeah. I thought of that and asked the teacher if Glimt's mother came to any of those Battle Bots tournaments. He said no. I didn't put this in my text, but he said a guy came sometimes. The teacher only talked to the guy once and didn't have a name. He said it was an older guy. Bald. And he said this guy and Glimt were close."

Vic's heartbeat quickened. He had a sudden vision of Steven's crime scene on Mt. Washington. Pittsburgh's two rivers, the Monongahela and Allegheny, merging from different directions to form the Ohio.

"Shit," Vic said softly.

"What?"

"We missed it." Vic's mind cleared. He pictured himself sitting in Drum's office, the wall behind Drum covered in framed photographs and one white certificate with blue lettering. He recognized what the letters stood for now. Fathers and Sons. The non-profit mentoring program connecting men to boys with no fathers. Maybe it was a coincidence, that Glimt had no father and Drum had volunteered for years to mentor boys who needed men as role models. To be the father figure to fatherless boys.

"When..." Vic scrunched up his face as he tried to remember. "When did

Glimt start working for Firefighters Health? Was it before or after Drum started at Veterans Health?"

"After, you said. Maybe a month."

"And Glimt was never a fireman or a paramedic, right? Jake was a union organizer, Drum a veteran. Glimt's the exception. I bet Drum recommended Glimt for the job, and Glimt got it because he could develop the app. It was Glimt who told us he knew Steven from college. So did Meera, but I bet Glimt told Meera that was how he and Steven met. Glimt was misdirecting us."

"I don't get it." Craig sounded confused.

"It isn't Glimt, it isn't Drum," Vic breathed into the phone, again picturing the rivers joining to become one. "It's both of them. They're working as a team. Drum is calling the shots, role-playing as Glimt's dad."

"Oh crap." As Craig spoke, the violin music drew to an end. "There's something else. You asked me to do background on Drum as well? Turns out his discharge from the Marines was a general discharge. Not an honorable one."

Vic's palms were suddenly moist. "Jake turned down Drum this morning. Wait, and this morning Drum told Jake that Steven told him about the Medicare fraud. Drum told us he'd never talked to Steven about it. What if Drum met Steven on Mt. Washington, and when Steven didn't back down about the fraud, Glimt showed up." Vic slapped the steering wheel, a realization the scenario could be playing out again. "Craig, I need you at Jake's office. Right now. Armed. I'm going back there now. Call the Braddock PD, tell them we need a wellness check on Jake right now. Imminent danger. I bet Glimt shows up next at Jake's office."

"On my way."

Vic checked the road, heart thumping, and did a U-turn in a squeal of tires. He gunned the car right at the traffic light and pushed the accelerator as far as he could on the windy, two-lane road. He slowed behind a pick-up and speed-dialed Liz.

"Vic?"

Liz sounded unreasonably calm. "I have something," Vic had to rein his voice back. "I talked to Craig. I think Glimt and Drum are in this together. Turns out Glimt could have written the code to put the app together using freeware. I also think Drum has been mentoring Glimt since high school. Grooming him. Drum does the planning, and Glimt does the dirty work. I bet Drum convinced Glimt to use the app to defraud Medicare, thinking they could do it for years. But two things happened. Steven spotted the fraud, and Brandon decided to do an IPO. They had to kill Steven to keep the fraud hidden, and stop Brandon's IPO, because to pull off an IPO, company financials have to be spotless. Due diligence would have found the fraud. Two different things came together, and Drum had to stop them. If they wanted to keep running the scam, Drum had to kill Steven and take over Brandon's job to bury the IPO."

Vic jammed his hand onto the horn to get the truck in front moving, the rest of the facts they'd learned falling into place. "If Drum's been grooming Glimt, it explains why Meera was surprised Glimt stayed here rather than go to Hollywood after college. Drum kept him here, got him a job at Firefighters Health, and promised him they'd be rich. Have enough money to work on whatever projects he wanted. Even gave him a bayonet. I mean hell, he gave one to Steven."

"That fits. Shit."

"Right. And this morning Drum asked Jake to join them, but Jake turned him down. I bet Drum did the same thing with Steven and maybe even Brandon. He had Glimt kill them because they said no. I'm headed back to Jake's offices. Call Jake and tell him to get the hell out of there, then call Sandy and tell her my theory. After that, turn around and get back to Jake's. Craig is calling Braddock PD to do a wellness check on Jake. I'll see you there."

Vic ended the call and tossed the phone on the passenger seat. He checked the traffic and swung around the slow-moving pick-up in front of him. He gunned the engine, and the truck's horn faded behind him.

Three minutes later, Vic shot down Braddock's main street and swung right into the street leading to Jake's offices. In the distance, a hunched form entered TU Health. Vic gunned down the street, ran the stop sign at the first intersection, and ground to a stop in front of the office door. No police cruisers were about. He cut the ignition, and, leaving the car door open, jumped out of the car and opened the door into the entry. At the second door, he looked through the glass and spotted Jake on the far side of the bullpen, sitting at his desk, his phone to his ear. Jake's back was to him, his feet up on the desk, encased in heavy, chunky boots.

Vic reached for the door handle with his left hand and felt for his Glock with his right. His holster was empty. With a start, he remembered sliding his weapon under the front seat. A shape he still couldn't make out moved near Edna's desk.

"Shit." Vic turned the door handle and slipped into the offices. "Police," he shouted, his right hand at his hip as if he was holding a holstered gun.

Jake didn't seem to hear him. Stillness in the bullpen. Vic stepped closer to Edna's desk, searching for the person he'd seen moments earlier. The phone on Edna's desk rang, startling him. Vic stepped closer to check the desk, and a shape launched itself from inside Edna's cube. Vic glimpsed short black hair, beard shadow, something shiny in the man's right hand. From boxing ring habit, Vic pivoted to his right to give the attacker the narrower target of his left side and shifted his weight back to counterattack. What he thought was a body punch landed on his left side. Instantly, Vic turned his hips, shifted his weight forward, and put all he had into a right cross. He'd aimed for an ear, but his fist landed higher, on the skull, and in a strobe of pain, bones snapped in his hand. Vic bellowed and staggered back. The man, swaying from the punch, rose to his full height. Glimt. In his right hand was a bayonet, red. In a distant part of his mind, Vic understood why, identified the stoked furnace of pain raging on his left side. He glimpsed Jake in his office, turning to them, eyes wide.

Vic leaped forward, got his body inside Glimt's right arm, and clamped it with his left. He drove forward, his right forearm on Glimt's neck. Glimt went over backwards, but Vic's forearm slipped off Glimt's neck before they hit the floor. They flailed their free arms, Vic only thinking to keep the arm with the bayonet clamped. His side burned white hot. He felt Glimt's face, an eye socket, but his fingers didn't work. He lifted his arm and jammed the heel of his fist downward on Glimt's nose. Something cracked, and Glimt made a huffing sound. Vic tried to lift his arm to do it again, but Glimt's right arm slithered against his left side, slick and lubricated. Vic couldn't keep the arm clamped. Dully, he knew why. Vic tried to get Glimt's right forearm into the crook of his left arm, hoping to yank upward and break Glimt's elbow, but didn't have the strength. Pain shuddered through him in waves. Glimt squirmed underneath him. Vic was losing. He knew it. Then, a crack and Glimt shuddered and went slack. A heavy boot on the end of a leg shifted through his peripheral vision, as if someone was resetting after a kick. The leg lashed out again.

Vic heard his name. Jake, he realized dully, Jake's chunky boot near his face.

Vic blinked and slid off Glimt's body. Glimt's shirt was covered with blood. Vic didn't understand why. Pain thrashed in his side like something gouging out pieces of him.

"This is the asshole that stabbed Stevie?" Jake's voice was distant. Vaguely, Vic noticed the swing of a leg again. A crunching.

"Vic, your side."

Vic rolled onto his back. He was too tired to sit up. He looked down. Blood. Everywhere. New boots appeared near his face. The cuff of uniform pants. Jake talking quickly, so fast Vic couldn't follow the words. The clatter of radio talk. Glimt being rolled onto his stomach, handcuffs clicking. Vic was suddenly cold. Terribly cold. He wanted to sleep.

He closed his eyes. He was aware of being watched. Blue eyes. He recognized them and sought them out. Dannie's face materialized, his daughter, watching him. Her face was kind. Patient. Waiting.

Dannie put a finger to her lips to shush him, as if he was a baby. As if she wanted him to sleep. He wanted to feel her arms around him.

"Vic." The word sharp. Nearby. "Vic!"

Vic forced open the heavy lids over his eyes.

Liz leaned close, her face twisted in anger. "Don't do this, Vic." Then a sob. "I can't lose you as well. Don't you dare fucking die."

Epilogue

A cluster of pink and blue balloons tied to a picnic table swayed and bobbled in the wind. A pinata of a zebra hung from a wire stretched above the brick patio, its belly gaping open, a metal baseball bat lying nearby. The candy from inside was long gone, stuffed into the pockets and mouths of Lettie's friends from kindergarten.

Liz stared at Lettie hunched over the picnic table. "She seems happy. Good birthday party for her."

"She's got something on her mind."

Liz turned to him. "What makes you say that?"

Vic smiled. "She was polite to everyone giving her gifts. But look at her. She's drawing, but she isn't really paying attention. She's withdrawn."

"I thought so, too," Anne chimed in. She placed her arm along Vic's shoulders. "Any thoughts what it is?"

"Well, she's seven. Must be the weight of all those years of living."

Liz looked at Anne. "You still putting up with this shit? He's been saying garbage like this since he got out of the hospital."

"I don't mind," Anne breathed, and squeezed Vic's shoulders.

Vic knew what she didn't say. That it was a miracle Vic was even wheeled out of the hospital, that he could shift his weight into their car for the ride home. He guessed that after everything that happened, she would take him any way he came. At least, he hoped that was true.

The back door closed, and Hana Richards, the DA, crossed to Vic. She was shadowed by a tall young man who looked uncomfortable he wasn't wearing a suit. He was the newly elected DA of a neighboring county, and had somehow convinced Hana to date him. Vic wouldn't admit it, but he was interested in how it might play out.

"Vic," Hana called, as she approached. "Great party, but we have to get going."

Vic straightened in his chair. "Thanks for coming. Lettie likes your gift."

"Glad to hear it." Her eyes narrowed, but her voice stayed light. "I hear you start work next week."

"I couldn't talk him out of it," Anne said, a note of disgust in her voice.

Hana turned to Anne. "I saw the therapist's report. The doctor says Vic's ready. And I wouldn't let him back without a green light from the psych folks."

Vic knew Hana was right. The wound in his side required two surgeries, and he lost three inches of small intestine. But with physical therapy, he'd been moving about well within several months. Enough so that Jake Kittery came over and helped him lay the brick for their backyard patio, as Conor Byrne sat in a yard chair drinking Diet Coke and wondering out loud why it was taking so long. The physical part of his wound had healed, but for months he'd still gasped awake in the night, still dreamed of Glimt underneath him, squirming and slick with blood. Felt the rush of fear, that overwhelmed him the instant Glimt freed his arm and the bayonet. Even the news that Jake's steel-toed boot left Glimt with permanent brain injuries hadn't put that to rest. Only the sessions with the psychologist had pushed them into the periphery.

Vic realized Hana was staring at him and he met her eyes.

"It sounds like that therapy did you some good," Hana said gently.

Vic shifted his legs. "Well, it didn't hurt."

"Oh, for Christ's sake," Liz muttered. "Men." She reached inside her purse and removed a small package wrapped in birthday paper. Held it out to Vic. "This is for Lettie, but you need to open it. After everyone leaves." She said goodbye to Hana and Anne, pointedly looked the young man next to Hana up and down, and headed for the kitchen. On her way, she stopped, said something to Lettie, and kissed the top of Lettie's head. Liz was rewarded with a broad smile. Vic noted that as Liz continued to the kitchen door, the serious expression returned to Lettie's face.

"Sandy is ready for you to start work," Hana added. "I just talked to her in the kitchen. She could use your help with the caseload."

"Liz told me Sandy has settled into the commander's job," Vic answered, drawing his attention back to Hana.

"Yes. No one called me about her." Hana gave him a sly smile. "And her call to bring in the FBI to find the Medicare overcharges was the right one. That's how we caught Drum. The money was going through cutouts into an offshore account he owned. Drum would have got away clean otherwise. Glimt isn't capable of testifying against him. So trust her and don't mess it up for her."

"Yes, ma'am."

Hana tapped the man next to her on the arm, and together, they headed to the kitchen door.

"I'll see them out," Anne said and followed them.

That left Vic and Lettie alone in the backyard. A light wind brought the sound of distant traffic. Interested, he turned the small package from Liz and slid his fingernail along the edge to cut the paper. Inside was a small box. He opened it. Nestled in white cotton wool was a gold coin attached to a chain. He lifted it out. It was like nothing he'd ever seen. He had a sudden memory of the small house in New Orleans, of entering the kitchen and seeing Liz stand up from the floor. It must have been lying there, and Liz picked it up.

He turned the coin in his hand and examined the front and back. So this was a doubloon. A small piece of paper was folded on top of the cotton wool. Vic removed it and read Liz's tiny, cramped writing. The doubloon was to help pay Lettie's college tuition.

Vic returned the note and coin to the box and slid everything into his pocket. He smiled. Liz, as honest as the day was long, had palmed and pocketed evidence. And he understood why she couldn't keep it. That coin was a reminder of Demond's death. He guessed when he asked her about it, she would simply say the coin needed to be used for good. That enough blood had been spilled over it already.

Vic rose slowly and stretched, feeling the crimp of his five-inch scar. He'd considered not returning to work, but knew if he didn't go back, he would always ask himself whether he could, or should have. He'd explained that to Anne, and knew she wasn't convinced by the argument. But she'd acquiesced.

"Papa?"

Vic looked down to find Lettie staring up at him. He sat down, and Lettie climbed into his lap. She was knobby-kneed and weighed more than he remembered. Even though part of her pressed on his injured side, he didn't feel any pain, and it gave him confidence.

"What's up?" Vic asked.

The serious expression returned to Lettie's face. She gazed at him. "I'm seven now."

"Yes. Yes, you are."

Lettie blinked in concentration. "I want to know about my mom. My friends all have moms. They were here today. I want to know what my mom was like."

Vic was overwhelmed by a rush of emotion. He remembered seeing Dannie in those moments after the fight with Glimt. He closed his eyes briefly and reopened them. "Then I have a lot to tell you." He remembered how Dannie convinced Susan Kim to save Lettie's life. Gently, he said, "You need to understand that your mother wanted you to be safe, and fought for you from the moment you were born. She wanted you to be happy. And that even now, I think she's still looking out for us."

A Note from the Author

Anyone who has lived or visited Braddock, PA, will know that in the writing of this book I took some liberties with the geographical locations of some places I describe. I also invented at least two business, including a local Braddock tavern and a health network designed to service the needs of retired union members. These choices were my own, and made in service of the story I chose to tell. They have no relation, connection, or are meant to reference or represent any actual businesses or entities. This is a work of pure fiction, as are the circumstances and characters I describe and portray.

Acknowledgements

This volume marks the sixth book in the Vic Lenoski Mystery series, a benchmark I never foresaw during the struggle to write the first volume. In those days I envisioned a trilogy, not a series, and only because I didn't know any better.

In truth, I wouldn't have reached this point without the patient and determined support of my critique partners, Annette Dashofy, Jeff Boarts and Mary Sutton (Liz Milliron). All three write lively and top-notch mystery series that can be counted into double numbers. The quality and quantity of their output is staggering, and reminds me of their exacting professional standards every time we meet. Between us, I do find that annoying, but my comparatively lackadaisical output is my own fault, not theirs.

I am fortunate to be part of a second critique group that includes Barb D'Souza, Caren Knoyer, Howie Ehrlichman, Janet McClintock and Steve Sharpnack, who were quick to spot various typos, inconsistencies and plot errors in the chapters I submitted to them. I appreciate every note and redline they provide on my work.

I must also thank two long-time friends, Steven Hastings and Tom Morris, who time and again have read my early drafts and helped me finalize my manuscript for submission. Given that you are both now retired, I'm hoping you will continue as readers. As you know, I pay in beer.

At Level Best Books, I once again give heartfelt thanks to Verena Rose and Shawn Reilly Simmons, who edited my final manuscript, and to Deb Well, who keeps me on schedule (did I mention I can be lackadaisical?). I truly appreciate their support, and the stunning opportunity they handed me six long manuscripts ago.

About the Author

Peter W. J. Hayes is a recovered marketing executive and author of the Silver Falchion nominated Vic Lenoski mystery series. His published short stories have been finalists for the Derringer and Al Blanchard awards, selected for The Best Mystery Stories of The Year (2024), and appeared in multiple mystery magazines and crime-writing anthologies. Peter can be found at www.peterwjhayes.com.

AUTHOR WEBSITE:
www.peterwjhayes.com

SOCIAL MEDIA HANDLES:
Facebook: Peter W. J. Hayes
Twitter: @PeterWJHayes
Instagram: Peter W. J. Hayes
Bookbub: https://www.bookbub.com/authors/peter-w-j-hayes

Also by Peter W. J. Hayes

The Things That Aren't There

The Things That Are Different

The Things That Last Forever

The Things That Secrets Cannot Hide

The Things That Stay True

www.ingramcontent.com/pod-product-compliance
Lightning Source LLC
Chambersburg PA
CBHW021457110726
47899CB00001BA/186